PRAISE FOR LIV CONSTANTINE

THE LAST TIME I SAW YOU

"Another clever whodunit jam-packed with enough twists, turns, and secrets to keep avid thriller readers second-guessing until the bitter end."   —*Library Journal* (starred review)

"Increasingly ingenious twists . . . expertly ratchets up the tension."
—*Publishers Weekly*

"An absorbing tale . . . fans of *Gone Girl* and its successors will appreciate an ending that puts a pricey shoe on one foot and then changes it again . . . and again."   —*Booklist*

"A transfixing novel full of twists and turns that will leave you breathless."   —*Westport Magazine*

"Liv Constantine delivers the goods with this cat-and-mouse thrill ride! As characters unravel and new suspects are revealed, Constantine keeps us guessing until the final, shocking twist."
—Wendy Walker, author of *Emma in the Night* and
All Is Not Forgotten

"Obsessions, secrets, decades-long grudges—*The Last Time I Saw You* packs all of these into a read reminiscent of the great Bette Davis/Joan Crawford thrillers. I couldn't put it down."
—Joseph Finder, *New York Times* bestselling author of *Judgment*

"Exactly what a good thriller should be—dazzling plot, haunting characters, wonderfully paced. Once again, Liv Constantine reaches deep into the psychic wounds of her heroine creating a deliciously satisfying and utterly compelling murder mystery."
—Aimee Molloy, bestselling author of *The Perfect Mother*

THE LAST MRS. PARRISH:

"Filled with envy, deception, and power, it's a great reading escape. And there is a thrilling twist at the end!!"
—Reese Witherspoon

"[A] wicked debut thriller . . . you'll relish every diabolical turn."
—*People*

"Utterly irresistible . . . pivots on an enormous and satisfying twist . . . the pages keep flying, flying, flying by."
—*USA Today*

"*The Last Mrs. Parrish* by Liv Constantine will keep you up. In a can't-put-it-down way. It's *The Talented Mr. Ripley* with XX chromosomes."
—*The Skimm*

"Wonderfully plausible, hypnotically compelling, and deliciously chilling and creepy—some of the best psychological suspense you'll read this year."   —Lee Child

"[A] haunting psychological thriller. . . . Engrossing."
                                                —*Real Simple*

"If you like your thrillers with an unexpected twist, this one's for you."—*New York Post*

"A bravura performance."   —*Sunday Times* (London)

"*The Last Mrs. Parrish* should be the very next book you read."
                                                —*Huffington Post*

"Fabulous. . . . I read this book in a flash, devouring every twisty, delicious detail."   —*Milwaukee Journal Sentinel*

"This terrific, noir-steeped tale written by sisters that go by Liv Constantine actually owes more to Patricia Highsmith's *The Talented Mr. Ripley* than it does to the likes of *Gone Girl* or *The Girl on the Train.* . . . The twists, turns, and mechanizations are a devilishly delicious delight."   —*Providence Journal*

"Captivating. . . . A deliciously duplicitous psychological thriller that will lure readers until the wee hours and beyond. With a plot equally as twisty, spellbinding, and addictive as Gillian Flynn's *Gone Girl* or Paula Hawkins's *The Girl on the Train*, this is sure to be a hit with suspense fans."
                                —*Library Journal* (starred review)

"Constantine's debut novel is the work of two sisters in collaboration, and these ladies definitely know the formula. A *Gone Girl*–esque confection with villainy and melodrama galore."
—*Kirkus Reviews* (starred review)

"To the pantheon of *Gone Girl*–type bad girls you can now add Amber Patterson, the heroine of this devilishly ingenious debut thriller. . . . The reader watches with shock and delight as Amber cold-bloodedly manipulates Daphne and Jackson and lays waste to anyone else who stands in her way. . . . Readers would have to go back to the likes of Ira Levin's *A Kiss Before Dying* or Patricia Highsmith's *The Talented Mr. Ripley* to find as entertaining a depiction of a sociopathic monster."
—*Publishers Weekly* (starred review)

THE

LAST

TIME

I SAW

YOU

ALSO BY LIV CONSTANTINE

The Last Mrs. Parrish

THE
LAST
TIME
I SAW
YOU

A NOVEL

Liv Constantine

HARPER

NEW YORK · LONDON · TORONTO · SYDNEY

HARPER

A hardcover edition of this book was published in 2019 by HarperCollins Publishers.

THE LAST TIME I SAW YOU. Copyright © 2019 by Lynne Constantine and Valerie Constantine. All rights reserved. Printed in the United States of America. No part of this book may be used or reproduced in any manner whatsoever without written permission except in the case of brief quotations embodied in critical articles and reviews. For information, address HarperCollins Publishers, 195 Broadway, New York, NY 10007.

HarperCollins books may be purchased for educational, business, or sales promotional use. For information, please email the Special Markets Department at SPsales@harpercollins.com.

FIRST HARPER PAPERBACKS EDITION PUBLISHED 2020.

Designed by Bonni Leon-Berman

Library of Congress Cataloging-in-Publication Data has been applied for.

ISBN 978-0-06-286882-4 (pbk.)

20 21 22 23 24 LSC 10 9 8 7 6 5 4 3 2 1

TO THE TUESDAY LADIES:

Ginny

Ann

Angie

Babe

Fi

Mary

Santhe

Stella

Incomparable models of friendship and loyalty.
You are greatly missed.

THE
LAST
TIME
I SAW
YOU

PROLOGUE

She screamed and tried to get up, but the room was spinning. She sat again, breathing deeply in and out, trying to focus. Was there a way to escape? *Think*. She rose, her legs wobbly under her. The fire was spreading now, engulfing the books and photographs. She sank down onto her hands and knees as heavy smoke filled the room. When the air became too dense with it, she pulled her shirt over her mouth, coughing as she moved across the floor toward the hall.

"Help me!" she croaked, though she knew there was no one around who would. Don't panic, she told herself. She had to try and quiet herself, preserve her oxygen.

She couldn't die like this. The smoke was getting so thick she couldn't see more than a few inches in front of her. The heat of the flames was reaching out to consume her. I'm not going to make it, she thought. Her throat was raw, and her nose burned.

With every last bit of strength, she inched her way to the entrance hall. She lay there, panting from exhaustion. Her head was fuzzy, but the cold marble floor felt good against her body, and she pressed her cheek against its cool surface. Now she could go to sleep. Her eyes closed, and she felt herself fading until everything went black.

1

Only days ago, Kate had been mulling over what to get her mother for Christmas. She couldn't have known that instead of choosing a gift, she'd be picking out her casket. She sat in numb silence as the pallbearers slowly made their way to the doors of the packed church. A sudden movement made her turn, and that's when she saw her. Blaire. She'd come. She'd actually come! Suddenly, it was as if Kate's mother was no longer lying in that box, the victim of a brutal murder. Instead, a different image filled her head. One of her mother laughing, her golden hair whipping in the wind as she grabbed Blaire and Kate by the hand, and the three of them ran across the hot sand, into the ocean.

"Are you all right?" Simon whispered. Kate felt her husband's hand at her elbow.

Emotion choked her when she tried to speak, so she simply nodded, wondering if he'd seen her too.

After the service, the long procession of cars seemed to take hours to reach the cemetery, and once everyone had arrived, Kate wasn't surprised to see that the line wrapped around it. Kate, her father, and Simon took their seats as mourners filled the space around the gravesite. Despite the bright sky, a few snow flurries fluttered in the air, precursors to the wintry days that lay ahead. Behind her dark sunglasses, Kate's eyes searched each face, assessing, questioning if the murderer might be among them. Some were strangers—or at least strangers to her—and others old friends she hadn't seen in years. As she scanned the crowd, her eyes came to rest on a tall man and a petite, white-haired woman standing next to him. Pain spread across her chest, an invisible hand squeezing her heart. Jake's parents. She hadn't seen them since his funeral, which until this week had been the worst day of her life. They were stone-faced, staring straight ahead. She clenched her fists, refusing to let herself feel that pain and guilt again. But how she wished she could talk to Jake, to cry on his shoulder as he held her.

The service at the grave was blessedly short, and as the casket was lowered into the earth, Harrison, Kate's father, stood there un-moving, staring at it. Kate locked her hand in his, and he lingered a few moments more, his face unreadable. All at once, he looked much older than his sixty-eight years, the deep lines around his mouth even more pronounced. Kate was suddenly overwhelmed with sorrow, and she reached out to one of the folding chairs to steady herself.

Lily's death would leave an enormous void in all of their lives. She had been the strong center around which the family revolved, and the organizer of Harrison's life, the one who arranged and managed their packed social calendar. An elegant woman who was the product of the Evans family's great wealth, she had been taught from childhood that her good fortune obliged her to give back to the community. Lily had served on several philanthropic boards and had headed her own charitable foundation—the Evans-Michaels Family Trust—which awarded grants to organi-zations dedicated to victims of domestic violence and child abuse. Kate had watched her mother over the years as she presided over her board, tirelessly raised money, and even made herself person-ally available to help the women who came to the shelter, and yet Lily had always been there for her. Yes, she'd had nannies, but it had been Lily who'd tucked her in every night, Lily who had never missed a school event, Lily who'd wiped her tears and celebrated her successes. In some ways, it had been daunting to be Lily's daughter—she seemed to do it all with such grace and ease. But at her core had been a strength of purpose that drove her, and Kate had sometimes imagined her mother finally relaxing her straight posture and perfect demeanor when she closed the door of her own bedroom. Kate had promised herself that if she ever had kids, she'd be the same kind of mother one day.

Kate put her arm through her father's, nudging him away from the canopy, where the cold air was thick with the nauseating smell of hothouse roses and lilies. With Simon on her other side, the three of them walked to the waiting limousine. She slid with relief into the cocooned darkness of the car and glanced out the window. Her breath caught when she glimpsed Blaire, standing alone, hands clasped in front of her. Kate had to stop herself from pressing the window down and calling out to her. It had been fifteen years since they'd spoken, but the sight of her made it feel like they had been together just yesterday.

Simon and Kate's house in Worthington Valley was a short drive from the cemetery, but there'd been no question anyway of holding the funeral reception at Lily and Harrison's home, where she had died. Her father hadn't returned since the night he discovered his wife's body.

When they arrived, Kate hurried to the front door ahead of the others, wanting a few moments to check on her daughter before people began to pour into the house. She quickly mounted the stairs to the second floor. Simon and Kate had agreed that it was best for their young daughter, just shy of five, to be shielded from the trauma of the funeral, but Kate wanted to check in on her now.

Lily had been so thrilled the day Kate told her she was pregnant. She'd adored Annabelle from the moment she was born, and had lavished attention on her without any of the limits she'd put on Kate, laughing as she said, "I get to spoil her. You are the one who gets to correct her." Would Annabelle remember her grandmother as the years progressed, Kate wondered? The thought made her falter, her foot slipping from the top step, and she gripped the banister as she reached the landing and headed to her child's room.

When she peeked in, Annabelle was playing contentedly with her dollhouse, looking mercifully sheltered from the tragic events of the last days. Hilda, her nanny, looked up as Kate entered.

"Mommy." Annabelle rose and ran to Kate and threw her arms around her waist. "I missed you."

Kate drew her daughter into her arms and nuzzled her neck. "I missed you too, sweetheart." She sat in the rocker, pulling Annabelle onto her lap. "I want to have a talk with you, and then we'll go downstairs together. You remember I told you that Grammy went to be in heaven?"

Annabelle looked at her solemnly. "Yes," she answered, her lip trembling.

Kate ran her fingers through the child's curls. "Well, there are lots of people downstairs. They came because they want to tell us how much they loved Grammy. Isn't that nice of them?"

Annabelle nodded, her eyes wide and unblinking.

"They want us to know that they'll never forget her. And we won't either, will we?"

"I want to see Grammy. I don't want her to be in heaven."

"Oh sweetie, you will see her again, I promise. One day you will see her again." She held Annabelle to her, trying to keep her own tears from falling. "Now, let's go downstairs and say hello to everyone. They've been very kind to come and be with us today. You may come down and say hello to Granddaddy and our friends and then come back upstairs to play. Okay?" Kate rose and took Annabelle's hand, nodding at Hilda, who followed them.

Downstairs, they made their way through the crush of well-wishers who'd arrived, but after fifteen minutes, Kate asked Hilda to take Annabelle back to her playroom. She continued moving around on her own, greeting people, but grief made her hands shake and her breath come in short gasps, as if the air were being gobbled up by the crowd. The living room was wall-to-wall people.

Across the room, Selby Haywood and her mother, Georgina Hathaway, stood in a tight circle with Harrison. Nostalgia swept over Kate as she looked at them. So many good memories—summers at the beach from the time she and Selby were kids, splashing in the surf and building sand castles while their mothers looked on. Georgina had been one of her mother's closest friends, and the two women had always loved that their daughters were good friends as well. It was a different kind of friendship from the one Kate had had with Blaire, though. She and Selby had been thrown together by their mothers—Kate and Blaire had chosen each other. They'd clicked from the start, as if there'd been a special understanding between them. She'd been able to open her very soul to Blaire, something she'd never experienced with Selby.

A hand on her elbow made her turn, and she was face-to-face with the woman who had been like a sister to her for so many of her formative years. She collapsed into Blaire's arms and wept.

"Oh, Kate. I still can't believe it." Blaire's breath was hot against her ear as she hugged Kate to her. "I loved her so."

After a moment, Kate pulled away and took Blaire's hands in hers. "She loved you too. I'm so glad you're here." Kate's eyes filled again. It was surreal to see Blaire standing here, in her home, after all their years of estrangement. They'd meant so much to each other once.

Blaire had hardly changed—her long dark hair hung in thick waves, her green eyes were still sparkling, the faint hint of laugh lines around them the only evidence that time had passed. Blaire had always been stylish, but now she looked sleek and expensive, like she belonged to another, far more glamorous world. Of course, she was a famous writer now. A swell of gratitude enveloped Kate. She needed Blaire to know how much it meant to her that she'd come, that she was the part of Kate's past that held so many good memories, and that she understood better than any of her other friends the anguish of this loss. It made her feel suddenly a little less alone.

"Your being here means so much. Can we go into another room where we can talk privately?" Kate's voice was tentative. She was unsure of what Blaire would say, or if she was even willing to talk about the past, but seeing her made Kate want that more than anything.

"Of course," Blaire said without hesitation.

Kate led her into the library, where they settled together on the deep leather couch. After a short silence, she spoke. "I know it must have been hard for you to be here, but I had to call you. Thank you so much for coming."

"Of course. I had to come. For Lily—" Blaire paused briefly before adding, "And for you."

"Is your husband here?" Kate asked.

"No, he couldn't make it. He's traveling for the new book, but he understood that I needed to be here."

Kate shook her head. "I'm so glad you are. Mother would be too. She hated that we never made up." She fingered the tissue in her hands. "I think about that fight a lot. The horrible things we said." The memories came flooding back, filling her with regret.

"I never should have questioned your decision to marry Simon. It was wrong," Blaire said.

"We were so young . . . so foolish to let it rip our friendship apart."

"You don't know how many times I thought of calling you, to talk it out, but I was afraid you would hang up on me," Blaire said.

Kate looked down at the tissue in her hands, now shredded into pieces. "I thought about calling you too, but the longer I waited, the harder it was. I can't believe it's taken my mother's murder to finally do it. But she would be so glad to see us together." Lily had been terribly upset about their fight. She'd broached it with Kate over the years, always trying to get her to reach out to Blaire with an olive branch. Now Kate regretted her stubborn resistance. She raised her eyes. "I can't believe that I'll never see her again. It was so brutal, her death. It makes me sick to think about it."

Blaire leaned in closer. "It's horrible," she said, and Kate sensed a gentle questioning tone in her voice.

"I'm not sure how much you've heard—I've been avoiding the papers," Kate said. "But Dad came home Friday night and found her." Her voice quavered, and she choked back sobs before going on.

Blaire was shaking her head, quiet as Kate continued.

"She was in the living room . . . lying on the floor, her head . . . someone hit her head." Kate swallowed.

"Do they think it was a break-in?" Blaire asked.

"Apparently a window was smashed, but there were no other signs of forced entry."

"Do the police have any idea who did this?"

"No. They didn't find a weapon. They searched everywhere. They talked to neighbors, but nobody heard or saw anything un- usual. But you know how secluded their house is—their closest neighbor is a quarter mile away. The coroner said she died some- time between five and eight." Kate twisted her hands together. "I can't bear to think that while my mother was being murdered, I was here just going about my business."

"You couldn't have known, Kate."

Kate nodded. She knew Blaire was right, but that didn't change how she felt. While she had been making a cup of tea or reading her daughter a bedtime story, someone had brutally taken her mother's life.

Blaire frowned and put her hand on Kate's. "She wouldn't want you thinking like that. You know that, right?"

"I've missed you," Kate sobbed.

"I'm here now."

"Thank you." Kate sniffled. They embraced again, Kate clinging to Blaire as if she were a life preserver that could keep her from sinking into her deep and terrible grief. As they were leaving the room, Blaire stopped and gave Kate a quizzical look.

"Was that Jake's parents at the church earlier?"

Kate nodded. "I was surprised to see them. I don't think they came to the house, though. I suppose they just wanted to pay their respects to Mother and leave." She felt a lump in her throat. "I can't blame them for not wanting to talk to me."

Blaire started to speak, then simply gave her a sad look and another hug.

"I guess I should get back to my guests now," Kate said.

She went through the rest of the day in a daze. After everyone had gone, Simon had holed up in his office to handle a work crisis while Kate roamed restlessly from room to room. She had been anxious for everyone to leave, for the day of her mother's funeral to be over, but now the house felt eerily quiet. Everywhere she looked, it seemed, there was another sympathy card or flower arrangement.

She finally sat down in the recliner in the study, leaning her head back, and closed her eyes, weary and sad. She had almost dozed off when a vibration at her side made her open her eyes. Her phone. In the pocket of her dress. She pulled it out, pressed her thumb to unlock it, and saw Private Caller where the phone number should be. She read the incoming text.

> Such a beautiful day for a funeral. I enjoyed watching you watch them lower your mother into the ground. Your beautiful face was mottled and swollen from crying. But I delighted in seeing your world fall apart. You think you're sad now, just wait. By the time I'm finished with you, you'll wish you had been buried today.

Was this some kind of sick joke?

Who is this? she typed, waiting for a response, but nothing came. She shot up from the chair, her heart thudding wildly against her chest, and ran from the room, her breath coming in short bursts. "Simon!" she yelled as she sprinted down the hall. "Call the police."

2

A deep sadness filled Blaire as she followed the long line of cars to the reception at Kate's house. It seemed impossible that Lily was dead, even more impossible that she'd been murdered. Why would anyone want to harm someone as kind and loving as Lily Michaels? Blaire fought back the tears that had been coming all morning. Gripping the steering wheel, she took a deep breath and willed herself to remain calm. She continued up the tree-lined driveway to Kate and Simon's elegant estate, where a valet greeted her. She stopped the Maserati and got out, handing the keys to the uniformed young man.

The stone house sat on a rise overlooking a green meadow that sloped down to large stables with a paddock. It was horse country, home of the world-famous Maryland Hunt Cup. Blaire would never forget the first time she'd attended the race with Kate and her parents on a sunny day in April. The excited crowd had gathered around cars and small tents as they tailgated with mimosas and waited for post time. Blaire, a novice, had been taking riding lessons at the Mayfield School, but Kate was practically born in the saddle. Blaire had learned during her lessons that timber races were much like a steeplechase. She watched in fascination as horse and rider scaled wood fences almost five feet high. Lily was in high spirits that day, spreading out the feast she'd brought in the wicker picnic basket on a beautiful flowered tablecloth she put down on a folding table. She'd always done everything with such grace and elegance. Now she was gone, and Blaire was just one of the crowd of mourners that filled Kate and Simon's home.

Blaire was so nervous about seeing her old friend, but the second she approached her, so many old feelings flooded back. Kate even pulled her aside for a heart-to-heart, and they were able to share a moment of grieving together for Lily. Looking around, Blaire thought the house was just as stately as the one Kate had grown up in. It was still hard to reconcile the image of the carefree twenty-three-year-old girl that Blaire had known with the mistress of this imposingly formal house. Blaire had heard that Simon, an architect, had designed and built it to look historic. Simon was one person who wasn't going to be happy that Blaire was back. Not that she cared about his opinion. She was ready to reconnect with the other friends she hadn't seen in years and put him out of her mind.

The library she'd walked past on the way to this room had made her want to stop and linger. It soared two stories high, with an entire wall of tall windows. The dark wood walls and ceiling gleamed in the sunlight, and a wooden staircase spiraled to the loft filled with more books. The dark Persian rug and leather furniture added to the antique feel of the room——a space where a reader could be transported back in time. Blaire had felt the urge to climb those stairs and run her hand along the thick wooden banister, to lose herself in the books.

But instead, she'd continued to the vast living room, where appetizers were now being passed by waitstaff and white wine offered on trays. The space was immense and filled with light, which made it cheerful, if not cozy. Blaire took note of the high ceiling with its intricate crown molding and the original paintings on the walls. They were the same kind of works that she'd seen in Kate's parents' house, with the smooth patina of age and wealth. The wide-plank floor was covered with an enormous oriental rug of dark maroon and blue. Blaire noticed the fraying fringe on one corner and a few spots that looked a bit threadbare. Of course—she smiled wryly to herself—it had probably been in the family for years and years.

She looked across the room at the gawky man standing by the bar, her eyes drawn to the bow tie around his neck. *Who wears a bow tie to a funeral?* She had never gotten used to the Maryland obsession with them. Okay, maybe in prep school, but once you were a grown man, only to a formal affair. She knew her old friends wouldn't agree, but as far as she was concerned, they belonged only on Pee-wee Herman or Bozo the clown. Once she registered his face, however, it made sense. Gordon Barton. A year or two ahead of them in school, he had trailed after Kate like a lost puppy when they were young. He'd been a weird and creepy kid, always staring at her for long moments in conversation, making her wonder what was going on in his head.

He caught her eye and walked over.

"Hello, Gordon."

"Blaire. Blaire Norris." His squinty eyes held no warmth.

"It's Barrington now," she told him.

His eyebrows shot up. "Oh, that's right. You're married. I must say, you've become quite well known."

She didn't really care for him, but his acknowledgment of her literary success pleased her nonetheless. He had always been such a tight-ass, so superior as he looked down his nose at her.

He shook his head. "Terrible thing about Lily, just terrible."

She felt her eyes fill again. "It's horrifying. I still can't believe it."

"Of course. We're all quite shocked, of course. I mean, *murder.* Here. Unthinkable."

The room was filled with people who had lined up to pay their respects to Kate and her father, who stood by the mantel, both looking as though they were in a trance. Harrison was ashen, staring straight ahead, not focusing on anything.

"Please excuse me," Blaire said to Gordon. "I haven't had the chance to speak with Kate's father yet." She made her way toward the fireplace. Kate was swallowed up by the crowd before Blaire reached them, but Harrison's eyes widened as she approached.

"Blaire." His voice was warm.

She moved into his open arms, and he hugged her tight. She was ricocheted back in time as she breathed in the scent of his aftershave, and she felt a poignant sadness for all the years they'd missed. When he straightened, he pulled a handkerchief from his pocket and wiped his face, clearing his throat a few times before he was able to speak.

"My beautiful Lily. Who would do such a thing?" His voice cracked, and he winced as if in physical pain.

"I'm so sorry, Harrison. Words can't convey . . ."

His eyes dulled again, and he dropped her hand, twisting the handkerchief until it was a tight ball. Before Blaire could say anything more, Georgina Hathaway strode over.

Blaire's heart sank. She'd never liked either mother or daughter. She'd heard somewhere that Georgina was a widow now, that Bishop Hathaway had died some years ago from complications of Parkinson's disease. The news surprised her. Bishop was always such a vibrant man, athletic and toned, with a runner's body. He'd been the life of the party and the last to leave. It must have been torture for him to watch his body wither away. She used to wonder what he saw in Georgina, who was more self-involved than Narcissus.

When the woman put her hand on Harrison's shoulder, he looked up, and she handed him a tumbler filled with amber liquid Blaire assumed was bourbon, his old favorite. "Harrison, dear, this will settle your nerves."

He took the glass from her wordlessly and swallowed a large gulp.

Blaire hadn't seen Georgina Hathaway in over fifteen years, but she looked practically the same, not a wrinkle to be found on her creamy skin, no doubt due to the services of a skilled plastic surgeon. She still wore her hair in a chic bob and looked smart in a black silk suit. The only jewelry she wore today was a simple strand of pearls around her pale neck and the exquisite emerald-and-diamond wedding ring she'd always sported.

Georgina gave Blaire a tight-lipped smile. "Blaire, what a surprise to see you here. I hadn't realized you and Kate were still in touch." She still sounded like a character from a 1940s movie, her accent some blend of British and finishing school lockjaw.

Blaire opened her mouth to answer, but Georgina turned back to Harrison before she could utter a word. "Why don't we go have a seat in the luncheon area?"

She certainly wasn't wasting any time staking her claim on Harrison, Blaire thought, though hopefully he had the good sense to avoid getting romantically involved with her. The first time Blaire had gone to Selby's house, it was a hot June day at the end of eighth grade, when Kate insisted on bringing her along to sit by the pool. She'd never seen an Olympic-sized pool at a private home before. It looked like something out of a resort, with potted palm trees, waterfalls, an enormous hot tub area, and a four-room pool house decorated more lavishly than Blaire's own house in New Hampshire. Blaire was wearing a new lime-green string bikini she'd just gotten at the mall and thought looked sensational on her. The hot sun felt good on her skin, and she dipped a toe into the sparkling blue water.

After they swam for most of the morning, the housekeeper had brought lunch out for them. They sat around the large glass table, still dripping from the pool, letting the hot sun dry them while they all grabbed sandwiches from the heaping platter. Blaire settled on a roast beef and Swiss and had just reached over to grab some chips from the bowl in front of her when Georgina's voice rang out.

"Girls, make sure you eat some raw veggies too, not just chips," she called as she sauntered over, looking chic in a navy one-piece and sarong.

Selby unenthusiastically introduced Blaire to Georgina, who gave Blaire a tepid smile and then stared at her for a long moment. She tilted her head.

"Blaire, dear. That suit's a bit revealing, don't you think? It's rather nice to leave something to the imagination."

Blaire dropped the chip still between her fingers and looked at the ground, her face hot with embarrassment. Kate's mouth had fallen open, but nothing came out of it. Even Selby was quiet for a change.

"All right then, enjoy your lunch." And with that Georgina turned around and went back inside. She'd been a bitch then, and Blaire would bet she still was.

She shook off the unpleasant memory just as she noticed Simon coming back into the room.

Blaire studied him for a moment before making her approach. He was still as over-the-top gorgeous as he had been fifteen years ago, leaning casually against the doorjamb, that lock of hair that never behaved grazing his forehead. Women were probably still falling at his feet. And she noticed that now everything about his look was expensive, from his exquisitely tailored black suit to his Italian leather dress shoes. The first time Kate brought Simon home over spring break, she had confided to Blaire that he felt out of his element. He had grown up on the Eastern Shore of Maryland in a family of modest means. His father's death of a heart attack when Simon was twelve had devastated the family, both emotionally and financially. His mother never really recovered, and if not for the scholarships Simon earned, it would have been impossible for him to attend Yale. When he and Kate married, he had finally been in a position to make his mother's life more comfortable, until her death shortly after Annabelle was born. And clearly he'd made his own life more comfortable too, Blaire reflected.

A young brunette woman was by his side. She was good-looking, but what grabbed Blaire's attention was the way she was looking at Simon, with a mix of adoration and expectancy. Simon smiled as she said something and touched his arm. Their body language made it clear that they knew each other well. Blaire wondered how well. After a moment, Simon seemed to end their conversation, though Blaire couldn't hear his words. The young woman's eyes followed him as he approached Kate. Then she turned and stalked away, stopping for a long moment in front of a mahogany sideboard. After she'd left the room, Blaire walked over to see what had caught the woman's attention. It was a silver-framed wedding photo of Kate and Simon, both smiling as if they didn't have a care in the world.

A bell tinkled, and a uniformed man announced that it was time for lunch. Simon was standing across the room alone, and Blaire seized her opportunity. As she approached him, his expression turned leery.

"Simon, hi. I'm so sorry for your loss," she said with all the sincerity she could muster.

He stiffened. "What a surprise to see *you* here, Blaire."

Anger surged through her like acid, starting in her belly and burning as it rose to her throat. The memory of what had happened the last time she saw him pushed against her with the force of a tidal wave, but she pushed back. She had to stay cool, composed.

"Lily's death was a terrible tragedy," she said. "Now isn't the time for pettiness."

His eyes were cold. "How kind of you to come running back." He leaned in closer, putting an arm on her shoulder in a way that a casual observer would have seen as friendly, and angrily hissed, "Don't even think of trying to come between us again."

She recoiled, incensed that he had the nerve to speak to her that way, today of all days. Squaring her shoulders, she flashed him her best author smile. "Shouldn't you be more concerned with how your wife is dealing with the murder of her mother than worrying about my relationship with her?" Her smile disappeared. "But don't worry. I won't make the same mistake again." This time, I'll make sure that *you* don't come between *us*, she thought as she walked away.

She was heading to the first-floor bathroom to freshen up before lunch when something outside caught her eye. She moved toward the window and saw a uniformed man standing in the shadows, next to the driveway. It took her a minute to recognize him as Georgina's driver. What was his name? Something with an R . . . Randolph, that was it. He'd driven them around whenever Georgina had carpool duty. Blaire was a little surprised he was still alive. He'd looked ancient to her all those years ago, but looking at him now, she realized he was probably only in his forties at the time. Then she saw Simon approach him and shake his hand before reaching into his coat pocket and pulling out an envelope. Randolph looked around nervously, then took it with a nod and got into his car.

Simon was already heading up the front walk, so Blaire quickly ducked into the powder room before he could see her. She couldn't imagine what business Simon would have with Georgina's driver. But she intended to find out.

3

The murderer was at the gravesite today—maybe even in our house." Kate's voice cracked as she handed her phone to Detective Frank Anderson of the Baltimore County PD. His presence comforted her, his manner sure and confident, and she was struck again by how his appearance of physical strength made her feel safe.

Taking a seat across from Kate and Simon in their living room, he read the text message with a frown. "Let's not jump to conclusions. It could be a crank who read about your mother's death and the funeral—there's been a lot of coverage."

Simon's mouth dropped open. "What kind of a sicko does that?"

"But this is my personal cell phone," Kate objected. "How would a stranger have gotten the number?"

"It's easy enough to get a cell number these days, unfortunately. There are plenty of third-party services people can use. And there were several hundred people at the cemetery. Did you know all of them?"

She shook her head. "No. We debated having a private funeral, but Mother was so tied to the community, we felt she'd have wanted it to be open to anyone who wished to pay their respects."

He was making notes as they were talking. "Normally we'd assume this was a crank, but since this is an unsolved murder, we will take it more seriously. With your permission we'll put in for a consensual Title Three wiretap. I'd like to add it to your home phone and computers as well. Then we can see in real time if you receive more threats, and we can track the IP address."

"Of course," Kate said.

"I have equipment with me that can take a mirror image of your phone. When we finish I'll do that, and we'll see if we can trace this text and find out who sent it. Whatever you do, don't respond if you hear from him again. If this is a crank, that's exactly what he wants you to do." He gave Kate a sympathetic look. "I'm very sorry that you have to deal with this on top of everything else."

Kate felt only slight relief as her husband walked Anderson to the door. She thought back to the last time she'd gotten terrifying news on her phone, that awful night when Harrison had found Lily. She'd seen her father's number pop up, and when she answered, he'd sounded frantic.

"Kate. She's gone. She's gone, Kate," he sobbed across the line.

"Dad, what are you talking about?" Panic spread through her body.

"Someone broke in. They killed her. Oh my God, this can't be real. It can't be true."

Kate had barely been able to understand his words, he was crying so hard. "Who broke in? Mother? Mother is dead?"

"Blood. Blood everywhere."

"What happened? Have you called an ambulance?" she asked him, her voice high-pitched, hysteria threatening to overtake her.

"What am I going to do, Katie? What am I going to do?"

"Dad, listen to me. Have you called nine-one-one?" But all that came through had been his hacking sobs.

She had leaped into her car and driven the fifteen miles to her parents' home in a daze, texting Simon to meet her there ASAP. She could see the red and blue flashing lights from two blocks away. When she neared the house, her SUV was stopped by a police barricade. As she got out of it, she saw Simon's Porsche pull up behind her. EMTs, police, and crime-scene investigators were going in and out of the house. Her panic swelling, Kate ran from the car and pushed her way through the crowd, but an officer barred her way, standing there with his arms crossed, legs in a wide stance, and an angry scowl on his face. "Sorry, ma'am. This is an active crime scene."

"I'm her daughter," she said, trying to push past him, as Simon rushed to her side. "Please."

The officer shook his head and put a hand out in front of her. "Someone will be out to speak to you. I'm sorry, but I'm going to have to ask you to step back."

And then they watched and waited together, horrified, as investigators came and went, carrying cameras and bags and boxes, putting up yellow crime-scene tape, and refusing to even look in their direction. It hadn't taken long for the television crews to arrive, with their cameras focusing on the breathless reporters, mics in hand, detailing every gruesome detail they could glean. Kate wanted to press her hands to her ears when she heard them say the victim's skull had been bashed in.

Finally she saw her father being led out of the house. Without thinking, she rushed toward him. Before she'd taken more than a few steps, powerful hands grabbed her and held her in place.

"Let me go," she yelled, struggling against the officer restraining her. Tears streamed down her face, and when the police car pulled away, she cried out, "Where are they taking him? Let me go, damn it. Where is my mother? I need to see my mother."

He had loosened his hold then, but not his expression. "I'm sorry, ma'am. I can't allow you inside."

"My father should be with her," Kate cried. Simon had appeared beside her, and she inhaled deeply, trying to calm herself. Even though she was still angry at him, his presence was comforting.

"Where have they taken him? Dr. Michaels, my wife's father—where have they taken him?" Simon said, putting a protective arm around Kate.

"To the station for questioning."

"Questioning?" Kate asked.

A woman in uniform approached Kate. "Are you the daughter of Lily Michaels?"

"Yes. Dr. Kate English."

"I'm afraid your mother is deceased. I'm very sorry for your loss." The officer paused for a moment. "We'll need you to come to the station to answer a few questions."

Sorry for your loss? So perfunctory. Glib, even. Is that how the families of patients saw her when she gave them bad news? She had followed the officer, but all she could think about was her mother lying dead, being photographed and scrutinized by investigators, studied by medical examiners, and finally taken to the morgue for an autopsy. She'd seen her share of autopsies in medical school. They weren't pretty.

"Have you eaten anything?" Simon asked, startling her out of her memories as he entered the room.

"I'm not hungry."

"What about a little soup? Your father said that Fleur made some homemade chicken rice."

Kate ignored him, and he sighed loudly, sitting in the chair next to a flower arrangement from her colleagues at the hospital, fingering the tip of a leaf as he read the card. "Nice of them," he said. "You really should eat, even a bite of something."

"Simon, please. Just stop, will you?" She didn't want him acting all husbandly and caring after all the tension of the past few months. When the arguments and bad feelings had reached the point where Kate couldn't concentrate on her work or anything else, she'd gone to Lily. It was just a few weeks ago that they'd sat by the fireplace in her parents' cozy den, warmed by the flames, Kate in her hospital scrubs and Lily exquisite in white wool pants and cashmere sweater. Lily had looked at Kate intently, her face serious. "What is it, darling? You sounded terribly upset on the phone."

"It's Simon. He's . . ." She'd stopped, not knowing where to begin. "Mother, do you remember Sabrina?"

Lily frowned, giving Kate a puzzled look.

"You remember. Her father was the one who sort of took over when Simon's father died, became a mentor to Simon? Sabrina was a junior bridesmaid at our wedding."

"Ah, yes. I remember. She was just a child."

"Yes, she was twelve years old at the time." Kate leaned forward in the chair. "Do you remember how, the morning of the wedding, as we were all here getting ready, Sabrina went MIA? I went to look for her. She was in one of the guest rooms, sitting on the edge of the bed and crying. I started to go in, but then I saw that her father was with her, so I stood to the side, out of sight. She was terribly upset that Simon was getting married. Told her father that she'd always believed Simon would wait for her to grow up and marry her. She sounded so pitiful."

Lily's eyes widened, but her face remained calm. "I'd forgotten that, but it was years ago. She was young and had a crush."

Kate's face had grown red. "But nothing has changed. I tried to understand and be kind, I really did. Her mother died when she was five, and I thought maybe I could be a good friend, even a confidante." Kate sighed. "She completely rebuffed my efforts. Oh, she was never rude in front of Simon, but when we were alone, she made it clear that she wanted nothing to do with me. And now, ever since her father died, she's clingier than ever, calling all the time, wanting more and more of Simon's time."

"Kate, what does that have to do with you, really? As long as Simon isn't encouraging her, you don't have anything to be upset about. And the poor girl is an orphan at such a young age."

"But that's just it. He *is* encouraging her. Whenever she calls with some sort of problem or something that needs fixing, he jumps. And she's calling more and more often. He's there a lot. More than he should be." Kate's voice was louder. "He says it's nothing, that I'm overreacting, but I'm not. Now that she's working with him, they're together all the time. They have dinners together, she comes riding at the house, she completely ignores me and gushes over him. I've reached the point where I just can't take it anymore. I've asked him to move out."

"Kate, listen to what you're saying. You can't break up your family over something like this."

"Well, I can't put up with this anymore. He never should have hired her, but her father asked Simon to look out for her on his deathbed. She asked Simon for a job right after he died."

Her mother gave her a look. "It doesn't sound like Simon had much choice. Things will settle down. Perhaps she's just grieving."

"Quite honestly, Mother, I'm tired of being the sympathetic, long-suffering wife. It's ridiculous for me to be treated like that and then have my husband tell me I'm being unfair."

Lily rose and began to pace. She walked to where Kate sat and put her hands on Kate's shoulders, her eyes locked on her daughter's. "I'm going to talk to Simon. Get this all sorted out."

"Mother, no. Please don't do that." The last thing she'd wanted was for her mother to call Simon on the carpet. That would make things worse than they already were. But she'd heard nothing more from her mother on the topic. If Lily had spoken to him, neither she nor Simon had mentioned it.

Now she looked at Simon as he leaned forward in the chair, his elbows resting on his knees.

"Please don't push me away," he said. "I know we've had our problems, but now is the time for us to pull together and support each other."

"Support? It's been a long time since you've been there for me. I never should have agreed to let you move back in."

"That's not fair." Simon frowned. "You need me here, and I *want* to be with you and Annabelle. And I'd feel much better being here to watch out for you both."

She felt a chill go up her arms and pulled the cardigan more tightly around her at the reminder: there was a killer on the loose out there. The last line of the text played over and over in her mind. *By the time I'm finished with you, you'll wish you had been buried today.* That implied more was to come. Had the killer taken her mother to punish Kate? She thought of the grief-stricken parents of the patients she was unable to save and tried to identify anyone who might have blamed her. Or maybe blamed her father. He'd practiced medicine for over forty years, plenty of time to make some enemies.

"Kate." Simon's voice broke through her musings again. "I'm not leaving you alone. Not with a threat against you."

She slowly raised her eyes to his. She couldn't think straight. But the idea of being alone in this big house *was* terrifying.

She nodded. "You can continue to stay in the blue guest suite for now."

"I think I should move back into the master bedroom."

Kate felt the heat rise from her neck and across her cheeks. Was he using her mother's death as a way to worm himself back into her affections? "Absolutely not."

"Okay, fine. But I don't understand why we can't just put the past behind us."

"Because nothing is resolved. I can't trust you." She stared at him, feeling like her eyes could bore holes into him. "Maybe Blaire was right about you."

He spun around, a dark look on his face. "She had no business coming today."

"She had every right," she replied hotly. "She was my best friend."

"Have you forgotten she tried to ruin us?"

"And you're finishing the job."

He pursed his lips and was quiet for a moment. When he finally spoke, there was a steely edge to his voice. "How many times do I have to tell you that absolutely nothing is going on? Nothing."

She was too exhausted to argue with him. "I'm going upstairs to tuck Annabelle in."

Annabelle was on the floor with a puzzle, Hilda in a chair nearby, when Kate walked into Annabelle's bedroom. What would she have done without Hilda? She was wonderful with Annabelle—loving and patient, and so devoted to Annabelle that Kate had to remind her that just because she lived with them didn't mean she was on duty all the time. Hilda had been nanny to Selby's three sons. When Annabelle was born, Selby had suggested that Kate hire her, since Selby's youngest would be going into first grade and would no longer need a full-time nanny. Kate had been relieved and grateful to have someone she knew and trusted to care for her daughter. They had known Hilda forever, it seemed, and her brother, Randolph, had been Georgina's driver for years, a reliable and trustworthy employee. It had worked out perfectly.

Kate knelt next to her daughter. "What a good job you've done."

Annabelle looked up at Kate with that cherubic face, her blond curls bouncing. "Here, Mommy. You do it," she said, handing her a puzzle piece.

"Hmm. Let's see. Does it go here?" Kate asked, and began to put it in the wrong space.

"No, no," she puffed. "It goes here." She grabbed it and placed it where it belonged.

"It's almost bedtime, sweetheart. Would you like to pick a book for Mommy to read with you?" She turned to Hilda. "Why don't you go ahead to bed? I'll stay with her."

"Thank you, Kate." Hilda ruffled Annabelle's hair. "She's been such a little trouper today, haven't you, sweetheart? It was a long day."

"Yes." Kate smiled at her. "It's been a long day for you too. Now get some rest."

From the bookshelf, Annabelle pulled out *Charlotte's Web* and brought it to Kate. She sat on the bed as Annabelle scrambled under the covers. Kate loved this bedtime ritual with her daughter, but the nights since Lily's death had been different. She wanted to gather Annabelle to her and protect her from tragic reality.

As soon as Annabelle fell asleep, Kate gently took her arm from around her daughter and quietly tiptoed out. She peered down the passageway to the last guest room at the end, the room Simon would occupy. His door was open, the room dark, but she could see a light shining from beneath his bathroom door and hear the water running.

She looked away, her thoughts turning to Jake. His parents hadn't come to the reception, so she'd never had the chance to speak to them—which might have been for the best, given how painful a reminder she must be. She and Jake had grown up in the same neighborhood and had known each other practically all their lives, but it wasn't until they went to high school at brother-sister schools that the two of them had fallen in love. Kate could still remember their senior year, Jake smiling up at her in the stands from the lacrosse field, and no matter how cold it was on those game days in February or March, she felt all warm and glowing inside. And he never missed one of her track meets, his deep voice cheering her on. They both applied to Yale, and it seemed all but certain that they'd spend the rest of their lives together—until the night everything changed. Through the years she'd relived the night of that party over and over in her mind, imagining it had turned out differently. If only they'd left ten minutes earlier, or if they hadn't been drinking. But of course, she couldn't change the reality. She'd lost him in the space of a few hours. When she'd gone to his house a few days after his funeral, the blinds were drawn. Days' worth of newspapers were scattered across the front porch, and the mailbox was overflowing. Eventually, his parents and two sisters moved away.

She continued down the hall to her bedroom to change for bed, though she knew sleep would be elusive. She padded into the bedroom, unzipped her black funeral dress, and threw it on the floor in a heap, knowing she would never be able to wear it again. When she flipped on the bathroom light and looked in the mirror, she saw that her hair was limp and her eyes red and puffy. Moving in for a closer look, she caught something dark out of the corner of her eye and froze. Sweat broke out all over her body, and she began to shake uncontrollably as she backed away in horror. She was going to vomit.

"Simon! Simon!" she screamed. "Come here. Hurry!"

In an instant, he was beside her as she continued to stare at the three dead mice, lined up in the sink, their eyes gouged out of their heads. And then she saw the note.

Three blind mice
Three blind mice
See how they run
See how they run!
They all ran after a charming life
He took their eyes with a carving knife
Did you ever see such a beautiful sight?
As three dead mice?

4

Blaire had played her reunion with Kate over and over in her mind through the years—what she would say to her, how Kate would beg to be her friend again, and the crushed look she'd get when Blaire told her it was too late. It would be Kate's turn to feel the pain of betrayal, just the way Blaire had felt when Kate kicked her out of her wedding after their terrible argument that morning. And then she'd elevated Selby from a regular brides-maid to maid of honor in Blaire's place. The truth was, Kate had never been far from Blaire's mind over the years—she'd heard news about her through their other friends and seen glimpses of her life in their pictures on Facebook. But since Blaire felt she was the injured party, there had been no way she was going to come crawling back—or so she'd thought. Lily's murder had changed all that. She'd known that the minute Kate had called. She had to come and pay her respects to Lily. And once she was there, she knew she had to do whatever she could to help them find the killer.

Now that she'd come back, she saw that not only had she been right about Simon, but that something was very wrong between him and Kate. Blaire had always studied people; it was one of the things that contributed to her success as a writer. The little things told the story—the looks that passed between two peo-ple, the choice of a phrase, an unreturned sentiment. From where she'd sat at the funeral luncheon, she'd had a clear view of the two of them, and Blaire had noticed Kate jump like she'd been burned when Simon's hand reached for hers, snatching it back and putting it in her lap. And then, of course, there had been the brunette in the short skirt.

She stood by the window and gazed at the Baltimore Harbor, the low December sun shimmering on the water in a dazzling geometric puzzle. When she called to make reservations at the Four Seasons, they'd told her they were fully booked, so close to the Christmas holidays. But as soon as she inquired about the presidential suite and gave them her name, the flat voice on the other end of the phone became animated, promptly apologizing and booking her reservation. She'd come a long way from that young girl who didn't quite fit in.

Blaire was still in touch with some of her friends from her school days in Maryland. It had been tough at first—they'd all known each other since kindergarten, and Blaire arrived on the scene in eighth grade. Her father had told her that she should be happy that she'd been accepted to such a wonderful school, that it would open up a whole new world for her. Enid, his new wife, said that she was languishing at her public school, that she would have better opportunities if she went to one of the country's top prep schools. They tried to make it sound like they were doing it for Blaire, but she knew the truth—that Enid wanted her gone, that she was tired of arguing with Blaire over every little thing. That's how she found herself going away to Maryland, where she knew absolutely no one, ten hours from her home in New Hampshire. And to add insult to injury, Mayfield insisted she repeat the eighth grade, since she'd missed so much school the year before when she'd had mono. It was ridiculous.

But once she got to Mayfield, Blaire had to admit that the school grounds were beautiful—grass so green it didn't look real and Georgian-style buildings dotting the campus, giving it a college feel. And the facilities were amazing. There was a tremendous swimming pool, stables, a state-of-the-art gym, and plush dorm rooms. It was a definite step up. Besides, her house wasn't hers anymore. Enid's touch was everywhere, her ridiculous homemade crafts all over the kitchen and living room.

Her first day at Mayfield, the headmistress had taken her around the campus. A woman of indeterminate age, she wore her hair in a tight bun, but she had a kind face and a soft voice, and Blaire had found herself suddenly wishing she would stay with her.

The headmistress opened the door to a classroom, and as the teacher welcomed them in, the room had grown silent and all the girls turned, their eyes settling on her. They were in uniforms: white button-down shirts, plaid skirts, white socks, shiny loafers, and navy cardigans. Upon closer inspection, subtle differences emerged—gold or silver post earrings, add-a-bead necklaces, thin gold bangles. Blaire curled her fingers into her hands to hide her chipped pink nail polish. The headmistress had already informed her that only clear polish was acceptable, but said she'd overlook it today.

As Blaire looked around at all the other girls, she laid eyes on Kate for the first time. Shiny blond hair pulled back into a sleek ponytail. A hint of clear lip gloss on her bow-shaped lips. Blue eyes the color of the Caribbean—or at least the way it looked in pictures. She could tell right away that Kate was the type of girl that everyone liked.

"Welcome, Blaire." Pointing to the beautiful girl, the teacher continued. "Go and take a seat next to Kate Michaels." Kate smiled at Blaire and patted the top of the empty desk next to her.

Later, at lunch, Kate introduced Blaire to her circle of friends. They'd all followed Kate's lead and been friendly and warm. Selby was nice enough, but the first thing she said when she introduced herself was "I'm Selby, Kate's best friend." Blaire had smiled at her. Not for long, she thought. And it hadn't been. She and Kate were soon inseparable.

It took a little longer for the other girls at the school to completely accept her. At first she was naive enough to believe that money was the great equalizer. Her father had made plenty of it, but he earned it selling tires at a dealership he'd founded twenty years before. Back in New Hampshire, they'd been one of the wealthiest families in their town, sponsoring Little League teams and the school backpack program. But here in Baltimore, she wasn't a big fish anymore. It hadn't taken her long to understand that there was a difference between old and new money, breeding and upbringing. But Blaire was a quick study; within a few years, no one who met her would have guessed she hadn't been born into that world.

Despite the somber reason for her return, she couldn't deny that it felt good—damn good—to have all of them looking at her differently. She was no longer the nobody from the boondocks who didn't know what a cotillion was. Thanks to the Megan Mahooney detective series that she'd created with Daniel, she was more famous than she ever could have hoped. She'd always had dreams of becoming a writer, and so she'd majored in English at Columbia and interned every summer for various publishing houses. When she graduated, she was hired as a publicity assistant at one of the major houses—the same one that published Daniel Barrington. With nine best sellers under his belt, he was not only well known but well loved. He'd written twelve thrillers in the serial killer genre. Blaire had read all of them and seen him interviewed on network talk shows. Assigned as Daniel's publicist's assistant, she had been delighted to realize how friendly and unassuming he was despite his success. She got to know him better when her boss was out on maternity leave, and she was able to fill in on two of his tour stops.

Blaire had seized the opportunity and made sure she looked her best that second night in Boston. After the signing, they grabbed a bite to eat around the corner from the bookstore. When Blaire ordered her cheeseburger with provolone, he'd smiled and told her that was the way he liked his burger too. For the next two hours there was never a lull in the conversation. They discovered they were both fans of the dark stories of Poe and Bram Stoker, and Blaire nodded in agreement when he'd said his favorite movie was *The Postman Always Rings Twice*. They talked about their undergrad years, when they'd immersed themselves in the tragedies of Aeschylus and Euripides, the poetry of John Milton and Edmund Spenser. And when, near the end of the evening, Blaire had made a reference to *Don Quixote*, Daniel had tilted his head at her and smiled. They were perfect for each other. Within a year, one of the book world's most eligible bachelors had become her husband. She hadn't needed an over-the-top wedding like Kate's. She and Daniel made it official at city hall between his tour stops.

It was Blaire's idea to collaborate on the Megan Mahooney series. His publisher loved the concept, and the first in the series hit the *New York Times* list within a week of publication and stayed there for over a year. After they'd written four books together, they signed a deal for a television show based on the series, and Blaire finally began to feel like she had made it.

During her years at Mayfield, it had seemed as though she'd never be in the same social or financial league as all of her friends. It had been hard, always feeling a step behind. But when her first million turned into double digits and she started being profiled in national newspapers and magazines, she finally felt like she could hold her own.

Walking over to the long dining room table, she sat and checked her email. She deleted the sales messages from Barney's and Neiman's, thinking she needed to start unsubscribing from all the junk mail filling up her in-box. She opened a message from her publicist about two conferences she and Daniel had been invited to speak at. She forwarded the email to him with a question mark.

Next, she googled "Lily Michaels," something she hadn't been able to bear to do since she got the news. The page filled with hit after hit. She clicked on the link from the *Baltimore Sun* to see a picture of beautiful, smiling Lily next to the headline "Baltimore Heiress Bludgeoned to Death in Her Home." She scanned the article, which included a statement from the police department. They were considering a wide range of suspects, it said. From research she'd done for her books, she knew the husband was always the first suspect. The police would be digging into every area of Harrison's life, and if they found even one shred of evidence that he had a motive to kill Lily, they'd latch on to him with the ferocity of a feral dog. He and Lily had always seemed happy to Blaire, but a lot could change in fifteen years.

Scrolling farther, she came to the obituary. It was a big article. Prominent. Just like Lily had been. It mentioned her charity work, her foundation, and all the wonderful ways she'd contributed to her community. Blaire felt a stab at her heart when she read that Lily was survived by one daughter and a granddaughter. She thought back to her senior year in college. Kate had been seeing Simon for a few months, and suddenly had less and less time for Blaire. It had been a Friday night when she'd gotten a call from Harrison asking if she knew how to reach Kate, who wasn't in her off-campus apartment or answering her cell phone.

"Is everything okay?" she'd asked.

"Lily had a minor car accident," Harrison had said.

"Oh no! What happened?"

"Someone rear-ended her. She has mild whiplash and a broken wrist. I'm on call tomorrow and was hoping Kate could fly down and help out over the weekend."

"Kate's probably already gone. She told me that she and Simon were going skiing in Stowe."

A sharp intake of breath had come over the line. "I see."

"What if I come?" she'd said impulsively. "I can catch an early train from Penn Station and be there by nine."

"Blaire, that's such a kind offer. Thank you."

She'd heard the relief in his voice. So she'd gone and taken care of Lily, and it turned out to be one of the nicest weekends she could remember. Just Lily and Blaire, talking, watching old movies, playing Scrabble.

Lily had hugged her tight and smiled widely, her eyes crinkling. She'd put her hand on Blaire's cheek. "Blaire, darling, I can't thank you enough. How lucky I am, to have not only one daughter but two."

Yes, Kate had lost her mother, and it was terrible, Blaire thought. But Blaire had lost her too—not once but twice.

5

Kate shuddered, her teeth clenched, as she got out of bed and looked at the bathroom door the next morning. She couldn't go in there. Not yet. Not while the rotten, decaying smell of the mice still clung to her. And those horrible eyes—every time she closed hers, she saw them, the empty sockets looking back at her. She'd asked her housekeeper, Fleur, to have her things moved into one of the guest bathrooms for the time being. The police had taken it all, the dead rodents and the note, and had swept the room for evidence. If they hadn't been sure that she was in danger after the text, the dead mice had convinced them, the concern apparent on Anderson's face as he'd stood at the sink. He'd cautioned her and Simon to keep the details to themselves.

First the text message and now this—who was watching her, waiting to hurt her? The nursery rhyme, with its mind-numbing tune, wouldn't stop playing in her head, over and over and over, until she wanted to scream. Did the killer have a third target in mind? And if so, who? Simon? Her father? Or, she shuddered to think, Annabelle? And what kind of charmed life was she supposedly running after, anyway? She'd worked her butt off to get into med school and to ace the MCATs. After medical school, she'd spent nearly five years in residency and another two years in a cardio fellowship. Kate had committed her life to saving others' lives. And her mother had been a generous philanthropist and advocate for women, admired by the community—except, it was now clear, by whoever was sending these notes.

As a precaution, Simon had hired private security. He'd done some architectural work last year for BCT Protection Services, a security firm in Washington, DC. He'd called his contact there, and there were now two guards stationed outside the house and two inside——one off the hallway in the small study, monitoring the premises via computer fed by the outside cameras, and the other doing hourly rounds of the first floor. The police had offered to station a car outside her house, but Simon had convinced Kate that they'd be better off with BCT, who could be on twenty-four hours a day. Anderson had told them that the size and scope of their property would make it a challenge to secure, especially with the huge expanse of woods adjacent to their thirty-five acres, but BCT had assured him they were up to the task.

Kate walked nervously down the hall to the guest bathroom, her robe tightly drawn around her. It was terrifying to think that the killer had been able to slip into her bathroom undetected in the space of a few hours. Granted, the house had been full of people during the reception, but that didn't make it better. The police and the security team had both done full checks of the house when they'd shown up, but she couldn't shake the idea that they'd somehow missed something, that whoever had left the mice was in her house right now, hiding somewhere, lurking behind a closed door, listening.

She'd spent the morning in bed, and now she only had a few minutes to get dressed for the reading of her mother's will, which was scheduled for ten o'clock that morning at Gordon's office. They'd considered canceling after the threats but decided it was better to get it over with. When she walked into the kitchen in the simple gray sheath she'd chosen, Simon was reading the paper. Her father sat at the table playing Old Maid with Annabelle. He hadn't gone back to his house since that terrible night, staying instead at the waterfront condo in downtown Baltimore that he and Lily had bought last year as a weekend retreat. Annabelle looked up from her cards and jumped down from her chair. "Mommy!"

Kate gathered her daughter into her arms, inhaling the sweet scent of her strawberry shampoo. "Good morning, sunshine. Who's winning?"

"Me!" she shouted and ran back to the table.

Kate followed her daughter to the table to lean down and give her father a kiss on the cheek, noticing again the gray cast to his skin and the dullness in his eyes.

"Good morning," Simon said, closing the paper and setting it on the table in front of him and rising. "How are you feeling?"

"Not great."

"Coffee?"

"Yes, thank you."

He poured a cup of French roast and handed it to her, but as she took it, her fingers trembled so badly that it crashed to the floor. Kate looked at the mess at her feet and burst into tears. At the sight of her mother's agitation, Annabelle began to cry too.

"Oh, sweetheart. It's all right. Mommy's all right," Kate said, hugging Annabelle until she calmed down.

"Kate, you need to eat something," Simon said, stooping to wipe up the coffee and carefully pick up the pieces of china.

She wiped her cheek with the back of her hand. "I can't."

He stood, holding the broken shards in his hand, and gave Harrison a look, but neither man argued with her.

"Will you ask Hilda if she's ready? And remind her to bring some things to keep Annabelle occupied while we're at Gordon's."

"Are you sure you want to bring Annabelle? Wouldn't she be better off here?" Simon asked gently. His eyes were pleading, and she wondered if he was trying to seem like a protector again, a husband she would want to stay with after all. In a way, she was touched by his attentiveness. It almost seemed like the way things used to be.

Though she knew that Simon was probably right, that Annabelle would be just as safe, or even safer, at home with all the protection they'd hired, Kate just needed to have her daughter near her for the time being. She walked out of Annabelle's earshot. "Her grandmother has just died," she whispered, though the words sounded as if they couldn't possibly be true. "Annabelle is sad even though she doesn't completely understand. She sees the police here, the security people. She's just a child, but she knows that something is not right. I want her with me."

"I guess I hadn't thought of it that way," he said. "I'll tell Hilda we're ready to go."

They got in the car and Kate realized she'd switched purses. She turned to Simon.

"Hold on. I need to go get my EpiPen in case we decide to grab a bite to eat afterward." Her peanut allergy necessitated that she always have it with her. Once they were on the road, Annabelle's chatter from the back seat was nonstop. When they pulled into the underground parking lot, Annabelle oohed and giggled at the sudden darkness, and Kate turned and smiled at her innocent joy.

Kate had gotten pregnant by accident in her first year of practice. She and Simon had been on the fence about having children. With two demanding careers, they didn't think it was fair. When they found out she was pregnant, though, they were both elated. She remembered lying on the exam table for the ultrasound, Simon in a chair at her side, while her doctor smeared the gel onto her belly and moved the probe across her abdomen. "Here's the heartbeat," the doctor said, and they'd looked at each other in wonderment. And once Annabelle was born, they couldn't imagine their lives without her.

Now Kate looked over at Simon's profile as he parked, and despite everything that had happened between them, felt a sudden urge to reach out and touch him. She loved Simon, or at least she had until the last few months. She'd met him in a philosophy class senior fall, when she was still in the grips of grief. She'd gone through that first semester after Jake's death in a fog, and Simon had been a good friend, helping her through her heartbreak. Then one day, he'd become more.

Simon was so different from Jake. He was a dark-haired heartthrob whose movie-star looks assured that he could get just about any girl he wanted, while Jake had possessed a combination of quiet confidence and fine intelligence. He'd never been one to draw attention to himself, whereas you couldn't help but notice Simon. Kate had initially dismissed Simon as a pretty boy. But she eventually saw there was more to him than his looks. Simon had made the class fun. His wit infused the discussions with just the right note of irreverence to keep the talk lively, and when he invited her to join his study group, she found herself looking forward to seeing him, her feelings shifting subtly as the term progressed.

She had surprised herself when she said yes to his proposal after graduation, the word coming out before she realized it had. But then, she'd thought, it would be good. He made her forget what she couldn't have. Together they'd forge a good life, their differences complementing one another. And wasn't that better than being with someone too much like you? Surely that would get boring. Her parents had thought the engagement was too fast at first, as she'd been dating him for less than a year and, they pointed out, still had four years of medical school at Johns

Hopkins. But in the end, they'd supported her, probably because they were just glad to see her happy again.

There had been a few times before Annabelle was born that Kate wondered if she'd made the right decision. On the day of her wedding, Blaire's angry words had echoed in her mind, and she wondered if she *was* just marrying Simon on the rebound. But Jake was gone. She allowed herself a fleeting moment to wish it was him waiting for her on the altar, and then pushed him out of her mind. After all, she did love Simon.

A loud horn made her look up as the five of them walked across Pratt Street to the offices of Barton and Rothman, a downtown Baltimore landmark of steel and glass that resembled a pyramid made from Lego blocks. Barton and Rothman went back to the days when Kate's great-great-grandfather Evans founded his real estate firm, which had grown into an empire, and Gordon's great-great-grandfather had invested and managed the money. From that day to this, their families had been intertwined, and her family's money had been in his family's capable hands. Gordon, who was a partner now, was an astute and shrewd investor, but unfortunately he had failed to inherit the charm or appeal of his forebears.

She shivered as the wind kicked up, pulling Annabelle closer to her as she adjusted her daughter's wool hat. The sidewalks were crowded with people—office workers, the men in suits and heavy overcoats, the women in stylish hooded parkas. There were sight-seers in bulky down jackets strolling around the Inner Harbor, where Christmas decorations blazed from every store window. Kate found herself searching faces again, looking for anyone who seemed suspicious, someone who might be watching her. The muscles in her face were tight, her whole body on full alert.

As soon as they entered the building, Annabelle skipped to the elevator bank. "Can I push the button?" she asked, hopping up and down.

"Of course," Kate said.

On the twenty-fourth floor, the elevator doors opened to the reception area of Barton and Rothman, the financial planning and advising firm. Sylvia, who'd been with the firm for as long as Kate could remember, rose from her chair behind the reception desk to greet them.

"Dr. Michaels, Kate, Simon," she said. "Gordon is waiting for you."

"Thank you," Harrison said.

Kate hung back a moment. "Sylvia, do you have an empty conference room or office where my daughter and our nanny might sit while we meet?"

"Certainly. I'll settle them in. You know the way to Gordon's office," she said and led Hilda and Annabelle down the hall in the other direction.

Gordon stood at his office door. "Good morning. Come in," he said, shaking Harrison's hand, giving Simon a curt nod, and then reaching out to Kate. His hand felt puffy and moist as it wrapped over hers, but as she attempted to pull it away, his fingers closed more tightly around hers, and he leaned forward to try and give her a hug. She took a breath, pulling away from him, and seated herself in one of the three leather chairs in front of his desk.

"Would you like coffee or tea?" Gordon asked, not taking his eyes off Kate.

Harrison cleared his throat. "No, thank you. Let's get this over with quickly."

Gordon walked back to his desk, bowed slightly, and pulled

at the bottom of his vest before sitting down. Simon had always said that Gordon was pompous, but Kate knew he also grudgingly respected his brilliance at financial management.

"It is a very sad task we have before us today," Gordon began, and Kate sighed, waiting for him to get on with it. He always managed to sound like he'd fallen straight off the pages of *Bleak House*.

"As I'm sure you know, Harrison, your wife's will states very clearly that half of her estate goes to your daughter, and a portion of that in trust for your granddaughter."

Harrison nodded. "Yes, of course. I was here with Lily when she made that provision."

Kate looked at her father. "I don't think it's right," she objected. "It should just be the trust for Annabelle. The rest should go to you." Kate didn't think she and Simon needed the money. They had plenty of income between their salaries and Kate's trust, and her parents had given them a very generous check that allowed them to buy the land and build their own home.

"No, Kate. This is what your mother wanted. Her parents' estate was handled the same way. I don't care about the money. I just wish she were still here . . ." His voice broke.

"Still—" she began, but Simon interrupted her.

"I agree with your father. If that's what she wanted, we need to respect that."

A look crossed Harrison's face, and Kate thought she read annoyance in his eyes. Simon's interjection irritated her too. It wasn't his place to say anything, really.

"I must agree with Simon on this," Gordon said, and Kate cocked her head, knowing how much he must have hated to agree with Simon on anything. "The estate is quite sizable. Thirty million to Harrison and thirty million to you, Kate, with ten of that put aside in a trust for Annabelle." Kate had known the number would be considerable, but she was still surprised by it. This new inheritance would be in addition to the millions that her grandmother had left her when she'd died. A good portion of that money had been used to create the Children's Heart Foundation, which provided free cardiac care to children who didn't have insurance. The foundation took care of all of the kids' medical expenses, along with housing for the parents while the children were in the hospital. Kate and Harrison, also a pediatric cardiothoracic surgeon, saw patients from all over the country, and the foundation allowed them to dedicate a significant amount of their practice to pro bono work.

Kate leaned forward in her chair. "I want to put some of the money into the trust for the foundation," she said to Gordon. "Will you set up a meeting with Charles Hammersmith at the trust and our attorney to discuss it?"

"Of course. I'll get right on it," Gordon said.

Simon cleared his throat. "Maybe we should take some time to think about how much should go into the foundation before we meet with them."

Gordon looked from Kate to Simon and back to Kate again, his eyes resting on her for an answer.

"Why don't you go ahead and set up the meeting, Gordon?" She turned to Simon and gave him a tight smile. "We have time to discuss it later," she said.

Gordon clasped his hands together and leaned forward. "I'm not sure how to bring this up, except to just tell you." He took a dramatic pause as they all looked at him expectantly.

"What is it?" Harrison asked.

"I received a phone call from Lily." Again he paused. "It was the day before she . . . ahem . . . anyway, she asked me to keep it confidential, but now that she's gone . . . well, she wanted to come in and make changes to her will."

"What?" both Harrison and Kate said at the same time.

Gordon nodded somberly. "I'm assuming, then, that you knew nothing about this?"

Kate looked at her father. His face had paled.

"No, nothing. Are you sure that's what she wanted to meet with you about?"

"Quite sure. She specified that she wanted a notary available. I had to mention this to the police, of course. I wanted you to know."

Harrison stood up, moving closer to where Gordon was sitting. "What exactly did my wife say?"

Color rose to Gordon's cheeks. "I told you. That she wanted to change her will. The last thing she said before we hung up was, 'I'd appreciate your keeping this between us.'"

Kate looked at her father again, trying to gauge his reaction. His expression was inscrutable.

"Is there anything else, or can we go?" Harrison asked, his voice tight.

"Just a few more things to sign," Gordon answered.

After the papers were signed, the meeting ended, and Gordon came around from behind his desk, once again taking Kate's hands in his.

"If there is anything, anything at all, I can do for you, please call me." He let go of her hands and pulled her to him in a stiff hug. There had always been such awkwardness to Gordon, from the time they'd been children together.

As a child, he'd had few friends, and that continued throughout his teen years. Kate wasn't sure that he'd ever had a girlfriend, certainly not when they were young. He had always been odd, eschewing jeans for checkered or printed golf pants along with starched shirts and bow ties when he wasn't in his school uniform. Although she never felt completely comfortable around him, she also never failed to defend Gordon when others made fun of him, so while she had never thought of Gordon as one of her friends, because of their parents' long-standing relationship, they'd been thrown together frequently growing up.

Once, at the Bartons' annual New Year's Day open house, when Gordon had just turned fourteen and Kate was almost thirteen, he'd cornered her.

The party was well under way when Gordon said, "This is boring. Come on. I'll show you something interesting."

"I don't think so. Maybe another time." As she edged away, he moved closer to her.

"Come on. You'll like this. I promise."

"I'll like what?"

"My new art project. I've been working on it for months. Follow me." He reached for her hand, but Kate clasped her hands together as he led the way out of the room.

She followed him to a wing of the large house where she'd never been before. After leading her down a long corridor, he stopped in front of a closed door and turned to her. "Mother gave this room to me for Christmas," he said. "For my art projects."

He pulled a key from his pocket and inserted it into the lock. Kate ran her tongue across her upper lip and tasted salty perspiration. The door opened, and Gordon flipped the switch. Soft light filled the room, making the small space look warm and cozy. The walls were painted dark red and covered in large black-and-white photographs of old downtown row houses.

"Did you take these?" Kate asked, moving closer to one of the framed images.

"Yeah, a while ago. But I want to show you what I'm working on now."

He pushed a button on the wall and then went to stand behind a metal desk where a computer and projector sat. Kate turned to look as a film screen rolled down.

"I'm going to dim the light," he said, turning on the projector.

Black-and-white images of houses appeared on the screen as the film opened, and then the camera focused on one house alone, slowly moving in closer until she could see the occupants. A thin blond woman sat on a sofa watching TV while two young children sat on the floor playing some kind of game. The camera then withdrew, and another house came into focus. The camera again moved in for a closer look at two women sitting at a kitchen table, while another one stood at the sink washing dishes. The film went on moving from house to house, recording the activities of the occupants. When at last it finished, Gordon switched off the projector and turned the light on.

Kate was stunned.

"Well, how do you like it? I've been working on it for months. I'm calling it 'Contemporary Mundanity,'" Gordon said. He'd been positively beaming.

"Gordon. You're spying on people!"

"I'm not spying. It's what anyone would see if they walked by and looked in."

"No, it's not. It's like being a Peeping Tom."

His face had fallen. "I thought you'd be the one person who would like it."

"You're a really good photographer, but I think you should find a different subject next time. Let's go back."

They left the room in silence. As crazy as it was, she'd felt sorry for him. He'd seemed genuinely excited about his project, and he wasn't without talent—but he also seemed to have no idea how violating the project was, and that had bothered her. It still bothered her, but he'd never shown anything but discretion in their business dealings, and he'd never crossed a line with her after that, so she'd kept with the family tradition of having a Barton handle her money. She'd tried to put it out of her mind, and the only person she'd ever told about the incident was Blaire.

Simon put his hand on her back as they all exited Gordon's office.

"We're all through, Sylvia," Kate said.

"Annabelle and Hilda are right down the hall. I'll take you to them," she said, and the three of them fell in behind her.

She opened the door, and when Kate stepped inside, her heart stopped. The room was empty. A box of crayons lay on the table, and a half-colored picture had fallen to the floor.

Kate's heart started pounding, and she felt as if she might faint. "Where is she?" She could barely get the words out. "Where is my daughter?"

"I, I . . . ," Sylvia stuttered.

Kate felt the room begin to spin, and then she felt her father's hand on her arm.

"Kate, honey, I'm sure they just went to the bathroom."

Without a second thought, Kate ran from the room, down the hallway, and pushed open the door to the ladies' room.

"Annabelle? Hilda?" she yelled, her voice rising hysterically. But there was no answer. A toilet flushed, the stall opened, and a young woman in a suit stepped out, looking confused.

Where were they? Running back out to the hall, she saw Gordon, who was now with the others.

"Kate—," Gordon began, but before he could finish, the elevator dinged, and the doors opened.

"Mommy, look what Miss Hilda got me."

Kate spun around and saw Annabelle standing in the elevator, grinning and holding an apple and a juice box.

Kate ran to her, stooped, and picked her up, burying her head in her daughter's shoulder and shaking with relief.

"Mommy, my juice is spilling," Annabelle scolded.

Kate brushed the curls back from her forehead. "I'm sorry, sweetheart."

"Daddy, look what I have," Annabelle said, and Simon took her from Kate's arms. She squealed with delight as he twirled her around.

Kate turned to Hilda. "You scared me to death. Why on earth did you leave like that?" Her tone was sharp.

Hilda shrank back as if she'd been struck. "I'm sorry, Kate. She was hungry, and I remembered there was a store on the ground level of the building. You know I would never let anything happen to her. I watched her like a hawk." She looked as if she were about to cry.

Kate was furious. Hilda had been told how serious it was that they all be on guard. Kate's face was still hot, but she held her tongue. She knew too well that spitting out angry words in a tense situation only upped the ante—calmness was an essential element in the operating room. They were all under enough stress as it was, but she was going to have a long talk with Hilda out of Annabelle's earshot when they got home.

"Everyone's nerves are a little fragile. Everything's fine. Now let's go," Simon said, giving Kate a reassuring look.

When they reached the parking lot, Kate whispered to Simon and then pulled her father aside.

"What was that all about? Why would Mother want to change her will?"

He shook his head. "I don't know, but I wouldn't worry too much about it. Maybe it had something to do with the foundation."

That made no sense to her. "But why would she ask Gordon to keep it a secret?"

She saw a flicker of anger in his eyes. "I told you, Kate, I don't know."

"Mommy, I'm tired," Annabelle called over.

"Coming," Kate answered, this revelation about her mother's wishes still weighing heavily on her mind.

They walked over to where Simon, Hilda, and Annabelle stood waiting. Harrison leaned down to give Annabelle a kiss on the cheek. "See you later, alligator."

Annabelle giggled. "After while, crocodile."

Kate put a hand on her father's arm. "I wish you'd stay with us. I hate thinking of you all alone at the condo."

"I'll be okay. I need to be among her things." He was quiet a moment, then spoke again. "I'm going back to the office tomorrow."

Kate had joined her father's cardiology practice after she'd finished her residency and fellowship. There was no way she could concentrate on her patients right now.

She was surprised. "So soon? Are you sure?" She wasn't sure when she'd be ready to go back, but it didn't feel like it would be any time soon. There was no way she would be separated from Annabelle while the killer was out there.

"What else am I going to do, Kate? I need to keep busy or I'll go crazy. And my patients need me."

Kate nodded. "I understand, I guess. But I can't. I need some time. I've let Cathy know to reschedule my patients for the next few weeks."

"That's fine. You take all the time you need. Herb and Claire have offered to take your surgeries until you're ready to come back."

"Please thank them for me," she said, giving him a kiss and going to the car.

As Simon pulled out of the parking lot, Kate listened to Hilda's gentle voice as she read to Annabelle in the back seat. Before they'd gone more than a few miles, passing Oriole Park at Camden Yards, Annabelle had fallen asleep. The three adults were silent the rest of the trip home, lost in their own thoughts. Kate was glad Blaire was coming over this afternoon. She needed to talk to someone. There had to be some kind of connection or clue she was overlooking, something that she was missing.

6

The first thing Blaire saw when she pulled into Kate's driveway was two men in dark suits and coats standing in front of the door. As soon as she parked and stepped out of the convertible, one of them walked over. "Are you expected, ma'am?"

He looked young. Too young to realize that women her age hated being called *ma'am*.

"Yes. I'm Kate's friend, Blaire Barrington."

He held up a finger and opened a notebook. "Your name is here, but I do need to see some ID, please."

He obviously didn't read her books. Though the truth was, despite her fame, few people recognized her face. Occasionally, usually at a restaurant, she'd get a request for an autograph. But for the most part, she lived her life in anonymity. Book signings were a different story. She and Daniel were used to long lines and throngs of people, leaving both of them exhausted and with aching hands by the end. Blaire thrived on it.

She pulled out her driver's license and handed it over, watching as he snapped a picture with his phone, then motioned for her to go ahead. The door opened before she knocked, and Kate stood in the frame, looking pale and drawn.

"What's with all the guys in black?" Blaire asked.

Kate started to say something, but then shook her head. "Simon hired them. Just in case . . ."

After Kate shut the door and engaged the dead bolt, she led

Blaire from the hallway into the kitchen. Turning to her, she said, "Selby's here. She came by earlier to check on me."

Blaire groaned inwardly. The last person she was in the mood for was Selby. They'd barely acknowledged each other at the funeral luncheon; Selby had sat with her husband, Carter, and not with the women. Now she'd have no choice but to talk to her.

When they walked into the kitchen, Blaire looked around in appreciation. It was fabulous, like something you would expect to see in a grand Tuscan villa of old. Beautiful terra-cotta flooring that looked so authentic she wondered if it had been brought over from Italy tile by tile. A skylighted cathedral ceiling with its rough-hewn wood beams cast a golden glow over the polished wooden counters and floor-to-ceiling cabinets. The room had the same refined and antique feel as the rest of the house, but with the added flavor of a bit of old Europe.

Selby was seated at a table that appeared to be a thick slab of wood carved from a single tree, coarse on the edges and elegantly simple. Annabelle was on her lap, and Selby was reading to her. Selby looked up, her expression turning sour.

"Oh. Hello, Blaire." Selby scrutinized her with the same disdain she always had, but Blaire didn't care anymore. She knew she looked good. If she wasn't quite as thin as she'd been in high school, her time at the gym and careful diet assured she could still rock a pair of jeans. And the hair that had been impossible to tame back then was straight and shiny thanks to the modern miracle known as keratin. Selby's eyes rested on the round eight-carat diamond ring on Blaire's left hand.

Blaire coolly returned the favor, grudgingly acknowledging that the years had been good to Selby. If anything, she was more attractive now than she had been in high school, the soft waves around her face streaked with subtle highlights that softened her features. Selby's jewelry was exquisite—large pearl earrings, a gold bangle, and a sapphire-and-diamond ring on her hand, which Blaire knew was an heirloom. Carter had shown it to Blaire a million years ago—before he'd acquiesced to his parents' insistence that he find a "suitable" prospect to settle down with.

"Hi, Selby. How are you?" Blaire said, turning away from her and pulling a stuffed purple unicorn out of her tote. She held it out to Annabelle. "Annabelle, I'm your mommy's old friend, Blaire. I thought you might like to meet Sunny."

Annabelle flew from Selby's lap, her arms outstretched, and hugged the stuffed animal to her chest. "Can I keep her?" she asked.

"Of course. I found her especially for you."

Breaking into a wide grin, the little girl squeezed it tighter. Blaire was pleased to see that it was a hit.

"Where are your manners, Annabelle?" Kate gently scolded. "Say thank you."

Annabelle regarded Blaire solemnly for a moment, then murmured a shy "Thank you."

"You're very welcome, Annabelle. Auntie Blaire loves to give presents."

Selby looked annoyed. "I didn't realize you were already on 'auntie' terms, Blaire."

Couldn't Selby put aside her pettiness for one day? Blaire thought. Not about to engage, she instead turned to Kate. "You don't mind if she calls me that, do you?"

Kate grabbed her hand and squeezed. "Of course not. We were like sisters—*are* like sisters," she corrected herself.

"Remember how we used to pretend that we were sisters when we'd go clubbing in college?" Blaire asked her. "And the fake names. Anastasia and . . ."

"Cordelia!" Kate finished, laughing.

Selby rolled her eyes. "Yeah, it was hilarious."

Blaire thought back to those years. Despite their completely different coloring, people believed them. They'd spent so much time together that they had begun to sound alike. They'd picked up the cadence and tempo of each other's speech and even had similar laughs.

Before she'd met Kate, Blaire had always wondered what it would be like to grow up in a normal family, to have a mother who cooked breakfast for you, made sure you had a healthy lunch for school, was waiting when you got home to help with homework or just ask how your day had gone. Blaire had been only eight when her mother had left, and she had quickly become the center of her father's universe. By the time she was in fifth grade, she'd learned how to cook better than her mother ever had, and relished making gourmet meals for her father. After a while, Blaire even liked taking care of herself and of him—it made her feel grown-up and in control. And then it all changed when Enid Turner came along.

Enid was a sales rep in her father's company who suddenly started coming to their house for weekly dinners. Six months later, her father sat Blaire down with a goofy smile on his face and asked, "How would you like to have a new mother?"

It had taken her only a moment to understand. "If you're talking about Enid, no, thank you."

He had taken her hand in his. "You know that I've grown quite fond of her."

"I guess."

He'd gone on, that stupid smile still on his face. "Well, I've asked her to marry me."

Blaire had shot off the sofa and stood in front of him, tears of fury blurring her vision. "You can't do this!"

"I thought you'd be happy. You'll have a mother."

"Happy? Why would I be happy? She'll never be my mother!" Blaire's mother, Shaina, had been beautiful and glamorous, with long red hair and sparkling eyes. Sometimes the two of them would play dress-up. Her mother would pretend to be a big star and Blaire her assistant. She'd promised her that one day they would go to Hollywood together, and even though she'd gone on her own, Blaire believed her mother would come back for her once she got settled.

She looked for a letter or postcard every day. She searched for her mother's face in movie posters and television shows. Her father kept telling her to forget about Shaina, that she was gone for good. But Blaire couldn't believe that she would leave her behind forever. Maybe she was just waiting until she made it big before coming back for her. After a year had passed with no word from her mother, Blaire started to worry. Something must have happened to her. She'd begged her father to take her to California to look for her, but he just shook his head, a sad look on his face. He told Blaire that her mother was alive.

She'd looked at her father in shock. "You know where she is?"

It took him a moment to answer. "I don't. I only know that she's cashing her alimony check every month."

Blaire was too young to wonder why he kept paying the bills after they were divorced. Instead, she blamed him, told herself that he was lying and deliberately keeping them apart. Soon her mother would come for her, or if Hollywood wasn't what she thought it would be, maybe she'd even come home again.

So when her father told her he'd decided to marry Enid, Blaire had run to her room and locked the door. She'd told him she would refuse to eat, sleep, or talk to him ever again if he went through with it. There was no way insipid Enid Turner was going to move into her house and tell her what to do. No way she was going to take Blaire's father away from her. How could he even look at Enid after being married to her mother? Shaina was vibrant and exciting. Enid was ordinary and boring. But nonetheless, a month later, they were married in the local Methodist church, with Blaire a grudging witness.

They quickly converted the den, where Blaire's friends used to come and watch TV or throw some darts, into a craft room for Enid. Enid painted it pink, and then she hung her "artwork," a collection of paint-by-numbers dog breeds, all over the walls, while Blaire's games and toys went down to the basement.

The first night after the room conversion, once Enid and her father had fallen asleep, Blaire had crept into her former den. Grabbing a Magic Marker from the dresser, she'd drawn eyeglasses on the cocker spaniel, a mustache on the golden retriever, and a cigar in the mouth of the black lab. Soon, she'd been doubled over with silent laughter, her body shaking as she held it in.

The next morning, Enid's cries brought Blaire into the room. Her eyes were red and puffy.

"Why did you do this?" Enid asked, looking wounded.

Blaire widened her eyes innocently. "I didn't. Maybe you sleep-walk."

"Of course I don't. I know you did this. You've made it quite clear that you don't want me here."

Blaire stuck her chin out. "I bet you did it, just so you could blame it on me."

"Listen to me, Blaire. You may have your father bamboozled, but not me. You don't have to like me, but I won't tolerate disrespect or lying. Do you understand?"

Blaire said nothing, and the two stared at each other. Finally, Enid said, "Go on. Get out of here."

Any time anything happened after that, Enid had blamed Blaire. Her father's devotion transferred from Blaire to his new wife; he had done nothing to defend his daughter, and it wasn't long before she hated going home and did anything she could to avoid it. It turned out to be a blessing that they had sent her away—living with Enid for over a year had been more than enough for Blaire. She went home for the summer after eighth grade, but in her second year at Mayfield, Lily had invited Blaire to spend the summer with them at their beach house in Bethany, Delaware. She was sure that her father wouldn't allow it, but Lily made one phone call and it was all arranged.

Blaire fell in love with the house the first time she saw it—the cedar-shingle dwelling had white decks and porches that stood out against the dark wood, as did the pure-white trim of the large paned doors and windows. It was so different from the boring colonial she'd grown up in, where the rooms were dull rectangles and all the furniture matched. The beach house was filled with breezy white-walled rooms, and big windows that looked directly at the ocean. Soft floral sofas and chairs were strategically placed so the view could be enjoyed while still sitting in cozy groups. But the most intoxicating things were the sound of the crashing waves and the air that smelled of the sea as it floated through the open windows. She'd never seen such an amazing house.

Kate had taken her hand and led her upstairs. There were five bedrooms, and Kate's, a large room next to the master, was painted a pale sea green. French doors led to a small balcony overlooking the beach. All the linens were white—the canopy over the bed, curtains, chair cushions—except for the comforter, which was a bright pink with mermaids embroidered all over it. The walls were decorated with mermaid pictures, and mermaid figurines lined one of the bookshelves. Kate's name was even spelled out

above her bed in sparkling blue sea glass. Kate had everything—
two parents who gave her whatever she wanted, including this
beach house. Suddenly Blaire couldn't breathe, the loneliness and
emptiness of her life closing in on her like a vise.

"Your room is great," she'd managed to say.

Kate shrugged. "It's okay. I mean, I'm getting a little old for the
mermaids. I've been asking my mom to get me a new comforter,
but she keeps forgetting."

Blaire was stunned. Kate had all this at her fingertips, and she
was complaining about a stupid bedspread? Before she could say
anything, Kate grabbed her hand.

"You haven't seen yours yet." Kate's eyes had shone with excitement.

"Mine?"

"Come on." She'd pulled Blaire to the room across from hers
and pointed to the name above the bed—it read "Blaire" in glittering sea glass.

Blaire hadn't been able to speak, hadn't known what to think or
how to feel. No one had ever done anything so generous and kind
for her before.

"Do you like it? My mother came down last week and took care
of it."

She'd run over to the window and pushed the curtain aside, a
wave of disappointment settling over her. Of course it wouldn't
have an ocean view—it was across from Kate's room, so it faced
the front. She hid her disappointment and gave Kate a forced
smile. "I love it."

"I'm glad. Course, we'll probably both sleep in the same room
anyhow, so we can talk all night."

And she had been right. They'd taken turns in each other's
rooms, lying there in the dark, spilling all their secrets. Blaire

hadn't really needed her own room, but Lily, wise woman that she was, had known that having it would make all the difference to her. Blaire spent every following summer with them at the beach—until the summer of Kate and Simon's wedding. She wondered if they still had the beach house, if Kate carried on the tradition with Annabelle.

Selby stood up and pecked Kate on the cheek.

"I guess I'll go now. Remember—whatever you need, I'm here for you." Selby grabbed her handbag. Blaire recognized the Fendi floral design. The cheerful flowers didn't suit Selby's personality at all, Blaire thought. She'd have pegged Selby as more of a *Traviata* fan, decidedly in black or dark green, holding it over her arm like the Queen.

"I'll walk you out," Kate said. She looked at Blaire. "Do you mind staying with Annabelle a sec?"

"Love to," Blaire answered, and then turned to Annabelle. "Would you like me to finish your story?"

The little girl nodded and handed her *The Giving Tree.*

"It's one of my favorites," Blaire said. They sat together at the table, and she began to read. Annabelle had one arm around Sunny the unicorn. She was an adorable child, with big brown eyes and a beautiful smile. She had a sweetness to her that reminded Blaire of Lily. What a shame that Lily wouldn't see her grow up.

"Auntie Blaire, read!" Annabelle demanded.

"Sorry, sweetie."

Selby came rushing back into the room with a frown on her face. "I don't know what's going on, but something is very wrong."

"What are you talking about?" Blaire asked as she readjusted Annabelle in her lap.

"The police came to the door with a package," Selby said.

"They're with Kate and Simon." She crossed her arms in front of her. "I'd stay, but I have a massage booked."

"You don't want to miss that," Blaire said.

Selby glared at her. "Maybe I should cancel it. I'm Kate's best friend. She needs me."

Why couldn't Selby give it a rest? They weren't in high school any longer. Blaire felt herself getting angry but took a deep breath, determined not to say anything she'd regret. She gently twisted a lock of Annabelle's hair around her finger and continued to stare at Selby, then said in a neutral voice, "I'm here. Go to your appointment. Kate will be fine."

Selby's face turned red. "Why did you come back? Didn't you cause enough trouble before her wedding?"

Was she serious? Their friend's mother had just been murdered, and all she could do was dredge up the past? Blaire let her anger bubble to the surface. Moving Annabelle from her lap, she got up and stood close to Selby, whispering so Annabelle couldn't hear.

"What's the matter with you? Lily is dead, and Kate needs all the support she can get. This isn't the time for your petty insecurities."

Obviously flustered, Selby opened her mouth, but nothing came out.

"Maybe it's time for you to go," Blaire said. "You clearly need to let out some of that tension."

Glaring at her, Selby grabbed her purse and stomped away.

7

Kate tapped on her husband's office door, which was slightly ajar. "Simon, the detective needs to speak with us."

Simon looked up from his computer and ran a hand through his hair as she walked in with the detective. "What is it? Have they arrested someone?"

"No, sir," Anderson replied from behind Kate. "But a box has been delivered."

"From where?" Simon's tone was impatient. "What's in it?"

Anderson entered the study as Kate eyed the package with dread. She put a hand on her belly, the all-too-familiar churning in her stomach making her dizzy. She wanted to run from the room before they even opened it.

"Please," Simon said. "Sit down."

Anderson set the box squarely on Simon's desk, and Kate noticed that its packing tape had been sliced through. "I've already seen what's inside. But I want you both to take a look."

"Yes, of course," Simon said, rising out of his seat.

"Just look, don't touch it, please," the detective instructed.

As he removed the top, Kate let out a gasp, stepping back in revulsion, her hand over her mouth. Three small black birds in a row—pierced by a metal skewer, all with their throats slit.

"What kind of sick bastard is doing this?" Simon roared, pushing the box toward Detective Anderson.

"These birds were most likely purchased from a pet store, just as the mice were," Anderson said. "They're parakeets, but they've been spray-painted black."

Kate felt the blood pulsing in her neck and shrank back. Her whole body shook as terror turned to rage, exploding inside her. She looked at Anderson. "Why didn't you warn us? To deliberately shock us? To see what our reactions would be?" Something else suddenly dawned on her. "Do you think we're hiding something from you?"

There was no regret in Anderson's eyes, only suspicion. "It's procedure," he said evenly. "Do you have *any* idea who might be doing this?"

"Of course not."

He replaced the box lid, took a plastic sleeve from his folder, and handed it to Kate. "This was on top of the birds." Inside the plastic was a sheet of plain white paper, with the same typeface as the other note.

> *Sing a song of sixpence*
> *a pocket full of rye*
> *3 little blackbirds*
> *simply had to die*
>
> *When the box is opened*
> *The birds no longer sing*
> *Wasn't that a pretty gift*
> *For someone to bring?*

"These morbid nursery rhymes," Kate whispered. She handed it to Simon, the words reverberating in her mind in a singsong. She doubled over, a wave of dizziness making her lean on the desk in front of her.

Detective Anderson took the note back and put it in his bag. "The killer obviously wants to taunt you. Based on my experience, I would say this is most likely someone you know, though maybe not someone you know well. Someone on the periphery of your life."

"Why do you think that?" Kate asked.

"We know it wasn't a robbery. No valuables were taken. Your father verified that the only thing missing was the bracelet your mother always wore. If someone had broken in to rob the house, they would have taken much more."

Kate considered this. "So you think someone deliberately targeted her to . . . "

Before he could answer, Simon interrupted. "Where are you with the investigation? Are you closing in on any suspects?"

"We're looking at everyone right now."

Simon sighed loudly. "I'd appreciate a little more detail. For instance, a short list of suspects. People's alibis. That sort of thing." He, Kate, and Harrison, as well as their household employees, had provided detailed alibis to the police in the days immediately following the murder.

"Mr. English. We're not in the habit of sharing the details of our investigation, because it can compromise our work. I assure you, we're being very thorough."

A silence hung in the room until Detective Anderson finally broke it. "Again, if there's anything else you can tell me, now's the time."

Kate turned to Simon for some kind of assurance, but his face, white and stricken, told her he was as filled with panic as she was.

"Were you able to trace the text my wife received?" he asked.

Anderson shook his head. "No, we need to do it in real time. But if they send another one, we'll be able to. I've also contacted the FBI behavioral unit. I'm going to fill out the paperwork to see if they can take a look at some of this. It could be a long wait, but we'll see."

Together, they walked to the front door. Detective Anderson pursed his lips again, shaking his head. "I know you're frightened. We're doing everything possible to protect you and your family, but please, be on guard too. Are you sure you can't think of anything out of the ordinary that's happened recently? Any hang-up calls? Any strangers who've approached you for directions or asked you for something seemingly insignificant? Anything odd at the hospital, Dr. English, or your firm, Mr. English?"

Kate thought about it for a minute but came up blank. She shook her head.

"I can't think of anything either," Simon said.

"Well, please get in touch if you do. Anything. I'd rather have extraneous information than miss something crucial."

"Of course," Kate and Simon said in unison. Suddenly drained, she leaned against him.

Before Anderson left, Blaire walked into the hallway with a crying Annabelle. "I'm sorry to interrupt, but Annabelle wants her mom."

As Kate reached out to take her daughter, Anderson extended his hand to Blaire. "I'm Detective Anderson. And you are?"

"This is one of my oldest friends, Blaire Barrington," Kate said. "She came in from New York for the funeral."

"Would you mind answering a few questions for me?" Anderson asked Blaire.

"Certainly."

Simon piped in. "You can use my office."

Blaire followed Anderson back to Simon's office.

Kate looked at Simon. "I'm really scared," she whispered. "Who could be doing this?"

Before he could answer, his phone rang. He held up a finger and looked at the screen. "Sorry, gotta take this."

Kate felt her back go up at his offhanded dismissal. She watched angrily as he walked back down the hall. Taking a deep breath, she took Annabelle back to the kitchen, where Hilda was putting together a snack for her.

"Would you mind taking Annabelle into the playroom?"

"I want you, Mommy."

"I'll come in soon, sweetie. I just need to talk to Aunt Blaire for a minute. How about a chocolate bar? Special treat for being a good girl." Kate winced as the words left her mouth, but sometimes bribery was the only way.

Annabelle was still pouting, but she nodded and took Hilda's hand.

Ten minutes later Blaire was back.

"What did Anderson want to know?" Kate asked.

"He was just verifying my whereabouts the night Lily was killed. I gave him the number of my doorman and the names of my neighbors. He also asked if you and Simon seemed happy."

Kate raised her eyebrows. She wondered briefly if Blaire had mentioned her feelings about Simon to Anderson.

"I told him we hadn't been in touch for a while, so I didn't know. I'm sure he's just looking at every angle. But what happened before? You looked like you'd just seen a ghost when I came into the hall," Blaire said gently.

Kate dropped into a chair, worn out by the stress. "I guess Selby left a while ago?"

"Yeah. She didn't want to be late for her massage. Is everything okay?" The concern was evident in Blaire's voice.

Kate took a minute to think. Could she tell Blaire what was going on? There'd been a time when she wouldn't have hesitated.

When they were young, Kate had no secrets from her. Before Blaire, Kate's confidante had been her diary. Bad moods and problems were frowned upon in her home, when she was growing up. Or at least they were kept hidden. Whenever Kate was upset, Lily had always comforted her—at least in Lily's own way. After a hug and some kind words, she never failed to remind Kate of how incredibly fortunate she was, that she should be thankful for all she had, that complaining or getting upset at her small problems was a sign of ingratitude. When Blaire came along, things had changed. Blaire had told Kate about her absent mother, indifferent father, and hated stepmother. She shared her insecurities and anxieties, and slowly, slowly, Kate opened up too. She had felt like a bird being set free from its cage, grateful to finally have someone tell her it was all right to be sad or angry or however else she felt for as long as she felt. It would be such a relief to confide in her, to let it all out. It took only a few seconds for her to decide to ignore Anderson's order of secrecy and plunge ahead. "Not a ghost," she finally said, "but something equally terrifying. A message from the killer."

Blaire's eyes widened in surprise. "Lily's killer contacted you?"

From there, it came out in a rush. The threatening text the night of the funeral, the mice in her bathroom sink.

"And just now he sent three dead blackbirds on a skewer with the nursery rhyme 'Sing a Song of Sixpence.'"

Blaire stared at her, unblinking, for a moment. "That's absolutely horrible! What do they think it means?"

Kate shook her head. "They don't seem to have any idea."

"Well, what's the plan?"

"They've cloned my phone and computers to see if they can trace who sent the text. They've questioned all of us, gathered the foundation files from Mother's office and the house. And they've talked to staff at the hospital and at Simon's office. Only one thing was missing from the house—her diamond bracelet. You remember, the one she wore all the time." Kate rubbed her eyes, the fatigue beginning to wear on her. "There was a broken window by the front door, but it could have been done later to make it look like a robbery gone wrong. At this point, Detective Anderson feels it's someone we know. Or at the very least someone Mother knew."

Blaire's porcelain skin looked even paler than usual. "Unfortunately, I think your detective is right," she said. "Did he give you any update on suspects?"

Kate shook her head. "He won't share the details, but he assured us he's being *thorough*."

"Well, he seems to be. When he questioned me just now, he told me he was going to talk not only to my doorman but also to a neighbor who saw me. I think he's good at following up. Let's run it down ourselves. You were home when your dad called, right? Where had he been?"

"He'd been home earlier that day and went back to the hospital."

"Okay, good. What about Simon?"

"He was at work. It was late, but that's not unusual."

"Was anyone there with him?"

Kate made her voice neutral. "Another architect. Sabrina Mitchell." She didn't want to get into the Sabrina situation right now.

"What if we make a list? Think of everyone you know. It could be anyone. Colleague, client, employee, extended family."

Suddenly, the idea of this evil psychopath being someone close to her was too much for Kate. She closed her eyes and stayed very still, hoping to quash the painful twisting in her gut. She felt a hand on her knee, and when she opened her eyes, Blaire was kneeling beside her.

"I'm going to call Daniel and tell him I'm staying on, that I want to be here with you."

"No, no. I can't let you do that. I'm sure he's missing you. And besides, it's almost Christmas. It's enough that you came for the service. It means the world to me."

"I want to be here for you now. There have been so many years we've missed." Blaire reached a hand out to Kate.

"But don't you need to get back to your writing?"

"It's December. The publishing world is quiet, and Daniel can do without me for now. He's finishing up our last tour stop, and then we were planning on taking off until January. I do write a detective series. Maybe I can finally put all my book research to good use here. I don't want to go anywhere until we find this bastard."

Kate felt her body go limp with relief. Despite what she'd said, she desperately wanted Blaire to stay. "Are you sure? I mean, I would love that, but . . ."

"I'm sure. Just try to get rid of me." Blaire smiled at her and rose. "I'll get going now. You should rest. Call me if you need anything. I don't care what time it is. I'm here for you."

Kate grabbed her hand and held it as they walked to the front door together. "Thank you," she said as she pulled Blaire into a hug, then watched her old friend descend the steps to her sports car.

Kate arched her back, trying to relieve the ache she felt. She needed to go for a run, to release some of this pent-up anxiety that threatened to consume her. She went to her bedroom and changed her clothes, grabbing her running shoes from the closet. Then she texted the security detail stationed outside. A return text informed her that Alan would be her companion for her run. She wasn't worried about whether or not he could keep up. Simon had reassured her that all the guards were either ex-military or heavily trained in martial arts and weaponry.

When she got downstairs, Alan was waiting outside the front door. Even though it was only four thirty, the sun was going down and the air was frigid. She put her earbuds in, but Alan walked closer.

"Sorry, ma'am. I'd prefer it if you didn't do that. I need to make sure you can hear me if I need to warn you."

She groaned. How was she supposed to run with no music? "I'll just leave one in." He started to object, but she took off, "Sweet Child o' Mine" playing in her left ear. Almost immediately she began to feel the tension leave as her stride lengthened and she picked up speed. She thought of nothing else but the pavement and her feet upon it as the cold air burned her cheeks. She wanted to run into oblivion, to go so fast that she would leave all the terror and grief behind. The hammering in her chest was so hard it felt like she would split in two, and she knew she was going way too fast. It felt so good to let herself fly, but she had to ease up. She gradually slowed her pace and put her hand on her chest, pushing against her breastbone.

She turned down the street and headed to the small pond that had a paved trail around it. There were other runners out there today, and she turned to look behind her, just to make sure Alan was keeping up. He gave a little wave. Before she faced front again, she noticed a runner approaching from behind, dressed all in black. Fast. She knew Alan was trailing her, but what if this man got to her first? Pushing her body, she picked up the pace, timing her breath to her strides. She threw another glance back at Alan and saw the black blur closer than it had been before. It had been a long time since she'd trained in sprints, but suddenly, she was doing just that, dodging oncoming pedestrians and fellow runners as she did. Her feet smacking the pavement, she felt the pace get out of control just as she came to a corner. She stopped cold and whipped around, the man running toward her, looking right at her. He was between her and Alan now—he *had* sped up, flying at her faster than she'd just been going.

Did she know him? He looked familiar. Maybe she'd just seen him out on one of her runs. Or maybe she knew him in some other way. Of course, maybe he was the killer . . .

Throwing her hands up to ward him off, she felt a wave of dizziness. By the time Alan reached her, it would be too late. A scream was working its way up her throat when the man blew right past her. She was flooded with relief so strong her knees buckled, and she rested her hands on her thighs, sucking in lungsful of air.

She had to get back to the house. She was too exposed.

Alan ran up to her, looking concerned.

"Let's go back. Can you stay next to me?" She hated feeling so weak.

"Of course," he answered, with no change in expression.

When they got back to the house, she ran upstairs, and turned on the shower, waiting for it to warm up. She threw her phone on the counter. It lit up, and her text tone sounded.

Private Caller. The pounding in her chest was instantaneous. She took a deep breath, picked up the phone, and read.

Did you like my gifts? Dead mice. Dead birds. Dead Kate?

"Stop this!" she yelled at the phone, tears springing to her eyes. Running to the bedroom, she picked up the house phone and dialed Detective Anderson. He answered on the first ring.

"I know," he said without preamble. "We've pinpointed the IP address and are heading there now."

"You know where this is coming from?" Kate asked, panting.

"The Starbucks on York Road. I'll call you as soon as I know more."

At least she knew the killer was miles away and not in her immediate area. And now they'd find him. Relief flooded through her. They would get this lunatic, and then she could breathe again. As she showered, she told herself that it was going to be okay. Anderson would find whoever was doing this and lock him up. She was drying her hair when her phone rang. Anderson.

"Did you get him?"

He cleared his throat. "By the time we got there, they'd turned the phone off and were gone. We know they used some sort of texting app that delivers over Wi-Fi. We were able to trace the IP address to that particular Starbucks. But once the phone is off, we can't track it."

"Did you question everyone? Maybe the person was still there."

"We did. The place was busy, but no one noticed anything unusual. I'm sorry. We'll be going through the video footage to see if anything looks suspicious—there are cameras everywhere. Of course, if they did it from the bathroom, we're out of luck."

The weight of her disappointment was crushing. She hung up the phone, dejected. Whoever was doing this was smart. Maybe too smart to get caught.

8

Tonight should have been a big night for Kate, Blaire reflected, the annual fundraiser for the Children's Heart Foundation. Originally it was to be held at Kate and Simon's home. But Kate was in no shape to host anything or go anywhere, and when Selby had stepped into the breach and offered to host the event at her house, Kate had asked Blaire to go in her place. Blaire was sure that Selby hadn't taken kindly to that, but she'd agreed without hesitation.

She pulled around the circular drive to Selby and Carter's enormous home in Greenspring Valley, which she had read about in *Horse and Rider.* They'd bought the seventy-five-year-old mansion right after they got married and spent five years on a meticulous restoration, pouring hundreds of thousands of dollars into the project. She stopped next to the fountain in the middle of the circle, and a valet opened her car door and extended a hand to help her out. Hugging her cashmere stole closer, she hurried up the expansive stairs to the black double doors, which were easily over ten feet tall. As she entered, she admired the elegance and sophistication of the grand foyer, with its silk pastel wallpaper and glittering chandeliers. She had to admit that Selby's taste was impeccable.

Blaire gave her wrap to a uniformed butler. As she walked past an immense dining room, its lengthy mahogany table awash with silver candelabra and serving dishes, she saw Selby coming toward her, Carter at her side. She'd seen him across the room at the funeral reception and wondered again how this overweight middle-aged man could be the same good-looking guy she'd almost married.

Selby nodded as they approached. "Hello, Blaire. Welcome to our home. How nice of you to step in for Kate." She shrugged. "I'd have been happy to do it, but I suppose your name probably will bring in more money, since you're so famous now."

"Well, I'm sure Kate thought it was enough that you opened up your home. Maybe she didn't want to put you on the spot to make a speech. You remember how nervous you used to get when you had to present at school. There was that one time——"

"Yes, well," Selby interrupted. "No need to go into that. I'm quite comfortable in the spotlight now." Her voice was sharp.

Carter didn't seem to notice the tension between the two women. He leaned in and kissed Blaire on the cheek. "Blaire, how good to see you." His eyes swept over her, taking her in. "You look absolutely wonderful."

Blaire was delighted by the admiring look on his face. The fiery red silk gown she'd picked up earlier at Octavia Boutique hugged her tall, slender frame. It was strapless, and her long dark hair brushed her bare shoulders. "Thank you." She gave him a confident smile, determined to show him he had no effect on her anymore. It had been so many years since she'd seen him, but the memory of her humiliation came racing back with the force of a runaway train. She took a deep breath, pushing the past from her mind, composing herself.

"Everyone will be so thrilled that you're here. A celebrity guest. How exciting! My mother is one of your biggest fans," Carter gushed. "She's dying to see you."

Blaire's eyebrows shot up. Really? His mother had wanted nothing more than for Blaire to be out of her precious son's life all those years ago. Now she was *dying* to see her?

"And I've read every one of your books," he continued.

"Carter," Selby interrupted. "We have other guests arriving."

He slowly dropped Blaire's hand, and Selby snatched his hand in hers. "If you'll excuse us, I'm sure you can find your way around."

Blaire spotted Gordon and headed toward him, relieved to see someone she knew. Even in a tux, he managed to make a bow tie look silly—probably because his was light blue with bulls and bears on it. Was it supposed to be some sort of stock market witticism? It was no wonder he was still single.

"Hey there," she greeted him.

"Blaire." A curt nod in her direction.

"Having a good time?"

He shrugged. "These things are not really my cup of tea. Just here to support Kate and her foundation. Of course, it's completely understandable why she didn't come."

"I'll be sure to let her know you were thinking of her," Blaire said. "Listen, Gordon. I was hoping to meet with you about some investments. I'd like more diversification in my portfolio, and I'm a little dissatisfied with my financial manager."

His face became animated. She had his full attention now.

"Is that so? I'd be happy to look at your portfolio. I think you'll find our firm knows how to strike just the right balance between risk and security . . ."

Blah, blah, blah. She tuned out the rest, impatient for him to wrap it up. Finally, he did, and she nodded.

"Great. How about if I come by Tuesday evening? Say around eight?"

He frowned. "Evening? I'm not typically at the office quite that late. Can you meet during the day?"

She tried her best to look regretful. "Sorry, but I've got interviews and PR obligations most of the week during business hours.

I guess I'm spoiled, but my current guy has always worked around my schedule. One of the few things I like about him."

He put a hand up. "It's not that I mind, but it's a whole thing with the security system at the office that far after hours."

"How about if we meet at your house, then? After all, we're old friends." His shoulder jumped, and she wondered if it was a tic or just a reaction to her suggestion.

"Well, yes, I guess that will work." He looked reluctant, and she wondered if he had something to hide or just wasn't used to guests.

"Terrific." She handed him a business card. "Email me the address, and I'll see you there."

She smiled. On Blaire's list of suspects, thanks to his weird fixation on Kate, Gordon was number two—right after Simon, with his bullshit alibi.

Glancing around the room, she noticed the woman she'd seen at the funeral luncheon, now chatting with an older man. Dressed in a backless black evening gown that clung to her slender frame, she looked stunning and very much at ease. Blaire wondered who had invited her. Once the man had moved away, she walked over and, giving the woman her best smile, held out her hand.

"Hello, I'm Blaire Barrington."

The woman appraised Blaire for a minute before answering coolly, "Nice to meet you. Sabrina Mitchell." If she recognized Blaire's name, she hid it well.

Blaire cocked her head. "Are you a friend of Kate's?"

Giving her hair a toss, Sabrina returned Blaire's stare. "No, I'm actually an old family friend of Simon's. I was hoping to see him tonight, but he just let me know that Kate couldn't pull it together to come. I thought about bailing too, but I'd already bought a new dress, so . . ."

Blaire looked at her in astonishment. "Her mother was just murdered. I don't think most people could 'pull it together' after something like that." This chick had some nerve.

Sabrina shrugged. "Well, it's a charity event, and people bought tickets expecting to hear from her."

"I'm actually filling in for her tonight."

The woman regarded her carefully. "And who are you again?"

Blaire wanted to slap her. "I'm one of Kate's oldest friends."

"Really? I've never seen you at any of their parties."

"I live in New York. I'm an author."

Sabrina gave her a bored look. "Anything I would have heard of?"

"The Megan Mahooney series. It's on TV too."

Sabrina stared at her a long moment. "Oh yes, I *have* heard of that." She shrugged. "I don't really watch television. I find it a waste of time. And I read mostly literary fiction."

She was some piece of work. Blaire arched an eyebrow. "I love literary fiction too. Who are some of your favorite authors?"

"Oh, you know, so many."

Blaire wasn't budging. "Like who?"

"Um, Virginia Woolf for one."

"Really? What's your favorite book by her? I personally love *Mrs. Calloway*," Blaire said.

Sabrina nodded. "Yes, so do I. Well, if you'll excuse me." She walked away before Blaire could burst out laughing. What a little fraud. Mrs. "Calloway" indeed. Blaire would have to keep an eye on her.

She decided to find her table and go over her notes for her speech, but before she could move, Carter cornered her. Blaire took in the faded blue eyes, the puffy face, and the buttons straining at his middle. It was hard to believe she'd once wanted to marry him. Harder still to believe he'd been able to make her feel like she was somehow less than he was when he ended it.

"I was hoping we'd find a minute to catch up," he said. "It's been so long, but you look exactly the same."

You sure don't, she felt like replying. When he smiled, his eyes practically disappeared into his pudgy face. "How sweet of you to say. You and Selby have turned this house into quite a showcase."

He smiled. "Thank you. It's home." He put a hand on her arm and continued, "I have to admit, I'm a bit awed. I loved your interview on *Ellen*. Who'd have thought one day you'd be in *People* magazine and doing interviews on television?"

I'd have thought, she wanted to say. Instead she simply said, "Thank you. It's a job."

"I'd say it's more than a job. You're like a superstar. My little Blaire, famous."

His little Blaire? He wished. There was no comparison between him and Daniel, and she wanted him to see that. "My husband is the real superstar." She pulled out her phone and found a picture of Daniel and her in Florence and showed it to Carter—the two of them on the Ponte Vecchio, Daniel with his thick black hair and killer blue eyes and Blaire smiling, tucked against his side.

"He looks like he could be in movies," Carter said. "Both of you do." The last part was clearly supposed to bring the conversation back to her, but she wasn't letting him off that easily.

Blaire smiled. "And he's as talented as he is good-looking. Looks like we both got what we deserved." She wondered if he really loved Selby, or if his was a marriage of convenience.

"Do you have kids?" he asked.

Blaire forced a smile. "Not yet."

From the corner of her eye, she saw Selby glaring at them.

Giving Carter a warm smile, she leaned in and grabbed his hand. "I think it's time for me to welcome everyone here. Shall we go?"

"Um, yes," he answered, gripping her hand tighter in his and leading her to the front of the room, where they'd set up a platform and microphone.

"May I have your attention, please?"

The room began to quiet.

"I have the pleasure of introducing Blaire Barrington, international best-selling author and good friend." His voice became somber. "As you know, Dr. English has had a death in the family and was unable to attend. Ms. Barrington has graciously agreed to speak tonight in her stead."

Blaire thanked him and took the mic. "It's an honor to be here tonight. Kate asked me to convey her deepest appreciation to all of you for your generous support." Blaire went through the acknowledgments Kate had given her, and then finished her speech with some stories praising Kate and her work on behalf of sick children. Twenty minutes later, she took her seat next to Elise, an old Mayfield chum who sent all four of her daughters to the school now. She could still pull off her preppy look because of her charm and youthful appearance, Blaire thought, smiling at her.

"Enjoying yourself?" Blaire asked.

"Yes, it's a lovely affair. So sad that Kate had to miss it. Are you planning to bid on anything?"

Picking up the brochure, Blaire looked it over. "Not sure yet. I'll see what catches my eye after the auction starts. You?"

"Maybe the Alaskan cruise. Whit and I could use a little getaway."

Soon the bidding began in earnest as trips, paintings, and other high-ticket items all went for double or triple their value. Finally, the biggest item came up—a golf trip to St. Andrews in Scotland.

Blaire sat back and watched in amusement as Selby and an older gentleman went at it. When Selby upped the bid another $500, he looked ready to quit but raised his number one more time and shouted, "Sixteen thousand."

Selby didn't have the good grace to pause. Her hand flew up, and she yelled, "Seventeen!"

The man cocked an eyebrow and shook his head in resignation.

Now it was Blaire's moment. She winked at Elise and raised her paddle. "Twenty thousand."

There was a collective murmur of surprise, and then the room went quiet.

Selby's lips disappeared into a thin line, and she threw her arm up again. "Twenty-one."

Blaire could play this game all day. "Twenty-five."

Selby shook her head and gave Blaire a murderous look. "Thirty!"

Blaire stood. Time to end this. "Fifty thousand dollars."

A ripple of shock went through the room. Carter put his hand on Selby's arm and whispered something to her. She yanked it away and placed her bid paddle back on the table.

The auctioneer looked back and forth between Selby and Blaire, cleared his throat, and then called out, "Fifty thousand going once . . . going twice . . . sold."

Damn, that felt good. Blaire remembered back to those times in high school when they'd be back from spring break and tell each other about where they'd gone—Gstaad or Tokyo or St. Barts. Blaire's father would have taken them to Florida or some other equally boring destination, while her friends were jet-setting all over the world.

Elise put a hand on Blaire's arm and laughed. "You're going to pay a lot more than fifty thousand for that little stunt."

"I'm not worried," Blaire told her. No matter what she did, Selby would take issue with her, so why not have a little fun?

"Does Daniel even play golf?"

Blaire cocked an eyebrow and grinned. "He can always learn."

Carter announced that the silent auction was closing in half an hour, and everyone started milling around again. Blaire got up, wanting to check on a pair of pearl drop earrings and a framed lithograph she had bid on. She looked around the room and saw Selby whispering to Carter. She looked angry. Good, Blaire thought. As she scanned the room, she suddenly wondered if the killer could be there, and a chill ran up her spine. Blaire knew as well as any cop that some psychopaths got off on watching their victims. If the killer had in fact come, he might have made a hasty retreat when he saw that Kate wasn't here. She'd ask Kate to have Selby give her a list of anyone who didn't bid on the silent auction or who left before collecting their winnings. Or maybe he was still here. It could be anyone, really. The thought that a cold-blooded murderer could be standing inches away from her made her shudder again.

9

Kate woke up drenched in sweat. The familiar feeling of dread washed over her as she opened her eyes, and it was a herculean effort to sit up and get out of bed. A wave of nausea made her sink back down. She took several deep breaths, trying to calm herself. Rising, she plodded to the guest bathroom and turned the water on for the shower while she brushed her teeth. She had hardly slept all night, primed to hear the *ping* of her phone and another menacing text message. Simon had tried to convince her to leave her phone downstairs, but she wanted it next to her in case she had to call 9-1-1. What if someone cut the lines to their home phone? The latest twisted nursery rhyme played in her mind, and she struggled to find a clue in its words. It didn't make any sense to her. Maybe someone was out for revenge. The police were going through the applications from patients who Children's Heart Foundation hadn't been able to help, but so far, they hadn't mentioned anyone to her.

After a quick shower in the guest bathroom, she went back to her bedroom and threw on a white cotton shirt over jeans. Blaire was on her way over, and Kate was hoping they might make some progress today. Kate was coming down the stairs just as Blaire arrived, and she took her friend right to the living room.

"Did you get any sleep?" Blaire asked.

Kate shook her head. "No. I can't stop thinking about these horrible texts . . . those dead animals." She lowered her voice when Fleur, a slight woman with prematurely gray hair, walked in with a French press of hot coffee and two cups. They'd asked the staff to be on high alert, but she didn't want Fleur to hear all the sordid details.

"Thanks, Fleur." Kate filled a cup and handed it to Blaire.

"Mmm. Thanks." She took a sip. "At least the police are monitoring them now."

Kate sighed. "For all the good it's done. This person is shrewd. It's like those stalkers you see on TV. I feel like I'm going crazy."

Blaire squeezed her hand. "I'm sorry."

"Let's talk about something else." Kate tucked one leg up underneath the other. "How did everything go last night?"

"A huge success. Everyone missed you, though."

"I'm sure they were excited that you were there."

"Everyone was great, for the most part. I did meet someone last night who gave me pause, though," Blaire said. "What's the story with Sabrina, the woman who works for Simon?"

"Why do you ask?"

Blaire arched an eyebrow. "I didn't like the way she was looking at Simon at the funeral luncheon. And when I introduced myself to her last night, she made a very inappropriate comment about you bailing on your commitments, or something like that."

Kate frowned. "Are you kidding me?"

Blaire shook her head. "No. And when I said you'd just lost your mother, she sort of breezed over it like it was no big deal. Said that she was hoping to see Simon, but he had to mollify you or something to that effect."

Kate felt the heat rise to her face. Why had Sabrina even gone the night before? "She's been a problem. The truth is, Simon and I were separated before Mother was killed. In fact, he had just moved out."

Both of Blaire's eyebrows shot up. "I'm sorry. I had no idea. What's going on?"

Kate shrugged. "We've been fighting about Sabrina. He swears there's nothing going on between them, but she's so . . . brazen. They have a long history together. He feels a loyalty to her because her father took him under his wing after Simon lost his own dad." Kate sighed. "Simon insists that I'm blowing things way out of proportion."

Blaire put her hand on Kate's arm. "Well, just watch your back."

"Believe me, I am." Kate was gratified to know Blaire was not only looking out for her but validating her impressions of Sabrina as well. It reminded her of how strong their friendship had been once, how they'd been completely in sync.

"Aside from her, so many people asked me to convey their good wishes to you and all the work you're doing. You have a lot of fans."

Kate tried to put Sabrina out of her mind. "That's nice to hear. Well, thanks again for going in my place. There's no way I could have faced being there with all those people. I'd have felt too exposed."

"Oh, Kate. They're going to get this person. And in the meantime, you're safe here."

"But what if I'm not? What if I'm next? And then Annabelle won't have a mother . . . or worse, what if they're after her? I can't lose her. Maybe this is all about me—take my mother, then my child." Suddenly she couldn't breathe.

Blaire put a hand up. "What-ifs are not your friend, remember?"

"I know, I know, but I can't help it. Someone is out there. Just waiting. Someone who's already killed my mother."

Blaire gripped each of Kate's forearms. "Look at me. Come on. Eyes."

Kate forced herself to breathe in and out and locked her eyes on Blaire's.

"What did we used to do?"

"One, two, three, four, I don't have to think it anymore."

"Five, six, seven, eight. Things get better when we wait," Blaire finished.

Kate gave her a weak smile. "Thanks." This was a method Blaire had come up with to help Kate when they were teens.

Blaire clasped Kate's hands in hers. "We're going to take care of this."

Just then they heard a commotion in the hallway and the sound of raised voices.

They looked at each other, panic-stricken, and sprang up at the same time to run into the hallway, where they almost collided with Simon.

"They've apprehended someone on the property. Coming from the woods!"

"Did you call the police?" Kate asked, her heart racing.

Simon nodded. "The security team already did. They told me to make sure we all wait here."

Maybe this was all going to be over now, Kate thought, feeling a surge of relief.

Blaire was looking at her with concern. "Kate, you're white as a sheet. Come on, sit down." She maneuvered her to a chair by the staircase.

Finally the front door opened and Brian, the lead security officer, was dragging someone in.

"You're making a mistake," the young man shouted, trying to pull away, but Brian had a hold on him and the guard behind him had a handgun trained at his back.

Kate and Simon walked a little closer. "That's Mack! He's one of our grooms," Kate said, feeling deflated, as if all the breath had left her body.

"I'm sorry, Dr. English." Mack's eyes darted around. "I had no idea you had security. I came in through the woods, like I always do." Mack had been working with the horses for over a year now. He was the son of friends of theirs whose house backed up to the same woods. He'd been away on vacation the past week.

"Let him go," Simon commanded. Brian dropped his grip, and Mack stumbled into the house.

"Sorry about this, Mack," Simon told him. "Come into my office, and I'll fill you in on what's going on."

Blaire raised her eyebrows. "Well, that was quite a scare."

Kate nodded. She should have known it was too good to be true.

"Are you going to be okay? I've got a call with my editor this afternoon—she's on vacation next week, and we have to iron some things out today. I can come back tonight."

Kate nodded distractedly. "I'll call you later."

She wandered around the house after Blaire left. She'd become more withdrawn, more in her own head, which she knew was in part due to the Valium her doctor had prescribed. But she needed something to help calm her right now.

How long was she going to be a prisoner in her own home? She looked out the window. The sun was warm today; so far it had been a mild winter. She stood. "I'm going to change and go for a hike," she said to Simon.

"I'll be in my office. I need to make a call."

"On a Saturday?"

"Just checking on a job."

A likely story, Kate thought. She pulled on her hiking boots and went past Annabelle's room before going downstairs. A couple of days ago, Kate had requested a guard to watch over Annabelle at all times, and she was glad to see Alan at attention just outside the child's door. She worried about Annabelle's isolation, but as long as someone was after her, Kate wanted her at home, even though it had become plain that there was no safe place.

The sun against her face felt wonderful, and she inhaled deeply as she walked through the field behind the house. She was grateful that Brian was the guard on duty today, as he always kept a discreet and silent distance. It was almost as if she were alone, birdsong and the crunching of broken twigs beneath her boots the only sounds. She walked for over an hour, stopping to look at a robin perched on a branch. Nature had always been her restorative.

As she approached the house, she saw Simon coming her way. "Enjoy your walk?"

"Yes. I think I really needed it."

Simon smiled at her. "It's so nice out. Why don't we ride? Be good for the horses to get some exercise. What do you say?"

Kate hadn't been back to the stables since Lily was killed. Riding had been one of their favorite pastimes, and when she was young they'd ridden together twice a week. Maybe it *would* be good for her to get back on a horse. She'd prefer not to have Simon along, but she was too tired to get into it with him.

"All right," she said. "I'll go change my boots."

He waved his hand at her. "Don't bother. You'll be fine. We'll take it easy."

They walked down the hill to the stables and saddled up Napoleon and Rembrandt. The wind was beginning to kick up as they walked the horses to the large arena, mounted, and trotted around for a while.

"Shall we take them out on the trail?" Simon said.

"I don't know. Will Brian be able to follow us?"

"We'll just stay on our property," Simon pressed. "Just for a little while. It's such a great day. Not many like this in December."

She sighed. "Okay."

They headed for the trail that led around the thirty-five-acre property. Watery winter sunlight bled through the leafless branches as they rode.

They had ridden in tense silence for about twenty minutes when they came to a clearing. The wind whipped across the open land, blowing a white plastic bag like a ghostly kite. Where had it come from? Kate wondered. The bag must have caught Napoleon's eye. Spooked, he snorted, then reared and bolted, sending Kate backward and out of the saddle. Her left foot got stuck in the stirrup as Napoleon galloped on. Her head hit the ground as she was dragged, the dirt and rocks tearing into her back and scalp. Her leg was wrenched, bent awkwardly. She was crying now, the pain excruciating, spitting out the dirt that filled her mouth. "Whoa! Whoa!" she screamed, terrified that she would break her neck. Her vision was blurred with caking soil and tears. Exhausted and finally calming down, Napoleon slowed to a halt, giving Simon time to catch up to them, free Kate's foot from the stirrup, and secure the puffing horse. He knelt beside her.

"Kate! Kate! Are you all right?"

Pain shot through her back and side. "Everything hurts. My ankle is throbbing," she said through tears, as she tried to sit up. "Maybe it's just bruised." She was angry with herself for not changing her boots.

"Don't sit up. I'll go back to the stables and bring the ATV up to get you."

"No." She sat all the way up now. "It's just sore. I can ride back."

"What if something is broken? You don't want to make it worse. It's going to be too hard for you to get back up on the horse."

She sighed. Maybe he was right. But she didn't want him to leave her alone in the middle of the woods. "Call Mack and ask him to bring it up."

He put his hand in his pocket and came up empty, patting his vest pockets too. "I don't have my phone with me."

"What? You always have your phone."

"I must have left it in the barn." He leaned over, putting his hands on her shoulders. "Don't you move. I'll be right back with Mack and the ATV." He jumped on his horse and rode away.

Kate hoisted herself up anyway, wincing as she put weight on her foot. She pulled her pant leg up. Her ankle was swelling. She must have sprained it. Had he planned to spook her horse? She jumped when she heard the sound of a branch falling. "Who's there?" her voice cracked as she called, but no one answered. The sun was going down and she felt chilled. What was taking Simon so long? She limped toward Napoleon and stroked his mane. Maybe she should try to ride back. She didn't like being all alone in the woods. She was about to try mounting when Simon and Mack returned with the ATV.

"Let me help you," he said as he reached for her hand.

She snatched it away. "I'll bet you want to help me. Right into an early grave."

"What? Why would you say that?"

She waved her hand. "Just take me home."

10

Blaire liked playing detective. Maybe it was because in her heart of hearts, she believed she knew almost as much as any real cop about crime. She hadn't spent hours sitting in on classes at the police academy, going on ride-alongs, and interviewing detectives without picking up a thing or two. But these stakes were much higher than figuring out the plot of the next Megan Mahooney book.

She'd been impressed by Detective Anderson's manner when he questioned her about her whereabouts the night of Lily's murder. She told him the truth—she'd been in New York at the time. Daniel had gone to Chicago for a talk he'd been invited to give at Northwestern and had stayed the weekend to see his parents, but Blaire's doorman was able to confirm her story. He'd seen her come and go several times that day, as had two neighbors on her floor. She'd tried to find out from Anderson if Gordon's alibi was solid, but he wouldn't give her any information. Blaire intended to find out more. Maybe he'd been cooking the books and Lily was onto him. Blaire couldn't really imagine him killing someone, but as she'd discovered from her research, it was sometimes the most mundane, docile-seeming people who had the most potential for violence—plus, he was clearly obsessed with Kate.

She was expected at Gordon's house in Baltimore's Federal Hill at eight. On the way, she stopped to grab a bite to eat at a small restaurant, ordering a tonic water with lime as she perused the menu. When she looked up, she was surprised to see Simon walk in with Sabrina. What was going on? They looked way too chummy, and Blaire watched as Simon held the chair for Sabrina, then sat opposite her. They were leaning in close, talking and laughing. No wonder Kate was so pissed off about her. Simon *was* still the same phony bastard. How could he be out on the town, especially with the woman who was causing all the problems in his marriage, when a killer was on the loose and his wife was terrified out of her mind? She pulled out her phone, put it on silent, and snapped some pictures of the two of them.

"Excuse me. Are you ready to order?"

She gave the server a tight smile, pulled a twenty from her wallet, and handed it to him. "Something's come up. This should take care of my drink."

Before he could answer, she slipped out the side door and got into her car, relieved to have left without Simon seeing her. She preferred that he not know she'd caught him out with Sabrina.

Twenty minutes later, she pulled onto Gordon's street. His brick townhouse was at the end of a charming row in this historic neighborhood full of quaint shops and taverns and the famous Cross Street Market. The view from Federal Hill onto Baltimore's Inner Harbor was magnificent.

Blaire pushed the doorbell and heard the chime inside. She stood shivering on the front porch, waiting for Gordon to open the door. When he answered, and she stepped inside, she was surprised; instead of being stuffy and boring, the decor was bold and stylish. The brick interior wall gave the living room a hip feel, and the sleek white furniture set it off perfectly. A red leather chair was the bright focal point in the room, but it matched the stripes in the geometric throw rug on the shiny hardwood floors. Gordon had taste in decor, if not fashion—tonight's bow tie featured little green frogs that matched his wool cardigan.

"Good evening, Blaire. Can I get you anything?"

"Not right now, thank you." She smiled as she took off her coat. "I'd love to use the bathroom, though."

"Of course. Right this way."

She followed him down a hallway, passing a den with a plush sofa and a large-screen television before coming to his office. After she'd used the bathroom, she snuck a quick peek on the way back. A large computer monitor was the only thing on the pristine wood desk—no papers or personal items littered its surface.

When she returned to the living room, he was sitting on the sofa.

"Maybe I will take a drink after all," she said. "But only if you'll join me."

"Sure. What would you like?"

"Do you have any bourbon?"

"Of course. Straight up?"

She nodded.

He returned with two tumblers filled halfway.

"Cheers," Blaire said, lifting her glass.

She took a small sip and watched as he drank half of his in one gulp. Interesting.

Blaire leaned back. "Gordon," she began. "I was wondering . . . you know what, never mind."

His brow furrowed. "What?"

She waved her hand. "It's nothing really. Just something I noticed at the funeral luncheon about Kate, and I wanted to get your opinion."

At the sound of Kate's name, his eyes lit up, and Blaire could see he was still besotted. She'd never forgotten what Kate had told her many years ago about Gordon pulling that stunt with the spying and his camera. He was odd. And he'd always been too fixated on Kate. Another reason she'd come tonight was to see if she could get more information about Simon's finances, but she wasn't ready to rule Gordon out either. If there was anything to find, it would be here, in his house, which was precisely why she had steered their meeting away from his office.

"Go on."

"Things seemed strained between her and Simon, and that new architect, Sabrina, seems to be hanging around him quite a bit." She put a hand on his arm. "I realize you can't discuss your clients, and I would never ask you to betray a confidence. I'm just wondering, as an old friend like me, have you noticed anything off?"

He took another sip from his glass and looked at his hands, then back at Blaire. "Well . . . as a friend . . . I've never thought Simon was right for her."

She leaned in closer. "Strictly between us, of course . . . I don't trust him. Do you?"

He shook his head. "I don't know what she ever saw in him. I think he's a bourgeois opportunist." Color rose in his cheeks.

Blaire nodded. "I couldn't agree more. You know, I never wanted her to marry him in the first place. It's the reason she and I have been estranged all these years."

He looked at her with renewed interest. "I didn't know that."

She nodded slowly. "Frankly, I'm worried. If it *was* a robbery, not much was taken from Lily's house. It's very possible that the killer was someone Lily knew." She gave him a long look. "What if it was Simon?"

Gordon's mouth dropped open. "What? Why would he kill Lily?"

"He says he was working late that night. Kate said Sabrina was the only one with him. She could be covering for him. And I just saw them both at a restaurant on my way here, looking very cozy.

I left before they could spot me, though." She paused and gave him a weighted look. "Maybe something's going on, and Lily found out. The police are being very close-lipped about who they suspect, though I hope they questioned Sabrina. Did they question you?" She tried to make her tone casual.

He nodded. "Yes, I think they've talked to everyone in Lily's circle."

She smiled at him. "Well, I hope you have a good alibi."

He made a face. "I was home that night, but they have no reason to suspect me."

She laughed. "Of course not. Back to Simon. I know that he and Kate have a prenup, that Lily insisted on it. And apparently he and Kate had separated right before Lily died. Now he's back in the house. Awfully convenient, don't you think?" She had to break Kate's confidence about the separation in the service of finding out more.

"I didn't know that." He picked up his drink and threw the rest back in one swallow, slammed the glass on the coffee table, then got up and brought the bottle of Blanton's back with him, refilling his glass. Blaire wondered if he always drank this much after hours, or if it was their conversation stressing him out.

Finally, he continued. "That phony baloney. Who knows what he's capable of? I tell you one thing, I'd like to wrap my hands around his neck for cheating on Kate." As he spoke, he balled one hand into a fist, his knuckles white and straining.

Blaire instinctively inched back farther in her chair. "I think I'll mention having seen them together tonight to the police, but I don't want to upset Kate further," she said.

A vein was bulging in Gordon's forehead, and for a minute, Blaire wondered if he was going to have a stroke. He was muttering now. "Thinks he's so damn good-looking with that mop of dark curls and his expensive clothes." He narrowed his eyes at her. "Do you know he has all his suits custom-made? Who does he think he is, royalty? If it were up to him, he'd go through all her money. I knew he wasn't the real deal the minute I laid eyes on him."

At least Simon didn't wear those stupid *bow ties*, Blaire thought, annoyed by Gordon's snobbery, even if he was giving her helpful clues. She took a deep breath and made sure she kept her tone even. "I suppose it's his choice to do what he wants with his money. After all, his architectural firm is so successful."

"Hmph. Not really."

Bingo. "Is his business in trouble?"

Gordon put his hands up. "I can't discuss my other clients."

She knew that unfortunately, he was a rule-follower, but she could still wheedle out a few details. She leaned in. "I'm not asking you to divulge any specifics. I just want to know if Simon could have had any reason for harming Lily. I mean, what if he needed money? What if Kate's next?"

His brow creased. "All I can tell you is that a friend of mine who works for one of Simon and Carter's biggest clients just told me that they switched architectural firms. That would be a huge financial loss for their company. It's common knowledge, so I'm not disclosing anything Simon has told me in confidence. In fact, he hasn't mentioned it at all." He cut his eyes to Blaire as he took another sip. "Even to Kate, as far as I know."

Blaire digested this information. If Simon's business was in trouble, that might give him a motive to kill Lily. But Kate had her own money as well. Why would he need to go to such lengths? Unless there was a different motive at play. How much might Carter know? Maybe it was time for a little rendezvous for old times' sake.

"Another thing," Blaire started.

"What?"

"At the house after the funeral, I saw Simon talking to Georgina's driver. What possible reason would he have for talking to Randolph?"

Gordon looked up a moment, then back at Blaire. "Well, their nanny, Hilda, is Randolph's sister. Maybe it had something to do with her."

Blaire supposed he was right. It could be that simple. She reached down for her briefcase. "Okay, enough gossip. I have my financials here, and also on a flash drive. Do you want to take a quick look first?" She pulled out the latest report from her financial adviser and handed it to him, pleased to see his eyes widening at the zeros following her account balances.

While he was reading over it, she hit send on the message she'd already loaded into her phone. Shouldn't be long now, she thought. Gordon was still engrossed in the report when a loud car alarm caused them both to look to the front windows.

"What the hell?" He rose and went to the window. "You've got to be kidding!"

Blaire jumped up. "What is it?"

"That's my car! Be right back." He ran out the door and down the steps.

She flew into action, going straight to his office. Pulling out the leather chair, she sat down and clicked the mouse. The screen lit up, but his computer was password-protected. She'd figured as much. She began opening drawers, but they were filled with the usual—pens, pencils, paper clips, stationery, household folders. She got up and went to the large bookcase on the opposite wall, scanning the shelves. Just books, pictures, and pieces of art. She knelt down and opened the cabinet doors beneath the shelves. Rows and rows of camera equipment with lenses of all sizes and shapes. In one corner was a stack of folders. She grabbed all of them, stood up, and plopped them on the desk, flipping through the notated tabs. Nothing to raise alarm bells. Until she reached the bottom of the pile. To the one marked "My Katie."

She gasped when she opened the folder. Photo after photo of Kate. She went through them as fast as she could: Kate in a coffee shop, sitting alone; Kate coming out of a yoga studio; Kate loading groceries in her car. There were hundreds of them—all of Kate, all candid.

He was still a stalker.

Was he a killer too?

She pulled out her phone to take some shots of the pictures but fumbled with her code. She heard the front door close. *Damn it, open!* Swiping to the right, she opened the camera. She quickly pressed the button and got a few shots.

"Blaire?" she heard him call from the hallway.

She quickly returned the files to their place and shut the cabinet door, her heart beating like a jackhammer. She turned away from the bookcase just as Gordon reached the doorway.

He frowned. "What are you doing in here?" He took a few steps closer, scanned the desk, and then looked back at her.

She smiled, trying to put him at ease. "I was just looking at your desk. It's exquisite. Where did you get it?"

He stared at her, his pupils narrowing into tiny pinpoints. Blaire stood still, trying to conceal her nervousness. He continued to stare at her as he ran a hand over the dark wood and said, "I had it custom-made."

"Well, it's just beautiful. I'd love to get the name of your designer." Her words sounded flat to her. "What happened with your car?"

A muscle in his jaw twitched. "Looks like some punk threw paint on my Jag. The police are on their way, so I'm afraid we'll have to reschedule this."

"Not a problem. I'll check in with you next week," she answered, anxious to get away from him. She wanted out of there now. Sweat dotted her upper lip, and she grabbed her bag, hurrying to the door. What if he *was* dangerous?

11

Kate's ankle was still swollen despite lots of icing and ibuprofen, and her arm was black and blue. Her head throbbed from the deep cut in the back, which surprisingly hadn't needed stiches. She'd been sure that her ankle wasn't broken, but to be safe her father had taken her to the hospital for a once-over and an X-ray. But besides the physical effects, she still felt shaken. Had it really been an accident, or had Simon had a hand in her horse being spooked? She was being overly paranoid, she told herself. Things like this happened all the time. Even if he had released the plastic bag, it could have easily fallen right to the ground or even spooked Simon's horse. She needed to get ahold of herself.

"Dr. English?"

Kate looked up at Detective Anderson, who was sitting across from her in the living room, a pen poised over the pocket-size notebook in which he always seemed to be scribbling.

"I'm sorry. What did you say?" She was having difficulty concentrating.

Anderson looked hard at her. "How did you get that bruise?" He pointed to her cheek.

Her hand went reflexively to it. "I fell from my horse yesterday. I'm fine."

He wrote something down and then asked, "Is your husband at home?"

"No. Simon had a business dinner tonight and said he wouldn't be home until later."

"I wanted to speak to you because some new information has come to light." He paused, and Kate waited for him to continue.

"Tell me. Did your parents argue a lot?"

That was the last thing she'd expected him to ask. "No. Occasionally, but I wouldn't say a lot."

"Were the fights heated?" he asked in a dispassionate tone.

"I don't understand what you're getting at. Certainly, they had minor disagreements now and then. But they didn't have shouting matches, if that's what you're implying." She was starting to get annoyed. Didn't he say he had information, not more questions for her?

He looked up from what he was writing. "I'm not implying anything, Dr. English. I'm just asking."

It didn't feel to her like he was just asking, but she took a deep breath and reined in her frustration. "Okay, fair enough."

"Did you know that your mother and father did, in fact, have a very serious argument a few days before she died?"

"No." She was a little surprised, but this didn't seem like earth-shattering news. People had conflicts when they shared their lives. "What does this have to do with the information that you have for me?"

"Your parents' cleaning lady called us. Apparently, she's been conflicted about whether to come forward or not."

"Molly?" Kate asked. She'd been with them for twenty years and was very loyal—and especially close to Lily. Kate thought back to the day of the funeral, when Molly had been a total wreck. Kate had attributed it to the circumstances, but was there another reason she'd been so distraught?

"Yes. Molly Grassmore. She says she overheard loud, angry fighting, doors slamming. Your mother was extremely upset. Crying."

Kate's hands tensed into tight fists at the thought of her mother in distress. Lily was *not* a crier. What on earth could have made her so agitated? And why hadn't her father mentioned it?

"Do you have any idea what they were fighting about?" he asked her.

She sat up straighter, her back rigid against the chair, and crossed her arms over her chest. What was he getting at? Some lunatic was stalking her, and he was wasting his time with this? She had to fight to keep her voice even. "My father hasn't said anything about any argument. Molly could be mistaken. Maybe she heard the television, mistook it for their voices."

"She seems pretty convinced, Dr. English."

"What did *she* say they were arguing about?"

"She couldn't hear very well. Just angry shouting, and tears."

"Why did she wait until now to come forward?"

"Because she didn't want to do something that might hurt your father. In the end, though, she decided the police needed to know."

"Maybe she's making it up." Even as the words left her lips, she knew it was unlikely.

"Why would she do that, Dr. English?"

"I don't know. People make things up. People fight. Why do you keep asking me?" But she was beginning to second-guess her own words. Her back and arms were starting to ache.

The detective leaned back in his chair and took a deep breath. His face remained impassive as he watched her. "Two days after the argument, your mother was dead."

"I don't know what to tell you. People argue. Did you ask my father?"

"We did. He won't tell us what they argued about, and his refusal to talk doesn't look good." He leaned forward. "One more thing. Were you aware that your mother had plans to change her will?"

She took a deep breath before answering. Gordon had said he'd told him. "No. I first heard that from Gordon Barton when we met to go over the will."

Anderson cocked an eyebrow. "You can see why we'd be concerned. Your parents argue, and your mother calls her attorney to change her will. Only before she can, she's murdered."

Was he trying to rattle her? What happened to his assertion that he didn't want to share details of the investigation? "My father was at the hospital when she was killed. Surely you've verified that."

"Yes, we have. However, there are a couple hours where his movements are unaccounted for."

She shook her head. "He was probably in one of the on-call rooms or sleeping. This is all out of context. Besides, my father would never send me these horrible messages and threaten me. It doesn't make any sense."

"But you're alive, aren't you? There've been sinister messages for you, but there's been no attempt on your life. Why?" He was being relentless.

She pressed her lips together and said nothing.

"Maybe your father only wants it to look like you are the next target to throw us off track. Maybe you aren't a target at all."

"I refuse to listen to this any longer. My father adored my mother," Kate said, eyes blazing as she looked at him.

Anderson flipped his notebook closed and returned the pen to his inside jacket pocket. Kate thought she saw a flicker of pity in his eyes as he got up from his chair, but it disappeared so quickly that she wondered if she'd imagined it.

He put his hand out, and she reluctantly took it in hers. "I'm very sorry," he said, as they shook. "I know this must be hard for you. I'm just looking for answers, and I go where the questions lead. I hope you understand."

"My father is innocent."

He cocked his head to one side. "Just be careful."

She hadn't been lying when she said that her father would never have murdered her mother, but she couldn't imagine him screaming at her either. And why had her mother wanted to change her will? Guilt washed over her at the disloyal thought. No. He wasn't capable of that. And she was sure he wouldn't taunt her and try to push her over the edge.

She'd talk to Molly and get this sorted out quickly. Kate googled the housekeeper's name for her phone number, and then punched it into her phone. After several rings a man's voice came on the line. "Hello?"

"Hello. This is Kate English, Mrs. Michaels's daughter. I wonder if I might speak to Molly Grassmore."

"I'm sorry. She's not here. Can I take a message?"

"When do you expect her?"

"She's out of the country. She left yesterday. Won't be back for a month or two."

Kate clutched the phone more tightly. "Who am I speaking with, please?"

"I'm her nephew. I'm house-sitting for her."

"I see. Thank you."

She hung up, her thoughts racing. Her parents paid their household staff well, but since when did Molly have the kind of money to leave the country for a month or two? Had her father sent Molly away to keep her quiet? Or maybe Molly had killed Lily, and she'd gone to the police to put suspicion on Harrison. It was pretty convenient for her to be unavailable for questioning now. Although why would Molly have killed her mother?

What Kate really wanted to do now was go for a run, but of course, there was no way she could with her sprained ankle. Instead, she went to the pantry and pulled out her stash of Hershey's Kisses, unwrapping one and popping it into her mouth. She had always made sure her family had healthy, organic meals. She ran every day—it kept her centered and cleared her mind as well. She didn't drink alcohol anymore, which was for other reasons, but it certainly contributed to her health. But chocolate—chocolate was her weakness, especially when she was stressed.

She thought about what Detective Anderson had told her. There had to be a reasonable explanation. Her father had always worshipped her mother. She unwrapped another chocolate and thought about a time when Lily and Harrison had taken a teenage Kate and Blaire to the beach house. They'd spent that sunny June day on the beach, swimming, reading, and relaxing. That night, Lily and Harrison had taken the girls to dinner in Ocean City at Fager's Island, a beautiful restaurant with windows overlooking the bay side of the small barrier island. They'd both worn white jeans and tank tops, Blaire's a hot pink and Kate's turquoise, to match her eyes. Kate smiled to herself as she remembered the two of them getting ready—applying thick mascara and shiny lip gloss. And then Lily had appeared, stunning in a cool white shift and simple gold earrings, her blond hair swept up with a few loose tendrils brushing her neck. Kate had felt like a grown-up as they'd all walked to their table and noticed heads turning. Even the waiter, who was around eighteen or nineteen, seemed to linger when he took their order and returned often to check on them once their meal had arrived. It had soon become apparent, however, that the object of his admiration was Lily. Harrison had chuckled after the waiter left the table and turned to Lily, smiling. "You are an enchantress, my love. I'm so lucky to be the one taking you home."

Later, as Blaire and Kate lay next to each other in the queen bed, Blaire had said to Kate, "That waiter was into your mom big-time. It was kind of weird."

Kate kicked the blanket off, pushing it down around her legs. She knew what Blaire was thinking——that Lily was too old, too much of a *mother*——for some young guy to be fawning over. He should have been flirting with them, not Lily. But it happened all the time. Men and women alike were drawn to Lily. Kate wasn't even sure her mother realized the effect she had. It was just part of who she was. Kate couldn't count the number of times her father had said how lucky he was to have married her. That couldn't have been an act. So they had an argument. But kill her? Never.

Wanting a distraction, she opened her work email and scrolled through to see if there was anything from the foundation requiring her immediate attention. Though her board had been giving her space to mourn, there were always requests coming in through the foundation's website that she needed to review. She sighed wearily when she saw there were over forty new emails. She methodically clicked each one, saving some to an action folder, forwarding others. Her hand froze when she heard the *ping* of a new email arriving. It was from Private Caller; the subject line was "Especially for You." Before she could think about it, she clicked on it.

There was no text, just an audio file. Her heart beat faster as the sound of an out-of-tune piano came from the speakers and a discordant version of "Pop Goes the Weasel" began to play. At first it was just the music, but soon a guttural voice, sounding distorted, like it had been through a mechanical voice changer, began to chant:

All around the mulberry bush
The killer chased the doctor
The doctor thought 'twas all in fun
Dead is the doctor

Kate grabbed her cell phone and fumbled as she tried to swipe it open; she had to put the passcode in three times before getting it right. She dialed Detective Anderson, gasping for air as the phone rang and rang. His voice mail eventually clicked on, and she choked out, "It's Kate English. I've received a threatening email. But I guess you know that. Please call me back."

She hoped the police would be able to trace the email to a physical address this time. She dialed Simon, but it went straight to voice mail. She pressed the end button in frustration. Why was no one answering? She called Blaire next.

"I was just going to call you," Blaire said.

"Can you come over?" Kate asked, the words gasping out of her.

"What's wrong?"

"Another message."

"I'm on my way. I'll be there as fast as I can."

She took a few deep breaths, focusing on the fact that Blaire would be there soon, that she had guards at the house. Unfortunately, the last thing anxiety did was accede to logic, but she had to try to calm down. She returned to her bedroom, and when she moved toward the bed, she noticed light spilling from the bathroom doorway. She hadn't used this bathroom since the mice had been left there, so why would the light be on? She took a deep breath and forced herself to open the door, exhaling when she saw that there were no dead animals waiting for her. There was nothing amiss. Someone had just flicked the light on, that was all. Maybe she had done it herself when she'd come upstairs, distracted as she'd been by the news of her parents' fight.

She turned it off and went to check on Annabelle, who was safe in bed, asleep. Kate tiptoed over to her and kissed her head, then backed out of the room, nodding to the guard on duty as she did.

As she came down the stairs, she nodded at the man sitting in the front hallway. Was that Jeff or Frank? She was having a hard time keeping them all straight. "Ms. Barrington is coming over shortly."

"Yes, ma'am."

"Can you please go around to all the rooms and double-check that all the windows are locked?"

He gave her a strange look, and then nodded. "Yes, ma'am, the house is secure, but I can check again."

"Please do. I'll check the kitchen."

All of the locks in the kitchen were secure, she discovered with relief. What was up with these nursery rhymes, though? Did they have a deeper meaning? She grabbed her iPad from the counter, went to Google, and typed "Pop Goes the Weasel Meaning." She clicked through article after article. One theory was that it was about pawning a coat to pay for a drink, another was that it referred to a spinning wheel. The only common thread seemed to be that it referred to the poor. Was it another dig at her for her wealth?

Her head was pounding. She poured herself a glass of water and downed a Valium from the high cabinet next to the sink, trying to shake off the feeling that someone was watching her.

12

Blaire was on the way back to the Four Seasons from Gordon's when Kate called. By the time she got to the house, Kate looked frantic, dark circles under her eyes.

"Kate, what's going on? I got here as fast as I could."

Blaire didn't miss the large black bruise on Kate's cheek, but before she could ask about it, Kate grabbed her hand and pulled her toward the stairs.

"It's an email on my desktop upstairs. I'm waiting for Detective Anderson to call me back. Come on." Kate held on to the railing, wincing as she favored her left leg.

"What happened to your face, and why are you limping?" Blaire asked as she followed behind.

Kate stopped and turned. "I fell off my horse yesterday."

"What?" Blaire exclaimed.

Kate sighed. "It was stupid. Simon and I were riding, and Napoleon got spooked. He threw me." She waved her hand. "I'm fine. Just a bruised ankle."

"Thank God you're okay. You have to be more careful!" Blaire wanted to tell her she was crazy for going out riding alone with Simon, but she didn't know how Kate would react.

When they reached the office, Kate plopped down into the chair. Blaire leaned over her shoulder to look at the screen.

"What . . ." Kate trailed off. "It was right here. It's gone!"

Blaire leaned in to look at the screen. "What do you mean, it's gone?"

"I mean it's not there." Her voice rose, hysteria edging it. "How could it just disappear?"

"I don't know. Check the trash. Maybe you deleted it?" Blaire suggested calmly.

Kate frantically looked through her deleted emails. "Nothing. I can't believe this! It was an audio file. 'Pop Goes the Weasel,' but the words were about me. 'Dead is the doctor.'"

"Okay, okay. Deep breath." Blaire gave Kate's shoulder a firm squeeze as she took a deep inhale herself and let it out slowly, a model for Kate to follow. "Let's go back downstairs and see if you can write down what you remember."

Kate turned and put her hand over Blaire's, squeezing it as she got up from the desk.

When they got to the kitchen, Blaire saw Kate's hand shaking as she pulled a pen and pad from the drawer. The landline rang, and Kate hesitated before answering it. "Hello?" She listened to the voice on the other end. "You saw it too? Okay, thank you." As she hung up, she said, "Detective Anderson is on his way back."

"It's late. Where's Simon?" Blaire asked.

"He had a business dinner tonight. I tried calling him, but he's not answering."

Business dinner my ass, Blaire thought. But she wanted to let Kate worry about one type of threat at a time—or maybe, at least only worry about one person at a time—while she dug in further to the nature of Simon and Sabrina's relationship.

They sat across from each other, and Blaire tried to think of a way to ease into what she had to say. "Listen, Kate. You know I told you I was going to start doing my own research for the case?"

Kate nodded.

"Well, I went to Gordon's tonight under the guise of hiring him."

"You went to his *house*?" Kate asked, her brows raised. "I've never even been there."

"Yeah. I told him I could only meet at night. I wanted to get a look around."

"Oh-kay."

"Someone vandalized his car while I was there, and he left me alone, which gave me the chance to snoop around."

Kate leaned forward with a furrowed brow. "You searched his house?"

"Don't worry. Gordon will never find out. The important thing is what I found."

"What was it?" Kate asked, her voice almost a whisper.

Blaire tapped the photo icon on her phone and handed the device to Kate. "This."

Kate took it from her, and all the color drained from her face. "What is this?" she breathed.

"Pictures of you."

Kate's hand flew to her mouth. "He's been following me around?" She flicked through the images. "These were taken in the summer. I'm wearing a sleeveless top here. And this one is just a few weeks ago. He's been doing this for months . . ."

"There were hundreds of photos in a file. I only had time to take pictures of a few. He's got all kinds of equipment too, cameras, telephoto lenses . . ." Blaire wished she'd been able to look through all of it.

Kate handed the phone back to Blaire. "How could I not have noticed him following me around? Am I really that unobservant?"

Blaire patted her hand. "He could have been really far away, with the equipment he has."

Kate shook her head. "Still, I never noticed someone *watching* me . . . Do you think he's the one? Could he have killed my mother?" Her breath was ragged, and her hands were shaking.

"I don't know. He's obviously still obsessed with you, but I don't see why he'd want to hurt Lily. Could he have been stealing money from the trust?"

Kate shook her head. "No, he doesn't have enough control of it on his own. Besides, he doesn't need it. His family is very well off." She shuddered. "This is like that crazy project he did years ago. The one I told you about."

"I think you'd better tell Anderson about it too."

As if she'd conjured him by saying his name, the detective walked into the kitchen through the swinging door. He nodded at Blaire and then turned to Kate.

"The email disappeared from our computer as well, but we *did* download the audio file before it disappeared."

Kate was shredding a napkin in her lap. "That horrible voice. And the chorus—dead is the doctor." She looked at the detective. "How could it just disappear?"

"There are services that allow you to send self-destructing emails. Our tech department will contact your email provider to see if the email can be found on their server. This is the email for your foundation, correct?"

Kate nodded. "Yes, it's easily found online." She paused a moment and then spoke again. "Detective, my father is not tech-savvy at all. I hope you're still working hard on looking at *other* suspects." Her voice had a hard edge.

What was she talking about? Blaire gave her a quizzical look.

Anderson merely nodded. "Of course. We'll continue to make sure to get screen shots and recordings on our end."

Blaire had never seen Kate look so haunted, at least not since Jake's death. It was clear she was shaken to the core.

Blaire drew her gaze from Kate and turned to the detective. "I have something to tell you as well." She felt uncomfortable under his scrutiny, watching his eyes narrow. "Gordon Barton has been taking pictures of Kate without her knowledge for months. Hundreds of them. I saw the folder at his house tonight."

"How did you happen to see them?"

She shrugged. "He stepped out of the house for a moment, and I took a look around his office."

Anderson scowled. "You have no business snooping around people's things. That's a good way to get hurt."

Blaire felt like saying, *If you were better at your job, I wouldn't have to.*

Kate bit her lip. "This type of thing is not unprecedented with Gordon."

Anderson frowned. "Can you elaborate on that?"

"It was a long time ago. We were just kids. But back when I was in eighth grade, he showed me a photography project he was working on. He'd used a telephoto lens to take pictures of his neighbors in their houses."

Anderson raised his eyebrows. "What kind of pictures?"

Kate shook her head. "Not *those* kinds of pictures. Nothing sexual or inappropriate. But . . . just normal goings-on—people cooking, watching television. He called it something like 'Urban Mundane.'"

Anderson heaved a sigh and shook his head. "How old was he?"

"Fifteen, probably?"

"Socially aberrant behavior like that often escalates. I'm very concerned to hear that he's been following you around." He looked at Blaire. "I'm going to need you to sign an affidavit confirming what you just told me, so we can get a warrant to search his house. In the meantime, I'll assign an officer to watch him, and we'll take another look at his alibi."

"I'm firing him immediately," Kate said. "I don't want him anywhere near me. I'll have his partner take over until we can find another firm."

"Please don't do that just yet. I don't want you"——he stopped and leveled a stare at each of them——"either of you, to say a word to anyone about this, especially him. If Mr. Barton *is* our man, we don't want to alert him. He could get rid of evidence before we've had a chance to search his house. We'll get the warrant as soon as possible."

"Fine," Kate said. "But once you have the evidence, he's gone. I don't care how far back our families go."

Blaire cleared her throat. "I think Gordon is a creep, but I don't see what he would gain by killing Lily. Besides, if he's obsessed with Kate, why would he want to hurt her? It seems more likely he'd go after Simon."

Anderson gave her an appraising look. "You don't know what kind of sick logic people have. Just stay away from him. Both of you."

Blaire wanted to bring up Simon, but she knew it wasn't the time. She chose her words carefully. "What about Sabrina? She's an old family friend of Simon's, right, Kate?" She looked at Kate. "She's made it clear you're not her favorite person."

Color rose to Kate's face, and Blaire couldn't tell if she was embarrassed or angry. "I don't know," Kate began. "I mean . . ." No one spoke as the implication filled the air. Kate turned to look at Anderson. "I've told you a little about her. Again, I'm not sure why she'd go after my mother." She fidgeted in her chair before she spoke again. "I'm wondering . . ." She stopped, and Anderson gave her a questioning look.

"There was a car accident the summer of my junior year in college. We'd been at a party." Kate hung her head. "My boyfriend was killed." She looked up at Anderson. "Anyway, I've felt like his parents always blamed me. They came to Mother's funeral. I was surprised they were there. They live a couple hours away now, in Pennsylvania. Do you think they could have something to do with this, that they might want revenge?"

"You said this happened when you were in college?"

"Yes."

"That was what? Fifteen or more years ago?"

Kate nodded.

"It's highly unlikely someone would wait so long to exact punishment, but if you give me their names, I'll check it out. I'll let you know if I think you have cause for concern." He stared back at Kate, his expression inscrutable. "I'm glad you told me about them, because you never know."

A chill went through Blaire.

"That's the problem. I'm beginning to trust no one and think everyone is *possibly* the murderer," Kate said, clearly exasperated and exhausted.

Anderson nodded slowly. "Everyone is."

13

After Anderson left, Kate tossed and turned, finally falling asleep a little past midnight. Even the Valium wasn't helping. And then the dream came back. She was driving up, up, up to a steep bridge that became almost vertical, her nausea growing the higher the car went. Then she reached the top, and the car perched precariously, tipping back and forth until it was propelled forward and she was plummeting, faster and faster, toward the hard pavement.

The dream had once come almost every night, but she hadn't had it in years, not after all the therapy and work she'd done to deal with her anxiety.

She called Blaire. "The dream came back."

There was a sigh on the other end of the phone. "Oh, I'm sorry. It's no wonder, though. Do you want me to come over now instead of waiting till dinnertime?"

"Yes, but no. Dad's coming over this morning, and we have to go over some estate business." She didn't want to fill Blaire in on Anderson's crazy suspicions.

"Okay. In the meantime, why don't you try some meditation? Try and clear your mind."

Kate heard Annabelle's sweet voice calling as she ran down the hallway to Kate's room. "Mommy, Mommy," she yelled, and came tearing into the room, jumping onto the bed. Hilda was right behind her.

"I've gotta call you back," she told Blaire and disconnected.

"It's all right, Hilda. Time for some cuddles. I'll bring her down for breakfast in a bit." She wanted Annabelle all to herself.

Hilda smiled and nodded. "Good. She loves her mommy time. I'll go downstairs and make some oatmeal. Would you like some too?"

"No, I'm fine. Thank you, though." She turned to Annabelle. "Come here, you little monkey." Kate plopped onto the bed and pulled her daughter into her arms. For the next ten minutes, as they wrestled and laughed, she forgot about all the danger and uncertainty surrounding her.

Hilda knocked on the door and stuck her head in. "Would you like me to get Annabelle dressed now?"

"I want to put on my bathing suit," Annabelle said.

"It's too cold for swimming, pumpkin. How about some snuggly pants and a sweater?" Kate suggested.

Hilda reached for Annabelle, and Kate reluctantly handed her over. She pulled a warm sweatshirt over her T-shirt and followed the tantalizing aroma of brewing coffee to the kitchen, pouring the steaming black liquid just as Hilda came into the room with Annabelle. A few moments later, Harrison arrived.

"Granddaddy!" Annabelle cried when she saw him come in.

"Good morning, my little peach. How are you today?"

"I was going to go swimming, but Mommy says it's too cold."

"I'm afraid she's right. I have to talk to Mommy for a little bit, but how about if we play Candy Land afterward?"

Annabelle pouted for a moment and then solemnly nodded. "All right."

"Good. Now sit down and finish your breakfast," Kate said, then stopped and stared at her daughter. She turned to Hilda. "Where did you get that sweater? I've never seen it before."

Hilda shrank back at the accusation in Kate's voice, and her brow creased. "From her drawer."

Kate felt a chill go through her. It was a green Christmas sweater with the words "Mice Scream for Ice Cream" stitched below a little mouse in between two red-velvet ice cream bars. The red in the bars reminded Kate of blood, and the mice immediately brought to mind the ones in her bathroom.

"Take it off her!" Kate insisted.

Annabelle started to cry.

"Kate, take it easy." Harrison picked Annabelle up and hugged her. "Sweetheart, Mommy needs to see your sweater."

"I don't wanna take it off! I like it!"

"I'll be right back," Kate said, and she ran to Simon's office and burst in. He was typing on his laptop.

"Did you buy Annabelle a Christmas sweater with a mouse on it?"

He looked up. "What? No."

She was keyed up, out of breath. "It was in her drawer. Hilda put it on her this morning. Come see."

He followed her back to the kitchen, but Annabelle and Hilda were gone.

"Where's Annabelle?" Kate demanded.

Her father walked over and put his hands on her arms. "Hilda took her upstairs to get her changed, like you told her to." He walked over to the island and picked up the sweater. "Here."

She grabbed it from him and shoved it at Simon. "Look. Don't those ice cream bars look like blood? And the mice . . . ? This was in her room! That maniac was in our daughter's room!"

Simon looked at the sweater and then back at Kate. "Kate, your mother gave this to her. She brought it over right after Thanksgiving, and you said something about her starting Christmas early this year, remember?"

Kate was seized by fresh grief. Images of her mother that day, her arms full of packages, saying "Wait till you see the darling things I picked up for Annabelle," flashed through her head.

Kate had told her Christmas was only a few weeks away, and suggested Lily wait to give the packages to Annabelle then.

Lily had thrown her hands up. "These are clothes *for* Christmas. And besides, no child wants clothes on Christmas morning. Look at this dress!" She'd held out a red-and-green-plaid dress. "Won't she look precious?"

She'd bought so many things, Kate must have missed the sweater. She'd have to apologize to Hilda for her outburst. Taking a deep breath, she looked at her husband and father. She was hot with shame at having reacted that way.

"I'm sorry. I guess I'm just a bundle of nerves. You must think I'm nuts."

Simon gave her a sympathetic smile. "Of course not. We're all on edge. It's okay."

His kindness endeared him to her for a minute, but she still couldn't let her guard down.

"If you're okay, I think I'll head back to my office, all right?"

She nodded and turned to her father. "Well, now that that's settled," she said, trying to lighten the mood. "How about we go to the family room? There's a fire going. Would you like a coffee?"

"I'd love one."

The room was large, but with several intimate seating areas, it still felt cozy, with its warm oriental rugs and river stone fireplace. Over the mantel hung a Turner landscape, a work that had been in Kate's family since the 1800s.

"I always enjoy this room," her father said, walking to the floor-to-ceiling windows.

He headed to the deep cushioned sofa facing the fire and sat at the far end from Kate, casually resting his arm on its back. Kate looked at her father's strong profile, the nose that was straight and proud. His dark hair had never lost its thick waviness, but the gray had taken over when he was in his early fifties. He was a great bear of a man, and she pictured her parents dancing together as they often had, her mother like a slim goddess in his muscular arms. He took a sip of coffee and placed the cup on the table in front of them. "So." He turned to look at her. "You sounded upset on the phone last night. What is it you wanted to talk about?"

She braced herself before she dove in. "I *was* upset. Still am. Detective Anderson was here last night. He told me things that don't make sense. Things about you."

His eyebrows drew together, and the frown lines between his eyes deepened. "What kind of things?"

"Did you and Mother have a big argument the day she died?" He said nothing, so Kate pressed him. "A shouting match, actually?"

"It's nothing for you to worry about," he said.

She looked at him incredulously. "But I am worried. He said Molly came to them. Said she heard you and Mom arguing. Screaming at each other. Is that true?" She watched his face carefully to see his reaction. Why was he being so evasive? He was behaving oddly, and she wondered if it had to do with more than just his grief.

"It's none of Molly's business."

"Did you send her away?"

His eyes widened in surprise. "What? Why would you ask me that?"

"I called her house, and her nephew told me she was out of the country."

"Good for her."

"Good for her?" Was he kidding? "What's going on?"

"Nothing is going on. She's been with your mother and me for ages. I can't move back into the house yet. I don't know if I ever will. But I couldn't put her out of work. I paid her a year's severance. I imagine she took that trip to Europe she's always wanted to take."

Kate didn't remember ever hearing Molly talk about going to Europe. "It looks a bit suspicious, Dad."

"Suspicious? You can't believe that I killed your mother!" He looked at her in shock.

She threw her hands up. "No. Of course not. But is it true about the fight?"

"Yes," he said. "We did have a fight. A bad one." He shook his head. "I'd do anything to take back what I said, but I can't."

Kate looked into his eyes, but they gave nothing away. He had his doctor persona on. She tried to do the same, but she was far too emotional. "What was it about?"

He rubbed his fingers across his brow. "That was between your mother and me. It has nothing to do with any of this."

Kate stared at him in disbelief. "You're not going to tell me?"

"It's private. Between your mother and me, as I said."

"Well, Anderson thinks it has something to do with her wanting to change her will. Is that what the fight was about? Was Mother going to cut you out for some reason?" She took a breath, and then continued. "Was there trouble in your marriage?"

He moved closer and tried to put his arm around her, but she pushed him away.

"Katie, you have it all wrong. I loved your mother, and she loved me." He held up his hands as if to show her he wasn't going to touch her again. He sighed. "Yes, we had a terrible argument, but I'm not getting into it with you. You'll just have to trust me that you don't need the details. She asked me to keep them private, and I'm keeping my promise."

"That's it? You sit here, telling me nothing, and then ask me to trust you? How can this secret be so important that you're willing to impede the police investigation? Mother is dead. Someone is threatening me. You've become a suspect. What on earth is worth protecting in the face of all this?"

"Lower your voice! You'll upset Annabelle."

She stood up and backed away from him. "Is that what you told Mother? Did you shut her up permanently?"

He rose from the sofa, his face twisted in pain. "Kate! How could you ask me that?" he said quietly.

"Please go. Leave. I don't want to see you again until you're ready to tell me the truth."

He put his hands up again and left the room. She stared after him, bereft.

What was he keeping from her? He must have done something to upset her mother enough for her to have made that appointment with Gordon. She sat there until she heard his car pull out of the driveway. Maybe she'd try and rest before dinner; she was exhausted and couldn't think straight anymore. She went to the kitchen and grabbed her cell phone from the counter. She was halfway up the steps when her text tone sounded. Her heart stopped when she saw it was from Private Caller.

Isn't it time to retire that old Yale sweatshirt?
You're turning into quite the slob.
Your mother would be appalled to see how you're falling apart.

She clutched the railing and looked down at her shirt. How did he know what she was wearing? She ran back downstairs and yelled to the guard by the door.

"Have the guards sweep the property! The killer is out there."

"On it," he answered.

She ran to the window in the kitchen, looking out, thinking about the expanse of woods behind them. Was someone hiding there, using binoculars and watching her? Or was the killer closer?

14

Everyone was in a state when Blaire arrived at the house. Kate had called her near hysteria, yelling something about the killer watching her. Now Simon was pacing, Kate pale and wild-eyed, and the guards searching the entire property. Anderson was the only calm one.

"Dr. English, Mr. English, I know this is very upsetting, but we don't know that the killer was actually here."

"Of course he was here! He knew what I was wearing. The text said it was time to retire my Yale sweatshirt."

Blaire put her arm around her friend and looked at the detective. "That *is* pretty specific. How could anyone know what she had on unless they could see her?"

"Maybe it was a lucky guess. It says on her practice's website that she went to Yale," Simon said.

"So what? That doesn't mean that's all I wear. Someone had to be watching me from the woods. It's the only explanation," Kate insisted, giving Simon a withering look.

"What if it's Gordon? He's got all that photography equipment," Blaire said.

Anderson shook his head. "Unlikely. We got the warrant to search his house early this morning and showed up around eight, much to Mr. Barton's surprise. The only things we found were the pictures that Ms. Barrington mentioned the other night. Nothing that could lead us to believe he had anything to do with your mother's murder or the current threats against you. He was home during the search, and couldn't have been anywhere near your house."

"What did that freak say about those pictures of my wife?" Simon asked.

"He was a little shaken, but he claims they are for an art project he's doing. They've all been taken in public places. There's no law against it. The paparazzi do it all the time."

Simon shook his head in disgust.

Kate stood up and began to pace. "Could you at least tell where the text came from?"

He shook his head. "Not this time. It wasn't over a recognized Wi-Fi. They used a VPN."

"What's that?" Kate asked.

"It's a virtual private network, which allows data to be encrypted and the IP address of the user to be masked," Anderson explained.

"We're never going to find out who this is," Kate whispered.

Anderson stood and walked over to her. "I promise you, I'm not going to rest until we do."

Was this how the parents of her young patients felt when they had to sit by and trust Kate while their children walked that terrifying line between life and death? It was a wonder those parents hadn't slapped her when she told them to remain calm, to trust her.

"Has anyone else been here today? Seen your outfit?"

"No. Well, my father," she said, her eyes widening.

Anderson raised his eyebrows. "I'll be in touch," was all he said as he left.

Blaire wondered what that exchange was all about.

One of the BCT guards entered the kitchen. "There's no one on the property or on the perimeter of the woods. We've got a team searching the rest of the woods now, but we've looked through all the video footage, and there's nothing."

"Big surprise," Kate said. "I'm going to go check on Annabelle." She looked at Blaire. "Will you come keep me company for a little while?"

"Of course."

Blaire followed Kate to the playroom, where Hilda and Annabelle were sitting together on the couch, watching a movie. Annabelle was so engrossed that she didn't look up as they entered.

Blaire and Kate stood behind the sofa. "What are you watching, sweetie?" Kate asked.

"Nemo," Annabelle answered distractedly.

They watched for a moment, and Blaire jumped when Annabelle screamed.

"It ate Coral!" Annabelle yelled as the barracuda's jaws started snapping. "No, her babies are gone too." She started to cry.

Kate scooped her up from the sofa and hugged her. "What's wrong with you?" she snapped at Hilda. "How could you let her watch this?"

Hilda's eyes grew wide, and she began to stammer. "She's seen it so many times. I had no idea it would upset her this time. I'm sorry. I would never have put it on if I'd thought it would frighten her like this." Kate pulled Annabelle closer, trying to soothe her.

"Well, maybe you should have thought about what effect it might have since all that's happened." Kate ran from the room with Annabelle.

Blaire gave Hilda a reassuring look. "Hilda, it's not your fault. Very bad timing, that's all. Kate's so upset with everything that's going on."

"I understand, and I'm trying to be sympathetic. But I can't seem to do anything right these days."

"Just be patient with her. She's not herself."

Blaire left Hilda in the playroom and went looking for Kate. She was in her daughter's bedroom, helping a calmer Annabelle with a jigsaw puzzle.

Kate looked up as Blaire came in. "That was intentional."

"What?"

Kate sighed and rolled her eyes, then stood and walked to the corner of the room. Blaire moved toward her, and Kate whispered, "The movie. Showing her a movie where the mother is killed. She's preparing her for my . . . you know . . ."

Blaire was stunned. "Kate! Come on. You can't watch a Disney movie without one or both parents being killed. It was just a coincidence."

Kate narrowed her eyes. "Was it? Maybe she and Simon are working together. I've seen *Finding Nemo*. After the mother is dead, the father and son live happily ever after."

Blaire was going to have to talk to Harrison. Kate was unraveling again. Right before her very eyes.

Blaire finally got out of bed at ten the next morning. She'd stayed at Kate's late into the night, doing her best to talk some sense into her friend. By the time she left, Kate had agreed to forget about the movie incident and give Hilda another chance. Blaire had fallen into bed exhausted when she'd finally gotten into her suite after two a.m. Now, slipping into her robe, she called room service and ordered breakfast. She went into the small kitchen and made a single cup of dark roast while she waited.

She opened her laptop and checked her email. She frowned. There was one from *her*. She hit delete. Then she saw one from her publicist, and clicked on it.

Thought you'd enjoy seeing these. Tour going well.

He'd attached some pictures from Daniel's talk at Waterstones in Trafalgar Square. There was a wall covered in copies of their latest book, *Don't Look in the Mirror.* It still thrilled her to walk into a bookstore and see their books prominently displayed up front. She never took that for granted. For as long as she could remember, she'd written. Short stories, poems, novellas. No matter what was going on in her home life, she could escape into the worlds she had created. She loved being the one to control everything, to decide who lived and who died, who stayed and who left. She was in seventh grade when she decided that she was going to be a published author one day. She'd talked to the school librarian, who helped her find a writing contest to enter. She read through the instructions on the bus ride home, eager to get her father to help her and mail it off right away.

She would never forget the look on his face when she showed him the entry form. She had expected him to be excited about it. He'd always complimented her writing and taken pride in her good grades. But when she handed him the story she wanted to submit, he pushed her hand away, not bothering to even look at it.

"You sound just like your mother." He said it like that was the worst thing in the world. "You're setting yourself up for disappointment. Do you know how hard it is to get published? Don't go setting your sights too high. You're a smart girl. You'll go to college, get a good job. Forget about all this writing stuff."

She'd run to her room before he could see the tears streaming down her face. For the first time since her mother left, she almost sympathized with her. Maybe if her father wasn't such a quasher of dreams, her mother would have stayed. It looked like he preferred someone boring and stupid like Enid. But Blaire wasn't going to let him hold her back. The next day she took the application back to school, and with the help of the librarian filled it out and sent it in. Three months later she received the letter that told her she'd come in second place, and that it would be published in the magazine. When she showed her father that night, he'd given it a cursory look, and an absentminded "That's nice, honey." Actually, even Enid had shown more enthusiasm, but Blaire didn't want Enid's approval. Her father's tepid support for her writing made it that much easier to say goodbye later, when they decided to send her to Mayfield.

Lily had been the first adult in Blaire's life who encouraged her dreams. It was Lily who in high school helped Blaire formulate a plan to increase her chances of getting into Columbia. She brought in a tutor to help Kate and Blaire with their SAT prep. She encouraged Blaire to get involved in the school paper, to submit her stories to magazines and other publications so that she could build a body of work. Lily took the time to hand-pick the appropriate charities and extracurricular activities best suited for each of the girls' dream colleges. By the time Blaire was ready to apply to Columbia, she had built up an impressive résumé—all thanks to the careful and loving attention of Lily. Blaire's heart ached at the thought of what had happened to her. She wished with all her heart that she could thank her again for all she'd done. She felt a tear slide down her cheek, wiped it away, and took a deep breath. It was too painful to dwell on, so she distracted herself by continuing to click through the pictures, lingering over one of Daniel next to a book-cover poster. It felt like forever since she'd been in his arms. She frowned. He was wearing that old gray sweater that she was always after him to throw out. Honestly, he needed better looking after.

She tried his cell phone, drumming her fingers as the phone

rang in that odd way it does when calling overseas. She sighed when she got his voice mail. The damn time difference was making it impossible to connect. She clicked reply to the email and answered.

> Thanks for the pics. Wish I could be there. Tell Daniel to drop by Good-hood and get himself a decent sweater. And tell him to call me! :) B

After scanning the rest of her in-box, she went to their Facebook author page and uploaded the London photos. Then a thought occurred to her, and she typed a name into the search bar. Three Sabrina Mitchells popped up. Blaire clicked on the photo of the Sabrina she'd met at the benefit. What a nitwit, Blaire thought—over three thousand friends, and no privacy settings. There was no way she knew all those people. Blaire clicked on her profile photo album. There were *lots* of pictures. Sabrina in a white bikini on a tropical beach, looking tanned and sexy. The next few at someone's wedding, Sabrina on the dance floor in a slinky strapless black dress, heels a mile high and her long hair trailing down her back. She looked fabulous. But the next ones were even more interesting. Pictures of Simon and Sabrina together—one at a construction site with hard hats on; another at a company dinner, their faces close together and a huge grin on hers. There was a photograph of a much younger Sabrina, maybe fifteen or so, on horseback with Simon and an older man. Blaire assumed it was Sabrina's father, the man who had been so good to Simon after his own father died. Another of her and Simon on horseback that Blaire recognized as being at Kate and Simon's property. She wondered if Kate had been on the little jaunt, or if it had been a romantic twosome.

There was not one photograph of Sabrina with any other man. All of her group photos included Simon, although to be fair, most of them were taken in some sort of work setting. But Blaire wasn't interested in being fair. It was completely obvious from Sabrina's dreamy expression in all of the pictures that she was in love with him. They went on and on, as if she were chronicling every moment of her life. And Simon's too. Kate wasn't in a single one of them. One thing was sure—the only person this crazy woman loved more than Simon was herself.

When Blaire reached the end of Sabrina's albums, she went to Selby's Facebook page, but she had clearly put up privacy settings, unlike that idiot Sabrina. Over the years, Blaire had occasionally gone to Selby's page to see if there were any pictures of Kate. She clicked on Carter's image in one of his wife's photos, and clicked through to his incredibly dull profile. Most of his posts were about his precious Lamborghini. There were pictures of him standing next to it, sitting behind the wheel, polishing it with a white cloth. Blaire scrolled through the pictures and saw a few shots of his kids at lacrosse games or—what else?—sitting in his Lamborghini. There were very few of him with his wife. Was it because Selby was camera-shy, or was the bloom off the rose? She impulsively clicked the Add Friend button. Why not? A little harmless flirting never hurt anyone. That's what her mother always used to say. Her mother would have loved Facebook. She could picture her now, looking up all her old beaus, as she called them, reconnecting and posting glamorous pictures of herself. How she loved having her picture taken.

One of the last days before her mother left was a Saturday, and her father had been at the dealership. Shaina had made pancakes for breakfast—a treat usually reserved for special occasions. Her eyes had been bright, her long copper hair piled on top of her head, and she'd run around the house excitedly. After breakfast, she'd called Blaire into her bedroom.

"Sweetie, can you keep a secret?"

Blaire had nodded.

"I ran into an old beau of mine last night at the grocery store."

"What's a beau?"

Shaina had laughed. "An old boyfriend. Your mama has lots of those. Anyhow, he knows some connected folks in Hollywood. I need you to take some pictures of me to send to him, okay?"

"Okay."

Shaina had handed her a camera. "Look through here and click." She'd shown Blaire how to use it.

"Okay, I'm ready."

Her mother struck a seductive pose, her red lips in a pout. She reclined on the bed, one hand on her hip, the other behind her head. As she changed poses, Blaire kept clicking away.

"Come here, let's take one together," Shaina said. Blaire turned the camera around and snapped one.

When they'd finished, she put everything away.

"Now listen, honey. Not a word to Daddy. He doesn't understand. But Mama is meant for greater things. California is waiting for me. Promise not a word."

Confused and nervous, Blaire had nodded. "Okay, Mama. But can I go with you?"

Shaina had smiled. "Absolutely. Not at first, of course. I have to get settled. But I'll come back for you, don't you worry."

Two weeks later, her mother was gone, but she'd forgotten the camera. Not knowing its contents, her father had had the roll of film developed. When he looked through the sleeve of photos, he shook his head in disgust and began ripping them in two. Blaire stayed silent until she saw him come to the picture of her with her mother. She put a hand on his. "Stop, Daddy. I want that one."

He'd given her a sad look. "Of course, honey." It was the last picture she ever took with her mother. Now, she realized what a horrible and selfish thing her mother had done. But for a long time, that photo was her most cherished possession.

15

The next day, Kate balled up the Yale sweatshirt and threw it into the kitchen trash. She knew that wearing it would only remind her of the danger she was in. They still had no leads on the texts or email. All of a sudden, it occurred to her that this person might have done the same thing to her mother before he killed her. Over the years, there'd been the occasional crank sending an angry letter or email, but they'd all been empty threats—except for the one incident that Lily had tried to keep from all of them. It was in the spring of Kate's senior year of high school, and Blaire was living with them by then. Kate heard the door chime in the middle of the night. She peeked into Blaire's room, but she was sound asleep. Kate had gone downstairs to see Lily tiptoeing down the hallway. Her hair was a mess, and she looked exhausted.

"Mother, where were you?"

"I had to take care of something," she'd whispered. "Everything's fine. Go back to bed."

A month later, the summons to appear in court came to the house. Her father happened to be home when the certified notice came, and signed for it.

"What's this?" he'd asked as he handed the official-looking document to Lily.

Kate had watched quietly as her mother's face turned red. "I was going to tell you."

"Tell me what?"

"It was last month. You were at the hospital. Margo called late at night. She asked me to pick her up."

He frowned. "Why?"

Her mother sighed. "Her husband had hit her. When he was asleep, she called and asked me to get her," she rushed on. "By the time I got there, he'd awakened and pulled a gun on us."

"What?" Kate's father exploded. "She should have called the police, not you."

Lily shook her head. "She had before. It never did any good. She just wanted to go . . . get to a safe house that night."

Kate had run over to her. "Mother! He could have killed you!"

She waved them both off. "A neighbor heard the yelling and called nine-one-one. The police got there soon after I arrived, and arrested him, so I have to testify."

It was one of the few times Kate had seen her father angry.

"I can't believe you kept this from me!" Harrison had shouted. "You could have been killed! What were you thinking, going out in the middle of the night by yourself?"

"I'm fine. Everything worked out. And now he's in jail."

"It is not fine," he'd roared. "You know as well as I do how dangerous those men are. You are not invincible, no matter what you think. You have to promise me never to do anything like that again."

Lily had promised, but Kate could tell it was lip service. Her mother was always going to do whatever her heart dictated in the moment. That's the way she was.

So it wouldn't be that far-fetched to think that she'd been getting creepy threats and had chosen to keep them to herself. Even though Kate was sure the police had scoured her mother's emails and phone records, she still made a mental note to mention it to Detective Anderson. If this was indeed the case, how long would it be before things escalated from texts and emails to the killer actually coming for her?

She walked over to the bookcase and pulled out a photo album, something she hadn't done since Lily's death. She smiled at a picture of her mother and grandmother and remembered the kind and quiet woman who always made her feel special. Each summer she would go and spend a week alone with Grandmother at her summer home on the Maine coast, and they would kayak and swim in the freezing cold water during the day and have marathon card-playing sessions each night. Kate's mother had had an especially close relationship with Grandmother. She remembered Harrison talking about a time during their engagement when Lily had spent months in Maine nursing her mother back to health after she'd had an unexpected heart attack in her late forties, cooking for her and making sure she was taking it easy. They'd even postponed the wedding by a few months so she was fully recovered. He'd said it was one of the things he admired most about his wife—her devotion to her family.

She returned the album to the shelf and went to the kitchen, pausing for a moment as one of the security detail walked back to his post in the hallway. Even though she was glad that Simon had stationed four guards around the estate, it felt like such an invasion, these silent sentinels who were strangers to her, as though there was nowhere she could be truly on her own. But what was even worse was that she was now terrified to be on her own. She picked up her cell phone and dialed her father. He answered on the first ring.

"I was just going to call you," he said.

"Dad, I'm sorry for yesterday, but we need to talk. I have to know what's going on. It's driving me crazy." She felt bad about the way she'd treated him, kicking him out of her house, and wanted to give him another chance to tell her what he and Lily had fought about. "Please tell me what's going on."

He took a minute to answer, then spoke in measured tones. "Your mother had lied to me about something that happened a very long time ago, and she had just told me the truth. I was shocked and, well, to say upset would be an understatement." He paused, clearing his throat, and continued. "However, what she told me has nothing whatsoever to do with you, and out of respect for your mother, I'm not going to divulge it to you. I hope that you know me well enough to respect my decision."

Kate's mouth dropped open. "That's it? Really?" She stood up and began to pace, gripping the phone tighter. "Are you going to *divulge* the details to Detective Anderson?"

"Yes. I'm going to call him this afternoon."

"Very well, then. I guess we have nothing more to discuss right now." She ended the call.

Kate sat alone for a while, trying to put together the pieces. What had happened to make her mother call Gordon about changing the will? It must have had something to do with whatever they had fought about. Why had he told her that her mother had lied? What was he trying to keep from her now? None of it was adding up. Everyone was hiding things. She felt her anxiety increasing, her mind concocting scenario after scenario. That night at dinner with Annabelle and Simon, she was barely able to hold a conversation. Her mind was racing, and she couldn't figure out how to stop it. At a little after seven thirty, she put Annabelle to bed, and continued to stew. She made a cup of tea and went into the living room.

What if her father had been seeing someone else, and her mother found out and threatened to divorce him? She thought back to the day her mother insisted she make Simon sign a prenup.

Her mother had made it a point to tell Kate that Harrison had signed one too. If they divorced, he'd lose millions. But still, he made plenty of money in the medical practice, and she knew he'd invested wisely over the years. She shook her head. But what had they argued about that would have made her want to change her will?

She felt as if her mind was spinning out of control. She'd worked so hard to tame it, to have a game plan for every day. Kate missed being in the operating room. She was in charge in her OR. Strong, competent, assured. Yes, there were sometimes surprises in surgery, but she never panicked, was calmness personified, her anxiety left in the scrub room. She trained hard for it, and had a plan for every contingency. But in the real world, where nothing was organized and ordered, it was a different story. She couldn't let herself fall apart again.

Simon came into the room, interrupting her thoughts. "I'm just going to run to the office to pick up some drawings. I'm going to work from home the rest of the week. With everything that's going on, I'll feel better being here."

She looked at him with suspicion. "It's getting late. You're leaving now? Can't it wait until morning?"

"It'll just be easier to get it out of the way tonight."

Or maybe he was meeting someone whose name started with an S. "Right."

He gave her a concerned look. "I'm trying to be supportive. I've got an early call, and I need those drawings beforehand. Otherwise I'll have to go into the office tomorrow morning, and once I'm there, it will be hard to extract myself. I won't be long."

"Fine."

After he left, she peeked into Annabelle's room and watched her for a few minutes. She loved to see her child sleep, so angelic and sweet. Kate's heart ached at the thought of not being able to see her precious little girl grow up. Suddenly, running to the bed, she scooped her up. Annabelle started to stir. "Shhh, it's okay. Come sleep in Mommy's room," Kate soothed her, and within a few minutes, she was back asleep in Kate's four-poster bed. Kate beckoned to the guard in the hall.

"Alan, I want you to guard my bedroom. No one is to come in. Do you understand? Not my father, not my husband, not the nanny. No one."

If he was surprised, his face didn't show it. "Of course."

She locked the door and pushed one of the wing chairs across the room and against it for good measure. She'd go online tomorrow and find some kind of door alarm too. She wasn't about to have anyone surprise her.

She needed to do something to try and calm herself down, but what? When she was a small child, Lily had affectionately referred to her as her little worrier. It was impossible for someone whose mind didn't operate that way to understand how debilitating anxiety could be. Whether it was stressing out over schoolwork or worrying about wearing the right outfit to a party, it seemed like she was always overthinking things. One of her earliest memories was her asking Lily how she was sure Santa wouldn't get hurt coming down the chimney. It wasn't until Kate became a teenager that her fears started getting worse. She'd lie awake in bed when her parents were out, unable to fall asleep until she heard the chime of the door alarm and knew they'd gotten home safely. Her imagination would run away with her as she envisioned them killed in a car accident or assaulted by a criminal. She'd toss and turn, trying everything to clear her mind of the horrible scenarios it concocted. Then they'd come home safe and sound, and she'd feel foolish—until the next time.

Even though nothing bad had happened, her happiness was tempered by the feeling that she was always waiting for the other shoe to drop. She would lie awake, imagining disaster. Then she learned that if she did math in her head, it helped her to fall asleep at night, her mind too occupied by equations to churn out unlikely, terrifying scenarios.

Blaire was the first person Kate had confided the extent of her anxiety to, one night toward the end of their first year at Mayfield. She was sleeping over, and they were lying in the dark, the house quiet, spilling secrets.

"Do you ever worry about something happening to your dad? Especially with your being so far away?" Kate had asked.

"Not really. What does my being far away have to do with it?"

"Well, um, I don't know. Sometimes I don't want to go to school . . . I'm afraid something will happen to my mother if I'm gone."

She heard Blaire shift next to her. "Something bad?"

Kate sighed. "Yeah. It's like when we're all together, I feel safe and good. But when I'm at school, I think about all the stuff she does and how she's out all the time. Like my dad is at work, and I guess I'm used to that. But my mom helps all those women whose husbands hurt them. What if they hurt her? Do you think I'm weird?"

Blaire reached over and took her hand in the dark. "Of course not. I understand that. But nothing's going to happen to her. She's too good of a person."

"How do you know?" Kate asked.

"Because. The world needs people like your mom. You just need to push the thought away." She looked up. "Let's see. Maybe we can think of something. You need a way to distract yourself."

"What will that do?"

"You'll stop yourself from focusing on the worry. You'll say it, and after a while you'll believe it."

She'd give it a try. They came up with their counting rhyme, and surprisingly, it had worked. At least most of the time. Then Kate joined the track team, got involved in more extracurricular activities, and before she knew it, she was too tired to worry—much. And Blaire was always there as a sounding board when she did. But by the time Kate was a freshman in high school, her therapist diagnosed her with generalized anxiety disorder and suggested she take medication. She'd noticed a difference right away. She wasn't obsessing over things anymore, not getting stuck like she used to. For the first time in a long time she felt like she wasn't walking around with a shadow over her. But after Jake died, everything changed.

Her fear of losing her mother had finally come true. It had taken many years, but part of her brain told her she was right in having been worried all that time. And of course, the accident that had taken Jake away was something she hadn't seen coming. Now, Kate could see Annabelle standing at Kate's graveside, sad and confused, while mourners threw roses on her coffin. Was her fear of leaving Annabelle motherless going to come true as well?

She had to take action. She swiped her phone open and searched "self-defense products." A variety of stun guns came up. So many choices. She clicked on one at a time, feeling herself begin to settle down as she read the descriptions. She'd talk to Alan and ask him which the best ones were. Now this was something that could help a lot more than a stupid little counting game.

16

The next day, Blaire stopped to pick up a box of chocolate-covered Berger cookies on the way to Kate's. Simon greeted her in the front hallway when the guards let her through. When he saw the box, he arched an eyebrow. "Cookies? Don't know that sugar is what she needs after the night she had."

Blaire didn't really care what he thought. "I guess we'll let her decide."

Simon cocked his head. "I think I know what's best for my own wife. She's coming apart, and the last thing she needs is you filling her head with sugar and panicky thoughts while you do your little amateur detective work."

"Me filling her head? That's rich. If I heard right, she kicked you out right before Lily died. So maybe you're not the best one to tell me what Kate needs." There was no way she would let Simon come between them again. Blaire had wondered over the years if perhaps she'd been wrong to caution Kate against marrying him. But now she knew in her bones that she'd always been right about him. And her connection to Kate was as strong as it ever had been. In the short time she'd been back, it had felt almost like they hadn't lost all those years.

"I'm back," he said firmly. "And I intend to stay."

Blaire laughed. "I wouldn't count on that."

Simon came closer to her, the small box of cookies the only barrier between them. "Listen. If you think I'm going to let you poison Kate's mind against me, you better think again. I'm the one she needs right now. When she came back to school after the accident, when I first met her, she was still fragile after her breakdown. I'm the one who helped her through. Not you. And I'll get her through again. You're not needed here."

Blaire felt her back go up at Simon's choice of words. He was making it sound like Kate was crazy. Her friend hadn't had a *breakdown*; she'd just gone through a difficult time.

"Is your ego really that big? Like you were the sainted hero who brought her back to life? She was already on the mend that fall. Anyone would have had a hard time coping with what happened. And now—Lily's death, the threats—anyone would feel the pressure. Kate's a strong woman. A surgeon. She's not going to lose herself. And you can bet your ass that I'm not going anywhere as long as Kate wants me here. I don't give a damn if you like it or not." And she didn't. He wanted Blaire gone because she was getting close to the truth.

After seeing her reaction to *Finding Nemo* two nights ago, she wasn't sure how strong Kate actually was now, but she wasn't going to let Simon know that.

She thought back to that Fourth of July weekend after their junior year in college when it had all come crashing down. A somberness had hung over the beach house as they grieved. Kate had been withdrawn and quiet, like a hurt animal. Blaire would hear her in the middle of the night, wandering around the house. She'd awakened early one morning and seen that once again Kate's bed hadn't been slept in. When she went downstairs, she found Kate in one of the rocking chairs on the screened porch, staring straight ahead as the chair moved furiously back and forth.

"Kate." Blaire had knelt beside the chair, resting a hand on its arm. "Are you all right? Have you slept at all?"

Suddenly the chair had stopped, and Kate glared at her. "Leave me alone," she shouted, jumping up from the rocker. "All of you. Leave me alone. Why are you bothering me?" She ran into the house in tears.

Blaire had been frozen for a moment, not understanding what had just happened, but as the days progressed, they all began to see it. Kate hadn't been sleeping or eating; she was tense and on edge all of the time, having angry outbursts over nothing. She stayed in the house, refusing to step foot on the beach or go anywhere, especially if it involved getting in the car. Late one night, when Kate seemed a trifle calmer than she had in the last weeks, Blaire saw an opportunity to try and talk to her. They were on the porch again, where Kate was spending practically all her waking hours. "I know how sad you are, Kate, how hard this is. But I'm really worried about you. It feels like you're sinking, like you're coming apart before my eyes. I don't know how to help you."

Kate was silent.

"Kate," she'd pressed. "Talk to me."

Kate had turned her head slowly and looked at Blaire. "I can't do this anymore. I can't." The rocker swung crazily as she jumped up from it and began to pace. "There's this pressure around my lungs, and it's going to suffocate me, like a bubbling in my chest that's going to explode. I can't think straight, I can't sleep—if I try, the nightmares come. I can't stop crying. I can't keep doing this."

"You need to talk to someone, Kate. Now."

But Lily and Harrison were one step ahead of Blaire. Harrison had already made arrangements for Kate to meet with her old therapist. She'd told them that Kate was suffering from acute stress disorder. She adjusted Kate's medicine and saw her three times a week the rest of that summer. When September came, and Kate returned to Yale, she was coping better, and was referred to a therapist in Connecticut who she saw as needed. And then she'd met Simon.

Blaire looked at Simon now. "Are you going to let Kate know I'm here, or shall I text her and tell her you're trying to get rid of me?"

He gave her a sour look, turned away without a word, and climbed the stairs.

"I'll be in the kitchen," she called after him, shrugging off her coat as she walked away.

She felt at home in Kate's kitchen now, and she pulled out some plates and napkins. There were three candles burning, filling the room with the smell of vanilla. The scent made her hungry. She was tempted to grab a cookie, but she had only used the fitness center at the Four Seasons a few times since she'd come to town, and her clothes already felt uncomfortably snug. Pulling a bottle of Fiji water from the refrigerator, she took a long swallow. She looked up when she heard footsteps and had to stop herself from showing how shocked she was at Kate's appearance. Her yoga pants were hanging off of her, and the circles under her eyes were practically black.

"Sorry to keep you waiting," Kate said. "I took a nap after lunch. Or at least I tried to." She spotted the box of cookies, and her lips curled into a half smile, the first one Blaire had seen in a while. "Bergers!" She lifted the box and peeked inside. "Bless you!" She took one out and bit into it. "Mmmm. Just what the doctor ordered."

"You look like you need to eat the whole box. Your pants are practically falling off."

Kate shrugged. "Well, having a killer after you does wonders for your figure."

At least Kate hadn't lost her sense of humor, Blaire thought. She looked over her shoulder to make sure Simon wasn't around and addressed her friend in a low voice. "Listen, I found some interesting photos on Sabrina's Facebook page. Is there somewhere more private we can talk?"

A flash of anger crossed Kate's face at the mention of Sabrina's name. "Sure, we can go to the study." When they entered the homey room with the dark green walls, Kate flipped the switch to the gas fireplace. Blaire stared a moment at the soothing flames. All the curtains were drawn, clearly in response to the text about the sweatshirt two days ago. Kate picked up her laptop, and they sat next to each other on the small love seat.

Kate opened her browser and turned to face Blaire. "How did you see her Facebook page? Did you friend her?"

"No," Blaire said, rolling her eyes. "The loony bird has no privacy settings. I'm thinking she wants the whole world to watch her live her amazing life. We should introduce her to Gordon."

"Not amusing," Kate said. "He won't stop calling me. I had to block his number from my cell phone. He even showed up here, and they told him they'd call the cops if he didn't leave."

"What a nut job. This was after you fired him?"

"Yes. Anderson gave us the okay after they searched his place. Simon is having everything moved to another firm. I don't want anything to do with him."

"Did you tell his partners about the photos?"

Kate shook her head. "No. As angry as I am about what he did, I'm not out to ruin his life."

Blaire didn't know whether she agreed with that decision. Those stalker types took any kindness as an encouragement. "Maybe you should get a restraining order."

"Simon wanted to, but I said no. But he did tell Gordon that if he comes anywhere near me ever again, he would. It's not a priority right now, seeing as how I'm practically a prisoner in my own home."

Blaire pulled up Sabrina's Facebook page. "Here, look." She pointed to the photos. "Half of them are her with Simon. You haven't ever looked at this?"

"No. I guess I'm the only person under forty who doesn't do Facebook. Selby set up an account for me a few years ago, but I just don't have the time or inclination. It all seems so pointless." She turned her attention to Sabrina's photos. As she flipped through picture after picture, she seemed mesmerized, her face growing paler and paler as she studied each one. She came to one of Simon and Sabrina standing against the railing of a boat, the sky dark behind them. There were party lights strung up and other people near them milling about with drinks in their hands. Sabina's smile was megawatt, and next to the photo was the caption "AIA Conference on Architecture: Emerging Professionals Party Cruise."

"Son of a bitch!" Kate blurted.

Blaire was taken aback. Kate never cursed.

Kate looked through the photos once again. "Look at these," she said in disgust. "You would think they were a couple."

"Were you there when any of these were taken?"

"Some. Not many, though. Definitely not the conferences. He's very conveniently made no mention of Sabrina attending any work-related functions." She slammed the computer shut and looked at Blaire. "What else is he lying about? I can't trust anything he tells me. He was so angry with Gordon. Probably all an act to make it look like he's worried about me."

"Do you think something is going on between them?"

"I don't know. Before Sabrina came around, I would never have believed he'd cheat. But things are different now. I'm starting to doubt everything. All those years ago, when Mother and I fought about making him sign a prenup . . . I wonder if she saw something in him that I didn't. He's never in all the years we've been together given me any reason to believe he married me for money. But lately . . . I don't know. . . . Some of the things he's said . . ." She looked at the floor.

"Like what?" Blaire asked, thinking back to what Gordon had told her about Simon's firm's financial problems.

Kate sighed. "Something at the reading of the will. It struck me at the time, but I dismissed it." She was staring at the floor again, miles away, it seemed. Blaire decided not to push her further today, sensing that Kate had said all she wanted on the topic.

Anderson was right about one thing: Kate had good reason to be suspicious of everyone around her. And Blaire was not going to stop until she had eliminated each one of them.

17

When Kate and Simon picked the lot on which they were going to build their dream house, she'd been happy about the seclusion and the expanse of woods that the house backed up to. Now it seemed like the perfect place for a killer to hide. The next morning, she strode with purpose around the house, peering out each window to see if anyone had snuck onto the property and was lurking somewhere in the dense brush. Satisfying herself that all was secure, she began her rounds again, opening every closet door in every room, searching for anyone or anything that might be hiding. She knew the house was surrounded by security, but it made her feel better to actually do something.

Christmas was in two days, and she was dreading it. The loss of her mother was too close to the holidays for Kate to believe she could ever forget the horror now attached to it. The threatening words of the nursery rhymes played over and over in her head, as if on a loop, and the image of those poor brutalized animals was seared into her brain.

She'd declined all the invitations they'd received, even low-key lunch dates with friends, needing to be at home. But when Selby had called to invite them to dinner, she'd caught Kate in a moment of lonesomeness, and she had relented.

Kate was quiet on the drive to Selby and Carter's. She sat with Simon and Annabelle in the back seat of the black Suburban supplied by the security company and driven by their bodyguard. The doors of the vehicle were apparently reinforced steel, the windows bulletproof. After yesterday, though, she was convinced that all the security in the world wasn't enough to save her. This person wasn't coming after her with a gun. Whoever it was would get in close and personal, just like they had with her mother.

Simon and Annabelle chatted the entire way, but Kate only half listened. She was beginning to feel the familiar signs: her pulse quickening, her breathing becoming shallow. This hadn't been a good idea.

"Simon, we should go home. This was a mistake."

"Kate, please. Try to relax." He put a reassuring hand on her arm. "It will do you good to get out a little, to be with good friends."

"Maybe." She supposed he could be right.

A little less than an hour later, Kate looked around the table as the white-gloved waitstaff served a first course of salmon rillettes. Selby had gone to a lot of trouble. The dazzling candlelight of the crystal chandelier made the damask-covered table even more luminous. Lily and Georgina had both been particular about how their tables were laid, but Selby was positively obsessive. There was hardly an inch of space on the surface of the table, it was so filled with china, crystal, silverware, and Christmas greens. Kate fingered the four sterling repoussé forks next to her plate, over a century old, the same pattern as her mother's own silverware. They were made by a Baltimore company, S. Kirk & Son, America's oldest silversmiths. She thought of sitting around her mother's dining room table at Christmas and felt her eyes fill just as Carter, at the head of the table, gently clinked his wineglass and lifted it in a toast.

"To our wonderful friends and family," he said. "Thank you for coming tonight. It's good that we can be together to help each other through this sad time."

Kate felt warmed by his words. It *was* comforting to be surrounded by old friends, and she was glad Simon hadn't listened when she suggested they turn around.

"Lovely sentiment, Carter," Georgina said.

Silence settled heavily as they raised their glasses. Selby's sons—Bishop, Tristan, and Carter IV—were holding wineglasses filled with soda, while Annabelle twirled a colorful cartoon cup in her hands, and of course Selby had made sure Kate's wine goblet was filled with her usual soda water. Kate smiled at Selby's brother, Palmer, who sat across from her. She had always liked him. Although he was two years older than his sister, he'd always been kind to Selby's friends, never making them feel like annoying little pests, like a lot of older brothers did. He'd lived in London the last sixteen years, working as a senior lecturer at the London School of Economics. She'd met his partner, a stage actor with the Royal Shakespeare Company, on two occasions when she and Simon were in England. Unlike Selby, he had escaped the rigidity of his mother's ordered and hierarchical world, where appearances mattered above all else. He had seemed content, happy and unguarded, very much at home in his adopted country.

"It's so good to see you again," Kate said, smiling at him. "How is James? It's a shame he couldn't come."

"He's busy. In rehearsal right now for *The Tempest*. Prospero. Opens in three weeks. He's either reciting lines or making illegible notes in the three annotated volumes he's studying."

"Sounds intense."

"Extremely. He hardly has time for anything else."

"Well, I'm sorry to miss him this time. When do you head back?"

"I'm leaving on the twenty-fifth. He and I will do Christmas on Boxing Day." His face became serious. "James only met your mother once, but he was enchanted. I'm so sorry. She was a lovely woman, Kate."

"Thank you." Tears sprang to her eyes.

"How is the investigation going?"

She felt the fear rise up in her as everything that had happened in the past few days ran through her mind. The police still didn't want her to tell anyone else about the messages and texts. She focused on keeping her voice even. "There's not much progress, I'm afraid. Everything seems to lead to a dead end."

Palmer shook his head in sympathy as the first course was being cleared.

Georgina's voice rang out. "Delicious salmon rillettes, Selby. Your cook has done a nice job." She looked her stiffly impeccable self in her cream-colored silk suit, not a blond hair out of place. She wore her customary three-strand pearl necklace, the same one she'd worn forever. She'd moved her engagement and wedding rings to her right hand; her left, the veins on it slightly raised, a few age spots beginning to appear, was bare.

"But, dear," Georgina said, fingering the holly on the centerpiece in front of her, "your greens look a bit tired. How long ago did you have them cut?"

Kate watched Selby deflate, the same way she had as a little girl when Georgina shamed her. She watched as Georgina took a delicate sip of wine, replaced her glass, and turned to face Harrison, who was sitting next to her. She leaned closer, until her lips were practically touching his ear, and whispered something. Harrison nodded as she spoke, his eyes cast down at the table.

Kate stared at them, frowning, and then leaned back in her chair as a server placed a steaming dish before her.

"All right," Selby said. "This is in homage to my brother and his unaccountable love of British cuisine. Roast lamb, Yorkshire pudding, gravy, roasted potatoes, and cheese cauliflower. Bon appetit, everyone."

A few moments of silence passed as everyone ate. "Perfect, Sis," Palmer said between bites. "James will be devastated he missed it."

"You know," Georgina said, putting her fork down and turning to Harrison, "this reminds me of the time the four of us went to England and France together. You and Lily and Bishop and I. Remember?"

"I do," Harrison said. "That was a great trip."

Georgina beamed, her blue eyes shining. "We stayed in that beautiful B&B in Kensington, near Hyde Park. You both worked so hard in those days, so many nights and weekends that Lily and I were practically single moms. Sometimes we even had to leave you behind for vacation. Remember that time she and I took the children to the Isle of Palms?" She leaned forward, warming to her subject. "We booked the most marvelous house, with a screened-in porch that looked right at the ocean. It had those wonderful ceiling fans that just kept turning lazily all day, keeping things just cool enough so that you didn't faint from the heat and humidity. Then it would cool down at night, and we'd enjoy the sound of crashing waves. In the morning, everything was damp and fresh. It was just divine." She took a sip of wine, her food untouched. "Anyway, the husbands never made it, of course, so there we were, all on our own with Palmer, Selby, and Kate scrambling around like wild little Indians."

"We don't use characterizations like that anymore, Mother," Palmer scolded good-naturedly. "Besides, you were hardly on your own, with two nannies and a cook."

At this there was laughter around the table.

Georgina gave her son a bright smile. He had always been her favorite, the child she doted on—the one who could get away with "teasing" his mother, and whose coming out of the closet she'd surprisingly not just accepted but embraced. "Don't laugh," she said, winking at Palmer. "It wasn't the same as being at our own beach houses. We were in a new and unfamiliar place where we didn't really know anyone. Lily convinced me that it would do us good to do some exploring, and we left the kiddies with the nannies and drove into Charleston, walked around, shopped, and then . . . we went to a drag queen show." She paused, letting the silence hover for effect.

Kate and Selby looked at each other in surprise.

"You never told us that," Selby said.

"You were only eleven years old. You didn't need to know what we were up to. Anyway, we had a great time, staying till closing and chatting with all the queens. They taught us so much about makeup." She laughed again. "And other things . . ."

"Mother!" Selby said, tilting her head toward her sons, who at this point were laughing and whispering among themselves.

"Mom, we're not babies. We know what a drag queen is," Carter Junior said, and the boys broke into laughter again.

"Sounds like you had a great time," Harrison said with a smile. "Lily never told me."

"There are lots of things wives don't tell their husbands," Georgina said, looking at Harrison.

What was that supposed to mean? Kate wondered.

"You and Lily were such good friends," Selby's voice interrupted her thoughts. "Just like Kate and me."

Kate glanced over at her. Selby had been a good friend to Kate over the years, the first one to offer help and advice when Kate suffered with morning sickness, the first one to be there, visiting and pitching in, after Annabelle's birth by C-section. Ever since Blaire's departure, the friendship between Selby and Kate had flourished, much the way it had before Blaire entered Kate's life.

Harrison turned to Georgina. "Remember Roger DeMarco?

He used to belong to the club before he moved away. He heard about Lily and reached out. Nice of him."

"How thoughtful of him. Where's he living now?"

"He's in Florida. Sarasota."

"Oh! I just love Sarasota," Georgina said. "There's a marvelous bridge tournament there every winter. In fact," she continued, "wouldn't it be great fun if we went together? You could visit your old chum, and we could both play in the tournament. If I remember right, you used to be a pretty wicked player."

Kate wanted to jump in, but it wasn't her place. She was bristling for her mother's sake, but perhaps Georgina was just trying to do for Harrison what he and Lily had done for Georgina when Bishop passed—keep him busy and social in spite of his grieving. This felt different, though.

"Uh, I don't know," Harrison said quietly.

"Oh, Harrison," she said, nudging his shoulder in a ribbing way. "Remember how we always used to joke that you and I should be married, that we were so much more compatible . . ." She laughed, her hand against her chest, as if embarrassed by her own words. "Just a little funny observation . . ."

"Have you lost your mind, Mother?" Palmer's voice interrupted her. "What a thing to say."

Harrison was staring at Georgina in bewilderment, just like the rest of them, but she stuck her chin out defiantly. "I didn't mean anything by it. I was just reminiscing. Goodness, if Lily were here, she would tell everyone to lighten up."

She was crazy, Kate thought. Her father and Georgina were nothing alike. She was seething at the suggestion.

"I hope you're not upset with Mother," Selby whispered to Kate, leaning in. "She doesn't always think before she speaks. As you well know."

The conversation after that was pretty desultory—the parts that Kate could focus on, anyway—and they were almost through dessert without any more tasteless comments from Georgina when they heard the doorbell ring.

Margaret, Selby's house manager, slid into the room and discreetly whispered into Selby's ear. She looked puzzled. "Kate, something has been delivered for you."

Kate felt a shiver go through her. "What?"

Selby shrugged. "I don't know. Should I have Margaret bring it in?"

"No!" Kate stood. Whatever it was, it couldn't be good, and she didn't want Annabelle to see it. Simon and Harrison both shot up from their seats. "Let's go see," Kate said, trying to keep her voice steady. She turned to Simon. "Stay here with Annabelle."

Georgina looked around at everyone in confusion. "What is going on? Where are you going?"

Kate walked from the room to the hallway as Selby and Harrison followed behind. A long cardboard box sat on the gold Parsons table. She lifted the top and saw a card perched on the tissue paper covering its contents. She felt a shiver go up her spine. She felt as if she might collapse, her legs suddenly made of jelly.

She looked around uneasily. "How did he even know I was going to be here?"

Selby gave her a puzzled look. "How did who know?"

"What does the card say?" Harrison cut in.

Kate took it from the box and handed it to him, watching his face for a reaction. His eyebrows shot up.

"It's from you. Did you forget that you had flowers sent to Selby tonight?" He handed the card to Kate.

Kate took the card wordlessly, her eyes scanning it.

Merry Christmas, Sel. I know white roses are your favorite.
Xo Kate

"But I . . ." She had to think. She hadn't sent these, but she *had*
thought about having an arrangement delivered. Could she have
mentioned it to Fleur and forgotten? Selby and her father were
both looking at her as if she were crazy. "Sorry, Selby. I've been
so stressed. I guess the florist just made a mistake in addressing
these to me. I remember now, I called them yesterday." She moved
back toward the box and pushed the paper back. White roses.

Simon came into the room, carrying a sleeping Annabelle.
"What's going on?"

"Just a little mix-up," Selby said, her voice too bright. "Kate,
these are lovely. Thank you so much."

"You're welcome. Sorry about earlier. I seem to be forgetting
things lately."

Selby patted her arm. "It's understandable."

Kate took a deep breath and looked at Simon. "I think we
should get going. Annabelle's out, and I'm feeling exhausted."

Once they were on the road, Simon turned to her. "What happened back there with the flowers?"

She leaned back against the headrest and closed her eyes. "For
a minute, I was afraid that it was another macabre message for
me. You didn't order those roses, did you?"

"You mean *you* didn't?"

"I must have mentioned it to Fleur. I hadn't realized she'd taken
care of it."

Her mind reeled as they drove home. She hadn't sent those
flowers tonight, despite what she'd told her father and Selby. And
she'd never discussed it with Fleur. But she wasn't about to let

Simon think she was losing it. She'd call the florist tomorrow and find out.

They were just pulling into the driveway when her text tone sounded. She knew before she looked who it would be from.

Simon reached across Annabelle and grabbed her hand. "Is it him?"

Kate saw the words flash on the phone before she swiped. "Yes," she said, her voice shaking. The blood in her veins froze as she read the text.

Did you really think you could take a night off? Pretty callous of you, being merry while your mother is decomposing in the ground. Are you as excited as I am to see what comes next? What might be in your coffee? Could your dessert be made with nuts? You'll have to wait and see.

The next day, the jangling of the house phone made her jump, and she reached out a tentative hand, hesitant to pick it up, but then saw Selby's name on the caller ID. "Selby. Hi."

"How are you?"

"Okay. Thanks again for last night. Sorry for the confusion at the end of the evening."

"It was my pleasure. Thank you for the beautiful roses. Do you want some company later? Or can I bring you anything?"

"Thanks, but I'm just going to lie low today. We'll talk tomorrow, okay?" Kate wanted to get off the phone.

"All right, talk then."

After she hung up, she went into the bedroom, where Annabelle sat on Kate's bed with a book in her lap.

Kate sat on the edge of the bed. "What are you reading, pumpkin?"

Annabelle closed the book and pointed to the title. "Look, Mommy. It's Cordree. You read it."

"*Corduroy*." Kate laughed. "Come on, snuggle up and we'll read it together."

When they finished, Annabelle jumped from the bed and grabbed *Harold and the Purple Crayon*. "Read this one now," she said, climbing back into bed beside Kate.

"Okay. One more, and then we get dressed." When she finished the story, she ran her fingers through her daughter's curls affectionately. "What would you like to do today, sweet girl?"

Annabelle wiggled closer to her. "Can we ride the horses?"

"Ooh, I don't know about that. Mommy's a little tired today. Maybe tomorrow."

"Maybe Miss Sabrina will come again, and I can go with her and Daddy."

Kate was very still. "Do you go riding a lot with Daddy and Miss Sabrina?"

Annabelle snuggled against her. "Sometimes she comes when you're at the hospital. She's a really good jumper, Mommy."

Kate's nostrils flared, anger coursing through her. So Sabrina was coming over when Kate wasn't home. What the hell was Simon doing?

Before she could ask anything more, Simon tapped lightly on the doorjamb.

"Daddy," Annabelle cried. She stood on the bed and jumped up and down.

"All right if I come in?" He stood there, waiting until Kate nodded, and then walked over, picking up Annabelle and swinging her around as she shrieked with laughter.

"Are you coming downstairs?" he asked Kate as he put Annabelle down. "I have to leave soon."

"Yes. I'll get her dressed and we'll be down." Her voice was cold.

Simon had told her last night that he needed to drive to Delaware this morning to see a client. He'd sounded worried, but when Kate questioned him, he'd brushed off her concern.

"There's nothing wrong. Just need to go over some items in the bid," he'd said, but his words rang hollow.

She knew him well enough to know when something was wrong, and he definitely had that "work worried" look on his face.

"I have to go," he'd said, "even though I really don't like being two hours away from you and Annabelle."

"If it's just to answer some questions, can't someone else go in your place?"

"No," he'd snapped, and then more calmly said, "They want to see *me*."

She'd been a little unsettled by his reaction, but that's where things were left when they'd gone to their separate rooms the night before.

There was a steaming mug of coffee waiting when Kate and Annabelle came into the kitchen. "I'm taking orders," Simon said. "What kind of eggs would you two ladies like?"

"Scrambled," Annabelle chirped.

"Nothing for me." Kate took a sip of coffee and sat down just as Simon's cell phone rang. The coffee tasted odd, but maybe it was because she'd just brushed her teeth. She couldn't let that stupid text actually convince her that everything was tampered with. That was what this person wanted, but she couldn't deny that it tasted funny.

He glanced at the display and rejected the call, quickly putting the phone in his pocket.

"Who was that?" Kate asked.

"Don't know. Didn't recognize the number. You sure I can't fix you something?" he asked.

"No, you should probably get going," she said, trying to tamp down her suspicion that he was lying about the phone call. Her paranoia was wearing her down. She took another sip of coffee. "What did you put in here? It tastes funny."

He shrugged. "Just milk and a stevia. The way you always like it."

She walked to the refrigerator and took the milk out, looking at the date. Still a week to go. She opened the top and smelled it. It hadn't gone sour. Had Simon put something else in the coffee? Her eyes narrowed as she looked at him. "Taste it." She handed him the mug.

He put his hand up. "I already had my coffee, and I've got to run."

After he left, she thought about the text from last night. She pulled it up on her phone. **What might be in your coffee?** What kind of game was he playing? But would he be that obvious? She poured the coffee down the drain.

Forcing a cheerful tone, she looked at Annabelle's plate. "Okay, girlfriend. You did a good job on your eggs. What do you say we go to the playroom and do some coloring?"

"Okay." Annabelle slid off the chair, and Kate took her by the hand.

Annabelle ran to the large box next to her easel and pulled out the box of crayons and five coloring books.

"Which one do you want, Mommy?"

"Hmmm. Let's see," Kate said, fanning the books out on the table. "I'll take *Moana*. Which are you going to have?"

"*Frozen*."

They were coloring together, Annabelle chattering away, and Kate tried to enjoy the moment. After a while, Kate closed her coloring book. "I think I'll try a different book. Maybe the one with all the animals," she said, sliding it to her.

She opened the book, flipping past the pages that were already colored, then past a hedgehog she had no interest in doing. When she turned the next page, she dislodged a page that had come away from the binding, one already bright with crayon. She bent to grab it off the floor and saw the image—a picture of a long knife, its blade colored with dark red dots that looked like drops of blood. Next to it was a woman wearing scrubs, her face distorted, the eyes and mouth drooping ghoulishly like melting wax. In the corner was a bed filled with stuffed animals, but empty of a child. She brought her hand to her mouth, stifling a gasp so as not to scare Annabelle, her heart thundering against her ribs.

What the hell use were guards and security when someone could sneak into her daughter's playroom?

That's when it dawned on her that this was precisely the message the killer was sending. *I can get to you wherever you are.*

18

*H*ot flames licked the floor, dancing their way toward her with alarming velocity. The room was so thick with smoke that she could barely see, and she croaked a dry plea for help even though she knew it was in vain. Why hadn't she listened to her intuition? She'd known something was off when he'd asked her to meet him here, in this shack miles from civilization. Was this really going to be her end? Tied to a rickety chair in a burning house like some clichéd movie character? Her eyes started to close, and she could feel herself fading. Maybe it was better this way—if she passed out, she wouldn't feel her flesh burning.

Blaire stood up and stretched. What next? Obviously, they couldn't kill Meghan off. But they needed to infuse some fresh blood into the series. She wished she could talk to Daniel, have one of their brainstorming sessions, but he was on a plane to Chicago to spend Christmas with his parents. She had to do something to keep busy until she could return to New York, so she was drafting some pages of the next book on her own. Usually they wrote for five hours a day across from each other in their apartment. Daniel would take her chapters and do his magic editing, and they'd sound brilliant. She was the faster writer, ideas churning furiously, while he labored over every paragraph. They complemented each other perfectly and were so used to each other's writing habits that they could tell just by the cadence of the keyboard whether or not it was okay to interrupt with a question. She sighed, wishing she could get back to her life with him, but she wasn't leaving here until she'd done everything in her power to find out who had killed Lily.

The room phone rang, surprising Blaire. "Hello?"

"Ms. Barrington, it's the front desk. There's a gentleman here to see you, a Mr. Barton. Shall I send him up?"

"No," Blaire said immediately. "I'll come down." There was no way she was going to be alone with Gordon.

When she reached the lobby, he was pacing and muttering quietly to himself. He looked up as Blaire approached. Her eyes were drawn to the bow tie du jour. Yellow with crabs on it. He looked angry.

He didn't bother with hello. "Is there somewhere we can talk privately?"

"The restaurant."

"I said privately."

She gave him a cold look. "The restaurant's as private as it's going to get, Gordon. Take it or leave it."

He said nothing while they waited for the hostess to seat them. As soon as she walked away, his eyes met Blaire's.

"What did you do?"

She leaned back in her chair and gave him a cool look. "What are you talking about, Gordon?"

His lips were pressed together, and he thrust his chin forward. "You know damn well what I'm talking about. You snooped around my house. Do you know the police came and tore everything apart? They said they had reason to believe I was a stalker!"

The waitress began to walk over, but Blaire caught her eye and shook her head. She wisely backed away.

Blaire tried to decide which way to play it. "As Kate's friend, I'm here to help her find Lily's killer. So, yes, I did look around your house. Imagine my surprise when I found a folder full of pictures of Kate." She leaned forward. "What kind of person follows someone around for months, taking pictures of them?"

"You don't understand. It's art. I did nothing wrong. I didn't sneak into her house or snoop around, like you did to me. All I did was take candid photos of a friend. It's an art project. That's all. Something I could enjoy. You're the one who's a criminal. You had no right to look through my things."

"So call the police."

He glared at her and went on. "Now she won't even talk to me. She fired our firm as well. It's all your fault."

She arched an eyebrow. "Are you kidding me? *My* fault? How about you stop spying on other people? You're lucky Kate doesn't expose your creepy little habit to your partners. What do you want from me? Why are you even here?"

"If you hadn't butted in, everything would be fine. You need to fix this. Talk to Kate. Tell her I'm sorry. That I would never hurt her. I didn't kill Lily. She has to know that."

"This isn't about Lily. It's about you not understanding proper social boundaries, Gordon. I can't help you. I would recommend that you seek help elsewhere—the professional kind."

His eyes held more than a hint of anger. "Your sarcasm is insufferable. Just like you."

She regarded him with distaste. "Are we finished here?"

He leaned forward, his elbows on the table and his fists clenched. "I never liked you, Blaire. You didn't belong back then, and you still don't. You'll never be one of us."

"Looks like you're the one who's out in the cold." She looked down as her phone buzzed. A text from Kate. Can you come over right now? Something's happened. Blaire typed back immediately. Of course, be right there. "Gordon, I have to go."

She stood, as he sat there, looking shell-shocked and a little ridiculous, the whimsical bow tie with little yellow crabs on it at odds with his sour expression.

"The police know all about you, Gordon. Stay away from me. And from Kate. Don't *ever* come near either of us again." She spun away from him and marched off.

She went back upstairs and quickly packed her bag, still rattled. Kate had invited her to stay over after Christmas Eve dinner that night. She closed down her laptop, checked to make sure everything was off, and left the suite. While she was waiting for her car to warm up, she fiddled with the radio. Despite the reason for it, there was something so comforting and familiar about having a sleepover with Kate again. It brought back her Mayfield days in a rush, when she'd escape the dorms some weekends to stay with the Michaels family.

She had enjoyed the dorms at first. In the evenings after dinner, she and her group of friends would get their work done. Teachers and prefects roamed the halls, open doors were mandated, and they made sure the girls were all in their rooms studying. At nine thirty, they had free time, and often ordered pizza, spending the next hour and a half before curfew and lights-out laughing and telling stories. Adding to their fun was the vodka snuck in by their favorite pizza guy. Then, in Blaire's junior year, one of the other girls got caught sneaking out one weekend. Security was tightened, curfews were moved up, and none of it seemed fun anymore. They'd limited how many weekends she was allowed to spend off campus, until Lily changed all that.

One Friday evening, the Michaels had taken the girls to Haussner's, a Baltimore landmark known for its hundreds of paintings covering practically every inch of the walls, and a favorite of Blaire's. Over dessert, Lily took a sip of her coffee and looked at Blaire.

"Blaire, darling. Harrison and I have something we'd like to discuss with you."

She remembered feeling panic-stricken. In her experience, a sentence beginning that way usually heralded bad news. She racked her brain, trying to think of anything she might have said or done to upset them. A glance over at Kate revealed nothing; she was looking at Lily.

Blaire cleared her throat. "What is it?"

Lily smiled, and all of Blaire's reservations evaporated. "We were wondering if you'd like to live with us instead of staying at the dorm."

"Um," Blaire said as Lily continued, "Before you answer, we just want you to know how much we've come to love you and, well, you're a member of the family now." Lily extended a hand toward Kate. "We're so happy that Kate has you. It seems silly for you to stay all alone in the dorm when you could be with us."

"I would love that," Blaire said, and turned to Kate. "Did you know?"

Kate had smiled and nodded.

That was a long time ago, but Blaire had always been grateful for the way Kate's family had so fully taken her in.

She put the car in gear and headed to Kate's. Now Kate was falling apart again, and needed Blaire. She knew that if these threats didn't end soon, it wouldn't be much longer before Kate cracked for good.

19

Kate heard the doorbell and walked to the front hall, nodding to Brian, the guard on duty, as she opened the door and let in an icy blast. The weather had turned dramatically yesterday. Blaire, in a down parka and gray wool hat, stamped her feet and rubbed her gloved hands together as she entered the house.

"So glad you're going to stay here for a few days. Let me take your coat," Kate said, grabbing a hanger from the hall closet. "Just leave your suitcase here. Fleur will take it up to your room." She was eager to show Blaire the picture she'd found in Annabelle's coloring book. She hung up the coat and turned back to Blaire. "Let's go to the study for a minute."

Kate shut the door. "Look." She pulled her phone out and swiped until she found the picture she'd snapped of the drawing and handed it to Blaire.

"That is . . . horrible. Where was this?"

"In Annabelle's coloring book! Anderson took it, of course, to check it for prints. I've been racking my brain trying to figure out who could have put it there." Kate shrugged. "But maybe it was there for a while."

"I'm sorry, Kate. Maybe he'll be able to pick up something from it."

"Doubtful. This creep knows how to cover his tracks. We were hoping to have the behavioral profile, but Anderson says there's a backlog in the FBI unit, and since this isn't some active serial killer case, we have to wait in a queue. But those roses that were sent to Selby's may turn out to be a break."

"How so?"

"He used a credit card to buy them. Anderson's already subpoenaed the records from the florist. Then I'll be able to prove to my father and Simon that I'm not crazy. That I'm not the one who sent them."

"That's great. When does he think he'll get the info?"

Kate shook her head. "Soon, I think." She sighed. "It's Christmas Eve—let's try and put it out of our minds for a few hours. I need to put on a good face for Annabelle."

"Of course. Where is she?"

"In the kitchen, making cookies with Hilda. I told her we'd come help, but I wanted to talk to you first." It was such a relief that she didn't have to keep secrets from Blaire.

"Aunt Blaire!" Annabelle came bounding into the room, her eyes bright. "Are you going to make cookies with us?"

"We'll talk later," Kate whispered as they followed Annabelle down the hall.

"Mmm. Smells like a bakery in here," Blaire said as they entered the kitchen.

With Hilda's help, Annabelle climbed onto a chair that had been pulled up next to the island in the middle of the kitchen, a large bowl of cookie dough in front of her. "We're making sugar cookies, Aunt Blaire. And guess what? I get to shake the fairy sprinkles on them."

"Ooh, can I help?" Blaire asked.

"Yes. But you have to wash your hands first," Annabelle said solemnly.

"Ha," Blaire said, "spoken like a true doctor's daughter."

Kate handed Blaire a rolling pin. "Here you go. See if you can get the dough as thin as Otterbein's."

"You're kidding, right? You remember my cookie-making skills, don't you?"

Blaire picked up a wad of dough, molding it into a ball before rolling it out. Watching her, Annabelle too picked up a hunk, and Hilda pinched off a piece of it, holding it in front of the little girl's mouth. "Here, taste. It's delicious, isn't it?" she said, as Annabelle took it into her mouth and chewed.

"Hilda!" Kate's sharp voice made them all jump. "What are you doing? There are raw eggs in that." What was wrong with the woman? She moved closer to Annabelle and cupped her chin, looking into her eyes. "You can't eat that, sweetie. We only eat cookies after they come out of the oven." She gave Hilda a disapproving look.

"We always ate the dough when I was a girl . . . ," Hilda said.

"I don't care what you used to do. It's not safe," Kate said. "She could get salmonella. And it's not just the eggs. Uncooked flour can transmit *E. coli*." Was this woman always this careless with her daughter's well-being, and she was only just now noticing? Was this another instance of Kate not being a good judge of the people around her?

Hilda looked embarrassed. "I'm so sorry, Kate. I didn't know that."

Everyone was quiet until Blaire said brightly, "Okay, time for the magic fairy sprinkles." She placed a baking tray of newly formed Christmas trees before Annabelle, who happily shook out the red and green sprinkles. Kate did her best to remain calm in front of Annabelle and smiled as she grabbed the tray and put it into the oven. They worked this way for the next two hours, until they'd filled four large cookie tins, Kate's mind churning the whole time.

The man in charge of their finances, whom she'd known since childhood, had been following her and taking pictures, her nanny was letting Annabelle eat raw eggs, and her father was still being secretive about his fight with her mother the day she was killed. Simon was, at best, disregarding her feelings and judgment about Sabrina, and at worst, cheating on her, and some psycho had been in her house despite a team of professionals they'd hired to keep her safe. Who else had she so horribly misjudged? Could she trust any of these people, in light of everything going on? The one person she'd always been sure of had been taken away from her, and now nothing else seemed certain, not even the sanctity of her own home . . .

"Dr. English," Fleur said, walking into the kitchen and pulling Kate from her thoughts. "The dining room table is set for tonight. Have you and Ms. Barrington eaten lunch?"

Kate looked at her watch. One thirty. "No. I didn't realize what time it was."

"I'll take care of the kitchen," Fleur said. "I made some soup this morning. Go have a seat in the conservatory, and I'll bring it to you."

"Thank you, Fleur." Kate *was* feeling tired—tired and jumpy, at this point. Food would do her some good.

A few minutes later, they were sitting in the conservatory while Fleur set a covered tureen and two bowls on the bleached oak table in front of them. When Kate lifted the lid, steam rose, and the mouthwatering smell of Old Bay filled the air.

"Maryland crab. I must be in heaven," Blaire exclaimed. "I can't remember the last time I had real Maryland crab soup."

"Do you remember the first time you tried steamed crabs?" Kate asked, bringing a spoonful to her mouth.

Blaire laughed. "Yeah. At first, I thought you were crazy, eating those alien-looking crustaceans."

Kate smiled at her. "But in your usual adventure-seeking way, you dove right in."

"I smashed the thing right in the shell with the mallet. I'll never forget the look on your dad's face. He gave me a detailed tutorial on the proper way to open the shell."

"That was such a perfect night." Kate was lost in the memory. Everything had seemed so innocent and uncomplicated back then. She thought about the twists and turns their lives had taken since those youthful days and felt a fresh wave of sorrow. "You know," she said, "the first time I went into Barnes and Noble and saw your book on the best-seller shelf, I felt such a surge of pride . . . and then sadness that I couldn't tell you how proud I was. I thought back to all the nights we'd lie in bed talking about the future, our dreams of writing books and practicing medicine. We made those dreams come true, but we lost each other along the way."

"I thought about you too. You were the one who always said one day you'd see my books in the bookstore. Being able to share it with you would have made it perfect."

"Mother was positively beaming that day, by the way. She bought ten copies of your book and gave them out to all her friends. She told me I should call you and congratulate you." Kate sighed and looked at the floor. "I was too stubborn," she said in a soft voice.

"It's okay, Kate. It's time to put our regrets away. We're together now. That's what matters."

"I've read all of them, you know. And I *am* so proud of you."

"Thank you. That means the world to me," Blaire said, her voice catching.

When they had finished, it was after two, and the sky was turning gray.

Hilda brought Annabelle in as they finished. "If you'd like, I'll take Annabelle upstairs and see if she might go down for a short nap before dinner. Or at least have some quiet time. She might be up late tonight, waiting for Santa."

"I want Mommy to do it," Annabelle said.

Kate smiled at her. "How about if I come up and help you pick out some books?"

"Okay," Annabelle said quietly.

They trudged up the stairs, Annabelle clinging to Kate's hand. Her poor baby was feeling the effects of all this stress. Kate pushed the door open and turned on the light. "Okay, sweetie, pick some books out for Miss Hilda to read, and I'll come check on you in a bit." Annabelle ran to her bookshelf and started pulling out books. As Kate turned, a bottle of cough medicine sitting on Annabelle's dresser caught her eye. "Hilda, what is this doing here?"

Hilda looked at the bottle and then back at Kate, her eyes growing wide. "You gave her some this morning, remember?"

Kate could barely contain her anger. "I put it back in the medicine cabinet. I would never leave it here, where she could get to it."

Hilda shrugged. "I know you wouldn't leave it there deliberately. Maybe you meant to do it and got distracted?"

"And you didn't see it before now and think maybe it should be removed from my daughter's reach?"

Hilda stood with her mouth agape for a moment, her eyes moving to Annabelle, who was watching them from across the room. "I'm sorry, Kate. I didn't notice it there. I would have certainly put it away if I'd seen it. I'll take care of it now."

Shaking her head, Kate picked up the bottle herself and took it to the bathroom, where she put it back on the top shelf. There was no way she would have forgotten to put medicine away. She felt the heat rush to her cheeks. She hadn't forgotten it. Someone had put it there, either to put Annabelle in danger or to make her think she was losing it. Maybe Hilda. She could have wanted to get back at Kate for embarrassing her about the raw eggs. No, that was ridiculous, Hilda would never hurt Annabelle. Could Kate really be so distracted that she could have thought she'd put it away but forgotten?

Maybe Simon did it. He'd been making insinuations about her state of mind a lot lately. She'd watch him more carefully. She went back downstairs, trying to push away the cloud of worry descending upon her. She found Blaire in the kitchen, making tea for them. "My father is coming at five thirty, so we'll have dinner around six or so. Hopefully Simon will be home soon."

"Where *is* Simon?" Blaire asked. "Don't most companies close, or at least close early, on Christmas Eve?"

"The company *is* closed today. But he claims he got a frantic call this morning about some structural integrity issue on a building downtown, something to do with the base building steel frames. He had to go meet with an engineer on-site." She would bet that the big emergency call he'd gotten that morning was from Sabrina. Probably pretending to need some comfort on her first Christmas without her father. Kate was convinced that Sabrina had a hidden agenda. She'd be more sympathetic, but she believed a good portion of Sabrina's grieving was simply an act to get attention from Simon.

"Claims?" Blaire prodded.

"Come on. It's Christmas Eve. Doesn't matter anymore. Besides, I have more important things to think about. When we find this killer, Simon's moving back out. The marriage is over."

"Excuse me, ma'am." It was Joshua, one of the security team.

"Yes?"

"Some flowers arrived for Ms. Barrington. We opened the box just to check everything was legit. Is it okay to bring them in?"

"Yes, please," Kate answered.

He came in with a box filled with two dozen red roses.

When Kate looked at the flowers, the image of last night's white roses—the ones she'd never ordered—came back to her. She turned away from the box.

Blaire took the card from him. "They're from Daniel. I told him you'd invited me to stay here tonight and tomorrow."

"He must be really missing you." When was the last time Simon had sent her flowers? She couldn't remember. But what difference did it make? She couldn't trust him anymore. An awful sense of fear and loneliness swept over her. Blaire had become her rock again, but of course, Blaire couldn't stay forever—she had her own life, her own husband, who sent her flowers, her own career to get back to. Doing her best to shake it off, she asked, "Want to help me finish wrapping Annabelle's presents?"

"I'd love to."

"Everything's upstairs in one of the guest rooms. I put the last of it there this morning." She glanced at Blaire as they climbed the stairs. "*Everything* makes it sound like a lot. I really only bought for Annabelle. Ordered some things online. I wanted to keep it happy for her, but my heart isn't in it."

"I'm sure it's not. Completely understandable," Blaire said as they reached the landing.

Together they made quick work of the wrapping, carried the presents downstairs, and arranged them underneath the nine-foot Christmas tree that filled the corner of the room.

They sat down together on one of the sofas facing the fireplace.

"Would you like a drink? Some wine? Or an eggnog?" Kate asked.

Blaire shook her head. "Nothing right now. I think I'll go up and get ready for dinner. I also want to give Daniel a call."

"Sure thing."

A few minutes after Blaire left the room, Simon walked in, still in his overcoat.

"Did you take care of your big emergency?" Kate asked.

He raised his eyebrows. "Things are under control, yes. I'm sorry I had to leave. I'm going to go shower before dinner."

After he'd gone upstairs, Kate went into the kitchen to arrange the serving platters on the kitchen counter. Her cook, Claude, had prepared the Christmas Eve meal earlier that morning. The pancetta-wrapped beef tenderloin and mashed potatoes were in a low oven, warming back up, and Kate would transfer everything to the platters once they were ready to eat. She uncorked a bottle of Silver Oak cabernet sauvignon and set it on the dining room table.

The doorbell sounded, and as Kate went to see who it was, Annabelle came bounding down the stairs with Simon close behind her. She was dressed in a little white sweater dress with red trim and red tights. Kate's eyes filled when she realized it was one of the outfits Lily had bought her a month before. Annabelle's blond hair was pulled into two curly pigtails tied with bright red ribbons, and her big brown eyes were shining with excitement. "Is that Santa Claus?" She danced around Kate as she neared the front door.

"I don't think so, sweetie. It's probably Granddaddy. Santa will come when we're all asleep. And he'll come down the chimney." Brian opened the door and let Kate's father in.

She managed a smile that felt somewhat natural. "Dad." She put her arms out to hug him as he came in. He looked weary, she thought.

"My favorite girls," he said, kissing Kate and stooping down to hug Annabelle. "Look at you. What a perfect Christmas girl you are."

"Granddaddy. Santa Claus is coming tonight."

"Is he?"

"Yes. And he's bringing toys for me."

"Shall we go into the living room?" Kate said. She was still upset with her father but had decided to put it out of her mind until after Christmas. She just wanted to get through the next few days for Annabelle's sake. After they sat, the phone in her pocket vibrated, and she pulled it out and swiped.

Food-allergy-related deaths spike during the holidays
All those home-baked treats with the potential to kill
It would be a shame for you to die before Christmas
Especially with so many packages under your beautiful tree
Is there one for me?

It felt like an elephant was standing on her chest.

"Kate, are you okay?"

She tried to speak, but nothing came out.

"Breathe, Kate. Where's your Valium prescription?"

"Kitchen."

He was back moments later with a glass of water and a pill.

She downed it. "How did he know . . . ? Every window in this house is covered."

As she held out the phone for her father to see, it rang, startling her. It was Anderson. "I know it's Christmas Eve, but can you come over?" Kate said by way of greeting.

"I was calling to let you know I'm on my way."

She sat still, as if in a trance. Harrison pulled Simon aside and whispered something to him. Simon's eyes widened, and he looked over at Kate, and then at Hilda.

"Hilda, would you please give Annabelle her bath before dinner?" Simon asked.

"But you haven't read *The Night Before Christmas* yet," Annabelle complained.

"I promise when you come back down, we'll read it."

When they'd left the room, Harrison showed the text message to Simon and Blaire. Kate felt as if she was floating above the room, seeing all of them through a misty lens. She watched grim faces having hushed conversations, unable to focus clearly.

Anderson arrived in what seemed like minutes, but when Kate looked, she saw it had been almost a half hour. She blinked, beginning to feel more in control, concentrating on his mouth as he spoke. "The text came from another VPN, so we haven't been able to track it. We're going to add protective custody. There'll be a police car outside your house." He looked at Simon. "I know you declined protection and have your own security, but now I insist."

"Of course," Simon said.

Kate was pacing. "I don't understand. . . . After that last text, we've made sure no one can see in. How does he know about the presents under the tree? And the food allergy . . . we made cookies today. It must be someone who has access to our house," Kate said.

Anderson shook his head. "It's Christmas. Everyone has presents under the tree. There's nothing specific in this text to indicate someone has access to your house. In fact, I'd say if this person did, the text would have included more details."

"But how does he know about Kate's nut allergy?" Simon asked.

Anderson cocked an eyebrow. "I didn't say this was someone you don't know."

"Everyone in our circle knows," Kate said. "I always have to make sure before eating anything that I check the ingredients with them."

"What about the security detail?" Blaire asked. "Any chance one of them is compromised?"

Simon gave her a withering look. "We're not in one of your murder mysteries, Blaire. I hired them *after* this started. I seriously doubt one of them is a mole."

"Okay, okay. No need to be sarcastic with each other," Anderson said.

"What about Hilda?" Blaire asked. "Could she have anything to do with it?"

Simon shook his head. "No, she's been with us since Annabelle was a baby. She was here when Lily was killed. There's no way she's involved. And Annabelle's already upset enough with everything. I don't want to take Hilda from her."

"I realize this isn't a mystery novel"—Blaire cocked her head at Simon—"but maybe you should have your security detail sweep for bugs anyway, because this person is getting their info somehow. We're only assuming that someone looked in the window when that last text came in. Maybe there's a camera or recording device in the house."

Anderson looked at Simon. "I assumed they'd already done that."

Kate sat there trying hard to follow the back-and-forth conversation. Blaire was right. There must be cameras somewhere. Her skin began to itch, as if there were things crawling all over her body. She looked up at the ceiling, her eyes moving along the molding from corner to corner, looking for a device that could be watching her every move. She was being spied on. The most intimate details of her life were known to some maniac who had killed her mother and now wanted her dead too. She lifted a hand to her throat and looked at Simon with suspicion. "You told me this security team was top-notch. Why haven't they checked the house for things like that? There were so many people here the day of the funeral. Anyone could have planted cameras. They could be anywhere."

"We had no reason to have them search for cameras until now," Simon said. He looked at Anderson. "Why would you assume they would check that? If you thought it was necessary, shouldn't you have done so yourself?"

Why weren't they doing something about this instead of just talking about it? It was maddening. Kate stood up. "Do it now! I can't stay here without knowing I'm not being watched."

Anderson picked up his phone and punched in a number. "I'll have a tech team dispatched. They'll check the house." He spoke into the phone, hung up, and then turned to Simon. "As you've pointed out, we had no reason to do so until now."

Kate studied Anderson's face as he spoke to Simon. He was pissed off. And there was something else in his expression— suspicion? Or just irritation? Did he know something she didn't?

20

When Blaire woke up early on Christmas morning, the house was still quiet. Not wanting to wake anyone, she tiptoed down the stairs and went to the kitchen. They'd all been up so late. The police had come over with all their equipment and scanned the house, even checking Kate and Simon's router to see if someone had tagged onto their Wi-Fi. Nothing was detected. Kate was still convinced that hidden cameras lurked somewhere, but the police had assured her that if that were the case, the camera had to be transmitting somewhere, and that was just not happening. Kate was devastated. Blaire didn't blame her, it would have explained everything. But now it was clear to them that whoever was doing this was someone very close.

Something else was nagging at her. Right after Simon finally got home from his so-called structural emergency the day before, an enormous box had been delivered. The two guards approached it, but Simon rushed over to them. "It's okay," he'd said, looking at the return label. "I ordered this. It's a Christmas present for Annabelle."

They backed away as Kate moved in closer. "What is this?" she'd asked, the unease in her voice obvious to Blaire.

Simon smiled and patted the top of the box. "It's that motorized mini Range Rover I've been looking at. She's going to love it."

"What? Have you lost your mind? How much was it?"

"It was only fifteen thousand. We can afford it."

"*Who* can afford it? You? Or me? Did you use your own money, or did you use mine?"

Blaire had watched Simon stiffen and his face go red. "I thought it was all *our* money."

"Do you realize we're hemorrhaging money with all this security? How can you be so cavalier?" She had pointed her finger at him, shaking. "We've talked about this before. Large purchases are to be discussed ahead of time. And I won't have Annabelle turned into a spoiled child."

"Fine. I'll return it," he said, his voice low.

"See that you do!" Kate stormed from the hallway, and Blaire looked at Simon before following her. He'd given Blaire an angry scowl and turned away.

Now Blaire put some coffee on and wondered if yesterday's argument would carry over into this Christmas morning. She walked to the French doors in the breakfast room, opening the long blinds and peering out. There was a light dusting of snow on the ground, with big flakes still falling. It would be a white Christmas.

It had snowed like this that first Christmas after her mother left. Blaire had still believed in Santa Claus and had written him a letter, asking him to bring her mother back to her. Her mother could be so much fun, but she could also be moody and angry. In her darker moods, she'd yell at Blaire to leave her alone, her face contorted in anger. Something as simple as a request for an after-school snack could elicit her rage. But then she'd be sorry, apologizing and trying to make up to Blaire. When Blaire would come home from school, she could sometimes tell how her mother was going to act. If she was playing fast music and dancing around, things would be good. She'd grab Blaire by the hand, and they'd laugh and dance, and she would tell Blaire how one day Blaire would go to the movies and see her mother on the big screen. Her eyes would be all bright and her smile big as she told Blaire about her plans. She was going to go to Hollywood and get discovered. Then, if Blaire was a very good girl, her mother would send for her and they'd live in a big mansion in Beverly Hills. Blaire didn't want to think of her mother going away, but when she said so, her mother became cold and told Blaire she was being selfish, so she'd pretend to be excited for her.

If her mother was playing sad music when she came home, Blaire knew that she had to be quiet. Otherwise her mother would yell and tell her how Blaire's father had ruined her life. That if she hadn't married him, she'd already be a famous movie star. Blaire never pointed out that if her mother hadn't married him, Blaire wouldn't have been born—but she thought it.

She glanced at the clock on the wall. Five thirty. It was too early to call Daniel and wish him a merry Christmas. They still hadn't connected, and she was getting frustrated. His flight from London had gotten in to Chicago the night before. She should be with him and his family today, not a guest in Kate's home. She knew it was important for her to be here, with Kate, but it didn't make it any less difficult to picture him with his parents and his sister, enjoying one another, laughing and exchanging gifts, while she was here. She poured herself a cup of coffee and rooted around in the cabinets until she found the sugar.

"Good morning." Hilda's voice startled Blaire, and she turned around.

"Good morning, Hilda. Merry Christmas."

Blaire had been surprised that Hilda wasn't spending Christmas with her own family, but Kate told her that Hilda had asked to spend Christmas here with Annabelle.

"Merry Christmas," Hilda answered.

Annabelle came running into the kitchen, followed by Kate and Simon.

"Merry Christmas! Did Santa come?" Annabelle asked, eyes wide and excited.

"I don't know. I haven't looked yet," Blaire answered, smiling. "I made coffee," she said to Simon and Kate.

"Bless you," Kate said.

Kate looked terrible, Blaire realized. The circles under her eyes gave her a hollow look. Her shiny blond hair had lost its luster, and she was thinner than ever.

"Come on, Mommy. I want to see what Santa brought."

"Okay, little one. I'll pour a coffee and we can go see."

Annabelle started to object, and Blaire came to the rescue. "You guys go in. I'll bring the coffees. Is your father up yet?"

"Yes. He's in the family room already."

"Great. I'll bring one in for him too."

"Let me help you," Hilda said, taking some mugs down from the cabinet.

Kate gave Blaire an appreciative look and took Annabelle's hand. Blaire noticed that Kate barely glanced at Simon. The tension between them felt like an actual presence in the room. She poured the coffees and a glass of orange juice for Annabelle, grabbed a few biscotti she found in a canister in the pantry, and put everything on a tray. When she set it down on the coffee table in the family room, she saw that the Christmas tree lights were on. Kate had told her that Simon insisted they put a tree up for Annabelle's sake. Blaire was glad to see the multicolored lights. Kate was obviously following her mother's tradition. Lily had always said that white lights were lovely and considered de rigueur, but she didn't care— Christmas trees were for children, and sparkling, colorful lights made children happier than plain ones.

Blaire walked closer to the tree, examining the ornaments. There were many from countries they must have visited, and some others that looked as if they might have special meaning. Blaire thought back to the Christmas of their senior year in high school, when Lily had given each of them an ornament—Blaire's a lion to represent Columbia's mascot, and Kate's Handsome Dan, Yale's bulldog mascot. Once again she was reminded of how much of Kate's life she had missed.

"Thanks for the coffee." Kate's voice broke into her thoughts. "Come and sit next to me."

Kate sat alone on the sofa, Harrison in a cushiony armchair near the tree. Simon sat cross-legged on the floor with Annabelle, surrounded by the pile of presents, and Hilda sat near them on a round ottoman. Blaire smiled as Annabelle began to tear off the paper, oohing and aahing at each present. There were dolls, stuffed animals, board games, Legos, and a shiny red bike with training wheels. Then Simon handed Annabelle a stack of presents all wrapped in paper printed with a design of animals wearing Santa caps.

"Books, right?" Blaire whispered to Kate.

Kate nodded. "I ordered them online. I had them wrap them for me, since I ordered so late." She rose from the sofa and went to sit next to Annabelle as she unwrapped each one. "Look, sweetheart." Kate took a book in her hand. "*Dragons Love Tacos*. We'll read it together later."

Annabelle laughed. "He's funny. I like tacos too."

"Wow. Lots of books. Let's see what else you have there," Harrison said as Hilda picked up the discarded wrapping paper and put it in a bag.

Annabelle tore the paper off the next one. "Look, Mommy. Why does this man look so mean?" She handed the book to Kate, and Blaire leaned forward for a closer look.

Alarm filled Kate's face. "Um, this book is not for you. Must be a mistake, sweetie."

Her blood ran cold when she read the title—*Watch Mommy Die*. It was the true story of a serial killer.

"Let me see it," Simon said, taking the book from Kate and flipping through the pages. His face paled.

"I didn't order that," Kate said in a trembling voice. Blaire could see how difficult it was for her to hold it together.

"You must have," Simon said.

"Of course I didn't!" She grabbed the book from Simon and jumped up. The way she was holding it, Blaire thought she was going to rip it apart.

Annabelle sat silently, looking back and forth from Simon to Kate, obviously upset at all the commotion. Hilda took the child onto her lap and tried to distract her.

"Maybe you ordered it by mistake . . . looking for a grieving book, and that came up," Simon said, his voice soft and calming.

"That's ridiculous. I didn't order this," Kate said. She'd lowered her voice so that Annabelle, now happily playing with her other presents, wouldn't hear.

No one said anything, and Kate faced them angrily.

"I'll prove it," she said, and ran from the room.

"She wouldn't have ordered that. It must be a mistake, don't you think?" Blaire said, looking first at Simon and then to Harrison.

"There must be a reasonable explanation," Harrison said. "Did you order any books?" he asked Simon.

Before Simon could answer, Kate came back in with her laptop and sat down. "I'll show you my order history. You'll see."

They exchanged looks as Kate clicked away. Finally, she looked up at them. "I . . ." She stood up, and the computer slid to the floor.

Blaire picked it up and looked at the screen. The book had been purchased the day after the others, but it was definitely an order that Kate had placed. Blaire swallowed. Kate's state of mind was clearly deteriorating.

"It's a mistake," Kate said, her hand at her throat. "I can't breathe. I can't breathe," she repeated, her body heaving as she tried to inhale.

Harrison jumped from his chair and ran to her, but Kate pushed him away. Simon stood, looking helpless.

"Mommy, what's wrong. Are you sick?" Annabelle looked close to tears.

"It's all right, Annabelle. Come with me. I want to show you something," Hilda said, leading her from the room.

Blaire went to Kate and drew her into her arms. She could feel Kate's heartbeat pounding against her as she held her, the extreme sharpness of her shoulder blades under Blaire's hands. "It's okay. I'm sure you're right. It's some sort of mistake. We'll get to the bottom of this," Blaire said.

It was just like the Kate of that long-ago summer, when she had slid into that deep dark place. If this reign of terror didn't end, Blaire wasn't sure Kate could come back this time.

Kate had gone to lie down before Christmas dinner. Blaire had stayed in her bedroom with her until she fell asleep. The others too were napping, and Simon was just coming up the stairs as Blaire was headed down.

"How is she?" he asked, civil for a change.

"She's sleeping."

"Good. I'm going to read awhile before dinner." Simon continued to the landing.

Blaire returned to the family room, where the presents had

been neatly stacked under the tree. Someone must have straightened up. She stretched out on the sofa and checked her phone, disappointed to see that she hadn't had a call from Daniel yet. She'd tried him earlier, but it had gone directly to voice mail. She called him now, but again had no luck. They'd probably gone to church in the morning and were now in the middle of getting everything ready for dinner. Blaire had always helped his mother with the cooking, feeling like part of the family.

Daniel had grown up in Forest Glen, a beautiful suburb of Chicago. His mother was an English professor at Loyola University, and his dad a successful ad executive. The first time Daniel took Blaire to meet them and spend the weekend, they'd immediately made her feel welcome. Barbara, his mother, had enveloped her in a warm hug, taken her hand, and pulled her into the kitchen so they could "get to know each other better." At first Blaire had thought Barbara wanted to grill her, but she relaxed when she saw how open and friendly she was. His parents were affectionate with each other and with Daniel, and it was apparent that they shared a great relationship. She could tell by the way Daniel and his family interacted that they really enjoyed being together, and it reminded her of Kate's family and all the good times she'd shared with them.

She'd been thrilled when Daniel's family had become hers too, and over the years, it felt like they loved her as much as they loved him. She knew that yesterday and today Barbara would be cooking everything from scratch—from the biscuits to the pies— while Neal, Daniel, and Daniel's sister, Margo, kept her company and chatted about everything from literature, sports, local events to world affairs.

She sighed, wondering if they were finished opening their presents and when they might be sitting down for dinner. Blaire missed all of them so much. She hated to think of them enjoying the day without her. She couldn't continue to lie there and think about how far apart they were, so she got up and walked into the dining room.

The table had been set plainly for their meal. She ran her hand along its polished burl wood. She'd expected an elaborate table—the kind Lily had always set, with exquisite china, crystal goblets, and monogrammed silverware. Lily had countless sets of china for different occasions. Blaire would never forget the first time she had dinner with Kate and her parents. Harrison had asked Blaire to pass the salt, and she'd done so, passing the shaker to him. Afterward, privately, Lily had taken Blaire aside and told her that when someone asked for salt or pepper, the polite thing to do was to pass *both*. There were so many things Lily had taught her about manners and etiquette, things that Shaina, and certainly Enid, hadn't had a clue about.

Blaire felt a tightening in her chest, and the pain of loss ripped through her. A sob escaped her lips, and she gripped the chair in front of her while taking deep breaths. There was so much she wanted to say to Lily, so much she needed to say. But some monster had taken Lily's life, and with it Blaire's last hope of ever seeing her again.

After a few minutes, she felt composed again and moved back from the table. It was set simply, six settings on festive placements, no candles, crystal, or greens. There wasn't even a centerpiece—but then again, Blaire realized, setting a nice table must be the last thing on Kate's mind.

She went to join the others when she heard Annabelle's chirpy little voice. Kate looked sleepy, but she was definitely less agitated when Blaire entered the family room, where everyone was now gathered.

"Feeling better?" Blaire asked Kate.

"A little. There's eggnog in the fridge," Kate blurted suddenly. "Would anyone like some eggnog? Dad, would you get the eggnog? Grab a cup for Annabelle too—there's no rum in it."

Blaire studied her. Kate was still on edge, jumpy. The Valium seemed to have helped a little, but not enough.

"Of course, sweetheart," Harrison said, his eyes troubled as he left the room.

Kate twisted her hands in her lap and stared straight ahead. No one spoke. As Harrison returned with a tray of eggnog, the doorbell rang.

Kate looked startled. "Who could that be?"

Simon shrugged. "Must be someone we know, if security let them past. I'll go see."

When he walked back into the room with Sabrina next to him, Blaire almost spit out the eggnog she'd just sipped. Sabrina looked stunning, in a body-hugging black dress that Blaire recognized as a Victoria Beckham, her lips painted a hot pink to emphasize their sexy plumpness. She held a large Neiman Marcus shopping bag.

"Merry Christmas, everyone. I don't mean to interrupt your Christmas, I just wanted to drop some gifts by on my way to my friend's house," Sabrina announced.

Simon gave Kate a plaintive look, and Blaire gripped her glass more tightly. Wow. She had some gall. Interrupting Christmas. And dressed like that?

"Hello, Sabrina," Kate said flatly. "Please come in."

Simon, visibly tense, offered her a drink.

"I'd love one," she said. "You know what I like."

Kate shot Simon a dirty look, but he was clearly avoiding eye contact with her. Blaire watched as he mixed up a martini. He handed Sabrina the drink, and she took a tiny sip and then put it down on the coffee table, not taking care to make sure it didn't splash onto the table, which it did.

Kate huffed and stood, blotting up the liquid and placing a napkin under the glass.

Sabrina looked at Kate. "Sorry, Kate. Didn't mean to wet your table." Without waiting for her to answer, she walked over to Annabelle.

"Hi, my sweetie, I have a gift for you."

Her sweetie? Blaire couldn't believe that Kate was just standing there, saying nothing.

"What is it?" Annabelle asked, smiling at her.

Sabrina handed her a box decorated in green foil, with a red velvet ribbon tied around it.

"Thank you," Annabelle whispered.

She opened it to reveal a Truly Me American Girl Doll. She had blond curls and brown eyes, like Annabelle.

"She looks like me!" Annabelle said.

"Sabrina, you didn't need to buy Annabelle a gift," Kate said, her voice strained.

Sabrina didn't bother looking up at Kate, but brazenly pushed back a curl from Annabelle's eyes. "I wanted to. Isn't she pretty, Annabelle?"

"What a nice gift," Simon said. "How thoughtful, Sabrina."

Blaire looked over at him. What a bastard. Parading his mistress right in front of his wife and his father-in-law. It was almost like he was getting a sick kick out of it. Blaire could imagine the two of them laughing about it later. She was going to unmask him, no matter what it took. How dare she play up to Annabelle like that! Blaire wanted to rip the doll out of her hands. The heat rose to her face as indignation and fury filled her.

Annabelle hugged her to her chest. "I love her!"

"There's more!" She reached in the bag and pulled out another box. This one wasn't wrapped—a box of Godiva chocolates. "Here you go, Kate. I know how much you love chocolate." She placed it on the table in front of her.

"Thank you, but we didn't get you anything," Kate said.

Sabrina smiled at her. "No worries, your friendship is enough. You and Simon have been so kind over the past few months. This is my first Christmas without my father. It's been hard . . ."

Kate gave her a strained smile back. "Yes, well, thank you so much for the gifts—it was very thoughtful," she said, her manners intact. "I'm sure you're eager to get to your own celebration."

A nervous laugh escaped Simon. "Sabrina, thanks for stopping by. I'll see you to the door."

The sound of low voices drifted in from the hall, but it was difficult to discern what they were saying. Everyone sat in strained silence, waiting for Simon to return. Finally Kate stood and smoothed her skirt. "What's taking him so long?" she asked, striding toward the hall just as he came back in. Her eyes were slits.

"Nice of you to join us. What took you so long?"

Simon shrugged. "I was just seeing her out."

Kate pointed to a bulge in Simon's pocket. "What's that?"

He sighed. "Can we talk about it later?"

Blaire looked at Harrison, wondering if he was feeling as uncomfortable as she was.

"What did she give you?" Kate's voice rose.

Pulling something from his pocket, he handed it to her. "It was her father's. She thought I'd want to have it."

Kate took it and opened the small box. Her mouth dropped open. "A ring? She gave you a ring?"

"I told you it was her father's. You know how close I was to him."

Blaire could tell Kate was ready to explode, and she couldn't blame her. That woman had a hell of a nerve.

"We'll discuss it later. I'm going to see to dinner." Kate's voice had an icy edge to it. "And Hilda," she said, looking back as she left the room, "get rid of that candy. It's not safe for me, which Sabrina probably knew."

After she left the room, Harrison walked over to Simon, and the two of them spoke too low for Blaire to hear. She imagined he must be taking Simon to task over what had just happened. Blaire was still so angry she could spit nails.

The pall over the rest of Christmas Day never abated. When it was finally time for bed, Blaire was relieved to retreat to the peace and quiet of the guest room next to Kate's bedroom. It was a large room with one entire wall of floor-to-ceiling windows, along which hung light gray silk curtains. A white deep-cushioned chair and ottoman sat in one corner, across from the king-size white sleigh bed. The colors were soft, muted shades of gray and white, giving the room a feeling of peace and tranquility, and the fireplace was the crowning addition on this cold December night. Blaire took a bath and had just slipped into bed to read when she heard the sound of angry voices coming from outside her room. She sat up and tried to decipher the words, but it was no good. She held herself that way for a few minutes, but as quickly as the voices had begun, they ceased, and she lay back and picked up her book once more. Her phone dinged and she picked it up, thinking it was Daniel. It was a Facebook message from Carter.

Thanks for the friend request ☺ Any chance you're free to meet for dinner? Would love some uninterrupted time to catch up xo

She smiled and began typing.

Love to. How about Prime Rib tomorrow night?

Seconds later he answered.

Can't wait. Meet you at 8:00?
It's a date.

21

The next morning, the events of Christmas Day came rushing back to Kate. She felt the rage course through her again at the memory of Sabrina coming to their house. Who did she think she was, giving Annabelle that doll? A Truly Me doll was not a spur-of-the-moment gift; she had to have ordered it ahead of time.

Kate picked up her cell phone and dialed Detective Anderson.

"Anderson," he answered on the first ring.

"I want you to take another look at Sabrina Mitchell."

"Dr. English?"

"Yes, it's Kate. Did you hear me?"

"You sound quite upset. Has something else happened?"

"That woman came over to my house yesterday with presents for my husband and my daughter. She actually gave my husband a ring. A ring!"

"What kind of ring?" he asked.

"It was her father's signet ring. She said some baloney like she knew her father would want Simon to have it. But I know what she's up to. She's acting like Simon is *her* husband. I told my mother she was trying to come between us." The words were pouring out fast now. "My mother was going to talk to Simon—she knew about Sabrina and him. What if they planned it together?"

"I'm on my way over."

She opened her door and was furious when she saw no one was standing outside the bedroom suite. Where was Alan? "Annabelle! Hilda!" she called as she ran downstairs to find them.

The guard in the hallway—was it Scott or Jeff? —called out to her. "Is everything okay, Dr. English?" She stopped and looked at him, catching a glimpse of herself in the mirror behind him. She was in her nightgown, her hair wild. She looked like a crazy woman. Taking a deep breath, she forced herself to slow down. "Where is Alan?"

"His shift ended at seven. Your husband told him it was okay to leave."

She was normally up by then, but still, she'd told Alan not to listen to anyone but her. She'd speak to him when he came back tonight.

"Have you seen my daughter?"

"I believe she's in the kitchen with her nanny, ma'am."

She gave him a curt nod and ran back upstairs to get dressed. All these people in the house spying on her—it was maddening. She rushed through her shower, threw on a pair of jeans, grabbed a T-shirt, and ran a brush through her hair. Taking a look in the mirror, she nodded. Better.

When she reached the kitchen, Annabelle looked up from her coloring book.

"Hi, Mommy. You slept late. Daddy said you didn't feel good."

"Where is Daddy?" she asked, looking at Hilda.

"He's in his office," Hilda answered. "And Blaire was just in here. She's doing some work in the study. She asked me to tell you to come find her when you got up. Can I get you a coffee?"

Kate shook her head, already moving toward the door. She needed to talk to Simon, and then she'd go find Blaire. She stomped down the hallway and stopped at his door. Her hand was poised above the knob when she heard his voice. Who was he talking to? She put her ear up to the door, trying to make out the conversation.

"Yes, I know. It's just . . ."

She leaned in harder.

"Of course, but you have to understand . . ."

He was talking to Sabrina. She opened the door and stormed in. "Hang up!"

He looked up at her incredulously and touched a button on his phone.

"Kate! I'm on with a client. What's up?"

"What's up? Really? After that stunt your girlfriend pulled yesterday and now you're in here whispering to her? Hang up the phone. We need to talk." She plopped down in the chair in front of his desk, crossed her arms, and waited.

He shook his head and held a finger up. "Barry, listen, something's come up. Can I call you back in a few minutes? Thanks."

Simon put the phone down. "Kate, you can't just barge in here like that. He's an important client that we've come close to losing."

She waved her hand. "Yeah, right. No one works the day after Christmas." She was about to tell him that she knew everything, that she could see it was him and Sabrina plotting against her, but then she realized that would only tip him off. She had to pretend it was just about his unfaithfulness so that he wouldn't know she was suspicious of him. "Listen to me, Simon. I wanted you out before all this happened, and I want you out even more now. I won't live under the same roof with you any longer."

His face turned red. "There's no way I'm going to leave you and Annabelle alone while a killer is after you."

"We have guards. And really, what have you done to protect us? We don't need you here."

He shook his head. "Kate, please. I love you. I'm sorry about yesterday. I've told Sabrina she can't come to our house again. And I told you, I'll give the ring back. You mean everything to me. You have to believe that."

There was a time that she had. Before Sabrina came back into their lives, she'd have bet her last dollar that Simon would never look at another woman. Her friends were always joking that if they had a husband that looked like Simon, they'd never let him out of their sight, but he'd never given her a reason to feel jealous, always making her feel as though she was the center of his universe. In many ways, he'd reminded her of her own father and how attentive he was with Lily. Simon would send her flowers to the hospital for no special reason, just to let her know he was thinking of her. At parties, she'd often catch him looking at her across the room, his smile broadening when her eyes met his. Even after fifteen years of marriage, he managed to make her feel like he was seeing her for the first time.

Before Annabelle was born, they'd easily spent a good part of each Saturday making love. At the beach, they'd often head back to the house in the afternoon and lie next to each other on the cool sheets afterward. As the sun would set, the French doors were opened, to let the salty breeze waft over their naked bodies. Then they would shower together, dress, and walk on the sand, holding hands and laughing, just enjoying each other's company. Even after Annabelle, they'd managed to get an evening out alone every few weeks, determined to keep their relationship a priority. But then Sabrina moved to Baltimore, asked him for a job, and everything changed. When he looked at Sabrina, Kate saw that same sparkle in his eyes, that same look of love that before then he'd reserved only for Kate.

"I don't have to believe anything of the kind. If you really love me, then fire her."

He looked like he'd just been told that his dog died. "Kate. I can't do that."

"Of course not! I guess your proclamation of love is just empty words."

"This isn't you. You're not an unfair person. How can you ask me to fire her when she's doing a good job? When if it weren't for her father, I probably would have never even gone to college and had a career? I can cut her off personally, but I won't fire her."

"Then we have nothing else to talk about. I'll expect you out by the end of the day."

His voice rose now. "I'm not going anywhere until you're out of danger."

She would call her attorney and see if there was a way to make him leave. "I'm just going to sit here, then. So if you want to get any work done, you'd better go to your real office." She wanted him out of the house while she talked to Anderson.

He stood up, grabbed his briefcase, and threw some papers in. "Fine. But I'll be back tonight."

She left the room and went back to the kitchen to check on Annabelle.

"Annabelle wants to go and see the horses," Hilda told her.

"All right," Kate said. "Just make sure you take a guard with you."

She heard the garage door opening. Simon was leaving—good. She poured herself a cup of coffee and pulled out a sheet of paper. She needed to write everything down for Anderson. Sabrina could have sent the flowers to Selby's if Simon told her they would be there.

A noise made her look up. Blaire had come in.

"Hey, you. How're you doing?"

Kate put the pen down. "I'm nervous. Simon was just talking to her on the phone. I've been thinking. What if Simon is the one who snuck that picture into Annabelle's coloring book? He's an architect; he can draw. For that matter, Sabrina can too."

"I guess that's possible."

"I told him to move out, but he refused. I did get him to at least go to his office today."

Blaire poured herself a cup of coffee and took a seat at the table. "So he'll be here for Annabelle's party tomorrow night."

"Yeah. I can't keep him from that, but I'm going to talk to my lawyer and see what I can do to get him to move out of the house. I called Anderson. He's on his way over now."

"I think you're on the right track," Blaire said.

"And you know what else? I think Mother must have said something to Simon after all. Maybe it was Sabrina who went to Mother's. Maybe she's the one who pushed her and killed her and then called Simon, and now they're lying to cover their tracks." She looked at Blaire in horror. "Now they're after me."

Blaire was looking at her intently, nodding slowly. "Your father told me that Lily mentioned the trouble with Sabrina. So it was definitely on her mind. Let's see what Anderson says."

The door chimed. "That must be him." Kate stood.

When Anderson walked into the kitchen, he looked surprised to see Blaire there. He nodded. "Dr. English, Ms. Barrington."

"Can I get you anything?" Kate asked.

"No, thank you." He took a seat across from Kate.

"I'm worried about having Simon in the house."

"Okay, we'll talk about that. But first I have some questions that are quite personal. Perhaps Ms. Barrington could leave us alone for a few minutes?"

Blaire stood up before Kate could answer. "Of course. I'll be in the study."

After she'd gone, Kate looked at the detective. "What is it?"

He sighed. "I need to ask you about the car accident when your fiancé died. That summer you were in therapy—intense therapy, apparently."

Kate's face was hot. She didn't want to talk about the accident. And how did he know she'd been in therapy? Her medical records were private. "What does that have to do with anything? And how did you even know about that?"

"Actually, when we questioned Ms. Mitchell, she told us."

Sabrina? Simon had to have told her . . . "How did she know? When did she tell you this?"

He studied her face a moment and then continued. "Your husband is her alibi and she's his for that night. They claim they were both working late. I called her back in for questioning yesterday, and she continues to insist she was working late that night with your husband. She mentioned that your husband was getting worried about your behavior, that it's been erratic and that he's concerned you might be having another nervous breakdown."

They were trying to make her look crazy to Anderson. But why? So he would dismiss her suspicions? She looked at Anderson. "First of all, I never had a 'nervous breakdown.'" She put the word in air quotes. "Not that it's at all relevant now, but I went through a tragedy. I saw a therapist that summer for trauma related to the accident. I'm not ashamed to say that I've dealt with anxiety most of my life, but I handle it—just like millions of other people. I am *not* delusional." She was up now, pacing.

Anderson said nothing; he watched and waited.

"Don't you see? The fact that she even knows about that summer, that the two of them are discussing my mental health, is completely inappropriate. What other proof do you need that they're plotting against me?"

"Dr. English, I'm not suggesting that you're crazy or delusional. And I agree that such discussions between your husband and Ms. Mitchell are inappropriate. But you need to try and remain calm."

"How am I supposed to stay calm when the killer could be living in my house?"

"I understand your concern, but I have no authority to make him leave your house. However, might I suggest you ask your father to come and stay with you for now? That might make you feel safer."

"I'm still upset with him. He hasn't told me what he and Mother fought about that day."

Anderson appraised her before answering. "We've cleared him. We have CCTV footage of his car leaving the hospital after she'd already been killed. And hospital staff can account for his whereabouts all evening before he left. Dr. Singer was on vacation when we first questioned the hospital staff and he's now confirmed that he was with your father during the two hours we couldn't account for his whereabouts. There was no way he was home when your mother was killed."

A wave of relief flooded her. Of course her father had nothing to do with her mother's murder. How could she have even entertained the thought for a minute? She would call him after Anderson left and ask him to come stay. Blaire had offered to stay with her for the next few days as well. Simon wouldn't try anything with both of them around. And she'd make sure the guard stayed outside her room, and that Annabelle was safely inside with her at night.

"I also wanted to let you know that we got some information back from the florist. Not surprisingly, a prepaid Visa card was used to purchase the roses. We've narrowed down the batch and will be trying to determine where it was purchased."

That was something, Kate thought.

Anderson stood. "Please take care of yourself. We'll be watching Ms. Mitchell, and I'll let you know as soon as we have any more information on that credit card."

"Thank you."

He left, and Kate went to the study to talk to Blaire. When she opened the door, she saw her sitting in a chair in the corner of the room, typing on her laptop.

"Am I interrupting?" Kate asked.

Blaire looked up. "It's a welcome interruption. I'm stuck on this chapter. What did Anderson want?"

Kate walked over and started pacing again.

"You're not going to believe this."

"What?"

"Sabrina told Anderson about the accident and my seeing a therapist that summer. She said that Simon is concerned about my emotional stability."

Blaire's mouth dropped open. "Sabrina? How did she know?"

"How else? Simon told her."

22

Blaire was due to meet Carter at the Prime Rib restaurant downtown at eight, so she made a hasty retreat after Detective Anderson left. She hadn't told Kate she was meeting Carter, because she didn't want her to get the wrong idea. The truth was, Blaire didn't have any lingering interest in Carter's few remaining masculine charms, only in whatever knowledge he was willing to share about his and Simon's business interests. It seemed like Kate was finally opening her eyes to Simon's treachery.

Back at her suite at the Four Seasons, Blaire opened the closet and pulled out the outfit she'd bought especially for tonight. After slipping into the slinky green dress—green had always been Carter's favorite color—she spritzed on some Clive Christian perfume and changed into the Miu Miu jeweled pumps that perfectly showcased her shapely long legs. On her lips, Cherry Lush by Tom Ford. She would be the complete opposite of his tamped-down, boring wife.

As she entered the restaurant and looked around at the old familiar haunt, she was glad she had suggested they meet here. It had a sensual feel, with its shiny black bar and soft gold lighting. She saw Carter waiting at the bar and gave him a warm smile as she walked toward him. His face lit up as he stood, his gaze traveling the length of her body. She gave him a hug and let her lips linger on his cheek just a moment longer than necessary, pleased to see the flush on his face when she pulled away.

"You look sensational! I'm so glad you reached out," he said as they took their seats on the black leather bar stools. "What are you drinking?"

She leaned back and crossed her legs, not missing the fact his eyes kept returning to them. "Bowmore. Neat. A double," she finally said, knowing he was a Scotch man, and he flagged the bartender over and ordered two. Good. She needed to loosen him up, and she knew he'd make himself keep pace with her.

She raised her glass to his. "To old friends." She paused. "And old lovers."

He clinked her glass and took a swallow. He was practically drooling. "I can hardly believe I'm sitting here next to you. You don't know how often I've thought about you over the years." He leaned closer to her. "I dream about you sometimes, you know."

He was making her sick with his hungry fawning, but she pretended to be flattered. "Really? I've wondered over the years if you still think about me."

He warmed to the subject. "More than you know. Have you thought about me?"

Only how you screwed me over and what a pompous ass you are, she wanted to say. "Of course," she replied instead.

He took another sip. "At my house the other night, you made it sound like you were pretty in love with your husband."

She tilted her head and gave him a flirty smile. "That's true, I am. I love my husband, but no one can really hold a candle to your first. You know?" She had to force out the words, almost choking on them.

His eyes widened. "I didn't realize. Oh, Blaire. If I'd known." He shook his head. "Why didn't you get in touch all this time?"

As if it would have changed things? She shrugged. "It doesn't matter now. We both have our own lives. But that doesn't mean we can't recapture a little of the old magic, right?" She took a long swig from her glass and watched as he did the same. "You have a nice life. Kids. Your own company. You really seem to have it all."

He beamed. "I guess it looks like that." His hand moved to her right thigh, and he ran it up and down. "But I don't have everything I want." He gave her a knowing look.

She gamely put her hand on top of his and gave it a squeeze. If enduring this could lead her to Lily's killer, then, well . . . it would all be worth it. "Well, who says you can't?" She moved toward him and pressed her lips to his, and he kissed her back, pushing his tongue into her mouth. She pulled away. "Maybe we should save that for later. We're in public, after all. My hotel isn't far from here."

He was staring at her, his eyes glazed, and she controlled the urge to slap him across the face. Breathe, she thought. Picking up her glass, she held it up again. "To later," and downed it all.

Carter followed suit. "I'm going to see if our table's ready. The sooner we eat, the sooner we can leave." He gave her a wink.

"Why don't we just have dinner here at the bar? It's so cozy."

"Great idea."

They ordered. A steak for her, and shrimp scampi for him. While they waited, she asked for two more drinks.

"I'll bet you're the one with all the great ideas at your firm," she ventured. "Simon doesn't strike me as all that brilliant."

Carter straightened his shoulders and gave her a slight nod. "Well, I guess I do come up with a lot of the creative ideas and new business contacts. But don't get me wrong," he rushed on, "Simon's a pretty good architect too."

She uncrossed and crossed her legs again. "But you're the real star, aren't you? Admit it, Carter. You don't have to pretend with me."

"Well—" He smiled and bowed his head for a moment, then looked up at her. "I guess you could say that."

Right. As much as she disliked Simon, she knew all too well how charming and winning he could be. And he was smart. She couldn't take that away from him. She would bet that Simon was the anchor around which the firm revolved, and the one the clients wanted to deal with. "I'm thinking you're probably the one who keeps an eye on the money too."

He gulped down the rest of his drink and sighed. "When there is money to keep an eye on. We lost a big job a few weeks ago. A longtime client."

"What happened?" she asked.

Before he could answer, the bartender was back with their food. "Will there be anything else?" he asked politely.

"Thank you, we're fine," Blaire said, turning back to Carter. "So . . . what was the story?"

"I'm not sure, exactly. One of Simon's accounts. But we need to make up for it, or we're going to have to put in more of our own money. A lot more."

"I see." She watched as he put a shrimp in his mouth. A trickle of butter ran down his chin, and she reflected again how very different he was from suave and sophisticated Daniel.

It was more of the same over the next half hour. They were losing money, and somehow he and Simon were going to have to come up with a considerable amount of cash to save the company. But Blaire wanted to have the full picture of the noxious mixture of ingredients that could make Simon a killer.

"What about that new hire? Sabrina, I think her name is?"

Carter stopped eating, his fork poised in midair. "Simon hired her. The last thing we needed was another architect on the payroll. But I have to admit, she's got a way with the clients."

Blaire was certain that Carter enjoyed ogling her as much as the clients did.

He shook his head. "In fact, I took Simon to task over the fact that he left her behind when he met with a potential client in New York. She was the one who'd reeled them in for the meeting. We'd probably have gotten the job if she'd went."

If she'd *gone*, Blaire wanted to say. So much for his expensive prep school education. She looked at him with curiosity. "Why didn't she?"

Carter threw his hands up. "Not exactly sure. But it was after he got a call from Lily."

Blaire's ears perked up. "Go on."

"I was in his office when his assistant patched the call through. Simon seemed a little surprised. After a few minutes, his face turned red, and he waved me out. Next thing I knew, he was telling Sabrina she had to stay behind."

"Hmm. So you think Lily said something about Sabrina to him?"

"Must have. You know you women and your jealousies. Maybe she was looking out for Kate, if Kate was feeling jealous. Although I think it was a bit inappropriate for her to interfere. Not to speak ill of the dead," he was quick to add.

Blaire wondered if Carter knew more about Sabrina and Simon than he was letting on. She took a deep breath and put her hand on his leg. "I'm a little jealous too. Thinking of you working side by side with such a gorgeous woman. How do I know something isn't going on between you and Sabrina?"

He put a pudgy hand on hers and tried to slide her hand farther up his leg. She didn't resist, curious to see how far he intended to push things. He stopped at the very top of his thigh.

"You have nothing to be jealous of," he leaned forward, whispering in her ear. "Sabrina can't hold a candle to you."

She needed to get this back on course. "I'm happy to hear that.

What about Simon, though? Do you think he's really getting a little extra on the side?" She cocked an eyebrow to make him think she was being playful.

"I honestly don't know. He could if he wanted to—it's clear to everyone at the office that she's got the hots for him. But he's a pretty discreet guy."

"No guy talk?"

"Nope. But I wouldn't blame him."

What a revolting pig. She pulled her hand off his thigh.

"How about a nightcap at your place?" he said, licking his lips.

"Gee, Carter. I've got this awful headache, all of a sudden. Can we just pay the bill and do that another time? I'll split it with you."

His whole body seemed to droop. "Sure. Another time." He picked up the leather check holder, looking crestfallen. "This is mine. I insist."

"Thank you, Carter. Next time it's on me."

But there wouldn't be a next time. Thank God.

23

When does my party start, Mommy?" Annabelle asked Kate, causing her to look up from the phone in her hand. She was on Facebook, looking at Sabrina's page to see if she'd added any new photos. Ever since Blaire had shown it to her, she'd been obsessively checking the site. She put the phone down.

"Everyone's coming at five, in just a few hours. You get to stay up late tonight." Kate and Simon had always made sure that Annabelle's birthday was fully celebrated despite the fact that it was a few days after Christmas. She never wanted her to resent it being so close to the holidays.

"But not too late," Hilda put in.

Kate bristled. "It's your birthday, and you can stay up as late as you want." She gave Hilda a pointed look, and Hilda said nothing.

Annabelle beamed. "I'm almost five!" Kate smiled at her daughter as they sat down to have some lunch. "Can I have some apple juice?"

"Sure, sweetheart. I'll get it," Hilda answered before Kate could.

Hilda stood in front of the open refrigerator door for a moment and then turned around. "Kate, why are your EpiPens in here?"

"What?" Kate rose and hurried over. "Who would've done that?" Everyone who worked at the house knew that the EpiPens had to be kept at room temperature.

Hilda pulled them out and shook her head. "I have no idea."

Kate felt heat rise in her chest. Hilda was looking at her like she thought Kate had done it. She snatched them from Hilda's hand and threw them into the trash. "They're no good now!"

Kate took her seat again next to Annabelle. She was trying to put on a cheerful face for her daughter, but her mood was dark. The day before, she'd gone through the house and checked all the expiration dates on the EpiPens. That text about the nut allergy statistics had made her nervous. She'd put them all back in their proper places, though, hadn't she? She *had* put a few high up on a cabinet shelf yesterday when Hilda interrupted her, asking some things about the birthday party. But Kate wouldn't have been so absentminded as to put them in the refrigerator, would she?

Hilda took the apple juice from the refrigerator and poured a glass for Annabelle. "I'll get one of the epis from the dining room." Her voice startled Kate. Maybe Hilda *was* trying to drive her crazy. Her phone buzzed. She glanced at the screen, bracing herself, and blew out a breath when she saw it was Blaire.

"Hey," she said.

"Hi there. Just wanted to see if you need me to pick anything up for the party tonight while I'm out."

"Thanks, but I think Fleur took care of everything. Do you have a lot of errands to run?"

"Just a couple. But I also decided my nails aren't fit to be seen, so I'm getting a manicure. I have to stop back at the Four Seasons for more clothes anyhow, so I'll have it done there. I'll be back to help before the party starts. You sound stressed."

Kate stood and moved from the kitchen to the hallway, out of Annabelle's and Hilda's hearing. "Blaire, my mind's racing. Someone put my EpiPens in the refrigerator. I think it was Hilda!"

"What?" Blaire said.

The words rushed out. "Maybe she's sabotaging me? Or Simon,

maybe. I don't know. Someone is trying to make me look crazy. When is this going to stop?"

"Try to calm down. Do something to try and relax. Make some tea? Have a bath? I'll see you in a few hours, okay?"

"A hot bath does sound like a good idea. See you later." Kate hung up and went to the kitchen. "I'm going upstairs. Will you bring Annabelle up when she's finished her lunch?"

Once upstairs, she sat on the edge of the bed, her leg jiggling. She thought about Hilda, and the way she acted like Annabelle was her child. Hilda's daughter had moved away a few years ago with Hilda's granddaughter, who was about Annabelle's age. What if the reason her own daughter had moved to California was because Hilda was unstable? There were plenty of stories about crazy nannies.

It could really still be anyone, Kate thought. Georgina had always been jealous of Lily, coveting her beauty and charm. Maybe coveting her husband as well? Or Selby. Maybe she'd only been pretending to be a good friend all these years. She was one of the few people who had easy access to Kate's house, to Annabelle. Could she be in on it with Georgina somehow? But she knew that seemed far-fetched. Simon was the more likely suspect. He'd admitted the other day that the client he was talking to was unhappy. And there was that urgent call he'd taken on the day of her mother's funeral. Maybe his business *was* in trouble. A lot of their cash was tied up in the foundation. Simon could have somehow been aware of Lily's intended provision for them. Money was a strong motive for murder.

She leaned back against the pillow and closed her eyes. She was so tired. Maybe she'd catch a few minutes of sleep. Her temples were pounding, and she felt as though a thousand voices were screaming inside her head.

"Mommy! Mommy!"

"What?" Kate snapped as her eyes flew open.

Annabelle's lower lip trembled, and she began to cry. "I was talking, and you didn't answer me."

Hilda was standing behind her. "I'm sorry, Kate. I knocked a few times. I wanted to make sure you're okay."

"I fell asleep for a second. You can leave Annabelle with me." She reached out her arms to her daughter. "I'm sorry, sweetheart. Come here."

Hilda looked surprised. "Okay. Are you sure you don't want me to take her, so you can get dressed?"

The woman really was trying to come between them. "No. Thank you very much."

Hilda gave her a strange look. "Okay, well, let me know. How about if I get her ready for the party when the movie is over?"

"How about you take the afternoon off? I'll get her dressed. I'll see you at the party."

Hilda left the room, and Annabelle jumped up on the bed next to her mother. "I miss Grammy. I want her to come to my party."

Kate blinked, holding back tears, pain spreading through her chest. When all of this was over, she was still going to have to grieve. "I miss her too. I wish nothing more than that she could be here. But she's in heaven. She'll be watching. I promise."

Annabelle jumped from the bed and stood in front of her. "I don't want her in heaven. It's not fair. She promised she would take me to a big-girl lunch in New York for my birthday. Why did she leave?"

"Oh, sweetie. It's not her fault. She didn't want to leave. Sometimes things just happen." Kate struggled to find the right words. She'd foolishly thought that Annabelle had accepted her explanation that it was time for Grammy to go to heaven, but of course the little girl didn't understand. She was far too young to grasp the finality of death. Kate had been so caught up in everything else that she hadn't focused enough on Annabelle's emotional well-being.

"Hilda said that a bad person hurt her."

Kate froze. "What else did she say?"

"I don't know," Annabelle said. "I want to watch *Beauty and the Beast*."

Kate didn't want to press Annabelle now, but she wouldn't forget to follow up. Hilda should not be telling Annabelle about Lily's murder, no matter how vague she thought she was being. "Okay, sweetie. I'll watch with you."

She streamed the movie, and the two of them snuggled on the bed, Kate dozing on and off while the movie played.

"It's over, Mommy."

Kate rubbed her eyes and looked at her watch. "Oh. It's time to get dressed."

She chose a cheerful pink sweater and navy slacks for herself, and made her voice bright.

"Okay, birthday girl, ready to put on your party dress?"

"Is it time for my party?"

"Almost."

When they entered Annabelle's room, her dress was already laid on the bed, along with her shoes, socks, and a bow for her hair. Kate got angry again. She'd told Hilda that she'd get Annabelle dressed. Did the woman think she couldn't pick out clothes for her own daughter?

"Let's find a different dress," she said to Annabelle.

"No, Mommy, I like this one."

Kate was not about to let Hilda win. "But you have so many other, prettier dresses. Come on."

Annabelle stomped her foot, her lips in a pout. "Grammy gave me that dress. I want to wear it. I picked it out this morning."

Kate was suddenly filled with shame. "Oh, honey, Mommy's sorry. Of course you can wear it. It's a beautiful dress."

Annabelle was still pouting, but Kate managed to get her dressed and downstairs without any more fuss.

When they entered the family room, Simon was finishing up the decorations. He'd transformed the family room—banners and streamers, enormous stuffed animals with colorful balloons attached to them. Kate hadn't given decorations any thought. When had he had time to buy all this? Had Sabrina helped him pick it all out?

"Daddy! I love my party room."

Simon scooped Annabelle up, twirling her around. "Anything for my princess—my soon-to-be-five princess!"

He put Annabelle down, and she ran over to sit on the stuffed pony in the corner of the room. Simon looked at Kate.

"You look very nice."

She smoothed her hair from her face and gazed at him. "Thank you," she said coldly.

Kate glanced at her watch. Four thirty. She'd hoped Blaire would have been back by now. She was about to text her when Blaire came into the room holding a huge wrapped box.

"I was just going to text you," Kate said by way of greeting.

"Sorry!" Blaire said, out of breath. "Took longer than I thought at the salon." She held her hand up to show Kate her red nails. "Where should I put Annabelle's gift?"

She pointed to a table against the wall. "What is it?"

Blaire shook her head and smiled. "Uh-uh. You have to wait till Annabelle opens it."

"Opens what?" Harrison said as he walked up to them. Kate's

smile wavered when Georgina waltzed in right behind him. Had they come together?

Blaire held the box up to show him.

He gave Kate a peck on the cheek. "Hello, everyone. Where's my birthday girl?" he called jovially, looking at Annabelle.

Annabelle ran up and threw her arms around him. "Granddaddy! I'm gonna be five tonight! Come see the new animals Daddy brought."

"Kate, dear." Georgina kissed the air next to Kate's cheek. She simply nodded at Blaire.

"I thought you were coming with Selby," Kate said.

"No, not enough room for me in her car. Besides, your father was already at my house, having lunch. He's turning into skin and bones. I wanted to give him a home-cooked meal."

Her father had spent the afternoon at Georgina's? He had other friends, couples, who'd be more than happy to feed him and keep him company. Why was he spending so much time with her?

"I don't remember your caring too much for cooking," Blaire said. "Or did you mean that your cook made him a home-cooked meal?" She laughed.

Georgina fixed her with a cold stare. "Harrison's quite used to staff doing the work. Lily didn't get her hands dirty in the kitchen either."

Blaire let it drop, but she didn't look at all fazed.

"Aunt Kate!" Selby's youngest, Tristan, ran up to her. "Thank you for the Warrior stick! It's way cool."

Tristan was Kate and Simon's godson and had practically been born with a lacrosse stick in his hand. She was grateful to Simon for remembering to get him a gift for Christmas—at least he was good to the children in their lives. Kate tousled Tristan's blond mop. "You're very welcome. Can't wait to come watch you use it."

Selby, right behind Tristan, gave Kate a hug. "You doing okay?"
Kate nodded.

"Hello, Selby," Blaire said.

"Blaire." Selby gave a curt nod. "Well, I'm going to go say hi to
the birthday girl. Where are you putting the gifts?"

Kate pointed to a table. "You already gave Annabelle such a
generous Christmas gift, the Pikeur riding habit. You're a doll,
but you've gone overboard again."

Selby smiled. "Well, you can't blame me for spoiling my girl."
She looked at Blaire. "She's my goddaughter, after all."

Carter had slunk into the room and now stood next to Selby,
looking nervous and jittery. He said a quick hello to everyone and
then walked over to the bar.

Annabelle's friend Morgan arrived, and Kate introduced her
parents around. The next few hours went by in a blur of chatter
and laughter. Kate watched from the periphery, feeling disconnected, as if she were hovering over the festivities, taking it all
in from afar. Georgina and Harrison sat huddled together, and
though every now and then Selby or one of the boys would invade
the duo's secret society, they seemed to remain completely indifferent to what was going on around them.

Her gaze moved to Simon, sitting with Annabelle, the big picture book on horses he'd chosen for her on her lap as they turned
the pages together. She couldn't hear what he was saying, only
saw his mouth moving and Annabelle exclaiming, her finger
pointing at the images on the page. Was he trying to prove that
he was enough for her? That she'd be fine without a mother? A few
weeks ago, she'd been worried about breaking up her family by
getting a separation. Now she was terrified she would leave Annabelle motherless. She felt like she'd lost her entire family—she
couldn't trust any of them.

Kate watched them all, her eyes moving from one to the next, imagining what they might be guilty of, what secrets they were keeping. She wanted them out of her house. Blaire was the only person she could talk to anymore.

Suddenly feeling sweaty, she decided to run upstairs and change. As she left the room, she stopped a moment to speak to the guard, who was standing just outside the room in the hallway. "I'll be right back. Make sure Annabelle doesn't leave this room. With anyone."

"Yes, ma'am."

She walked up the stairs, wincing as she tried to keep the weight off her sprained ankle. Sweat dotted her forehead, and when she reached her room, she sat on the bed to catch her breath. After a moment she rose and went to her closet, looking through her shirts, trying to decide what she wanted to wear. She stood there, befuddled, suddenly overcome with indecision.

What was the matter with her? Snatching a navy T-shirt and throwing the hanger on the floor, she pulled off her sweater and pulled on the tee. She walked down the hallway to the guest-suite bathroom to put on a dash of lipstick, but as she pushed the door open, a flickering shadow caught her eye. Was someone in here? Her eyes swept the room. It was empty, but three of her pillar candles from downstairs were sitting on the rim of the bathtub. Lit.

She spun around, her pulse beating so hard she could feel it in her temples. She dropped to the floor and looked under the bed. Jumping up, she ran to the windows and threw the drapes aside, half expecting someone to leap out at her. There was no one in the bedroom. Back in the bathroom, she blew the candles out, then splashed some water on her face. She raced downstairs to find Blaire and pulled her aside.

"What's the matter?" Blaire asked. "You look freaked out."

"I found candles lit in my bathroom. I don't remember lighting them," Kate whispered, looking around furtively. "I only do that when I take a bath, and I didn't take one today."

A sympathetic look crossed Blaire's face, and she cleared her throat. "Honey, remember you said you were going to take a bath before the party. Are you sure you didn't light them and forget to blow them out?"

Kate shook her head wildly. "I didn't end up taking a bath. I fell asleep, and then I watched a movie with Annabelle." She remembered calling Blaire this afternoon . . . but had she taken the candles upstairs? The doctor in her knew that it was possible that her mind was playing tricks on her—she was tired enough and distracted enough—but still, Blaire had to be mistaken.

"Excuse me, Dr. English. Where should I set these?" Fleur was holding a large tray of sandwiches.

"Why don't I show her? Go sit for a minute, Kate," Blaire said.

Kate looked around the room, and her eyes came to rest on Simon. He was talking to Selby. They were probably discussing her. He was probably telling Selby how crazy she was, about all the nutty things she was doing. When Simon looked her way and saw that she was staring, he quickly turned back to Selby.

Selby started laughing. Was she laughing at Kate?

Carter had cornered Blaire now. He was standing close to her, invading her personal space, and Blaire kept backing up. What a jerk, flirting right in front of his wife and clearly making Blaire uncomfortable.

Kate strode over. "Excuse me, but I need Blaire for a moment."

"Everything all right?" Blaire asked as they walked away.

"Just rescuing you, that's all."

Blaire smiled at her. "Thank you. He had one of the tuna sandwiches, and his breath was horrible."

For some reason, Kate found that hilarious, and she started giggling. They were both laughing now, but soon loud guffaws were coming from Kate and she was holding her side, unable to stop. The room went quiet, everyone turning to look at her. It made her laugh even harder, until tears were running down her cheeks.

Simon walked over and pulled her to the side. "What's so funny?"

She pushed him away. "Why don't you go back to talking to Selby? You were doing quite a bit of laughing yourself."

He looked at her like she was crazy. "What's wrong with you? We were just talking."

"You always have an excuse, don't you?" She walked away.

She walked around in a daze awhile longer, anxious for the evening to end. The original plan had been to wait until eight to sing "Happy Birthday" and cut the cake, but Kate needed the party to be over before she completely fell apart.

At seven thirty she decided to hurry things along. She looked around the room for Simon so that he could help with the presents, but he was nowhere to be seen. Naturally he would be somewhere else when Kate needed him. She loaded as many of the gifts as she could carry into her arms and took them to the dining room, setting them down on the table, and then went to the kitchen to find Fleur. As the two of them gathered the cake and dishes, the door from the garage opened, and Simon walked in.

Kate looked at him, annoyed. "I was looking for you. Where have you been?"

"Nowhere. Just remembered I left my phone in the car." He patted his pocket. "What did you need?"

"Just get the other presents from the table in the hall and take them into the dining room," she said, not bothering to look at him as she left.

Kate gathered everyone into the dining room, and as soon as

Simon turned off the lights, Fleur brought the cake in, candles blazing, along with Kate's sterling cake knife. Simon hurried in with the rest of the gifts as they sang "Happy Birthday." When Annabelle blew out the candles, the room was plunged into darkness.

"Daddy, turn the lights on," Annabelle's frightened voice rang out amid soft laughter.

The lights came on, and when Kate looked down, she saw that all of the wrapped packages were now on the table. But the cake knife . . . The knife was gone. She was about to cry out when she saw Simon holding it, poised to cut the cake, and breathed a sigh of relief.

"Here, sweetheart," he said, placing Annabelle's hand over his. "Let's cut the cake together. The first piece is for you, because you're the birthday girl."

Kate smiled at her daughter. "After everyone's had their cake, you get to open your presents."

"Goodie," Annabelle said, as the cake was passed around. She took two bites of her own and put her fork down, looking up at Kate. "That's enough, Mommy. I'm finished. Can I open my presents now?"

Kate laughed. "Of course." She slid the packages closer to Annabelle, who chose first a square box wrapped in blue paper and a huge yellow bow. She struggled to remove the bow until Kate came to her rescue, and in a few seconds, Annabelle had torn off the paper, opening the box to reveal a SparkleWorks Design & Drill. It was one of the gifts Kate had bought.

"Ooh, just what I wanted," Annabelle said.

As Annabelle reached the middle of the pile, she picked up a small rectangular box wrapped in plain white paper decorated with red glitter. "Look, Mommy. It's so pretty."

Annabelle unwrapped the box and lifted the top. Kate leaned

over the child, tilting her head to get a better look. "Let me see that," she said, taking the box from Annabelle and looking at it more carefully. "Who gave you this? Where's the card?" Kate's voice trembled.

"What is it?" Simon rose from his chair.

"Mommy, I want my present!" Annabelle reached out and tried to take it from Kate.

Kate looked around the room, panicked, and then back at the box she held. Inside was a small wooden coffin, hexagonal and tapered at one end in Wild West style. She inhaled sharply and moved away from the table as she lifted it out of the box.

"What is it?" Simon asked again.

Kate stood in front of the sideboard, away from the others, and opened the tiny coffin. As she pushed the top open, movement caught her eye. A feeling of dread washed over her. Suddenly the room began to spin, her stomach heaving. The box was teeming with white slithering blobs. They were moving, wiggling, climbing up the sides of the coffin. Maggots! Squirming, slimy maggots. The hammering in her ears was deafening. A guttural cry came from her as she flung the box to the floor, but now the swarming mass was spread out beneath her, several of them on her right foot and moving.

A new wave of dizziness overcame her, her stomach pitching up and down like an out-of-control roller coaster. She was going to be sick. She shook the crawling parasites from her foot and backed away, scanning the room, but the sea of faces blended together. Simon was coming toward her, taking the box from her, as she shrank away from him in fear.

"Stay away from me." She held her hands out in front of her. "Blaire," she called, searching the room through eyes blurry with tears. "Get the police in here. Hurry."

24

The police had told everyone to wait in the dining room, where one of the officers kept watch while they took each guest, one by one, into the study for questioning. The tension in the room was unbearable, with everyone looking at one another, trying to assess who among them might be guilty. It reminded Blaire of that Christie book *And Then There Were None*.

She was nearly the last to be summoned. A police officer escorted her in.

"Please have a seat, Ms. Barrington," Anderson said, gesturing to the chair across from him.

Blaire sat and waited for him to speak.

"Do you have any idea if that box was among the presents that Mr. English brought into the room?"

"No, I don't. There was a big pile of presents. I can't be sure if it was there or not."

"Did you see anyone bring it into the house when they arrived?"

She shook her head. "No."

"Did you happen to see anyone leave the dining room before the gifts were opened?"

"No. It was dark. We had just sung 'Happy Birthday.'"

"How about right before? Did you notice anyone leave the dining room before the singing began?"

She thought a moment. "I can't be sure. I wasn't really looking around. I was watching Annabelle."

"Try to remember," he prodded.

She looked up and tried to picture who'd been around the table. Simon and Kate were on each side of their daughter, Carter was across from her with Selby and their three boys, and Harrison and Georgina and the parents of Annabelle's friend were on the same side of the table. She shrugged. "Everyone was there. I mean, Fleur brought the cake in, Simon turned off the lights, and we sang. It was only dark for a few seconds after Annabelle blew out the candles."

"Which present was yours?" he asked.

"Annabelle hasn't opened it yet. It's big. A life-size mechanical dog." She stared at him. "She never got to it, unfortunately."

"I see. Have you been here all day?"

"No. I had some errands to run, and then went back to my hotel for a manicure and to pick up some things."

"And which hotel was that?"

"The Four Seasons. Downtown."

He wrote in his notepad, stopped, and looked at her again. "Was anyone acting strangely? Nervous?"

"No. It was a party. Everyone was happy . . . well, as happy as could be expected, given the recent circumstances. Kate was on edge, but who could blame her?"

His brow creased. "More on edge than the past few days? Was she wary of anyone in particular?"

Blaire hesitated only a moment. "Simon. She's afraid of him. Thinks he's doing things to make her doubt herself."

"What kind of things?"

"Moving things around where they shouldn't be, making her think she doesn't remember she's done something, that sort of thing."

He arched an eyebrow. "Do you think that's possible? Or could she be imagining it? How do you think her state of mind is?"

She hesitated, thinking about Kate's hysterical laughter earlier in the evening, and the candles in the bathroom. If she told Anderson about it, he'd definitely discredit Kate's judgment. But since Kate wasn't a suspect, she saw no reason to tell him any of that. She needed him to take Kate's suspicions of Simon seriously.

"I think Simon could definitely be doing these things. I've never trusted him. Maybe you already know this, but that night I was at Gordon's, I found out that Simon's lost some big clients lately. He also told me that almost all of Kate's money is in the foundation, and I know he signed a prenup. Did you? Kate inherited a lot of money when Lily died. According to Carter Haywood, his business partner, they need a cash infusion for their business."

He stared at her. "I see. Do you know any more specifics about Mr. English's financial difficulties?"

"I really don't know any more than that. Only that Gordon Barton thinks Simon's in big trouble. Can't you look into his company's financial records?"

"We can. It will take some time."

This man was exasperating. "Why? How much time?"

"There's a little thing called the Fourth Amendment, Ms. Barrington. We can't just access people's financial records without their permission or a warrant."

"I'm well aware of that," she said coolly. "I write about crime."

"I know that you do. And I work at it in real life. I appreciate the information. We'll look into it. Is there anything else?"

"The only other thing is that I think you should look further into the relationship between Simon and Sabrina Mitchell. Earlier in the evening of the night I found the pictures at Gordon's, I saw the two of them out together at a restaurant downtown. He told Kate he had a business dinner."

"We're aware of that. Anything else?"

That was interesting. "Are you having Simon followed?"

He gave her an impatient look. "Again, Ms. Barrington, is there anything else?"

"One more thing."

He raised his eyebrows and waited.

"Carter Haywood told me that just last month, Simon received a call from Lily at the office, and that immediately afterward, he changed his mind about taking Sabrina on a business trip. It sounds to me like Lily had known something was going on with them, and told him he had to stop."

He looked up at her. "Thank you for this. We'll follow up on it. Don't hesitate to call me if you think of anything else."

He turned to the officer standing by the door. "Please escort Ms. Barrington out, and bring Mr. English back in."

She rose and went back to the dining room, where Harrison was sitting alone.

"Where's Kate?" she asked.

He looked up. "She and Annabelle are sleeping in her room. I'm glad you're staying. Kate needs you. I told her I'd stay as well, and I promised her I'd get Simon to leave."

How was he going to do that, Blaire wondered? The door chime sounded. "I guess Anderson's heading out."

Simon came into the room, looking exhausted, his shirttail half out, his hair a mess. He slumped into a seat. "I don't know how much longer I can take this. How the hell did that present get in here? Who could be doing this?"

"Maybe it's someone on your staff," Blaire said. "I know Anderson's looked into them, but it's the only explanation. It's certainly unlikely that it was Annabelle's friend's parents. That just leaves Selby, Carter, and Georgina. And us."

Harrison was quiet a moment and then looked at Simon. "Why

is Kate so suspicious of you? I took your word at Christmas that nothing was going on with that woman who showed up. But now . . ."

Simon stood, his face red. "You can't be serious."

Harrison's voice rose. "I'm completely serious. Someone has killed my wife and is now threatening my daughter. Someone very close, apparently. If she's afraid of you, then you need to leave."

Simon looked pained. "You can't honestly think it's me? Harrison, come on!"

"I don't know what to think. All I know is that my daughter is scared out of her mind, and if you care so much for her, you'll give her space. If for no other reason than her peace of mind."

"But she's not safe. I can't leave her alone here."

"She's not alone," Blaire said. "I'm here, and so is Harrison. And there are plenty of guards and the police."

Simon narrowed his eyes. "Fine. I'll stay on the couch in my office, but just temporarily. Until we find the person doing all this. Then you'll both be sorry for accusing me."

25

Kate felt better with Simon out of the house. As she got dressed the next morning, she felt slightly lighter for the first time in days. There was one more thing she had to do, though. Opening the door to Annabelle's room, she smiled at her daughter.

"Hi, sweetie. Granddaddy and Aunt Blaire are in the kitchen. Why don't you go down and see them? I need to talk to Miss Hilda."

Hilda gave Kate a questioning look as Annabelle ran past her and down the stairs.

"Is everything okay?"

Kate raised her eyebrows. "Does it look like everything's okay? Are you in on it with him?"

Hilda took a step back. "I don't understand what you're asking me."

Kate scoffed. "The candles, the EpiPens, the cough medicine, the sweater—you're working with Simon. I almost believed I was losing my mind. Now I see, you're trying to get rid of me, so you can be the only woman taking care of Annabelle."

Kate had done some research that morning. She'd gone back and reviewed Hilda's employment application and found her daughter's number, listed as the emergency contact. But it was an old number, from before she'd moved away, and Kate couldn't find a new one. Kate had found her right away on Facebook, though she'd only been able to scroll through a handful of pictures due to the privacy settings. She'd been right. Hilda's daughter, Beth, had a little girl Annabelle's age. She even looked like Annabelle—long blond hair and big brown eyes. Then she'd googled Beth and found a blog about mothering. No mention of Hilda anywhere, but there was a post about getting toxic people out of your life. That was proof enough to Kate that Hilda was bad news.

"Kate . . ."

Kate put a hand up. "Don't bother. I'm sick of your lies. Pack your things and get out. You're fired."

Tears sprang to Hilda's eyes, and her face paled. "Kate, you're wrong—"

"Wrong?" Kate's voice rose. "I'm not wrong. *You're* wrong if you think you can trick me anymore." She turned and walked away before Hilda could say anything else. Marching down the stairs to the kitchen, she walked in and called over to Harrison and Blaire sitting at the table. "Now we're safe."

Annabelle looked up. "What, Mommy?"

"Don't worry, sweetie. Everything's fine."

Harrison rose and walked over to Kate. "Kate, are you okay?"

She gave him a triumphant smile. "I am now. I just fired Hilda. Another traitor gone." Why did he look so upset?

He put his hands on her arms. "Katie, Katie. Hilda's not a traitor. Where is she?"

Kate narrowed her eyes at him. "She's packing. I want her gone."

He started to say something, and then stopped. "Okay. I'll just go and make sure she leaves."

"Thank you very much."

Harrison walked back to the table and whispered something to Blaire.

"Hey, no secrets!" Kate called over.

Blaire smiled over at her. "Of course not. Why don't you come sit down, and I'll make you some breakfast?"

"I can make my own breakfast. Anyway, I'm not hungry." Kate made herself a cup of coffee and walked over to the table. "Why don't we go do something fun today? How about the zoo?"

Annabelle's face lit up. "I love the zoo! Can we go see the monkeys?"

"Um, it's maybe a little cold for the zoo," Blaire said. "There's snow on the ground."

Kate looked out the window. "I guess you're right. Well, how about the aquarium?"

"Okay, if you feel like going out."

"I'd love to join, but I need to go to the hospital," Harrison said. "I'll be back early afternoon." He turned to Blaire. "You'll be here all day?"

Blaire nodded.

"Great." Kate exhaled. Now that Simon was gone, it was as if a weight had been lifted. "I'm going to go check my work email, and then we can go."

She ran upstairs to her office and clicked the mouse. She breathed a sigh of relief when she scanned her emails and saw nothing out of the ordinary. She read through the new ones and was about to get up when she heard the *ping* of an incoming message. The subject line screamed at her: TIME IS RUNNING OUT. She held her breath as she clicked on the email.

You really loved Jake, didn't you?

Well, not enough to save him

But don't worry, you'll be joining him soon

You can sleep with ten guards outside your room

It won't save you

This is the last message you'll get

Because it's the last day you're going to live

She tried to yell, but nothing came out. She dialed Blaire's number on her cell.

"Kate?"

"I'm in my office. Come here," she panted.

Kate took a picture of the screen while she waited, and then Blaire was next to her.

Blaire leaned toward her and got closer to the screen. She took the mouse. "Um, Kate . . ."

"What?" Kate was staring off into the distance, numb.

"This is from you."

"What are you talking about?"

Blaire pointed to the From field. "Look. It's your personal email address. K English thirty-four at gmail dot com."

Kate shook her head. "I didn't send this!"

Blaire was quiet, staring at Kate with a look she had never seen before.

"Why would I send this?"

Blaire leaned down farther, to be eye level with her. "You're under a tremendous amount of stress. You know as well as I do—"

"No!" Kate pushed her away and stood up. "I'm not crazy," she insisted. But she was starting to wonder.

Just then her cell phone rang. It was Detective Anderson.

Kate answered the phone. "Did you see it?"

"Dr. English. We traced the IP address. That email came from your Wi-Fi."

26

Blaire could see that Kate was doing her utmost to appear calm, the only outward sign of anxiety the constant thrumming of her fingertips against each other as they sat in the living room, waiting for Anderson.

"They think I sent that email to myself, don't they? I didn't. You believe me, don't you? You don't think I'm crazy, do you?" Kate was sitting ramrod straight in the chair, now absently rubbing her hands together.

Blaire decided to take a middle road. "Of course you're not crazy. I'm sure there's a reasonable explanation."

Kate looked dubious. She had a perpetually gaunt and haunted look these days. She wasn't eating, existing on coffee and Valium. Blaire watched Kate push the food around on her plate, never bringing it to her mouth.

"I'm really, really sure it wasn't me. It wasn't, was it?" Kate pleaded. "How could they have traced the IP address to here?" She brought her hands up to her face, crying softly.

It didn't matter how many assurances Blaire might try to give her—Kate was clearly second-guessing herself, believing she might actually have sent the email. Blaire was anxious for the police to arrive. She wondered if they would be able to put Kate's mind at ease and finally figure this out.

When they heard the sound of the doorbell, Kate stood, wiping the tears from her face.

Brian ushered Anderson into the room. There was another man

with him, one Blaire hadn't seen before, though she assumed he was a colleague.

Anderson took off his hat and nodded at them. "Dr. English, Ms. Barrington." He indicated the man who had come in with him. "This is Detective Reagan. He's with our technical unit."

"Hello," Kate said, and looked expectantly at him. "Are you sure this is where that email came from?"

"There's no mistake, ma'am," he said. "Your home is the location of the IP address."

She turned to Anderson. "I didn't send it, though."

"We know that."

Blaire saw a look of surprised relief cross Kate's face and waited to hear what Anderson was going to say next.

"The sender's email address was not yours," Reagan said.

"But——" Kate began.

"The sender's address was K English one three four at gmail dot com. You must have glossed over the numeral one when you looked at the address."

Kate scrambled to get her laptop from the side table and opened it. "Yes, yes. You're right. It's not my address."

"Who does the account belong to?" Blaire asked him.

Anderson turned to Reagan, who said, "It's been deactivated. There's no way to definitively know."

"We need to find the device from which the email was sent. It's here. Somewhere in your house," Anderson said.

"But how is that possible?" Kate asked. "You see everything outgoing and incoming from our phones and computers. How can it be coming from my house?" She still had that wild-eyed look on her face.

"We've only been monitoring the devices you gave us permission to monitor, Dr. English. Any other smartphones, tablets, or laptops that were used here would use your IP address but not be monitored."

It was the first time Blaire had heard such patience in his voice. She hoped he was going to start in Simon's office. It was all she could do not to open her mouth and suggest it.

"Well," Kate said, seeming to have regained some equilibrium. "Where do you want to start?"

Anderson gave her a curt nod and stood. "Your husband's office."

As they left the room, the two men slid gloves on, and the two women trailed behind them.

Simon's desk was a light wood—maple, Blaire guessed—and completely clear of paperwork. There were two silver-framed photos resting on it—a portrait of Kate looking beautiful, and a picture of Kate, Simon, and Annabelle together.

Anderson moved behind the desk. "Do we have your permission to search these premises, Dr. English?"

"Yes. Absolutely," she said, her voice wobbly.

Anderson began with the desk, opening drawer after drawer. Blaire and Kate watched as Anderson picked up a globe from its stand, examining it as he turned it around and around.

"Does your husband have a safe?" he asked.

"Yes, in our bedroom. You can check it, but I just put my wedding ring in last night. There's only jewelry in there."

"We'll check that later. Let's finish in here first," he said to Reagan.

Anderson walked the perimeter of the room, checking behind each painting and award hanging on the wall. He turned to Reagan. "Let's check the bookshelves."

The two of them began to search the shelves behind Simon's desk while Blaire and Kate stood in hushed anticipation. The rows of books went almost to the ceiling, and it looked as if Anderson and Reagan were going to open every single one. This could take forever.

"Why don't we sit down," Blaire said to Kate. "They might be a while."

Kate sat, but she couldn't seem to stop her foot tapping anxiously. She had that faraway look again. Reagan was on the step stool, pulling books from the next to the last shelf, when suddenly he stopped and handed one to Anderson. Blaire and Kate stood, craning to see what he held. It wasn't a book at all—it was a leather box that looked like a copy of *Moby-Dick*. He stared at the contents and exchanged a look with Reagan, who came down from the ladder.

"What is it?" Kate asked, moving closer to him.

The corners of his mouth turned down, and he shook his head as he held the box out for them to see. Inside was a black smartphone. Nestled beside it was a plastic baggie—containing a gleaming diamond bracelet.

Blaire heard a sharp intake of breath. "Dear God, it's my mother's bracelet," Kate said, just before she hit the floor.

27

Kate felt a dull pounding in her head and opened her eyes to see Blaire hovering over her. "What happened?"

"You fainted."

It took a moment before everything came rushing back. Simon. The phone. Her mother's bracelet. She tried to sit up, but a wave of dizziness made her fall back against the pillow and close her eyes.

"Dr. English?" Detective Anderson's deep voice jarred her. She opened her eyes and pushed herself to a sitting position. She felt as though she were seeing and hearing everything in slow motion.

"Here you go." Blaire held out a bottle of water. "This might help."

Kate took a small sip and then handed the bottle back to Blaire. She felt like she was going to throw up. Even though she'd wondered about Simon—his fidelity and his guilt regarding the threats and her mother—she was still utterly shocked when confronted with the hard evidence. How could she have lived with him all those years, and not known he was capable of murder and psychological warfare? She couldn't grasp it.

She needed answers, something to make sense of this. What kind of a monster kills his mother-in-law and plots against the mother of his child? If he'd wanted out that badly, she'd have given him a divorce. She'd have been generous with the settlement, despite the prenup. Another thought occurred to her, and she felt seized by panic. What if one of the security people had been helping him? She could still be in danger.

She looked up at Blaire. "Get rid of the security team. Simon hired them—I don't feel safe with them around."

"I don't think you want to be without protection until he's been arrested," Blaire said. "There's a firm we use for crowd control at events when we tour. Do you want me to call them?"

Kate nodded, then ran her hands through her hair, her eyes closed.

"Dr. English?" Detective Anderson called to her.

Kate and Blaire looked up at the same time.

"We've found something else." He cleared his throat. "Rat poison."

Kate doubled over, the wind knocked out of her. Every new revelation felt like a fresh assault. He'd planned to poison her. She remembered the funny-tasting coffee and wondered if he'd already started.

Blaire went to Kate, putting an arm around her shoulder. "I'm sorry, Kate. I'm so sorry."

Kate slumped back onto the chair.

Detective Anderson tapped the smartphone. "All the texts and the emails came from this phone."

"He really wanted to kill me. Does he hate me so much that he also had to torture and taunt me?"

"Obviously he wanted it to look like someone else was doing it, or to make you seem like you were crazy," Blaire said. She looked at Detective Anderson. "One thing I don't understand is why Simon would use a similar Gmail address. Wouldn't it be more effective to make Kate look bad if he'd used her own?"

Kate shook her head. "He doesn't know any of my passwords." Something odd had occurred to her, though. "My husband isn't here. How did he send the email, if the phone was here?"

"It looks like this email was scheduled," Detective Reagan said. "He could have set it up days ago."

"Simon must have forgotten to take the phone with him when your dad made him leave," Blaire said. "That's why it wasn't turned off this time."

"Lucky break," Anderson said.

By the time Harrison arrived, Reagan had left, and only Anderson remained.

"Kate, what's happened?"

"Sit down, Dad," she said.

"What's going on?" Harrison asked, continuing to stand.

"They found Mother's bracelet."

"Found it where?" he demanded.

"Right here, hidden in Simon's shelves." She began to cry, her shoulders shaking. "I'm so sorry I brought him into our lives, Dad. Mother would still be alive if I hadn't . . ."

He stood, perplexed, as if she were speaking a foreign language. "Are you saying that Simon killed your mother?"

"Yes."

Suddenly her father roared to life, his eyes blazing. "I'll kill the son of a bitch. I'll kill him with my bare hands." He was ranting, saying things she couldn't decipher, his face red and spittle spewing from his lips.

Kate understood his fury, but the force of it frightened her nonetheless. She feared he was going to go into cardiac arrest.

Detective Anderson went to him, putting a hand on his shoulder. "Hey, take it easy. Nothing is certain yet. I'll take the evidence, and we'll see what they come up with." He turned to Kate. "Is Simon at his office now?"

Blaire answered for her. "Supposedly."

The thought of facing her husband filled Kate with dread, as did the thought of everything that was about to unfold, ripping their lives further apart.

Anderson pressed his lips together and sighed. "We'll go and arrest him now. You should probably call your attorney."

"Attorney? Why would we get him an attorney?" her father asked. "He can rot in hell."

"Okay, I'll be in touch," Anderson said, and was out the door.

Kate turned to her father. It was painful to see his earlier rage turn back to suffering, to see the misery in his eyes.

He took her hand in his and stared beyond her, a vacant look in his eyes. "Why? Why?" he kept repeating. "It doesn't make sense." He looked at Kate. "At least we know. And now you'll be safe." He pulled Kate into his arms.

That was small consolation, she thought.

The following morning, Kate stood just inside the front door and waved goodbye to Annabelle as Harrison drove away with her. Though the police had arrested Simon last night, she was still a nervous wreck, and they'd all agreed it would be better for Annabelle to have some time away with her grandfather. He was taking her to the beach house—a place of tranquility and peace in the off-season. The house was quiet without all the security around; Blaire had gotten rid of them right after Anderson had left. The team that Blaire used on tours was coming later that day. She and Kate wanted to be sure that if Simon hadn't been acting alone, she'd still be safe.

Kate had spoken to Detective Anderson earlier that morning, and he'd told her that Simon had hired an attorney. Kate had already contacted her lawyer and filled him in. There was no way she'd contribute to the defense of the person who'd taken her mother from her.

Her eyes were swollen from crying, and her head was fuzzy

from the Valium she'd taken earlier as she paced the downstairs, going from room to room, straightening a picture, moving a magazine, anything to keep herself from going crazy.

Blaire popped into the living room. "How're you holding up?"

Kate shook her head. "I don't know. All I do is rehash everything in my head until I think I'll go crazy."

Blaire brought a mug over to her. "Here, I made you some tea. Let's sit."

Kate took it from her. "Thanks. Ugh, the house is so empty without Annabelle. Maybe I shouldn't have let Dad take her to the beach. What if they have a car accident?" She jumped up, panic-stricken. "I'm going to call him. I don't want her that far away."

"It's okay. They'll be fine. Don't call while they're on the road. You'll distract him."

Kate took a deep breath. Blaire was right. She could *cause* him to have an accident. It'd be better to call him later.

"You haven't eaten since yesterday. Let me get you something."

Kate waved her hand. "No, not hungry."

"Kate—toast, something. You're going to get sick. Annabelle needs a strong mother."

Kate relented. "Just a half piece."

"Be right back. Drink your tea."

Kate took a few sips and leaned back against the sofa. Why was her heart still beating so furiously? Simon had been arrested. They had her mother's killer. She was safe now. She imagined Simon in handcuffs, professing his innocence while being dragged away. She'd wanted to go, to be there watching behind the two-way glass as he was questioned, but Detective Anderson had told her it was a bad idea. And in the end, she had to agree.

Blaire came back a few minutes later. "Here you go." She handed Kate a plate with a piece of toast cut in half and covered in jam.

"Thanks." Kate took a small bite and felt her stomach turn with nausea. Putting the plate next to her, she took another sip of tea. "Mmm, this is good. Peppermint?"

Blaire smiled. "Yes, I remember how much you always loved it. I'm still a die-hard coffee drinker." She stretched and yawned. "So what should we do today? Now that you don't have to be a prisoner in your house any longer, we should celebrate."

Kate arched a brow. "I don't know if finding out my husband is a killer is a reason to celebrate."

"Of course not—that's not what I meant. Don't you want to get out of here, though? Even just walk around the mall. Something."

The idea of being able to do whatever she wanted without worrying about being watched *was* a liberating thought. "Actually, that's a great idea. I'd love to go to a bookstore and just wander around."

Blaire stood. "You won't get any objections from me." She smiled at Kate again. "Let's go."

Kate held a finger up. "Do you think they've gotten to the beach yet? I want to connect with them before we leave."

"Give it another half hour." Blaire sat back down. "It's been ages since I've been to the beach house. Probably looks completely different now."

"Not too much. We've updated some of it. The rooms are pretty much the same. Annabelle has my room now. Still has the mermaids. Mother never did get around to changing that. But Annabelle loves it."

"What about my room?" Blaire asked, an edge to her voice.

Kate was taken aback. "Oh, um, Simon uses that as his office."

"Of course he does."

Kate gave her a confused look. "What does that mean?"

"Nothing, I just meant that he takes whatever he wants with

no regard to anyone else." She leaned back in the chair across from Kate. "Well, he's out of your life now. I'm just relieved we found out the truth before he could have hurt you or Annabelle."

Kate swallowed. She hadn't considered that he could actually be a threat to his own daughter. She was still trying to figure out why he'd killed her mother. "I don't get it. Do you think he killed Mother as a cover-up? So that he could kill me, and the police would attribute everything to some crazed psycho?" Kate swirled her spoon around the mug, lifting the tea bag up and down unconsciously.

Blaire gave her a sympathetic look. "Yeah, I do. I'm sorry, sweetie. I've been waiting until you were strong enough to tell you what I found out. Carter told me your mother *did* call Simon. Sabrina and he were supposed to go on a business trip to New York, but he made her stay behind after speaking to your mother. Lily must have tried to talk some sense into him. Obviously he didn't appreciate that. I think he and Sabrina planned this whole thing. I mean, he knew all about your anxiety. How to push your buttons. And what kind of sick bastard tortures innocent animals? I mean, seriously, killing those poor parakeets and painting them black. That's beyond sick."

Kate's head snapped up. What had Blaire just said?

"Why don't you try your dad now? Then we can get out of here."

"Okay." Kate pulled out her cell phone and tried him. It rang four times before going to voice mail. "No answer. Maybe they hit some traffic." She was still thinking about Blaire's words from a moment before.

"Why don't we get going now? You can try them again from the car," Blaire said. "I'll drive."

Kate was still thinking about the birds. How did Blaire know the birds were parakeets, and that they'd been spray-painted? Kate had never told her that, had she? She was sure she'd only said they were blackbirds.

"Um, you know what? I've got a splitting headache. I think I need to just rest a little before we go out. Do you mind terribly running over to CVS and picking up some Tylenol for me? I've run out."

"I've got some Advil with me." Blaire started to get up. "Let me go get it."

Kate shook her head. "No, I can't take ibuprofen. It bothers my stomach. I hate to ask, but it's not far from here, only a few miles up the road." She was lying, but she needed to get Blaire out of the house.

Blaire stared at her for a minute and smiled. "Sure. I'll be right back."

As soon as she heard the door chime announce Blaire's exit, Kate limped up the stairs to the guest room where Blaire was staying. The room was immaculate. All of her things were neatly stacked on her dresser, her suitcases zipped and next to each other on the wooden luggage valet in the corner. Kate unzipped the Mulberry duffel first. Rifling through as quickly as she could, she pulled out some books, a makeup bag, boxes holding jewelry. She didn't even know what she was looking for. She put everything back, trying to make sure it was in the same order she'd found it. Next, she unzipped one of the suitcases. Neatly folded jeans and shirts. She lifted the clothes out and placed them carefully on the bed. A leather journal sat on the bottom of the suitcase. Kate picked it up and opened it. Blaire's bold handwriting jumped out at her. She flipped through the pages and came to one dated the day of her mother's funeral.

*I'm coming back to town. It's not the way I would have
planned our reunion, but there's no way I'm missing Lily's
funeral. This isn't the way it was supposed to be. All these
years I've been kept away from her. You're to blame for
keeping us apart and for depriving her of my love and me
of hers. It could have been so different. We could have been
a real family, but your pride was more important. You don't
deserve my friendship, but I'll pretend to offer it. I'll be
right there, giving you my sympathies, pretending to feel
sorry for you, maybe even holding your hand. But inside,
I'll be seething, planning my next move, relishing the look of
suffering and terror on your face.*

She sank to the bed, horrified and turned the page to the next
entry.

*If only I could have seen your reaction when you found the
mice. Did you scream, or has your job inured you to the sight
of death? Do you wonder if the same fate awaits you? I hope
my little present at least snapped you out of your stupor. I
know you're upset, but honestly, Kate, you had guests, and you
didn't do a very good job of taking care of them. Lily raised
you better than that, didn't she? She would have been appalled
to see the coffee run dry, the creamer gone, and no one
overseeing the staff to refill it. I was always a better daughter
to her than you. You weren't worthy of her. And now I'll never
get to see her again because of your selfishness.*

Blaire was behind everything? Kate felt the sour taste of bile
rise, burning her throat. Her hands were cold, her fingers tingling.
She was going to be sick. *Blaire* had killed her mother?

"What are you doing in here?" Blaire's voice cut through the silence.

Kate jumped, looking up and closing the book. "It was you?" She could barely get the words out, her breathing labored. "You killed her?"

Blaire's eyes blazed as she looked at the journal in Kate's hand. "That's private!"

"Blaire! What did you do? Why did you kill her?"

"I didn't. I promise I didn't."

Kate threw the journal at her. "What is this, then? You hate me!"

"No! I did at first. When you called to tell me about Lily, I blamed you. I came back to hurt you. But after being with you . . . my feelings changed. Look." She opened the journal again and pointed.

"See, here I'm talking about how happy I am that we've made up. And that justice is served for Lily. I started out for revenge, but I've forgiven you for what you did."

Kate's heart started beating faster. "Blaire, you're scaring me. I don't understand. I loved you—why would you do all this? You sent me those mice, the birds, those horrible maggots, when you knew how fragile I was. I thought you were here to help me."

Blaire's expression turned plaintive. "I *was* trying to help you." She shook her head. "In the beginning it was to get back at you, but then, when I realized Simon was guilty, I had to keep going so he'd be caught. The last time I tried to tell you about him, you kicked me out of your life. Remember?"

Kate began to tremble, her body going cold. "Blaire, I'm sorry. I was young." Her mind was working as fast as it could. This was not the Blaire she'd known years ago. She tried to remember what she'd learned in her psych rotation in medical school about dealing with the mentally ill. "You were right," she said in a calm voice. "I see that now. I should never have married him."

"No, you shouldn't have. I needed to make you see that. That's why I planted the bracelet and the phone while you were running around accusing poor Hilda."

"Simon is *innocent*?"

Blaire was pacing now. "He's not innocent! He's guilty of everything. Just because I had to help the police get enough evidence to nail him doesn't mean Simon is innocent! I told you. Your mother called him and told him to stop messing around with that tramp."

"But your journal . . . you sent the mice. Are you working with him? Are you *involved* with him?"

Blaire gave her an incredulous look. "What? No. He didn't do anything but kill Lily. Everything else was me."

"But how did you know what I was wearing . . . the sweatshirt?"

"I put a camera in your bedroom. Pretty smart of me to suggest the police search for equipment. Of course, by then, I'd taken it out. I've learned a lot of technical skills doing research. It wasn't hard to trick you."

"You did all this to make him look guilty? My mother loved you. I loved you." It was too much for Kate to take in. "Why did you kill my mother?"

Blaire gave her an exasperated sigh. "You're not listening! I didn't kill her. I loved her! I came back to solve the murder, and to make you suffer for taking her from me. But I told you, Kate, I changed my mind about that when I saw that our bond was just as close as ever. Over Christmas . . . staying here with you . . . it brought it all back."

Kate tried to keep her voice even. She didn't believe Blaire. She had Lily's bracelet. She had to be the killer. "You had her bracelet, Blaire. Just tell me the truth."

"I bought another diamond bracelet. They're not that hard to find, and I remembered what it looked like. I was there when your father gave it to her at their twentieth anniversary party." Blaire tapped on her temple and shook her head. "Seriously, Kate, use your head."

"I don't understand. Who killed her, then?"

Blaire's voice rose. "I told you. Your husband. Who else?"

Kate pushed past her and hobbled down the stairs as fast as she could, her ankle throbbing. She had to get Anderson here immediately. She could hear Blaire's footsteps right behind her.

"Where are you going? Kate, stop!"

Where had she left her cell phone? She went to the living room. When she went to pick it up, she felt a hard smack on her hand that caused her to yell out. She brought the hand to her chest. Blaire was holding the fire poker.

"Sit down, Kate. You're not making any phone calls."

"Blaire, put that down," Kate pleaded.

Blaire shook her head. "You're going to call the police. Tell them about what I did. I can't let you do that. They'll let Simon out of jail, and he'll get away with it. That can't happen. You really can't have them send me away, not before I tell you something else."

Kate threw her hands up, trying to show Blaire that she was no threat to her. She kept one eye on the poker still poised in Blaire's hands. "Okay, okay. I'm listening."

Blaire sighed. "I got a letter from Lily. It arrived two days before you called to tell me she'd been murdered." Tears were streaming down Blaire's face now. "Kate, listen to me. She was my mother too."

"Blaire, I know you thought of her that way. And I'm sorry, truly sorry, for all the years you missed, and I accept the blame, but I can't take it back now."

Blaire's expression turned hard. "You're not listening. I didn't *think* of her as my mother. She *was* my mother. She gave me up for adoption."

Kate suddenly felt as if she couldn't get a breath. Blaire was delusional. What was she talking about? "That doesn't make any sense. How can she be your mother? We're the same age. It's impossible." But even as the words came out, something was nagging at her.

"No, silly. I'm a year and a half older, remember? The only reason we were in the same grade is because Mayfield made me repeat eighth grade. Lily conceived me while she was engaged to your father."

Kate was confused. "Because she was pregnant before she got married, she gave you up? Why wouldn't she and Dad have just moved up the wedding?"

Blaire took a moment to answer. "Because Harrison is not my father."

"What are you talking about? This makes no sense. Who is your father?"

"I don't know. She was going to tell me. But then . . ."

Kate didn't know what to believe. Was this some fantasy Blaire had concocted, or could it possibly be true? All she knew was that she had to calm Blaire down and get her to put down that poker.

"Listen, Blaire. I'm so sorry. If we're sisters, then we need to start over."

"You're willing to just forget everything I did? Forgive me?"

"Of course," Kate lied.

Blaire began to pace. While her back was turned, Kate's hand moved slowly to open the drawer in the table next to her. She felt around for one of the EpiPens, curled her fingers around it, brought it back to her side, and dropped it between the sofa cushions before Blaire could notice. If she could use the EpiPen on

Blaire, the shock might give her the advantage, and she could get away. She watched her old friend carefully, waiting for the right time to make her move.

"How do I know I can believe you?" Blaire looked away, and Kate raised the EpiPen, ready to plunge it into her neck. Before she knew what was happening, Blaire turned back and lunged at her, grabbing the EpiPen.

"How could you? Even now, when you know the truth, you're still betraying me." She wiped her face with the back of her hand.

Kate had to calm her down. "Blaire, please, I won't call the police. Just sit down so we can talk. I love you. We're sisters. We can work this out. Let me help you." Kate's mind was racing furiously, trying to keep one step ahead of Blaire.

"Sisters?" Blaire sneered. "You threw me away. Just like my adoptive mother did. Just like my father did. Just like Carter did. I thought you were different, but you're just like the rest of them. I can see that I've given you a chance you don't deserve. I'm sorry, Kate, but you failed the test. But at least I'll have Annabelle."

"Don't you dare hurt Annabelle," Kate yelled.

"*Hurt* her? I don't want to hurt her. She's my niece. My flesh and blood. She'll be better off without you. I'll come and visit her after you're dead. I'll tell her all the horrible things you did when she's old enough to understand. She'll know that it's all your fault. That her poor Auntie Blaire could never have children because of her own mother's selfishness. Then she'll love me and never leave me."

"My fault? What are you talking about?"

"The accident, Kate. The one we had because you were so out-of-control drunk that you distracted me. Leaning over the seat, playing with the radio, when I kept yelling at you to sit back down. Maybe I would have been able to avoid that driver hitting us, if you'd have just listened to me."

"But you weren't even hurt. Jake died that night. Don't you think I've tortured myself over it every single day of my life since? I will live with that guilt forever. But we were kids, Blaire. Stupid kids."

"Is that your excuse for everything? Youth? Take some responsibility. You were too wrapped up in your own misery to see what it did to me. Did it occur to you to ask why Carter broke up with me?" Her voice was rising. "I was pregnant. And your recklessness cost me both the baby and the man I was going to marry."

The thought that she'd also been responsible for the loss of a pregnancy overwhelmed her. "Oh, Blaire. I'm so sorry. I didn't know you were pregnant."

Blaire brought her face close to Kate's. "I'm sorry, I'm sorry," she mimicked in a mocking singsong. "It's too late for your sorrys. The miscarriage caused an infection. My husband's walked out on me because I can't give him a child, and it's all your fault."

"What do you mean, he walked out on you? He sent you flowers. And that beautiful note."

"*I* sent those flowers. I couldn't let everyone in Baltimore know my husband doesn't love me anymore."

"Blaire, please, listen to me. You need help. I can help you. Please, we can work this out."

Blaire gave her a sad look. "You broke my heart, Kate. Twice. You've left me no other choice. I can't let you tell anyone the truth."

Kate's fear gave way to desperation. "So, what's the plan, then? Let Simon go to jail for something he didn't do, and kill me?"

Blaire had gotten a gleam in her eyes. "I'm not going to kill you. The fire will. Everyone knows how much you love candles. In fact, you keep forgetting to blow them out. No one will be surprised when you burn to death because of your carelessness. They may even think you did it on purpose. You've been acting pretty loco lately. Too bad I was out shopping when it happened. Between the Valium and the candles, you didn't stand a chance. What a shame all the security is gone, and the staff left for the night—the ones you haven't fired, that is."

Kate looked around the room again, frantic. "You would really kill me? You're not a murderer, Blaire," she said, trying to focus.

"You've left me no choice." Blaire took the poker and smacked Kate on the head. Dazed, Kate fell to the floor in agony. Blaire pulled a lighter out of her pocket and lit the two candles on the coffee table in front of her. Next to one of them she'd placed a tea towel. Knocking the candle over, she watched as the towel caught fire and then consumed the newspaper she'd spread on the table. The fire detectors were screaming now. But Blaire figured it would take the fire trucks too long to get to Kate in time, given how fast the fire was spreading.

"Bye, Kate," she said, walking away.

"Blaire, no! Wait! Please help me," Kate screamed. She tried to get up, but she kept losing her balance. She sat again, breathing deeply in and out, trying to focus. *Think*. She rose again, her legs wobbly under her. The fire was spreading now, engulfing the books and photographs. The smoke was filling the room so fast! She sank down onto her hands and knees as it closed around her. When the air in the room became too dense, she pulled her shirt over her mouth, coughing as she moved across the floor toward the hall, wincing as she dragged her leg behind her.

"Help me!" she croaked, though she knew there was no one around who would. She couldn't panic. She had to try and quiet herself, preserve her oxygen.

She couldn't die like this and leave her daughter alone. Simon was already in custody. Annabelle would be orphaned. The smoke was getting so thick that she couldn't see more than a few inches in front of her. She felt the heat of the flames reaching out to consume her. I'm not going to make it, she thought. Her throat was raw, and her nose burned.

With every last bit of strength, she inched her way to the entrance hall. She lay there, panting from exhaustion. Her head was fuzzy, but the cold marble floor felt good against her body. She pressed her cheek against its cool surface. Now she could go to sleep. Her eyes were closing, and she felt herself fading until everything went black.

28

Blaire was just out the front door when she stopped. If she left now, Kate would be dead. It would all be over. There would be no more chances to make things right. She'd just given Kate shocking news. Maybe when she had time to think about it, she'd realize that blood was thicker than water, and that Blaire had only done what she thought she needed to do to save Kate from Simon. But if Kate died, that could never happen. She needed to save her. No matter what Kate had done, she was her sister. She couldn't leave her to burn.

She turned and yanked the front door open, relieved to find it hadn't locked behind her. She ran back inside, determined to pull Kate out. Maybe there was some way she could make Kate see that everything Blaire had done, she'd done for her. Certainly Kate could see why Blaire had been so angry. She'd been kept from her mother for over fifteen years over a stupid argument. And over a man who didn't even deserve to be with Kate—a cheater and a murderer.

Kate would have to forgive her for what she'd done, just as she'd forgiven Kate. After all, what Kate had done was much worse. All Blaire had done was scare her a little and help to get rid of the man who had taken their mother from them, a man who deserved to suffer for the rest of his pathetic life. Kate would eventually see that. And in the end, Blaire had saved Kate's life. Maybe Kate would see that everything Blaire had done had been necessary to get Simon out of her life. Without Blaire's help, they would never have caught him. Yes, Kate would see that sometimes drastic measures were required. She'd always had Kate's back, and she still did.

She started to cough as she walked back into the smoke-filled room. She had to be fast. She saw that Kate had made it all the way to the hallway but collapsed there. The fire was raging in the living room, and now it was spreading out to the hall. She grabbed Kate under her arms and began to drag her toward the front door. The flames were licking at the wallpaper in the foyer. Blaire could feel the heat on her face as she backed out of the house with her sister. Suddenly Kate's outstretched legs bumped against a table near the wall, sending a large vase crashing to the marble floor. Blaire felt a sharp sting on her wrist.

When she finally got Kate outside and into the yard, Blaire dropped her hands and began CPR. Blaire's wrist was bleeding where a shard of glass had made a deep cut.

Surprised to see a police car pull up the driveway, she stood, waving her hands. As the two officers ran to her, she yelled out, "Call the fire department! Hurry, she's passed out. I think she's inhaled too much smoke."

One of the officers knelt down next to Kate and checked her breathing. The other one looked at Blaire. "What happened here?"

"I don't know how it started. I got home, and the house was on fire! I ran in and found her. Thank God I got back in time! When I walked in the house, the flames had almost reached the hallway."

"It's a lucky thing you did," the officer said.

Kate still hadn't come to. Suddenly Blaire was seized with panic. What had she done? What if Kate didn't make it?

Minutes later she heard the wail of the fire-truck sirens approaching.

29

When Kate opened her eyes, her father was standing over her. She blinked, unsure of where she was, and turned her head against the pillow. The strong smell of smoke hit her, and it started to come back. The fire. Blaire saying crazy things. It got hazy after that.

"Kate," her father said, the relief obvious in his voice. He sat on the edge of the bed, holding her hand.

Her body ached, but she sat up as quickly as she could. "Dad, what happened? How did I get here?" She could hear the panic in her own voice.

"Easy, easy. Calm down." Her father tried to soothe her. "You're in the hospital. There was a fire."

How long had she been here? "You were all the way at the beach. When did you get back?"

"You've been in and out for the last few hours. I came as soon as Anderson called me."

Kate shook her head. "Blaire." She began to cry.

Her father held her to him, patting her back, then pulled away to look at her. "Blaire's okay—she's resting up on this floor. She pulled you out of the fire, you know."

She wanted to push back—she knew she needed to tell him something, but she couldn't put her thoughts together, and there was something she needed to know first. "Annabelle?"

"Don't worry, she's with Georgina. I called Georgina and asked her to meet me here and take Annabelle while I was with you. I wasn't sure what kind of shape you'd be in, or if Annabelle would be able to see you. Georgina's taking her to her house now."

"Thank God." She fell in relief against the pillow and looked at her father. "Is the house gone?" she whispered, her voice hoarse and throat sore.

"The damage is pretty extensive, but they got the fire out."

Kate thought of all the family pictures, notes, and cards from her mother, years and years of memories that might have been lost. At least she and her daughter were safe. That was all that mattered.

"Kate," her father said gently. "Tell me exactly what happened."

She told him as much as she could remember, watching as his face grew redder and his brow more furrowed. Suddenly he sprang from the edge of the bed.

"She thinks Mother is her mother." She waited for the look of shock on her father's face, but saw something else instead. "Dad, did you hear me? She thinks Mother gave her up for adoption before you were married."

He looked away, his face white, and then shook his head. "I didn't know she was the baby," he whispered.

"What?"

His eyes turned slowly to Kate, filled with sorrow. "Kate, you wanted to know what your mother and I argued about the day she died." He paced in the small cubicle, finally stopping and sitting again. "She told me that she'd slept with someone else. Just once. One night while we were engaged, and I was in medical school in California. That she'd had a child and given it up. That's what we were yelling about. She wouldn't tell me who the father was, or anything else about the child. She said she needed to talk to the other parties first." His face was red now, and he balled his hands into fists. "I didn't want you to know. To have your mother's memory tainted. I was furious." He paused and took her hand. "I still am, but what's worse is that I can't forgive myself for the fact that the last words I spoke to your mother were angry and cruel."

It couldn't be true! Her mother had had a one-night stand? There had to be more to the story. But now, with what Blaire was saying . . . there must be some truth to the story somewhere.

"The father could be the one who killed her. Have you thought of that?" Kate asked him. "How could you hold this information back from the police?"

He shook his head. "I told them. But Lily promised me I was the only one who knew. She was going to tell me who the father was. She said she wanted to wait until I had calmed down more."

"So that must have been why she wanted to change her will. To include Blaire." It all made sense suddenly.

Harrison nodded. "It must have been."

She lay back again and closed her eyes, suddenly spent. Exhaustion overtook her, and as the sound of voices and the hum of machines drifted into the cubicle, she found herself dozing off.

30

Blaire was waiting for the doctor to release her. It was all so unfair. Kate was going to make her look like the bad guy once again. She thought back to the last time she'd been in a hospital bed, after the night that had changed everything. Carter had had to get a passed-out Jake in the back, and Blaire had insisted that Kate let her drive, given that she was the only sober one. Carter got in the passenger seat, while Kate crawled into the back with her boyfriend. It was raining, and they were on one of the dark country roads. Blaire had turned off the radio so she could focus better. Kate was having none of it. She'd leaned up from the back seat, fumbling with the radio dial until she turned it on again.

"Come on, I like that song," she slurred.

Blaire pushed her hand away. "Kate, cut it out. I'm trying to concentrate."

But Kate persisted. She turned the knob again, and the music blared. Kate was singing at the top of her lungs. Looking down, Blaire tried to find the button to turn the radio off, but the car was unfamiliar. When she looked back up, a pickup truck was careening toward them. She could still see the blinding lights from the truck. The sounds of screeching wheels and crashing metal were the last things Blaire heard before waking up at this same hospital. She'd appeared relatively unscathed, some scratches and bruises but nothing else, and still they'd insisted on examining her.

Jake had been pronounced dead at the scene.

Carter had broken an arm.

Kate didn't have a scratch.

The authorities determined that the other driver was at fault, with an alcohol level twice the legal limit. Blaire remembered the guilt that had gnawed at Kate afterward, the guilt that kept telling her Blaire might have been able to get out of the way if Kate hadn't distracted her.

It hadn't been until two days later that the bleeding started. No one but Carter had known Blaire was pregnant, and they had planned to elope before Christmas. Blaire had desperately wanted to confide in Kate when she found out, but Carter had begged her not to say anything until they were married, for fear word might reach his family if the news got out. His mother would have eventually accepted Blaire, especially when she gave her a grandchild.

When the bleeding got worse, she'd called Carter, and he'd taken her to a clinic in Philadelphia, somewhere they knew no one would see them. A kindly doctor told her that she was hemorrhaging. The accident had caused a miscarriage. She'd lost their baby and gone back to school, no one the wiser. Then he'd called her and broken it off. Maybe if she'd called the clinic when the fever started and gotten antibiotics, things would have been different. Instead, ten years later, she sat in a Manhattan fertility clinic while a doctor told her that the ensuing infection had scarred her uterus and closed both fallopian tubes. There was no way she could conceive or carry a child.

She and Daniel "tried" for three more years before he began pestering her to adopt. The last thing she wanted was to take care of someone else's child. But he was relentless, finally giving her an ultimatum: either say goodbye to Daniel and the life they had built together, or find a way to start a family. He couldn't leave her, take away her livelihood, take his wonderful family away from her.

Blaire was finished being left. Shaina had left her. Her father had chosen Enid over her. Carter had left her. And Kate, her best friend, her actual sister, had left her for Simon, replaced her with Selby, and Lily had been forced to take Kate's side. Because of Kate, she'd lost Lily forever, and she'd lost any chance of having a family of her own. And now, Kate didn't even seem to care that they were sisters. That Annabelle was her niece. Kate had just cut her out of her life—until Lily died. She'd thrown their bond away because of a stupid little fight.

Leading up to Kate's August wedding, Blaire had done her best to keep her mouth shut and pretend to be happy for her. She'd gone to all her gown fittings and thrown her a bachelorette party. She had even refrained from commenting on the fact that they'd had to forgo their usual month at the beach due to wedding planning, even though it was the last summer before they all joined the real world, and Blaire had been looking forward to it for months. Instead, they were stuck in humid Baltimore, working on place settings and party favors. But the kicker had been at the rehearsal dinner, when Selby, newly engaged, had raised her glass to Simon and Kate.

"Next summer, it will be Carter and me. Think of all the fun the four of us are going to have."

Simon smiled. "Carter, thanks so much for putting in a good word for me at Bachman and Druthers. I'm looking forward to starting my internship when we get back from our honeymoon."

"Happy to do it," Carter said, smiling back. "One day we'll have our own architectural firm. Partners."

Selby had looked at Blaire then. "We married folks have to stick together."

Simon had laughed. "I have a feeling we'll be spending lots of time together."

Kate had been the only one who noticed Blaire's discomfort,

giving her sympathetic looks throughout the evening, especially while Selby lorded it over Blaire about being together with Carter. Blaire had been seething inside. Selby was going to occupy the space in Kate's life that rightfully belonged to Blaire. And Simon, that idiot, acting like he belonged when he'd only just come on the scene months before. She'd stewed all through the dinner, and by the time they were back at Lily and Harrison's that night, she'd been ready to explode.

By morning, she'd known she had to do something to stop it. Harrison and Lily were upstairs getting dressed, and Kate and Blaire were in the kitchen, making breakfast.

"You're making a mistake," Blaire said.

Kate whirled around from the refrigerator. "What?"

"Marrying Simon. He's not right for you."

Kate sighed and came over to the table. "Blaire, please don't do this. We're about to get married this afternoon. I know you were skeptical of him at first, but you promised you'd support me."

"I'm sorry. But I'm your best friend, and I can't sit back and say nothing while you ruin your life."

Kate's face had turned red. "I'm not ruining my life. Simon's a wonderful guy."

"Aha! See. You didn't say you love him. You're not over Jake. Simon's just a rebound."

Kate's expression turned dark. "Don't you think I've cried enough tears over Jake? He's gone. I have to move on."

Blaire could see she wasn't getting anywhere. She changed her approach. "I'm sorry. I know how hard it's been, but I can help you through it. I don't have to go back home. I can stay here, find a job. You don't need Simon."

Kate shook her head. "I'm getting married today. I love him. You're my maid of honor. Act like it."

The anger and frustration felt like it was burning through Blaire. She was just trying to look out for Kate's best interests. Why couldn't Kate see it? "I *am* acting like it. It's ridiculous. You're starting at Hopkins in less than a month. You'll have plenty to get your mind off Jake. Simon is a pretty boy with no substance. It's a dishonor to Jake's memory." She knew that would hit the mark, remind Kate of who she really was, of who she really cared about.

But Kate was trembling with anger. "How dare you try and make me feel guilty about getting married? You're being a jealous bitch."

"Why shouldn't I try to make you feel guilty? You don't seem to feel guilty about killing Jake." As soon as the words left her lips, she knew she'd gone too far.

"I knew you always blamed me! Get out! I don't want you in my wedding. I don't even want you to come to my wedding. I don't want you in my life!"

"Kate, calm down . . . I didn't . . ."

"Go! I don't even want to look at you."

Blaire could admit now that her comment was insensitive, but everyone said things they ended up being sorry for in the heat of the moment. That didn't mean you cut them out of your life. But that's exactly what Kate had done. Hours before the wedding, Blaire had packed her things and left in tears, not even saying goodbye to Lily and Harrison.

Everyone thought Kate was such a hero. Saving lives, doing good. Kate had perfected the facade so well that she probably even believed it herself. Everything came so easily to her. She'd never even particularly wanted children, but the universe had given her Annabelle, because of course, she got everything. And once Annabelle arrived, did Kate appreciate her? No, she worked just as hard and left all the mothering to Hilda. That woman was more a mother to Annabelle than Kate had ever been. But did Kate care? No. She fired Hilda for no good reason.

When Kate called her to tell her about Lily, Blaire was crushed. Over the years, they'd stayed in touch sporadically via email, but she'd gotten Lily's letter and its news only two days earlier. After the initial shock, she'd been furious. How could Lily have never told her the truth? She almost ripped the letter to shreds, she was so enraged. But then she realized that she still had a family. Lily wanted her to come back to Baltimore. To take her place with them. She needed a family—the one she had made with Daniel had completely fallen apart.

He'd been frustrated with her resistance to adoption. She'd tried to explain it to him, but he didn't get it. She wanted her own child, someone connected through blood. Now, knowing what she did about her own history, she wondered if Shaina had ever really felt connected to her. Was the fact that Blaire wasn't her biological daughter the reason it had been so easy for her to leave her behind? And her father—sending her away once he'd gotten married, making Enid a priority over her. She wanted to know what it felt like for someone to share her blood. Even Kate had been able to replace her with Selby at the drop of a hat. She wanted a child who would never be able to leave her.

She was devastated when Daniel left, and on an impulse she'd called Lily. They normally emailed every few months, but it had been a long time since she'd heard Lily's voice.

"Hi, Lily." She'd choked back a sob. "It's Blaire."

"Blaire? Darling, what's wrong?"

"He left me. Daniel left me. I'm all alone. No one's left."

They'd talked for hours that night, and before they hung up, Lily spoke the last words Blaire would ever hear from her.

"It's going to be okay, I promise. You're not alone. Trust me on this: things are going to get better."

And then, a week later, she'd gotten Lily's letter. She couldn't call her father and demand to know why he'd never told her. She had never had any idea that she was adopted. But he was gone now, and she wouldn't give Enid the satisfaction of asking her.

Blaire thought back to the last time she'd seen either of them. She had gone back to New Hampshire for the next-to-last time after Kate kicked her out of the wedding. She'd tossed and turned that night, furious, lying uncomfortably on a hard cot that had been shoved into her old room, a room that was now filled with more of Enid's crafting junk. She imagined Selby next to Kate at the ceremony, fixing her train, holding her flowers, and then giving a speech at the reception. They were all having fun and celebrating, without a thought to Blaire.

Her father had been impatient and short-tempered that weekend, and she assumed he didn't want her there. Neither he nor Enid told her the truth. So she'd decided to leave the next morning. She asked her father to lend her some money to move back to New York while she looked for a job. He'd written her a generous check, and she left. Six months later, she got a call from Enid.

"Blaire, can you come home? Your father's not doing well."

"What are you talking about?"

A long sigh came over the line. "He made me promise not to tell you. He's been sick. He's suffering from congestive heart failure. For the last two years. The meds aren't working any longer. I don't think it will be long now."

Why had he kept it from her? If she'd known that was the reason for his ill humor, she'd never have left. She would have taken care of him, angry as she still was about Enid's intrusion into their lives.

Blaire had rushed back to New Hampshire to find him hospitalized, hooked up to all kinds of machines. After ten days, he was gone. Enid had made out well. She'd inherited Blaire's father's dealerships and the millions he had in the bank, while Blaire inherited a measly hundred thousand dollars.

When Kate called to tell her that Lily had died, Blaire couldn't believe it. What a cruel trick for fate to play. Just when she'd found her again, she'd lost her forever. Now she'd never get the chance to know her mother's love. Never have the chance to make up for all the years they'd lost. She'd wanted to scream at Kate, tell her that it was all her fault. That she was responsible for keeping Lily from her. She was so consumed with hatred and anger, she wasn't sure she'd be able to hide her true feelings from Kate. But she had to make her pay. Someone finally had to make Kate pay. It was easier than she'd thought, with Kate so oblivious to Blaire's pain. And of course, she wasn't leaving until she found the person who'd taken Lily from her and made that person pay.

At first she was unsure who had done it. But it soon became apparent to her that she'd been right about Simon. He was cheating on Kate, and he was only out for himself. Once Carter and Gordon had filled in the picture for her—a man with money problems and a wandering eye—she put it all together. When she discovered that Lily had known about Sabrina, had actually called Simon about Sabrina, she knew he was the one. But she couldn't prove it. That's when she modified her plan.

At first, seeing Kate slowly break down as she received message after message had been gratifying. It had been so easy to make it look like the killer was after Kate as well. But after spending time with her and seeing that their bond was as strong as ever, Blaire realized she wanted Kate back. Blaire might not have a mother, but she had a sister, after all. So she'd made Kate depend on her again. Helped her to see that Simon was guilty. And this time, Kate would choose Blaire over him.

If Simon hadn't come on the scene, she'd have never lost Kate and Lily in the first place. Kate was still responsible for taking Blaire's ability to have children from her, but now that Blaire was back, she'd share Annabelle with Kate. With Simon in jail, it would be like Annabelle belonged to both of them. She'd bet that Kate would even let Blaire take her to New York for some weekends. But now they were all suspicious of her.

Heavy footsteps stopped outside the curtains, and she heard the familiar voice of Detective Anderson call in.

"May I come in and talk to you, Ms. Barrington?"

"Yes," she answered.

He looked serious as he came in and pulled up a chair, notepad in hand. "Ms. Barrington, I'd like to ask you about the fire." His eyes were cold as he cleared his throat. "Can you tell me what happened today?"

"As you know, I've been staying with Kate. Harrison and Annabelle were away, and Kate needed me to go to CVS to pick up some Tylenol. When I got back, there was smoke pouring out of the chimney, and all the alarms were going off. I knew Kate was still inside, and I ran in to find her passed out, and pulled her out. Thank God I got back in time." Blaire studied Anderson's face, but he remained impassive.

"I see. Did you pick up any more prepaid Visa cards while you were at CVS?" He sat back and crossed his leg, a slight smile playing on his lips.

"Why would I need a prepaid Visa? I have excellent credit," she said calmly.

"There's video footage of someone who looks an awful lot like you buying one. Coincidentally, whoever ordered the roses that were sent from Dr. English used a card from that same store."

She wasn't rattled; she'd been too careful. They would never be able to identify her on that video. "Well, that *is* a coincidence."

"You have a very successful career as a writer, don't you, Ms. Barrington?"

Blaire eyed him, her antennae up.

"You've sold millions of books." He stopped, silent for a moment. "You and your husband," he said at last.

Blaire continued to stare at him.

"You did a bit of writing on your own, isn't that right? Before you began your collaboration with Mr. Barrington," Anderson went on.

"I don't know what you're talking about."

"You don't? Your short story. Very interesting reading, I must say."

She wanted to rip that mocking look off his face. She was tired of playing games. "Get to the point, Detective."

"The point, Ms. Barrington, is that the taunting nursery rhymes that Dr. English was sent were very similar in tone to those in that story you wrote. A few of them nearly word for word. That doesn't look very good for you, wouldn't you say?"

"You really enjoy asking rhetorical questions, don't you?"

He gave her a dry look.

"Anyone could have read that story and picked up the nursery rhymes to pin this on me. You know that as well as I do, don't you?" She smiled widely at him. "How's that for rhetorical?"

Anderson clicked his pen a few times and started to say something else. Then, seeming to think better of it, he stood up. "That's all for now. We'll probably have some follow-up questions."

Yeah, right. This would be the last she saw of Detective Be-hemoth. "I'm being discharged soon, then heading back to New York."

He moved to the curtain surrounding the emergency room cu-bicle and then stopped and turned around to look at her. "By the way, Dr. English is going to be fine. Just thought you might want to know."

"I know she is. It was the first thing I asked the nurse."

Once he'd gone, Blaire lay back against the pillow. *Good rid-dance, smart-ass.* He thought he was such an ace detective.

She got off the bed and sat in the cubicle's plastic chair, waiting until, finally, twenty minutes later, she'd signed her papers and was ready to go. She pushed the curtain back and began walking toward the double doors that led out of emergency. None of this had transpired as she'd planned, but as soon as she was back in New York, she'd figure a way to get Daniel back.

31

Kate didn't know how long she'd been asleep when someone gently shook her arm.

"Dr. English." It was Detective Anderson.

She blinked, her eyes still dry from the smoke. "What are you doing here?" she asked Anderson as she sat up in the bed.

"I wanted to see how you were and update you on a few things."

He pulled up a chair and sat. "There was something about all those nursery rhymes that kept niggling at me. No one that we were looking at as a suspect struck me as someone who would take the time to make all those twisted poems up. I had picked up one of Ms. Barrington's books and did some research on her, looked into her background. I found a short story that she wrote under her maiden name—Blaire Norris. It was published more than ten years ago in the *Strand Magazine*. I got a copy of it, and guess what? The killer sends nursery rhymes to his victim."

Kate felt conflicting emotions flood through her. "I guess we have proof now."

"I've spoken to her. She denies everything. And anyone could have read the story. We also tracked the prepaid credit card used to send those roses to a CVS on York Road. We've looked through hours of video. We have someone on tape that could be Ms. Barrington, but we can't definitively identify her. It was enough to convince me you were in danger, though, so I sent a unit over to check on you, and that's when they saw the fire."

"You saved my life." She reached out for his hand, and he

squeezed it. For the first time, his eyes looked warm to her. "Thank you. Do you think Blaire killed my mother? She denied it, but . . ."

He released her hand as he continued. "No. She was definitely in New York the night your mother died."

"She claims she bought another bracelet like my mother's. But I don't know."

"The bracelet we found in your husband's study was different from your mother's. Not the same carat weight."

Kate digested this news. It was a relief to know that Blaire really hadn't been the one to take her mother's life. But if it wasn't Blaire, then who was it? "Are we ever going to find who did this?"

Anderson's phone rang, and he looked at the screen. He stood. "Excuse me a minute. Have to take this."

Kate leaned back and closed her eyes again as he left the curtained area and went into the hallway. A few minutes later she heard him walk back in the room. She opened her eyes.

"We've had a break in the case! Another witness has come forward."

Kate pushed herself up in bed. "Who?"

"Randolph Sterling, Georgina Hathaway's driver. He drove her to your mother's house the night she was killed."

"What? Georgina was there?" She was suddenly alert. "What else did he say?"

"He claims she was concerned about being implicated, so she asked him not to tell anyone she was there that night."

"Why would she lie about it? Unless she had something to do with it." All of a sudden, panic seized Kate. Georgina had Annabelle.

"Don't worry, I'm on my way over to question her now."

Her voice rose in alarm. "She has Annabelle. She has my daughter! You've got to get over there before she can hurt her."

As soon as Anderson had left, Kate had jumped from the bed, almost colliding with her father as he came back into the room.

"Kate, what's going on? You need to be in bed."

"Georgina! She was there that night. We have to get Annabelle!" Her breath came in ragged gasps, and she began to cough.

"What are you talking about? Georgina was where?"

She pulled the hospital gown more tightly around her, and then grabbed the blanket from the bed to put over it. "She was there the night Mother died. Randolph lied for her, but he just came clean."

Harrison's mouth dropped open. "I don't understand."

She grabbed his hand. "Come on, we need to get over there. Now!"

"But you haven't been released."

"Dad! What if she had something to do with Mother's death? What if she hurts Annabelle? We need to go!"

It finally seemed to register in his brain, and they both hurried from the room, Harrison helping her as she favored her good ankle. When they got downstairs to the hospital entrance, he turned to her. "Wait here. I'll get the car. It's too cold for you to come outside, dressed like that."

She couldn't stop rubbing her arms up and down as she waited for him to pull the car around. It was taking forever. Why had Georgina hidden the fact that she was there? Had she been a part of it? It made no sense, but Kate worried that Georgina could be crazy. Jealous of Lily. What if she decided to use Annabelle as a hostage when the police arrived at her house?

Harrison finally pulled up, and she ran and jumped into the passenger seat of his Infiniti, shivering from the cold. "Hurry, Dad."

"This makes no sense. There has to be a reasonable explanation for why Georgina lied."

Kate tapped her foot nervously. "I can't think of any."

They were quiet the rest of the way, both lost in their own thoughts. He drove just above the speed limit, reaching Georgina's house in under fifteen minutes.

When they stopped in front of the imposing Roland Park colonial, she saw that Anderson's car was already there. Kate bolted out and walked as fast as she could up the steps to the front porch, wincing as a pain shot through her ankle. She pressed the doorbell over and over, until a uniformed servant opened the door, just as Harrison reached her side. "Mrs. Hathaway is waiting for you in the living room," the young woman said, escorting them in.

"You poor thing," Georgina said, holding out her arms and pulling Kate into a hug. "You must be just devastated." She turned away from Kate and gave a haughty look to Detective Anderson. "I still don't understand why you're here. I've already told you everything I know."

"Where is Annabelle? I need to see Annabelle," Kate blurted out.

"She's fine, Kate," Georgina said. "She's in the playroom. My maid is with her. She's having a lovely time playing with Selby's old dollhouses. Don't you worry. You just sit yourself down on that sofa and warm up by the fire." She pointed to the sofa nearest the fireplace.

Kate shook her head. "No, I want to see her."

Georgina pressed an intercom button and spoke. "Bring Annabelle downstairs."

A few moments later, Annabelle stood at the top landing. "Mommy!" Relief flooded Kate as Annabelle came running down the steps to her. "Mommy, Miss Lucy and I are playing dollhouse. Come see."

Kate gave Annabelle a tight hug before smoothing her daughter's hair while she stared at her face for a moment. "You go back and play, sweetheart. Mommy will be up in a little while."

Georgina smiled at her. "See? Everything is fine. Now sit down."

Kate remained standing. "Why did you—"

Anderson cut her off, giving her a warning look. "Please, Dr. English. Let me ask the questions."

Anderson stood by the fireplace, his elbow on the mantel. "Some clarification, really. Did you go to the Michaels house the night Lily Michaels was murdered?"

Georgina raised her chin, her eyes steely. "Of course not. Why would you ask me that?"

"Your driver has come forward and told us he took you there."

"Th-there m-must be some mistake," she stammered. "He must have the day wrong."

"There's no mistake, Mrs. Hathaway."

"I most certainly did not see her that night." Georgina looked at Kate. "The detective just told me that Blaire is the one who started a fire at your home this morning. I never liked her. That girl was trouble from the very beginning, Kate. She came between you and Selby. Selby and I lamented that fact. She was never the sort who would fit in with us. She was jealous of Selby, jealous of your friendship. As I said, I never liked her." Georgina's voice dripped with disdain.

"Raking through the past is pointless," Harrison said. He stared hard at Georgina. "The question now is, were you at the house that night?"

"I've told you I wasn't." She turned to Detective Anderson. "It's Randolph's word against mine. This is ridiculous."

Anderson watched her for a moment before speaking again. "He keeps detailed logs. What possible reason would he have for lying? Especially as it could cost him his job."

Kate was watching everything with mounting frustration. Anderson was right. Why would her driver lie? Georgina must have been there that night.

Anderson gave her a stern look. "Tell us the truth—otherwise the wrong person will go to jail. Simon English has just been charged with the murder."

Georgina turned to Detective Anderson. "Why would you charge him? If Blaire tried to kill Kate in the fire, she's probably the one who killed Lily. You should arrest her."

"Ms. Barrington may be guilty of other things, but murder is not one of them. She was in New York the night Mrs. Michaels died. We have incontrovertible proof of that. I have no reason to arrest her."

"She admitted to Kate that she was the one who sent all the messages," Harrison said. "You must be able to prove that and charge her."

Anderson shook his head. "We have no proof of any of it. She's made it look like Simon sent all those messages.

"At this point," Detective Anderson went on, "Ms. Barrington denied planting that evidence, so it's her word against Dr. English's. Mr. English has no alibi other than his claim that he was at the office working late, and we now believe that Ms. Mitchell is not a reliable alibi witness."

"But surely . . . surely, you'll see your mistake and release him," Georgina said.

"Everything points to him."

Kate ran her hands through her hair, catching a whiff of the smoke that still clung to her.

Anderson crossed his arms in front of him. "You were there that night, weren't you, Mrs. Hathaway?"

"I told you, I wasn't." Her voice shook.

At once, all eyes turned to the entrance as a tall figure strode in, clearing his throat. "I can't let this go on without coming forward," Randolph said. "I am not mistaken, and I am not lying." He looked at Georgina. "I'm prepared to testify in court that I drove you to Mrs. Michaels's house the night she was murdered."

Georgina stood up straighter, her eyes flashing. "How dare you. You've forgotten your place."

"No. My place is here. In this room. Telling the truth."

Kate watched Georgina's face go white, her nostrils flare. "I won't have this, Randolph. You're dismissed. Get out at once."

He shook his head. "Fire me. I don't care. You know I'm not lying. I took you there that night. You were in the house for over an hour. I waited for you." He looked around the room at the others. "I'll defend Mr. English no matter what. He's a fine man who's never done anything but good by me."

Anderson spoke quietly. "It will be better if you admit it now, Mrs. Hathaway. The truth will come out. I have a warrant right here." He pulled a document from his pocket. "For your house and your car. Tell me, are we going to find any of Lily Michaels's blood on the leather or the floor mats?"

Georgina's face turned a mottled red. She walked to the fireplace, put a hand on the mantel, and let her head hang. She stood there for a minute without saying a word. Finally, she heaved a sigh and turned to face them. "I was there."

Kate couldn't follow what Georgina was saying. She opened her mouth to speak, but the older woman went on.

"But it was all a terrible misunderstanding—"

"It was you!" Kate's hand flew to her mouth as she looked at Georgina in shock.

"Georgina, what are you saying?" Harrison said, and Anderson put a hand up as if to silence him.

Georgina's face was red, and she narrowed her eyes. "Lily called me that night. She told me she needed to see me right away. She sounded so upset, so I went right over." She paused and ran a shaking hand through her hair. "Lily told me about your argument," she said, looking at Harrison. "Said she'd admitted to getting pregnant while you were engaged. What she hadn't told you was that the father was *my* Bishop."

Kate felt sick. Bishop? Selby's father and her mother had slept together?

"What are you talking about?" Harrison thundered. "She and Bishop were having an affair?"

"She said it only happened once. When you were still at Stanford. Palmer was just a baby. They went to a party together." Her voice turned angry. "We were all supposed to go together, but then Palmer wasn't feeling well. I told Bishop to go on without me. Stupid me, I thought nothing of it when he came home late, stinking of booze. What a fool I was. He'd been with Lily. But I thought she was my friend. My best friend. Ha!"

Harrison's face was white. "Did Bishop know about the baby?"

Georgina shook her head. "No. Apparently, Lily never told him. They made fools of both of us, Harrison."

"What happened that night?" Kate asked impatiently. "What did you do to my mother?"

"When she told me that she'd slept with my husband, I saw red. It didn't matter that it happened all those years ago. She was my best friend. How could she have done that to me? How could she have lied to me all those years, betrayed me, pretending everything was normal? I was out of my mind. I pushed her. She fell. Backward against the coffee table. She wasn't breathing. And there was so much blood. I knew she was dead. Oh God . . . forgive me." She began to sob, her hands in a prayerful pose and her small body heaving. "I panicked. I thought if it looked like a robbery . . . I don't know. That's when I took the bracelet. Smashed a window. And then I took a bookend from the shelf and hit her on the head.

Oh dear God, I'm so sorry, I'm so sorry. I didn't mean to kill her. It was an accident. I didn't mean it." She was hysterical now.

Kate doubled over, gasping for breath. Georgina had killed her mother? The image of Georgina smashing her mother's head in flashed in her mind. "How could you?" She flew from her seat and grabbed Georgina by the shoulders, shaking her. She felt arms pulling her away. Kate lifted her hands to her face, and it was wet with tears.

Detective Anderson picked his coat up from the chair. "Please come with me, Mrs. Hathaway."

32

Blaire was preparing to go back to New York. Despite Anderson's best efforts and Kate's statements, he didn't have enough evidence to make an arrest. Blaire had denied everything, claiming Kate had made it all up. Simon was still in jail when Blaire left, but the next day, she heard on the news that he'd been released. He'd actually been innocent. Well, innocent of Lily's murder anyway. Blaire didn't regret what she'd done, though. After all, he'd still been cheating on Kate. And more important, he was the reason Blaire had lost Lily all those years ago. Simon had been responsible for taking away the only real mother Blaire ever had. There was no punishment harsh enough for that.

Kate had refused to take any of her calls, but Blaire was surprised to get a message from Harrison at the hotel, asking her to meet him at Baltimore Coffee and Tea the next morning. He was already there when she arrived, and she grabbed a latte and joined him in the corner.

"Hello," she said carefully, not knowing what to expect.

He nodded. "Blaire, I called you out of respect for Lily. If it were up to me, I would never see you after what you've done."

She stirred her coffee and waited for him to continue.

"I won't beat around the bush. I've discovered who your father is."

She felt her heart skip a beat. Was it possible that she still had a chance with a family member? Leaning forward, she asked, "Who?"

He stared at her. "Bishop Hathaway."

Blaire blinked, the words taking a moment to sink in. "What? Selby's father?" Her heart sank as another thought occurred to her. "Selby and I are sisters?"

"I'm afraid so."

Stunned, Blaire sat back in her chair, thoughts racing as she tried to picture Bishop in her mind. She'd only met him a handful of times over the years, but she could still picture the tall athletic man with dark hair and a winning personality.

"Are you sure?" she asked.

Then he told her the rest of it. How Georgina had been the one to kill Lily in what the police thought was a jealous rage. She claimed it had been an accident, but she'd just found out a secret that her best friend and husband had been keeping from her for almost forty years. No way was it an accident. Blaire hoped they would lock her away forever. How ironic. Selby, the woman that she hated most in the world, was related to her. It didn't matter what the blood said, though. They would never be sisters.

"Does Selby know?"

"Yes, of course. Georgina's been arrested. It's all come out now."

Blaire's only consolation was that Selby would be even more upset than Blaire to discover they were related. That snob, looking down her nose at Blaire all those years, when they were cut from the same cloth. Well, the scandal would ruin everything for Selby. She and Carter would be knocked down a peg in their social circle. And now she would lose her mother too. It served them right.

Harrison stood. "If there's nothing else you need to ask, I'll go now."

"Wait."

"What is it?"

She handed him an envelope. "Please give this to Kate. It's a copy of the letter that Lily sent to me. No matter what you think of me, I loved Lily."

He nodded and took the envelope from her. Then he turned and walked away.

The next morning, Blaire left for New York.

The first thing she did when she got home was call Daniel again. She had tried him numerous times while still in Baltimore and left messages, but he hadn't called her back. When she finally reached him a few days later, he sounded weary.

"Blaire. I told you that anything you have to say to me can be told to my attorney." His tone was exasperated. He hadn't even asked her how she was.

"Why are you being so cruel? I don't want to talk to your attorney. Why are you shutting me out like this?"

A loud sigh came over the line. "Kate called me."

She gripped the phone. "How did she even get your number?"

"She got in touch through my agent. Listen, Blaire. She told me everything. You need help."

Blaire felt her face flush hot. She hadn't missed that he'd said "my" agent, not "our." "What did she tell you?"

"Everything. How you sent her all those horrible messages. The dead animals."

"She's lying. Her husband is a gold digger, and she doesn't want to see it. He's been cheating on her. I have pictures I can show you. She's putting this all on me to save her reputation."

"Blaire, she told me about the fire. That you tried to kill her and frame her husband."

"No, no. She's choosing Simon over me all over again, and now she's trying to turn you against me."

There was silence on the other end of the line, and she heard a loud exhale. "I'm sorry, Blaire. But this is just too much. Things were already bad between us, but this . . . I don't even know who you are anymore. You need to get help."

"No!" she screamed, banging her fist against the wall. "They're all liars. Can't you see it? Daniel, you have to come back to me. I need you."

"I'm hanging up now. Please don't contact me again. My attorney will be in touch."

She threw the phone across the room and let out a bloodcurdling scream. Running into the dining room, she began to pick up crystal glasses and hurl them at the wall. When her rage was spent, she sank to the floor, sweat dripping down her face, and stared unmoving at the wreckage.

After she had calmed down, she poured herself a whiskey and pulled out an old photo album from high school. Most of the pictures were of her and Kate together. There were shots of them at the beach, at Kate's house, Blaire's dorm room. Parties and events. She looked at their two faces, trying to see if it was obvious that they were sisters. Did they have the same dimples around their smiles? Graduation and holidays. She paused a moment at a photo of Lily and herself outside the Booth Theatre in New York. Her mother. Her real mother. Beautiful and kind. There were pages and pages of wonderful times and proof of Lily's and Kate's affection for her. Proof that she'd been part of a loving family once. She felt something wet on her hand and realized she was crying. She'd loved them all, hadn't she? Given them everything until she had nothing left. But it wasn't enough. Why did they all leave? Why did everyone always leave?

She pulled out a second album, this one full of pictures from signings and book events and articles about her and Daniel. Shots of the set the first day of their television show. The two of them had been perfect together. They belonged together. She studied each photo, dispassionately evaluating her looks. She was still a knockout. She'd easily find another husband. But this time she'd make sure it was one who didn't want kids, or maybe one old enough to have grown children. That way she'd have a ready-made family. She thought about one of the actors on her detective show. He'd be perfect. Late fifties, sexy in a silver fox way, and always giving her the eye.

Daniel might be gone, but she still had her fans. They adored her. But would they still love her if she didn't produce any more books? Fans could be fickle too. They'd forget about her eventually. Blaire wasn't stupid. She had great ideas, but without Daniel, the series was done. Maybe she should get into acting. Then everyone would really love her. She'd be famous, not just at book events but everywhere she went. That was it. She'd put a plan in place tomorrow. She had plenty of connections now because of the series. She knew producers, actors, money folks. She just needed to do her research, figure out which prospect to go after, and chart her course. It could be fun. A new start for her.

She closed the album, went into the kitchen, and opened her laptop. She'd started over before, and she could do it again. Time to find a new life.

33

Kate held Lily's letter in her hands and wept. She'd read it over and over.

My dearest Blaire,

Have you ever done something that changed everything forever? One impulsive act, the consequences of which are more far-reaching than you could have ever imagined? One bad decision that led to another and another. My darling, Blaire, I sit here, pen in hand, wondering how to begin. How to make you understand why I did what I did.

You know the world in which I was reared. A world of privilege, abundance, and responsibility. I'm not complaining. I was well loved, and my life was easy. I knew what was expected of me; my world was well defined and my future assured. But at times, the strictures of that world were utterly suffocating. I met Harrison at a party the summer after I graduated from Smith. He'd just started medical school at Stanford. It was a whirlwind romance, and he was everything I was looking for. We knew it would be difficult to sustain a relationship three thousand miles apart with three years until his graduation, but somehow we did. Over summers and breaks and letters every week, our romance blossomed. We got engaged the summer before his final year in California.

After we got engaged, Harrison changed. He worried about me more, cautioned me not to stay out late, urged me to begin settling down. I'm sure it was hard for him, being so far away, but I was young and nervous. I was about to make the biggest commitment of my life, and he was telling me to act like I was already married. I began to feel suffocated again, wondering if I was making the right decision.

I was in a reckless mood the night of the party. The usual crowd was there, along with some new faces. The music was loud, and Donna Summer's "Bad Girls" was blaring through the speakers. That's how I felt that night. Every pent-up urge pushing to get out. I'd never done any drugs before, but that night I wanted to try something new. I won't make excuses or blame anything else. I joined in when the pills came out, and the next thing I knew, I was in one of the bedrooms with the wrong guy. I didn't know anything about drugs—someone told me they were quaaludes, something to make the party more fun. Afterward, I was horribly guilt-ridden, and we swore never to tell anyone. And I realized then that I did love Harrison, and a life with him was what I desperately wanted. How could I tell him what I'd done? He would never forgive me. And the man I'd been with was also committed to someone else. It would have ruined his life as well if anyone found out. We vowed to put it behind us and pretend it never happened. But forgetting wasn't so easy. Three months later, I discovered I was pregnant. It was too late to terminate, but I felt a connection to the baby already and wouldn't have been able to do it anyway.

I never told him the truth, but he must have suspected when I left town a few months later under the guise of caring for my mother in Maine. It was her idea to pretend she was sick, and Father went along. They wanted to protect my reputation, after all. The hardest thing I've ever had to do was to give you up. Mother and I found a private adoption agency and interviewed dozens of couples. Your parents seemed so perfect. How could I have known that your mother was unstable and would leave you when you were still so young? I've stayed in touch with your father your entire life, and it was my idea to bring you to Mayfield when he married Enid. My heart overflowed when you and Kate became so close, and you can't imagine how many times I wanted to tell you. How often I wanted to gather you in my arms and tell you that you were mine. I convinced myself it was almost as good as the truth coming out. You moved in with us, and you were a daughter to us in everything but name. And I got to love you.

I know you'll believe that I chose Kate over you after that terrible fight. But it wasn't that simple. I know now that I should have come out with the truth then. But I told myself that by staying in touch with you over the years, I'd still get to be in your life without upending the lives of so many others who would be affected. And then you had your own family—Daniel and his parents, and I hoped, one day, children of your own. But now, finding out you've already lost a child, and can never have another because of that terrible accident, I can't bear to think of you all alone. It's time for the truth to come out. For you to come home and take your rightful place in this family—if you can find it in your heart to forgive me. Take your time. When you're ready, call me, and we'll arrange a time to meet and talk about this before I make it public. I know you will have so many questions. I'll tell you everything then.

All my love,

Lily

How differently things might have turned out if her mother had revealed the truth sooner, Kate thought. Who knows, perhaps she would have rejected Blaire, knowing that she was the product of her mother's illicit liaison with a family friend. She didn't understand how Lily and Bishop could have kept the secret all those years. The families had socialized together, even vacationed together. Georgina and her mother had been friends since they were girls. The only rationalization that Kate could come up with was that Lily felt too guilty to cut the friendship off. After all, what excuse could she have used? But it must have eaten her alive over the years. And Bishop, he was a married man at the time of Blaire's conception. Even if her mother had no clue about how those pills would lessen her inhibitions, Bishop must have known. He was an experienced criminal attorney, with well-heeled clients who paid handsomely for his cunning and connections. Kate was certain he'd defended a client against a drug case more than once. Had he intentionally steered Lily toward taking them? He'd always struck Kate as bit of a letch. She remembered the way he'd looked her and all of Selby's friends up and down when they were swimming at the pool, making her uncomfortable. And she'd heard rumors about his liking the paralegals and secretaries a little too much. But Lily wasn't blameless, regardless.

Now that Kate knew the truth, it made sense to her that Lily had given Blaire her own bedroom at the beach, that she'd engineered her living with them in high school. She wished her mother had trusted her enough to confide in her. Kate realized she'd concocted an image of perfection about her mother. She'd put her in her own ivory tower, where everything she did was right and proper. But Lily had been human, of course, just like the rest of them, and fallible. It pained her to think of her mother bearing the burden of this secret for over twenty years after her own mother and father passed. Had she been able to go to her mother and mourn the child that she'd lost, or had it all been taken care of and swept under the rug, never to be discussed again?

Kate hadn't seen Blaire before she left. She couldn't forgive Blaire yet for what she'd put Kate through. Or maybe Kate couldn't forgive herself for her part in depriving Blaire of the mother she needed. All she knew was that she couldn't face her yet. The memory of her systematic and cruel campaign of terror was too fresh.

Simon had been released the following day. Kate asked her father to pick him up, nervous at how he'd react to seeing her after the way she'd treated him. Even if he had been cheating on her, the fact that she'd believed him capable of killing her mother and terrorizing her made her feel ashamed. They needed to have a long talk about what they would do going forward, and how they would co-parent Annabelle. She'd rented a suite at the Sagamore Pendry while the house was being inspected for structural damage, and she'd asked her father to wait until evening to bring Simon over, so she could get Annabelle to sleep and they could talk privately.

Harrison and Simon walked in, and Kate rose from the sofa in the living room, tentative.

He looked terrible—his skin ashy, his clothes wrinkled. It had only been a few days, but she could see jail had taken its toll.

"How're you doing?" she asked.

He ran to her and pulled her into his arms. "Thank God you're okay. I almost lost you."

Surprised, she began to return his embrace, but then she remembered Sabrina and pulled away. "Simon, we have to talk."

"I'll be in the lobby," Harrison said. "Just call if you need me."

Simon and Kate sat down, and she began. "I'm so sorry for the way I behaved. I just sort of lost it. The anxiety really took over, and I wasn't myself. Can you ever forgive me for believing that you could have hurt my mother? I think I always knew deep down that you could never have done that."

He visibly relaxed. "I forgive you. These have been the worst days of my life. Sitting in that cell, knowing that you believed I had done such a horrible thing. Thank God Randolph came forward."

Kate thought of what Randolph had said. "He intimated that you'd been good to him. What was he talking about?"

Simon shrugged. "His grandson's financial aid for college fell through. He came to me for help in arranging for another loan. I remembered how hard it was for my mother after my father died, so I gave him the money. We can well afford it. I knew Hilda would want to help her brother, and I didn't want her to deplete her savings."

Kate was touched. "Why didn't you tell me?"

"He asked me to keep it between us. Speaking of Hilda, your father said you fired her?"

Kate groaned. She'd really messed that up. "I'm afraid my paranoia got the best of me. I wrote her a long letter, apologizing and letting her know about my history with anxiety. I haven't heard anything from her yet. I can only hope she'll forgive me and come back."

"I think she will."

Kate was still bothered by one thing. She had to know the truth about Simon and Sabrina once and for all.

"Just tell me. Are you in love with Sabrina?"

"Of course not."

She wanted to believe him, but she was struggling. "Why did you tell her about what happened to me in college?"

He looked confused. "What do you mean?"

"She went to Anderson. Told him I was crazy. That I'd had a breakdown in college, and that you were worried about me." Kate felt herself getting angry at the memory. "How could you do that? Discussing such intimate details of my life with *her*?"

"Kate, I never . . . Your father and I spoke after Annabelle's birthday party. He stopped by the office to see me. She must have overheard."

Kate narrowed her eyes. She could ask her father about that later.

"What about the night you said you had a client dinner? Blaire saw you and Sabrina. She showed me pictures of you and Sabrina together."

"It *was* a client dinner. He was over an hour late. Stuck in traffic behind an accident. That's why the dinner went so late. But, still, I should have given more credence to your concerns. I guess because *I* knew nothing was going on, I just couldn't understand why you didn't believe me." He shook his head. "But you were right about her. She came to see me in jail. Went on and on about starting a life together. Said she didn't blame me for getting rid of Lily. Told me she'd find a way to get me out, all the time believing that it was true, that I'd done it. Can you believe that?"

Kate was stunned. "She really is crazy."

"I don't pretend to understand. I loved her father so much. I didn't want to break my word to him. It would break his heart to know the way she's turned out. She changed when he got sick. I think because I was the only other person that had been so close to him, in a way, being with me was a way for her to hold on to her father. You don't know how hard it was when my dad died. My mother fell apart, and I was pretty much on my own from the age of thirteen. If it hadn't been for Sabrina's father, I really don't know where I'd have ended up. I didn't want to let him down after everything he did for me." He put his hand up. "I'm not making any excuses, Kate. I was wrong to defend her, to ignore your concerns. I see now that she had no regard for your feelings, and I shouldn't have let her treat you that way. My loyalties were divided, but they should have been with you. I'm so sorry."

"What now?"

"I'm going to tell her she needs to resign. I'll give her a good severance package and a glowing letter of recommendation. I'm sorry for everything. I should have nipped this in the bud a long time ago."

"Did my mother call you about Sabrina?"

Simon nodded. "Yeah. She was upset that we were separating. She told me that it didn't matter if I was innocent if the appearance of impropriety was going to ruin my marriage. So that's when I told Sabrina she couldn't travel to New York with me."

Kate studied him for a moment.

"She didn't think you were cheating?"

He shook his head. "No. She said she knew I loved you too much to do that." He put his head in his hands. "I miss her."

Kate thought about that for a moment. Maybe Lily had seen something in Simon that Kate had never been able to see. "I'm sorry that my mother had more faith in you than I did." She pulled a pillow onto her lap and wrapped her arms around it. "I've been doing a lot of thinking after all that's happened."

Simon shifted in his chair.

"I've walked around all these years tortured with guilt, regret, grief. I've cheated you of the kind of love you should have had from a wife. After the accident." She stopped. "After Jake died, I never got over it. It didn't matter that the other driver was drunk, that the accident was his fault." She was crying. "I'd been drinking too. I was acting crazy, playing with the radio. It's my fault that Blaire didn't see that car coming until it was too late."

He sat quietly, waiting for her to go on.

"I've always regretted it. It's crippled me, made me feel like I was always hiding this horrible secret, that I was an awful person. That's why I never drink now. I was too ashamed to tell you the real reason. Every time I thought about Jake, he became this tragic hero, a bright light I had snuffed out." She studied Simon's face.

"He's always been there, between us."

She nodded. "You're right. I never gave myself all the way. I never allowed you to become to me what I thought Jake had been. I made him larger than life after he died." She paused and looked at Simon with tenderness. "You would never have been able to live up to the ghost of Jake."

They were both quiet for a few moments.

"I tried, Kate, but you were always so strong, so self-sufficient. Don't get me wrong," he hurried to add, "I admire that about you. Your strength and determination." He gave her a half smile. "I knew the moment you walked into Philosophy 101 that day that you were the one. Before we even spoke. That's why I asked you to be in my study group, before anyone else could ask you."

"Simon, I—"

"No, let me finish," he said. "You've always been the one, Kate. I fell in love with you from the very beginning. I knew there would always be a place in your heart for Jake, and I didn't resent that. I really didn't. But he took up so much of your heart that there wasn't enough room for me. You kept me from getting too close."

Kate hung her head and wiped away silent tears.

Simon put a gentle hand under her chin and lifted her face to his, looking into her eyes. "You're an incredible woman. I so respect and admire your dedication to your work, the mother you are to Annabelle, the amazing person you are. The only thing I've wanted all these years was to be the person by your side, supporting you, loving you. I wanted to take care of you. Letting someone take care of you doesn't mean you're weak. We have to take care of each other."

"Can you ever forgive me? I've thrown away so much while I've stayed mired in the past, in the mistakes I've made. Punishing myself. And you. Our family. I'm so sorry."

"I love you. I hope one day you'll understand how much, and that we can begin again."

"I hope so too, Simon." She squeezed the hand holding hers. "I hope so too."

34

FOUR YEARS LATER

t was the premiere of Blaire's movie debut, and she was putting the finishing touches on her makeup. Her husband, Seth, was already waiting in the limo for her. She smiled inwardly, thinking of him. He was the king of Hollywood, its most prolific producer and director, and founder of the biggest studio in town. She'd met him at a party thrown by the producer of the Megan Mahooney series. He'd been married at the time, one of the few Hollywood icons to still be with his first wife. But Blaire knew that meant that his wife took him for granted. And once he'd met Blaire, he was a goner. He told her that she was the perfect woman, the one he'd waited for all of his life. At forty-two, Blaire was smart enough to realize that no matter how well she could act—and let's face it, she'd been acting her whole life—she'd never break into films without a little help. Once she was married to Seth and he'd cast her in his latest movie, no one was going to argue. And she'd been brilliant. Everyone had told her so. It was lucky too, because she'd had to leave New York and the literary world.

After Blaire and Daniel split up, the Megan Mahooney books were finished. Daniel had offered to buy her out so he could keep writing the series on his own, but there was no way she was going to let him bask in the glory of *her* fans. It hadn't taken him long to go back to writing solo again, and she'd been furious to see that he hit the *Times* list immediately. She'd tried her hand at writing solo too, a book about a friendship gone wrong, and waited eagerly for it to surpass Daniel's in sales. The first few weeks it sold well on her name alone, but then it slipped further and further down the lists, until it disappeared altogether. The crowds at her signings began to dwindle as well, until she pleaded exhaustion and put a stop to her tour. But the worst were the reviews. Scathing one-star reviews filled with vitriol and criticism. Every morning she'd go online and read them, skimming over the positive reviews and ruminating on the bad ones. One particularly bad day, she'd had enough, and she began to respond. She'd read the review out loud, her heart beating faster with each word.

Total garbage. I guess we know now who had the talent. Blaire Barrington's solo debut should be her finale. Clunky sentences, clichéd characters, and meanderang prose. Take a pass.

Blaire had hit the comment field and started typing. When you learn how to spell, you can criticize my work. It's meandering, you idiot. Go back to English class.

It felt great. She'd gone to the next.

Totally unrealistic! I have lots of friends and none of them has ever behaved like the protagonist in this book. And the ending was so predictable. Hated it.

Blaire's hands were poised over the keyboard while she thought.

Maybe your friends are as stupid as you are. Or maybe you don't have any friends. How could it be unrealistic and predictable too? Go screw yourself.

She was laughing, really enjoying herself. She spent the rest of the day answering the bad reviews. That would show them. Who did they think they were? Had they written tons of books? They were probably frustrated writers who were jealous of her. It was about time someone stood up for authors.

Her agent called the next day.

"Blaire, what's going on? Please tell me that you've been hacked."

"I wasn't hacked. It's about time someone did something about those trolls."

There was silence on the other end.

"Are you still there?" Blaire asked.

He sighed. "Yes. Blaire, the publisher is threatening to cancel your contract. Everyone's buzzing about this. It's bad."

"Oh, come on. What's the big deal? Why is it okay for them to say horrible things about me, but I can't say anything about them? That's not fair."

"Because it's just not done. You've stooped to their level, and it's made you look insane and vindictive."

A few weeks later, her publisher had indeed dropped her, then her agent, and no one would touch her after that. But none of that mattered now. Being a movie star was way better than being a best-selling author. She couldn't wait to see herself on the silver screen. She looked at her Cartier watch. It was almost time.

There was a knock at her door.

"Come in."

"It's time for your medication, Ms. Barrington."

Where was her assistant? Who was this woman?

"What are you doing in my bedroom? It's time for my premiere. Where's my assistant?"

The woman smiled at her. "You're right. It's almost time for the movie to start. But you need to take your pills first, remember?

They make you feel better." She wheeled in a cart and took a little white cup from it and a cup of water, handing them to Blaire.

It wasn't a bad idea to take something to calm her opening-night jitters. She took the cup and downed the pills. "Please call down to the limo and tell my husband I'll be right there."

"Yes, Ms. Barrington," the woman said as she left the room.

Blaire took a final look in the mirror. She could only see herself from the waist up. Why hadn't Seth gotten her a full-length mirror yet? How was she supposed to see how she looked in this crappy little mirror? She opened the door and went out into the hallway.

"Blaire, come on. I've saved you a seat."

A young woman in a robe grabbed Blaire's hand and pulled her toward the next room, where folding chairs had been set up in front of a television set.

"I have to go now—it's my premiere, Isabel. They'll be waiting for me on the red carpet."

"Come on, the movie's about to start," Isabel said.

Blaire didn't want to miss it. She sat in the front row. Where was Seth? Oh well, the opening credits were rolling. They'd have to start without him. There she was. She had to give it to the makeup artists. They'd done a spectacular job. She barely even recognized herself. She sat, entranced, as the movie played. Her favorite part was coming up, the one in the department store where she and Bette Midler had the big fight. Bette was a great actress, but Blaire had held her own. *Beaches* was going to be a smash hit. She would probably even win an Academy Award.

Wait till all her friends heard about it. They'd be sorry they'd turned their backs on her.

35

Kate's flight had gotten into LAX late the night before. Simon was initially concerned about her plan, but in the end, he'd understood. After all, Blaire was her sister, and Kate knew that, despite everything, Lily would want them to move past everything and begin again. And Kate wanted it as well. Kate had worked hard, with the help of a therapist, to control her anxiety. She and Simon had spent that first year after Lily's death in counseling. They had learned that secrets were poison to a marriage. But the first hurdle that Kate had to overcome was her anger. She was still struggling to come to terms with the fact that her mother's oldest friend had been the one to end her life. Kate wanted vengeance, and the few years Georgina got for involuntary manslaughter seemed paltry in comparison to what she'd taken away. Her sentence had been reduced, and she'd already served her four years. She was out now. Free and alive. Unlike Lily.

Kate had severed ties with Selby and all the Hathaways. She thought about the last time she'd spoken to Selby, a few days after Georgina was arrested, when she'd stopped by the hotel where Kate was staying.

"Kate, I'm so sorry. I don't even know what to say." Selby had reached out and embraced Kate, both of them in tears.

"Come sit," Kate said, struggling to come up with something to say to the daughter of her mother's killer. "I assume you know everything?"

Selby wrung her hands and shook her head. "Yes. Your father

and my mother. I don't understand. I'll never understand. How could she do that to my mother?"

Kate was surprised that Selby was completely missing the point. "Let's talk about Blaire. She's related to both of us."

Selby's eyes flashed with anger. "I hate her! Because of her, your mother is dead, and mine might go to jail. It's all her fault."

"Her fault? How is it her fault?"

"If she hadn't come here, snooping around, doing all those crazy things, all this wouldn't have come out. She should have just paid her respects and left. But instead, she led the police right to Mother. It was an accident. Kate, you have to do something. Tell them to let my mother go."

Kate felt the anger surge through her like hot lava. She stood and looked down at Selby. "Your mother *killed* mine! Let her go? I hope she never gets out of jail. She pushed my mother and smashed her head in. You have the nerve to blame Blaire for that? Your mother would have let us live the rest of our lives not knowing what happened."

"She didn't mean to do it. They argued, and your mother fell!"

Their loud voices brought Simon into the main room of their suite. "What's going on?"

"Get her out of here!" Kate could feel the hysteria taking over. "Before I do something I'll regret."

Kate had done her time in the therapist's office over the past several years, and she could truthfully say that life was good again. It was as if the guilt she'd carried for all those years had finally lifted. She was a better partner, a better mother. And she, the fixer of hearts, had finally opened her own.

And then there was Blaire. How many hours had she spent in therapy talking about Blaire? Kate had come to realize that she bore some responsibility for Blaire's progression into madness. She wasn't taking the blame for Blaire's actions, but she did have to admit that she'd never considered what taking Lily and Harrison from Blaire would do to her. Even if Lily hadn't been her biological mother, she was more of a mother to Blaire than anyone in her life had ever been. Kate had known all about Shaina. Blaire had told her about the way she'd waited day after day to hear from her. How she would run to the mailbox after school every day, looking in vain for something, anything, to prove that her mother hadn't forgotten about her. Blaire suffered in all those years before Kate ever met her, coming up with excuse after excuse for her mother never having come back for her. And then, just when Blaire had started to move forward, Enid had come into her life and taken the only stable person left—her father. Kate's family had become Blaire's family. But in the end, they'd all thrown her away—even Lily. It was no wonder Blaire went over the edge when she found out the truth.

So many wasted years. It made Kate so sad. The first few years after Blaire moved away, Kate was so busy with medical school and marriage that it was easy to put her old friend out of her mind. And when she mentioned the idea of calling her to Simon, he'd always discourage her and remind her how Blaire had tried to break them up. But she couldn't lay all of this at Simon's feet.

Blaire had been her touchstone, helping her through her anxiety through high school and then her depression after Jake's death, never adding to Kate's burden by telling her that her reckless actions had caused Blaire to lose her baby. And then Kate had turned her back on Blaire because of one fight. She would never be able to absolve herself of that. This new Blaire, though, the one who had done all of those horrible things, was someone who Kate didn't know how to connect with. She was at a complete loss, and though she wished she could take back all the years of silence, there was no going back. But when she got a call from Enid, of all people, telling her that Blaire had had a complete breakdown, she knew she couldn't stay away. This was her sister! After all, Blaire *had* pulled her out of the house at the last minute. She hadn't been able to hurt her, when it really came down to it. And Kate's therapist had explained that in Blaire's twisted logic, she truly believed that what she had done to Kate had a noble purpose. She was trying to save Kate from Simon, who she believed was the villain.

Enid told Kate that Blaire had gone to Hollywood, as her mother had done so many years before her, in search of fame. Her connections had all turned their backs on her—they had all seen her disgrace play out online, and no one would return her calls. Then one day, she totally lost it, tried to stab a producer at the Polo Lounge, and was arrested. Her lawyer had been the one to get in touch with Enid, who'd flown out and helped to get Blaire into Los Angeles's finest private psychiatric facility to avoid jail time. Even though Blaire had more than enough money, Kate had insisted on paying for her extended stay. She didn't know what Lily's intended provision for Blaire had been, but she felt responsibility as a family member and someone who had contributed to Blaire's decline. Still, this was the first visit she had made.

Enid met her in the lobby of the stately facility, more like a luxurious country club than a medical institution. It had been years since Kate had seen Enid, and she looked so much older.

Enid walked slowly toward Kate. "Thank you for coming," she said.

"I'm glad you called. Is there somewhere we can talk before I go in to see her?" Kate was nervous and wanted to get her bearings first.

Enid nodded. "There's a lounge outside her wing. The elevator's this way. You'll sign in upstairs."

They rode in silence to the fifth floor, where Kate followed Enid to a seating area.

"I have to say I'm surprised you're here," Kate said. "I thought you and Blaire hated each other."

Enid took a deep breath and shook her head. "I never hated her. I tried to be a mother to her, but she wanted nothing to do with me. I won't lie to you, Kate. There's no love lost between us. But I did love her father. And I promised when I married him to do my best to take care of his child. I tried to keep up with her over the years, but she cut me off after her father died. I had put money in a trust for her." She shrugged. "But by the time it matured, she didn't need it anymore and told me where I could put it. I've sent her emails through her author website, but she never answered. I'm just glad her lawyer was able to get in touch when this happened."

Kate shook her head. "Blaire always acted as though you didn't want her around."

"I wanted to try and help her. It was her father's decision to send her away. Once we married, she was merciless in her campaign to get me out. She'd hide my blood pressure medicine. Or sneak outside and put my car windows down in the rain. Once, she went through my closet and threw half my clothes in a dumpster down the street."

Kate was shocked. Blaire had never mentioned any of this to her.

Enid put her hands up. "She did a lot of angry things. We had her evaluated, but she was only twelve, so they wouldn't label her with a personality disorder. But I could read between the lines. Shaina was a narcissist and had borderline personality disorder. Even if they didn't share a gene pool, she raised Blaire in those formative years."

"What did the doctors who evaluated her say?"

Enid shrugged. "To make her feel loved. Try and undo the damage done by her adoptive mother's abandonment. I never agreed with Ed about keeping the adoption a secret, but he wouldn't budge. He was afraid she'd never forgive him for lying in the first place." She sighed. "We took her to therapy for over a year, and she hated every minute of it. Wouldn't open up to the doctor. She had a hole in her heart that was too big to fill."

Kate turned to Enid. "How could I not have seen it? She was my best friend. She even lived with us, and I thought she was happy. She was always so much fun."

Enid gave Kate a sad look. "She puts on a good front. She always had a bit of the actress in her."

"I didn't realize how much she needed my family."

"When she came home, all she talked about was how much better Lily and Harrison were than her father and me. It about killed Ed."

Kate wondered about Blaire's mother. When they were in college, she'd asked Blaire if she was going to try and find her, but Blaire had said she wanted nothing to do with Shaina. "Do you know what happened to her mother?"

Enid nodded. "She died when Blaire was in college. Drug overdose. She still had Blaire's father listed as her next of kin."

Kate digested this news. Why hadn't Blaire ever told her?

"What do the doctors here say? What's her state of mind?"

"She's had what they call a split. She's delusional. A complete break with reality. She thinks she's a big star and that her husband is Seth Ackerman."

Kate's eyes widened. "I don't know what to say to her."

Enid looked at Kate. "It doesn't matter. Just be kind and follow her lead. Tell her you loved her in her latest movie. Just let her believe that you're still her friend. It won't matter what you say. Only that you came."

Kate looked at Enid, the woman she'd believed to be a wicked stepmother all these years, and felt a keen sadness for her and for Blaire. Maybe she wasn't the kind of mother Blaire yearned for, but she *had* cared for her stepdaughter. And Blaire hadn't been able to see it. She'd been so scarred by Shaina's leaving that she saw everything through a distorted lens.

Kate got up and walked to the nurse's station outside the locked door.

"Ms. Barrington is in the last room at the end of the hall," the woman told Kate.

She felt her heart skip as the door was buzzed open and she walked through. She took her time walking down the hallway, taking deep breaths and trying to stay calm. When she reached the end of the hallway, the door was shut. She knocked.

"Who is it?" The voice was guarded.

"Kate. It's Kate." Her voice trembled.

"Katie! I've been waiting for you," Blaire answered, her voice happy. The door swung open, and Kate walked in.

ACKNOWLEDGMENTS

There are so many wonderful people without whom this book would not have become a reality. First and foremost, to our dear friend and agent, Bernadette Baker-Baughman, thank you for supporting and encouraging us every step of the way. You are our touchstone and center, and we're so lucky to work with you. Heartfelt thanks to Victoria Sanders for always cheering us on and lending your wise counsel. And a big thank-you to Jessica Spivey for your support.

To our first editor, Gretchen Stelter, thank you for walking alongside of us from the earliest drafts and taking such care to help us develop the story over many subsequent drafts until it was ready to turn over. To Emily Griffin, the miracle worker, who always challenges us to produce our best work, and then challenges us again until it is truly ready, thank you for your dedication and guidance. Gratitude to Julia Wisdom, our UK editor for her keen eye and championship. Thank you to Jonathan Burnham, Doug Jones, Heather Drucker, Katie O'Callaghan, Mary Sasso, Virginia Stanley, Amber Oliver, and the passionate Harper US team. To the HarperCollins Global teams, we also thank you for your hard work and dedication to excellence. And a hearty thanks to Dana Spector at CAA.

Thank you to the experts in their fields who helped us to authenticate plot points. Any errors are solely our own. Carmen

Marcano, PhD, for always helping with our psychological profiles; Detective 2nd Grade, Allan D. Wong, NYPD, for making sure our detective knew procedure (and didn't violate anyone's rights); Lieutenant Steven B. Tabling III, retired from the Baltimore City Police Department, for sharing your experience and knowledge about the Baltimore police department; our brother, Stanley J. Constantine, JD, for always picking up the phone when we need to understand the law; Tracey Robinson for help with all things horse related; Trevor Rees for boarding school tips; and Leah Rumbough for her advice on etiquette.

We have a group of dedicated beta readers who help us to see holes in the plot, confusing bits, and provide other helpful feedback. Deepest appreciation to: Amy Bike, Dee Campbell, Honey Constantine, Lynn Constantine, Leo Manta, and Rick Openshaw.

As always, heartfelt thanks to our families for their encouragement, support, and love.

READ ON FOR
AN EXCERPT FROM

THE WIFE STALKER

BY LIV CONSTANTINE.

AVAILABLE IN HARDCOVER, E-BOOK,
AUDIO, AND LARGE PRINT
IN MAY 2020 FROM
HARPERCOLLINS PUBLISHERS.

PIPER

Piper Reynard pulled into the parking lot of the Phoenix Recovery Center and parked in her reserved spot. When she'd been forced to leave San Diego ten months ago, she wasn't sure where to go, only that she wanted to be as far away from the West Coast as possible. It had to be somewhere near the water, though, so that she could still sail on the weekends. And it needed to be a place where she could start over without standing out. After extensive research, she'd settled on Westport, Connecticut, a jewel of a town on the coast of Long Island Sound. The former home of Paul Newman and other celebrities, it had a sophisticated vibe and was just over an hour away from New York City by train. But best of all, it was the kind of place that attracted people from all over, rather than the kind of small town where everyone's family had lived for generations, making them nosy about newcomers. She'd found the perfect house—a sprawling white clapboard on the water—and joined a yacht club, where she kept the sailboat she'd bought as soon as she came east.

The one problem she had to overcome was how to reinvent herself. She couldn't continue with her counseling practice, as her license was in her real name, so the next best thing was a business in a similar field. She'd been incredibly lucky to find an existing one for sale and bought the Phoenix Recovery Center a few weeks after moving to Westport. All she'd had to do was have a lawyer set up an LLC for her under the name Harmony Healing Arts. It had already been a thriving business, offering meditation retreats, mindfulness, recovery programs, and nutrition and yoga classes.

She grabbed her briefcase from the passenger's seat, slid out of her Alfa Romeo Spider, and walked toward the entrance of the building, feeling a sense of pride as she looked up at the sleek, two-story building of glass and cedar. She unlocked the front door and went directly to her office. It was still early, six thirty a.m., but Piper liked to be there well before the center opened at eight. It gave her time to get centered before she thrust herself into her busy day. She took a quick look at her calendar to check the time of her appointment with Leo Drakos. He'd called her out of the blue last week and asked to discuss a client he was defending in a murder case. He spoke to her about Fred Grainger, who had been in one of the center's support groups for the last four months and was about to go to trial for the murder of his actress girlfriend. She'd googled Drakos and seen he was a well-known defense lawyer, prominent or perhaps even famous in his field. Based on her knowledge of Fred, she didn't think he was guilty, and she was glad Drakos had taken his case.

She opened her laptop to check the social media accounts for Phoenix. Instagram first. Another three hundred followers. Excellent. It must have been the podcast episode she'd uploaded yesterday on filling your well before trying to fill someone else's. Twitter next. Thirty-five retweets of her blog post on selfishness being the new selflessness. And on Facebook, the center had hit ten thousand likes. A very good morning indeed.

She dimmed her office lights and pressed Play on her iPad. As the soothing sounds of Debussy filled the room, she closed her eyes and leaned back in the chair. Maybe things were really going to be different here. They had to be. She couldn't keep starting over and finding new places to hide.

JOANNA

Leo's finally coming out of his depression. After three long months of his barely communicating with me, lost inside his head, he suddenly seemed to perk up. He was starting on a new murder case next week, and I could see that having it to immerse himself in was a good thing, but I knew from experience that it would also be exhausting. I convinced him that a few days away at the house in Maine before the trial started would be a nice break for all of us. The bracing sea air and magnificent views were always restorative, so I'd already called ahead to Lloyd, the caretaker, to ready the house for us.

As soon as we drove up and opened the front door, fresh flowers greeted us on the entry table, and the rooms seemed to welcome us back. Stelli ran through the house ahead of us like a tornado, and when I heard a whoop of delight, I knew he'd found the surprise I'd arranged to have waiting in his bedroom. A minute later, he came barreling down the stairs holding two remote-control bumper cars and ran to his sister, Evie.

"Look what was in my room! Come on, let's go play."

Evie, a grown-up eight to his six, gave him a measured look, then spoke. "Let me put my things away first."

She was such a sweet child that she didn't ask if there was anything waiting in her room, which of course there was. I'd ordered her a pink wireless karaoke microphone and asked Lloyd to place it on her bed.

As Leo unloaded the car, I went through the house, turning lights on, unpacking our bags, and getting us settled in. Opening the door to the deck, I took a deep breath of Maine air. It was a perfect spring day, 62 degrees, according to the thermometer on the outside wall, but the sun made it feel warmer. The sea was calm and the sky a brilliant, cloudless blue. I sat in one of the white lounge chairs and breathed in the salt air, closing my eyes as the warmth of the sun spread across my body.

"Are you asleep?"

Leo's voice startled me from a light slumber, and I sat up, turning to look at him standing at the open sliding glass door. "No, just resting," I said. "Where are the children?"

"In their rooms, playing."

"Why don't you sit down and join me?"

He shook his head, his expression serious. "No. I think I'll go inside and rest for a bit."

I tried not to show my exasperation. "Leo. The sun and sea air will do you some good. Come sit."

He sighed reluctantly. This is how he'd been the last few months—keeping to himself, sleeping most of the time, or staring off into space. Finally, he stepped onto the deck and took the lounge chair next to mine, but he looked straight ahead at the water, not saying a word. I put my hand on his arm.

"Leo, let's try to make this trip a good one for Stelli and Evie. They love it here. It would be good to make some happy memories for them."

He continued to stare at the water. "I'll try, Joanna. I know I've not been the easiest person to be around these last months." He turned to look at me and attempted a weak smile. "You've been wonderful, you really have, and I'm grateful. I don't know what I would have done without you."

Even though we'd been together for many years, it was still a thrill to hear those words, to know he appreciated me. There was no one I cared about more than him and the children, and I was relieved to see that he was starting to come back to me.

"I will always be here for you, Leo. No matter what," I said.

Tears filled his eyes, and he blinked, then turned to hide them from me. Seeing him like this made me hope he was emotionally prepared for this case, which would be another high-profile one. I'd been telling him it might be good for him to get counseling, but he wasn't interested, even when I reminded him how much it had helped me. My therapist, Celeste, advised me not to push him, so I'd backed off. But after something he'd said in passing, a possible solution occurred to me. I just had to figure out a way to frame it so that it sounded like a good idea to him, too.

ABOUT THE AUTHOR

LIV CONSTANTINE is the pen name of sisters Lynne Constantine and Valerie Constantine. Separated by three states, they spend hours plotting via FaceTime and burning up each other's emails. They attribute their ability to concoct dark story lines to the hours they spent listening to tales handed down by their Greek grandmother. Lynne lives in Milford, Connecticut. Valerie lives in Annapolis, Maryland.

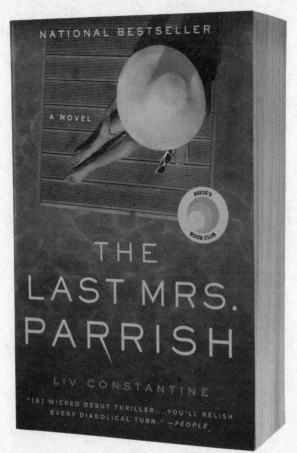